Men of Iron

By

Col. Cline Williamson

Other works by the author available on Amazon.com at booksbyclinewilliamson or Legionbooks.net

SOG Series	RVN Series Series	Adventure
Tempting the Devil Shame	Men of Iron	A Crying
Don't Mean Nothing Revenge	Code of Honor	Hitler's
Private Enterprise	The Chosen Few	Bishop
Driving On	Hired Help	Stecker's Run
Last OP, Armageddon	Bad Moon Rising	Sadler's Gold
Code Word Prairie Fire Keepers	The Frenchman	Finder's
Shadowman	A Hard Way to Die	

RVN Series

I

Preface

The ground war in Vietnam was, in some ways, identical to all of America's other modern wars. Men on both sides tried their hardest to kill each other with new weapons and technology employed by small unit leaders, making life and death decisions daily. In most American infantry units, as in WWI, WWII, and Korea, there was usually a shortage of junior officers as platoon leaders, especially as the war wore on. In those cases, the platoons were commanded by senior NCOs, and that was probably a good thing for the troops in those platoons.

By and large, the senior NCOs had much more leadership experience than a new second Lieutenant and were far more used to handling men in stressful situations. By contrast, new second lieutenants, fresh out of the Infantry Officer's Basic Course, or Officer's Candidate School, were young, untested, and generally had no previous leadership experience at all.

Especially the kind necessary to lead men under the stressful conditions of combat.

Generally, the ROTC officers knew barely enough to get by in a peacetime environment, much less effectively leading men when they first assumed command of a platoon in combat. This lack of experience was especially debilitating in Vietnam because it was a war fought at the small unit level. The VC or the NVA employed guerrilla-style tactics against the American units they engaged. Worse, their tactics and doctrine were not taught to young American officers during their training.

Instead, they were hit-and-run ambushes conducted where and when the NVA or VC chose and were utterly unfamiliar to a new second lieutenant. The NVA rarely used traditional tactics by holding a piece of terrain or standing and fighting.

In contrast, the US Army didn't have any doctrine that espoused counter-guerilla warfare, so the younger officers had to learn "on the job" once they got to Vietnam and got into a firefight. If they survived, the learning process for them began. However, they had to experience more than one firefight before gaining the combat experience necessary to lead men while being shot at effectively.

Complicating the situation, a young officer's actual time in-country lasted only one year. Of those twelve months, over two were devoted to administrative time involving processing, assignment, and R&R. Then a two-week orientation course of initial in-country training and acclimatization, and finally, a week of out-processing when your tour ended.

All totaled, that meant a junior officer had only ten months to learn what he needed to run a platoon in combat. Unfortunately, his tour was over just about when he became effective at it. That was the nature and the result of the Army's personnel assignment policy during the Vietnam conflict.

It was a short-sighted and inferior personnel management system resulting from the Army's lack of foresight, probably due to the war's poor popularity back in the States. Whatever the reason, it severely curtailed the Army's ability to obtain and enhance any depth of experience for its junior officers in any combat units.

Despite that, many junior officers did a reasonably competent job as platoon leaders during their limited assignments. But a great deal of credit for that probably belongs to the senior NCO they had as their platoon Sergeant and the squad leaders working under him. With their assistance, advice, and experience, a platoon leader's job was much easier, which saved lives.

This novel is about an NCO who became a junior officer by a battlefield commission during that conflict. During the war, there were numerous instances of this occurring.

Although the characters and situations in this novel are fictional, they are based on real-life figures in similar cases in the heat of combat during that war.

This book is dedicated to all those NCOs, young Lieutenants, and Captains who served in the Nam, and it is a thank you for the job they did. Probably the only one they will ever get for their service there. Because, unlike today, when they came home, there were no victory parades, no Wounded Warrior Projects, no yellow ribbons, not even a polite Thank You or Good Job from any of their countrymen, and that was especially true of their government.

Instead, if people said anything to the Vietnam vets, it was never a grateful acknowledgment for putting their lives on their country line. More probably, it was an apathetic stare or a *"who gives a shit"* attitude.

Unfortunately, Vietnam was a war where soldiers sent to fight were never treated as heroes when they returned. Instead, most of their countrymen were ashamed of them. So, as the war's misfits, they ultimately became its scapegoats.

As a result, the Vietnam Vet and his comrades that served with him all share a common yet strange bond. It is a compact forged in combat fires, which will never let them forget or forgive, and they will go to their graves with that resentment. They will also continue to distrust the government that was responsible for it.

That sad and disgraceful chapter in American history will finally be closed only when the last Vietnam vet dies. What the government did was a national disgrace and one of the most despicable and shameful acts ever perpetrated on its veterans. It will never be forgotten or forgiven, and the politicians responsible should be hung.

Chapter One

Pike already knew what was coming. Although the news was just what he had expected, it certainly wasn't what he had wanted. He was part of the small formation waiting for more bad news, the kind he usually received in this unit. The kind that meant more of his men would die because its leaders were so incompetent. So, he could feel the new orders coming in his gut before the CO opened his mouth. Still, when the Company commander gave his subordinates the word, the words hit the senior NCO like a sucker punch, and the air rushed out of him. His small world was rocked, and he suddenly felt a nasty, bilious taste in his mouth.

"We're going back into the valley tomorrow morning," The company commander told the assembled group. "I just got the word from battalion."

There was a collective groan from the NCOs. Then some muted bitching in angry, subdued undertones. Hearing it, the Captain stared unsympathetically at his subordinates until it subsided. He was a weak and incompetent leader who projected an uninspiring and frail personality. It was doubtful if he even understood why his subordinates were griping. He only knew he didn't like it.

His men weren't thrilled with him either. Or by the fact, he was their commander. They no longer trusted him since he had already proven himself indecisive under fire, even cowardly. Unfortunately, he was so incompetent; that he wasn't even aware of that or any of his shortcomings. Worse, the Company's casualties that morning apparently hadn't yet registered with him. Or if they had, he didn't care and had ignored them. He certainly didn't blame himself.

"Is he that clueless and uncaring?" Pike wondered. *"or simply that ignorant and incompetent."*

"Or is he simply oblivious about the men he's responsible for?"

In truth, the Captain was all those things. He was entirely out of his depth. He had no concept of leadership, no knowledge of tactics, and no fundamental understanding of his job. At best, he was a weak product of the ROTC training program at his no-name college and a pretend soldier. He had no genuine desire to even be in the Army. In his mind, he was simply repaying the college debt he had incurred by accepting his ROTC scholarship by serving his required three-year service obligation. He was merely marking time until he became a civilian again. The fact that he was in a war seemed to be an unfortunate but minor irritant on his way to becoming a civilian once again

Unfortunately, he had barely paid any attention to any of his compulsory initial training, short as it was. He hadn't been that interested since he considered it something he had to endure as payback for his education. He hadn't retained any knowledge of the tactics he had been taught either since the subject matter bored him. Instead, he concentrated on other subjects, like post-service plans and social life.

He never figured he would have to remember his training anyway, much less use it, especially in combat. In sum, he had either forgotten or disregarded what little military training he had received. Despite that, he was in a war he never expected and in a situation, he was entirely unprepared for. He was in command of an infantry company in combat, and his leadership was worse than the blind leading the unwilling.

He was inept, incompetent, and had no business trying to command anything, in any environment, especially over a hundred men in the hell of Vietnam. He was totally unsuited to the task in manner, knowledge, and ability. He had proven that by his actions that very morning.

When the firefight began, he had been frozen with fear and incapable of assessing or dealing with the situation, much less giving orders or telling his subordinates what to do about it. Instead, he had been so frightened he had hugged the ground in terror in a fetal position, oblivious to all the soldiers around him awaiting his orders and dying in the process.

Unfortunately for them, as the firefight continued, he never recovered. He never issued any orders or gave any instructions. He just moaned in fear, hugged the ground tightly, and cried.

So, with no direction, the Company had gotten mauled, and shot to pieces because of a lack of orders. Only the insertion choppers, turning around on their own, had saved them, and even then, not all of them. The insertion had been a setup: a preplanned trap and a disaster, easy meat for the waiting NVA.

Thanks to the lead pilot of the insertion package, the unit's salvation was rendered by an old grizzled Chief Warrant Officer who was the lead pilot. He was a true hero, while the Captain had been a coward and a failure. He returned to the LZ independently and extracted the stricken unit without orders.

Now, this idiot of a commander was getting ready to replicate his same, earlier mistake. Compound it by going into that exact location tomorrow morning and getting even more men killed by his incompetence and fear. Worse, he hadn't even apologized for his actions that morning and didn't even act ashamed. Apparently, he didn't need his men's acceptance or respect anyway. He believed his rank trumped all that.

"D company is going to cover our western flank after we insert," the Captain droned on.

He was simply regurgitating what he had been told in the operation's order given to him minutes earlier at Battalion headquarters.

"We'll be the lead element of the attack, so we'll take the brunt of the enemy's fire."

"*Jesus,*" Pike thought disgustedly. "*What's this "we" shit?*"

"You acted like a terrified child in this morning's firefight."

"You were so goddamned scared you couldn't even issue any orders."

"Your own RTO had to pry you out of the hole you were in just to get you back into the extraction chopper."

"As a leader, you're a fucking joke."

The Captain didn't hear him. Even if he had, he would have disregarded him and probably disciplined him. Pike was an NCO, a lowly Sgt, so his opinion didn't count.

The Captain was so inept he hadn't even read the operations order before issuing it, much less considered its ramifications reference his unit regarding it. He hadn't even modified it to fit his company, as he should have.

He was simply a mouthpiece repeating what he had been told with no thoughts of his own. Someone clueless as to his job and completely unqualified when he tried to accomplish it.

As such, he was completely unaware of his platoon leader's and NCOs' concerns and reservations about the upcoming operation. Consequently, he just droned monotonously like some pre-programmed robot.

A good commander would have at least gotten some input and concerns from his subordinates, then tried to find ways to alleviate them. But not him. He wasn't that smart or that competent. He simply didn't care. He was just there because he had to be.

"The choppers will be here just after first light," he continued, simply mouthing words.

"We'll insert on the valley's north end in four sorties."

"We'll be first in, followed twenty minutes later by elements of D Company on the third lift."

"Once both companies are on the ground, we'll sweep south, down the valley floor, while artillery supports us and covers our flanks."

"It should be a relatively easy operation," he opined. "Especially after this morning."

"The NVA will undoubtedly vacate the area tonight." He predicted. "Since they know we'll probably be coming back in tomorrow in strength."

"They were just lucky today and caught us off guard."

"They'll leave tonight because they'll want no part of us tomorrow."

"They'll be too scared."

Pike stared at him in astonishment. The man was brain dead if he believed what he had just said.

"Christ," the NCO thought, sucking in his breath. *"doesn't this idiot or the morons at Battalion even know what's in that valley?"*

"Haven't they ever read any after-action reports about the place?"

"Haven't they at least studied any of the histories about Indochina or the wars regarding it?"

"Are they that ignorant and clueless?

"Or do they think we will prevail simply because we're Americans, and Americans are regarded as the good guys?"

"Please tell me they aren't that naïve, that incompetent, or that stupid."

But they were. The proof was standing right there in front of him.

"The French lost an entire demi-brigade in this same valley twenty years ago," Pike thought to himself. *"Fifteen hundred men."*

"It went in and simply disappeared without a trace."

"Worse, about a year ago, the 1st Cavalry Division made that same damn mistake, in the same place!"

"As a result, they lost almost three US battalions because of it."

"Now, this battalion will go back into that same area a little over a year later with two shot-up companies?"

"Whoever dreamed this operation up must be insane!"

"A low-level cretin," Pike scoffed in disbelief under his breath. "That is a complete retard."

"The Dicks will kill every single one of us tomorrow and in record time."

"Hell, they own that fucking valley."

"It's been their fortified sanctuary for over thirty years, despite every attempt the French and Americans have made to take it."

"And after our moronic display this morning, the NVA are just waiting for us to do something stupid, like come back tomorrow."

"Hell, killing off two American infantry companies will be nothing more than a training exercise for them."

"They won't even work up a sweat."

"Didn't our intelligence people brief the battalion staff about the place, or don't they know about it either?"

"Christ, we'll get our asses handed to us."

"We're being led by ignorant morons who are advised by clueless lunatics!"

"Delta's going to cover our western flank," Pike mimicked to himself in disbelief. *"Hell, there won't be any flank left to cover, you imbecile."*

"Not by the time they get there."

"We'll all be dead by then, and so will Delta Company if they're stupid enough to land."

"The NVA are going to chew us up so fast; they won't even have time to spit us out."

"Sgt Pike," the Captain continued obliviously, unaware of Pike's thoughts. "your platoon will be first in tomorrow."

"Wonderful," Pike thought disgustingly, *"it gets even better."*

"We get to get killed first, again."

"Just like this morning."

"As soon as you're down," the Captain ordered as he plowed ahead indifferently. "Head for the eastern wood line and form a perimeter."

"The rest of the company will assemble on you once we've landed."

"The rest of the company will get shot right out of the air before it even hits the LZ," Pike thought in disgust. *"As for us, we'll never make it to the wood line."*

"The NVA will shoot us to pieces as soon as we clear the choppers if they even wait that long."

"This entire plan is insane."

"Whoever planned this abortion ought to be the first man out of the first chopper tomorrow."

"Let him get his ass ripped for his stupidity."

"The dumb SOB doesn't have a clue as to what we're going up against."

"That's the Ia Drang Valley, for Christ's sake," Pike thought in disbelief. " a known NVA stronghold for over thirty years."

"Ho Chi Minh established it in WWII when he sent his first cadres into South Vietnam to occupy it."

"Since then, they've had over forty years to fortify the place."

"Now we're going to try and take it in one day with two lousy shot-up companies!"

"That's not even a sick joke; it's a travesty, a pipedream."

But it wasn't a sick joke. It wasn't a joke at all. Pike's battalion was about to enter that NVA stronghold and attempt to seize it with less than two hundred men the following day. It would be two hundred against ten thousand. Odds so bad they guaranteed a disaster.

"Where are the Battalion staffs' brains?" Pike wondered.

"Christ, they're as fucked up as this idiot Captain."

"Not only is their plan fucked up," Pike muttered in disgust. *"the LZ we're using is the only one within seven miles of the valley and the same one we used today."*

"The Dicks certainly know that."

"Hell, they're not stupid, and they can read a map as well as we can."

"So, they'll be dug in around it about three deep in the same hole, just licking their chops and waiting for us."

"Once we land, they'll rip us to shreds."

"We'll have two Snakes supporting our insertion." the Captain babbled on.

"If you need them, Pike, you can direct their fire until the rest of the company lands."

"I'll take over once the company is in a perimeter in the wood line."

Pike had no more words. Instead, he and the rest of the NCOs just stared at the imbecile in amazement. They were appalled by his complete ignorance and lack of concern. The man was incompetent, an egotistical prick, and obviously unconcerned.

He had completely fucked up today's insertion so badly his unit had to be hastily extracted under fire by someone else because he was so scared and incompetent. The Warrant officer pilot leading the choppers had to do his job for him. The entire company would be dead if it weren't for him and his actions.

Even worse, once the shooting started, the Captain had turned mute, frozen with fear, and unable to issue any orders. Only the NCOs taking charge of their platoons had saved what was left of the Company from being killed outright. Now the ignorant ass was about to try and get them all killed again tomorrow morning.

"Where did this misfit get his commission?" *they wondered.*

"Was he asleep when the Army supposedly trained him?"

"What he knows about leadership or handling an infantry unit in combat here in Vietnam can be summed up in one word."

"Nothing!"

"What did we do to deserve him?"

"Assembly on the PZ will be at 0730 hrs. tomorrow morning," the CO concluded, oblivious to the apparent dissatisfaction on his NCO's faces.

"Brief your people, draw whatever you're short on, and get them ready," The Captain concluded.

"Dismissed."

Pike picked up his weapon, shaking his head in disgust. He had no more words or thoughts. He and his men had just become innocent victims, again, scheduled to die because some inept asshole was in command.

He wearily started walking back to what was left of his pitiful platoon, manning some bunkers on the eastern side of the firebase. He was trying to think of a way to give them the bad news. But as of yet, he was unsuccessful. He only had twenty-seven bodies left. He had lost eight people that morning, including his new platoon leader. Four died, and four were wounded because he had a moron for a company commander.

His latest platoon leader, a baby-faced 2nd Lt named Mickelson, hadn't lasted a week. Pike hadn't even known the poor bastard long enough to learn his first name. Now he was headed stateside in a dull aluminum casket. Apparently, none of his superiors in this fucked up battalion even cared.

This morning's firefight should have been a wake call to the disaster that awaited any future company-sized action in the valley, yet it wasn't. The battalion commander and his staff would implement their idiotic plan regardless. After all, *they* weren't inserting into a deathtrap, just the poor grunts in the line companies they were responsible for. The grunts were simply cannon fodder, barely educated, and easily replaceable. For most of them, Vietnam was their senior trip following high school graduation. The ultimate reward.

The company's remaining members were high school dropouts, already scared shitless by this morning's action. However, none of that mattered. All of them would be even more frightened when they learned they were going back into the same area again tomorrow morning and with fewer men than they had today. They would undoubtedly be thrilled when they heard the news. Especially the remaining members of Pike's platoon. They had already had their ass handed to them that morning as the first element on the ground. Tomorrow, they were going get a second chance to get killed first again. They would undoubtedly absolutely love that. It would be another chance to die early. Another opportunity to avoid the rush and get in the express lane.

The rest of the company had also been chewed up in that morning's combat assault, but not nearly as bad as Pike's platoon. He had been the first platoon down on the LZ with the remainder of the company behind him. But not a single man had even gotten off the LZ before the entire company had been lit up.

Shot up so bad they had to be extracted under fire, minutes later. The NVA hadn't even waited for the Slicks to depart the area before they started chopping pieces out of the unit.

With a total of ten dead and sixteen wounded in A Company alone, you'd think the stupid bastards at battalion would have learned something from that and changed their plans accordingly. Apparently not. Both A and D Companies were being ordered back in tomorrow by the same cretin who had planned this abortion. Another incompetent moron.

"Sgt Pike," a loud voice behind him barked suddenly. "You didn't appear enthusiastic when you heard the battalion was going back tomorrow."

Pike turned in midstride and glanced back. It was the new Battalion commander standing beside his incompetent Company commander. They were two of a kind, complete morons, and promoted well above their actual level of competence. Both were total fuck ups, especially the Battalion commander. He was even worse than Pike's company commander.

He was an arrogant man full of himself, who thought he was George Patton reincarnated. He was even dressed for the part with crisply starched fatigues, spit-shined jungle boots, and sporting a camouflaged scarf as an ascot. He looked like he had just stepped out of a recruiting poster or was going to a parade. Compared to his battalion's dirty grunts, his dress alone revealed just how out of touch he was with his unit. Still, he had a *know-it-all* smirk plastered all over his face. Typical.

The ass looked like he was about to hold a press conference touting his intelligence and heroics instead of leading a combat infantry Battalion. The same one that had just had its ass kicked that morning. That alone made it evident to everyone but himself that he was as poor a leader, just like Pike's Company commander. Neither man knew shit, and both were failed leaders!

Pike hadn't noticed the pompous ass before since he had been too engrossed in his thoughts. Perhaps he was just another loser, like the men in his battalion thought he was. Or maybe he wasn't that noticeable, to begin with, despite his recruiting poster dress. Still, he was a senior officer, so Pike wearily came to a position of attention and waited.

Good leaders listened to their subordinates, took advice, and learned. But this moron wasn't a good leader. He was even worse than the idiot Captain he commanded. Now, he was going to prove it to Pike.

"You know something about this operation we don't, Pike?" the Battalion commander asked nastily, a tight smile on his face.

"No, Sir," Pike lied, not wanting to get into a pissing contest with the pompous ass.

"You can't talk to people like him," Pike thought as he stared straight ahead.

"They already know all the answers."

"If you don't believe it, just ask them."

"This asshole is the poster child for jerk-offs like that."

"Mr. "I'm a LtCol, and therefore, I know everything," Pike thought in disgust.

26

"The silly shit is so stupid he couldn't pour piss out of a boot if he had directions printed on the heel."

"He's been poured out of the same mold as the Company Commander."

"They're both classic, ignorant dumbasses who are in charge only because of their rank."

"How the moron ever made Lt Colonel is a complete mystery."

"He must be a world-class ass kisser because he doesn't know shit about commanding troops in combat in the Nam."

"Shit, in that regard, he's even worse than our Company Commander."

"The idiot has never even been shot at before!"

But Pike didn't voice any of those thoughts, even though he wanted to. He couldn't. NCOs didn't tell LtCols they were incompetent morons. That wasn't done in the Army. So, he just remained silent, standing at attention and waiting for LTC Motormouth to finish. No sense trying to tell the idiot anything; he would be just wasting his breath.

"Well, you're certainly not happy about something," The LTC pressed nastily. "It's written all over your face."

"So, what's your problem, Sgt?"

"Nothing, Sir," Pike said, just wanting to leave.

"If this idiot didn't already understand the fucking problems with the operation, he wouldn't let a mere Sgt. educate him."

"Bullshit," The LTC demanded, all pretense of niceness evaporating now.

"Spit it out, Sgt." He ordered.

Pike hesitated. The Battalion commander made an irritable come-on motion with his hand, so Pike decided to speak his mind.

"This is your first tour, isn't it, Sir?" Pike asked the LTC, trying to be tactful.

"And the Captain's too?"

"Yes, it is," the Battalion commander replied, not liking a lowly NCO questioning his credentials.

"What's that got to do with anything?"

Another idiotic remark uttered by a moron.

"I was here in sixty-six with SF, Sir," Pike continued.

"I was stationed at a Special Forces A camp about fifty klicks north of here."

The LTC just stared sullenly at Pike. He was obviously completely unimpressed and ready to dismiss any point Pike made. Typical.

"That valley we're going into is called the Ia Drang, Sir," Pike continued, already aware that he was wasting his time.

"The NVA own the place."

"They've owned it since even before the French were here."

"It's been an NVA stronghold since the mid-forties when Ho Chi Minh first established it as a base area against the Japanese."

"He later used it against the French, and with great success."

"The French Foreign Legion lost an entire fifteen hundred man demi-brigade there in 1953 when they first tried to clear it," Pike said, continuing his history lesson.

"They marched in, disappeared, and were never heard from again."

"And although the French High Command tried in several later campaigns to find out what happened to them, they never did."

"They also never succeeded in taking the valley."

"Even after several more attempts."

"It remained an NVA stronghold all through the remainder of the Indochina war."

"Less than two years ago, just after the US Army came into Vietnam in force," Pike continued. "the 1st Cavalry Division put two battalions into that same valley.

"Into two LZ's called: LZ X-Ray and LZ English."

"After insertion, the battalions fanned out and were about two miles apart when the NVA hit them."

"The first battalion got massacred during their first twelve hours on the ground," Pike said, his voice tight as he remembered. "Almost to a man."

"The second one didn't fare much better."

"They got so severely mauled, the Division had to reinforce them with two more battalions, just to keep them from being overrun, and even that force had to have the support of almost continuous TAC air."

"Aircraft were stacked up from five thousand feet, all the way up to God," Pike explained. "But even that made little difference."

"That three battalion force was in the valley for a total of five days, continuously supported by TAC Air, artillery, and gunships," Pike continued.

"Yet in all that time, with all that support, they were only able to advance a total of maybe six hundred yards, getting the shit kicked out of them during the entire process."

"Finally, the NVA pulled back into the mountains of Laos at the north end of the valley to resupply."

"When they did, the 1st Cav gave up and extracted what was left of their three battalions."

"I know, Colonel," Pike said heatedly. "I listened to the entire battle on the radio."

"I even saw part of it when I flew as a Covey Rider with one of our FACs, and I can tell you it wasn't very pretty."

"The 1st Cav found out the hard way that the Ia Drang Valley was home to the 103rd NVA Division."

"It's been their base area for thirty years."

"Now," Pike asked incredulously. "less than a year later, we're going into that same valley with only two shot-up companies to clear it?"

"That's not only impossible; it's insane."

"About two minutes after we land," Pike predicted. "we're going to be up to our asses in NVA."

"So is the rest of the battalion if you put them in behind us."

"The NVA are going to have our asses for breakfast, just like they had the 1st Cav's two years ago."

"This morning was only a preview of what we can expect tomorrow, Sir."

The Battalion commander's face turned livid at Pike's prediction, and Pike's history lesson went right over his head. He was so angry he could barely speak.

"This is my plan," he thought furiously. *"I designed it, and I intend to see it implemented."*

"So, who is this lowly Sgt to question it?" he thought angrily.

"Who is this smart-assed NCO upstart to tell me I don't know what I'm doing?"

"He's just some undereducated and ill-informed NCO who is probably scared."

"So this is his way of trying to get out of doing his duty."

"But it won't work."

"He's going back in tomorrow with the rest of the battalion."

"You don't honestly believe the NVA are still in that same valley after two years, do you?" The LTC asked with a look of disbelief, replacing his smirk.

"Why wouldn't they be, Sir?"

"Who's pushed them out since then?" Pike asked logically.

"We both know they were certainly there this morning, don't we?"

The LTC's face turned red with embarrassment, and he was furious. He had been caught by his own words and by a lowly Sgt.

"That's ridiculous," the LTC exclaimed, his anger seething. "The NVA wouldn't be that stupid."

"The unit we encountered this morning was just a small force probably transiting the area when we surprised them with our airmobile insertion," he explained, grasping for a rebuttal, but being so ignorant, he didn't have one.

Pike just stared at him, dumbfounded by his stupidity.

"There are certainly some NVA in that valley." the LTC reluctantly admitted lamely after realizing his mistake.

"We accidentally ran up against them this morning."

"But nothing even close, numbers-wise, to what you think is there, Pike."

"Our Intelligence estimates that there may be a battalion of them in the area at most," The LTC pronounced with finality, wanting to end this discussion before he looked like an even bigger ass than he already was.

"But even they're spread out."

"Then intelligence is wrong," Pike said determinedly.

"And you're right," the LTC said, the smirk returning. "is that it?"

"Sir, you asked for my opinion," Pike said, barely able to contain his anger. "If you don't like it, I'm sorry."

"Pike," the LTC said sarcastically. "as a multi-tour veteran, I guess you're entitled to an opinion."

"But opinions aren't facts, are they?" he sneered.

"And your entire argument is based on something that happened nearly two years ago."

"A lot has happened since then, Sgt," He reminded Pike unnecessarily.

"The U S Army here in Vietnam has gotten much smarter for one thing," he pointed out.

"We've also gotten a lot bigger."

"We even have newer and better equipment."

"By this time, the NVA also realize we have the advantage of overwhelming firepower on our side and much more mobility."

"Shit," Pike thought. "We had all that two years ago, and it didn't make a damned bit of difference."

"The 1st Cav still got the shit kicked out of it."

"So, the NVA would be stupid to still be using that valley as a major staging base," The LTC explained. "And we both know they aren't stupid, don't we?" The LTC concluded as he continued to display his ignorance.

Pike remained silent.

"It's a waste of words trying to convince this idiot of anything," He thought. "He already has all the answers."

"We'll find out who's right tomorrow morning, won't we?" the LTC concluded smugly.

"You're an egotistical idiot, Colonel," Pike thought. "You're probably the moron who dreamed up this entire, fucked up operation, to begin with."

"Your stupidity and stubbornness will get a lot of good people killed tomorrow, you silly ass."

"I just hope you're one of them."

But again, Pike didn't voice any of those thoughts. Instead, he just looked at the LTC in disgust for a long moment.

"I guess we will, Sir," he said instead.

Chapter Two

Pike shoved the mess tray back untouched. The food smelled good, but he had no appetite. His stomach was still in knots after his run-in with the idiot battalion commander the previous afternoon. As a result, the NCO wasn't interested in eating, even though he knew it might be his last hot meal in a while. Maybe his last meal ever. He sipped his coffee instead and gazed at the members of his platoon in the firebase's small, open-air mess hall.

They were mostly kids. Draftees. Teenagers with low to average IQs. Almost men fresh out of high school and people who had no desire to be in the military. High school seniors who got sent to Vietnam on their senior trip. That alone ensured they were less than enthusiastic about being here. Even so, they were good soldiers.

They were driving on, despite their youth, and doing a pretty fair job of it. They couldn't even legally purchase a drink in the United States, but here they were, risking their lives daily for their country. Fighting in a country most of them couldn't even find on a map while enduring the hostile climate, suppressing their fear, and watching their friends die regularly.

Pike was an excellent leader, so they trusted him, did what they were told without complaint, and rarely bitched. They endured the heat, the monsoons, the insects, and the eighteen to twenty-four-hour days, week in and week out. They faced danger and death daily and somehow underwent all the other miserable things a grunt must sometimes face, mainly with a good-natured attitude. They did that while others of their generation demonstrated in America's streets and openly sided with the North Vietnamese, the very people trying to kill them.

They all looked up to Pike like little puppies, dependent on their mother. Pike was a bloodied veteran with two previous tours in the country and had managed to survive them both. As such, he knew what the hell to do in a firefight. He knew which way to jump when the shit hit the fan. They had seen him do it. He had taught them to do it. He was their leader and their father figure, and a good one.

Consequently, when Pike gave an order, his men obeyed it instantly and unquestioningly. If they stood a chance of surviving, it would be thanks to Pike, and they all knew it. For that reason alone, they trusted him, obeyed him, and hung on his every word.

"Okay, ladies," Pike said, smiling. "finish it up."

"I don't want any of you getting fat."

Laughter bubbled up everywhere. Papa had just made a joke, a good one. Especially since nearly every one of them was at least fifteen pounds underweight thanks to the conditions, they endured daily.

"Showdown inspection at the Platoon CP in ten minutes." He ordered.

There was a chorus of good-natured groans as the platoon members got up, as Pike smiled and shook his head. Moments later, he drank the last of his coffee, got up too, and then walked back to the bunker that served as the Platoon's CP in the firebase. Ortiz, his RTO, was already there when he arrived.

"Morning, Boss," Ortiz said, a grin on his brown Mexican face.

"Good morning, Paco," Pike replied. "You get breakfast?"

Ortiz nodded.

"Half hour ago," he replied. "I came back early to pack my ruck."

"Take extra batteries, Paco," Pike ordered. "And extra ammo."

"Forget the extra food this trip."

"Use the space it'd take up in your ruck, for the ammo."

"Why the extra ammo, but less food?" Paco asked curiously.

"That shit will weigh a ton, and I already got the radio and batteries to hump."

"You can get hungry lots of times, Paco," Pike replied. "You can only get dead once."

"And I don't want that to happen to you because you ran out of ammo."

"Take the extra rounds."

Paco nodded, removed the excess rations, then started cramming extra M-16 magazines into his ruck. The rule in the Platoon was simple.

"When the man spoke, you listened."

"If you wanted to stay alive, that is.

Seeing Paco jamming extra ammo into his rucksack, Pike turned to his own ruck and checked it one last time. He had already packed it the night before with extra ammo and water. When he picked it up and put it on, testing its weight, he discovered Paco was right. With all the extra ammo and water, it did weigh a ton. But that couldn't be helped.

A few minutes later, the platoon formed outside Pike's bunker, their squad leaders putting them into a loose formation. Pike walked out and looked them over, made a few adjustments to some of their gear, and asked a few questions as he inspected them. But his inspection was mostly cursory, just another way to put his people at ease and reassure them. Let them know that he was concerned with their welfare. It was just his way of saying he would do his best to take care of them today. But maybe his way of saying goodbye to some of them, especially today.

When Pike looked over his platoon, he noticed everyone was overly anxious about going back into the Valley. That was normal, especially considering what had happened the previous day, but it wasn't good. Not today. He needed his men alert and very watchful today, not nervous and scared. They'd stand a better chance of surviving that way.

Scared men make mistakes, and mistakes get people killed. He had less than thirty-five men left because his idiot company commander had made a mistake the day before. He couldn't afford another one.

"All right, girls, listen up," He said, smiling at their youthful, strained faces.

"If you haven't already got it, draw extra ammo and grenades."

"As much as you can carry."

"Take extra water too."

"Draw a five-quart water bladder from Company supply and strap it to the top of your ruck after you fill it."

"And don't anybody start bitching about all the extra weight either," He warned.

"Once we get on the ground, you'll be glad you've got plenty of rounds and extra go juice."

"It's liable to be very hot once we get there, and I'm not just talking about the temperature."

The kids all let out a collective groan. They already knew what to expect and weren't happy about it. They were scared instead. They had seen their ranks shot to pieces the day before and didn't want it to happen again today. They trusted Pike to make sure it didn't.

"Once we're down," Pike explained, ignoring their reluctance. "There isn't going to be any resupply for a while."

"That's why we're taking what we need in with us, including extra ammo and water. "

"We may be out there for a while."

"Hell, some of us may be out there permanently if things go south." he thought.

"If we are, you'll need the extra ammo." He finished.

"You ever run out of ammo in a firefight, Sarge?" A youngster asked curiously.

"Yeah," Pike answered. "back in '65 up in II Corps.

"We were in a very nasty firefight at the time."

"What happened?" the youngster asked wide-eyed.

"After I ran out of ammo, I had to use my knife," Pike replied with a deadpan face.

"And after it broke," he said with a sly smile. "I had to bite the rest of them to death."

"I haven't been able to get the taste out of my mouth since."

The rest of the Platoon howled with laughter, and the tension was broken. The anxiety was gone, and there were smiles again. More reassurance they needed.

"When we hit the LZ," Pike ordered when the platoon stopped laughing. "forget running towards the wood line and setting up a perimeter, like the order said."

"Form on me, instead."

"If and when I think we're clear, we'll move to the wood line as a unit."

"But we'll do it when and if I give the word, and not before," He warned.

"If we do move," he added. "you squad leaders keep your people spread out and low."

"Don't get ahead of the unit on your flank."

"But if we take fire when we land," Pike explained. "hit the deck as soon as you clear the chopper, then form on me, and wait for my orders."

"I think the bad guys will be waiting on us when we go in this morning, and there'll probably be a shitload of them," He predicted.

"So, remember what I said, keep cool, and don't do anything stupid."

"Just do what I tell you, and I'll try to get you through this alive."

"Whatever you do," He warned. "don't panic."

"If you do, you're going to get waxed, sure as shit, along with some of your friends."

"Stay loose, keep cool, and control your emotions."

"You've all been shot at before," Pike reminded them. "so you all know the Dicks can't shoot worth a shit anyway."

"If we start taking fire, I'll tell you where to go, when, and what to do when we get there."

"But when we move, keep low." He warned everybody again.

"You stand up; you're going to get killed."

"So, keep your ass glued to the ground and crawl when you move."

"Got me?"

Young heads nodded in response because everyone was listening very closely now. Pike was the man. He knew what to do when things got messy. So, you paid attention when he spoke and followed his orders. Exactly.

"Squad leaders," Pike ordered. "check your people."

"Make sure everybody takes extra ammo, grenades, and water; no exceptions."

"If your people need anything, like water bladders, have them go get it now, and be quick about it."

"We've about ten more minutes before moving to the PZ."

"Standard loading order on the birds when we get there," Pike continued.

"We'll be in the first four birds, and I'll go in with first squad."

"Now, get what you need and be ready to move to the pickup zone in ten mikes."

"Will this operation be bad, Sgt Pike?" A lone voice asked a few minutes later after everyone had returned.

Pike turned back towards the platoon. Anxious young faces waited for his answer, and he didn't want to lie. Not intentionally.

"I don't know, son," Pike finally said, not wanting to tell the whole truth and scare the shit out of everybody. "But I'm not taking any chances."

"And neither are you."

"That's why we're going in heavy with all the extra ammo."

"That's why you won't be running to the nearest wood line when we touch down."

"And that's why I told you to form on me as soon as we unass the choppers."

"Clear?"

Everyone nodded.

"If we get hit, listen to your squad leaders, do what they tell you, and you'll be fine," Pike predicted.

"Don't freeze up and panic."

"Remember," Pike told them. "we got guns too."

"So, use them, and hit something when you fire."

"Don't just shoot to make noise and waste ammo."

"Pick a target and knock it down when you fire."

"We will, Boss," another young voice promised enthusiastically.

"We're badasses."

"You made us that way."

"That's right," another kid boasted.

"We bring smoke when we light something up."

"We know how to shoot and scoot."

"Yeah," another youngster said, joining in.

"Charlie fucks with us; we'll clean his clock and put the Damn Damn on his ass."

"Damn right," someone else echoed, caught up in the enthusiasm. "We're the big dogs in this barnyard."

"You fuck with us; we'll bite your ass."

"We will kick some NVA ass if they mess with us."

"Big-time!"

"Jesus," Pike thought, smiling and watching his people get fired up. "I hope we don't even see any NVA today."

"Much less meet any on the LZ."

"I hope I'm dead wrong about all this, and this entire operation turns out to be a walk in the park."

"I hope that idiot battalion commander was right."

"All right, A Company," the CO yelled from his CP five minutes later. "move to the PZ and stand by to load."

"The birds are inbound."

"Move it out, ladies," Pike told his platoon. "It's time to go to work and earn your pay."

"Uncle Sam isn't giving you all those big bucks to lay around on your asses over here and get a tan."

The platoon chuckled. They were thinking of the thirty pitiful dollars they each earned monthly. Apparently, that's all their lives were worth. Pitiful. Afterward, they started moving to the PZ, Pike leading them.

Ten minutes later, the first lift was airborne. It was part of another heavy package. Nine Slicks, two guns, plus a Command-and-Control bird. The C&C bird contained the battalion commander, who would control the insertion. The two Snakes accompanying the Slicks would provide fire support.

Pike's platoon was in the first four birds. Second Platoon, plus the Company headquarters, were in the last five. The company's third platoon would come in on the second lift with Delta Company's first platoon. At least that was the plan.

Pike had serious doubts about that happening. As he watched the ground fade away when the bird gained altitude, his stomach knotted as he reviewed the flight time involved.

"The flight to the LZ will take twenty minutes," he calculated.

"It will take another twenty-plus minutes for the Slicks to unload and get back to the PZ."

"Five more minutes to load up again with the second lift and "another twenty more minutes to bring the second lift back to the LZ!"

"That means a total of forty-five minutes between lifts."

"That's an eternity if the Dicks are waiting for us."

"It could all be over, and we could all be dead before the second lift even gets back to the LZ to reinforce us!"

"Hell, the second lift could even be shot off the LZ and have to abort because of heavy ground fire, and that would make a third lift impossible."

"It would have to wait at least another full hour and a half, minimum, because the birds would have to return to the airfield and refuel before returning to the firebase, picking the third lift up and then ferrying them back to the LZ."

"Who dreamed up this abortion?" Pike thought angrily, tasting the bitterness in his throat as he watched the green jungle flow beneath him.

"This plan is so bad it's a fucking disaster just waiting to happen."

"That means that tight-assed, smiling LTC obviously doesn't know shit about planning an airmobile operation either."

"Or anything else for that matter."

"He probably never considered the flight time to and from the PZ to the LZ when he dreamed up this cluster fuck."

"Much less the required refueling between lifts."

"That fact alone will split the battalion in two."

"Half of it on the LZ and the other half still on the PZ, sitting around waiting while the rest of us are getting our asses shot off."

"Given that, if we run into trouble, we'll be in shit so deep we'll be swimming in it."

"When the shit hits the fan on the LZ, we're going to be all by our lonesome, with Dicks all over us before the second lift can get back to help us," Pike realized.

"God help us."

Pike looked over at Paco, his RTO. The little Mexican was fidgeting with his web gear, and his eyes were so wide you could see their whites highlighted in his brown face.

"He's nervous," Pike thought correctly. *"Did he pick it up from me?"*

Pike quickly glanced at the rest of his men on the helo. Eyes were darting, and hands were fidgety. They were scared too.

"Jesus," he thought, genuinely surprised. *"am I that obvious?"*

"Is my concern about this fuck up rubbing off on them?"

"That's the last thing I need," He worried.

A moment later, the copilot yelled back. "Two minutes."

"Get ready."

Pike nodded his acknowledgment.

"Too late now," he thought. *"we're committed."*

"Lock and load," he ordered.

Pike pulled the charging handle back on the M-16 and chambered a round. The bolt slid forward with a satisfying clunk, seating the new brass cartridge into the chamber. He then slapped the bottom of the magazine to ensure it was seated correctly. Everybody else did the same. It was almost time.

Faces were tense now as sweat poured off frightened bodies. Beads of it started to pop out on brows, and dry lips were licked continuously. Fun time was over, and everyone knew it. If the LZ was hot, the dying would begin shortly. Time to get busy living or get ready to die.

Pike's platoon knew that. They were already sweating furiously despite the cool air pouring into the helo. Pike even caught a whiff of the rancid odor of fear coming off Paco. The young Mexican was terrified as he edged over closer to the helo's side door, getting ready to unass. Suddenly, the helo nosed over abruptly and dove for the LZ.

"Christ," Pike realized, with a knot in his gut. "we're here."

"Please, God, at least let us at least get off the choppers before they open up on us,"

"At least give us that much of a chance," Pike prayed.

"These are good kids, Lord, and they deserve that much."

"At least let them have a fighting chance to stay alive."

Seconds later, the bird flared, its skids kissing the dry paddy with a slight bump. Pike jumped off immediately, Paco following with the other six men. They all hit the ground and buried themselves in the waist-high elephant grass with debris from the helo's rotor wash temporarily blinding them when it lifted back off. The bird's engine screamed, and a moment later, it was gone. The platoon was down, and the nightmare was about to begin.

A second later, Pike heard the first explosion, and the firing started. He seemed to be surrounded by it. He whirled around quickly towards the sound and stuck his head above the grass. When it did, the jungle around the LZ erupted in a new avalanche of weapons fire. The sixth helo in the formation was on the ground on its side and on fire. Men with burning clothes were stumbling out of it when its fuel tank suddenly exploded into an orange fireball with a loud Whoomph, encompassing everything around it.

"Shit," Pike spat, half in anger and half in disgust, as he hit the ground again. *"I knew it!"*

"The bastards were just waiting on us."

"We're in for it now."

"Dawson," he screamed at the 1st squad leader. "get your people back into that depression behind us."

"You too, Pardee," he yelled at the second squad leader.

"And tell Martin and the third squad too."

Dawson waved his hand in acknowledgment and started moving his squad, shouting orders. Everyone was in a low crawl. They couldn't get any closer to the ground because their shirt buttons were in the way. Pardee's and Martin's squads followed, fear etched on their young faces.

"Paco, get me the gunships," Pike screamed over the noise of the firefight.

Then he waited. 7.62 AK-47 rounds tore through the elephant grass all around them, shredding it like green confetti, while green NVA tracers created miniature rainbows as they buzzed overhead. RPD machine guns sounded like industrial sewing machines hammering out dungarees, and RPGs blew the ground up like miniature volcanoes.

Pike's situation was terrible and turning worse by the second. The NVA had the company surrounded, outnumbered, and outgunned. He and his platoon would die within minutes unless the situation changed dramatically. They were pinned, and the NVA had them cold.

A moment later, Pike had the lead pilot of the two gunships on the horn.

"We're taking heavy fire from the eastern tree line of the LZ," he reported urgently.

"I need it hit hard, as soon as you can."

"WILCO," the pilot replied. "we see the tracers."

"We're rolling in hot now."

"Hang on,"

"We'll fire them up for you."

Pike watched as the gunships made two passes over the tree line moments later, firing rockets and miniguns. The ordnance tore into the tree line savagely, and pieces of vegetation and trees flew into the air with each pass. Still, the firing continued unabated. It was like trying to kill an elephant with a BB gun. As the gunships raked the area, he and Paco crawled back to the depression and joined the rest of the platoon.

Just as they reached it, the guns made another pass. But Pike noticed that the gunship's murderous fire had little effect on the dug-in NVA. The tree line's wall of lead barely diminished after the gunship strikes. Apparently, the NVA were there to stay and were determined.

On their third pass, the lead gunship wobbled violently over the wood line as it came in and took heavy fire. The Dicks were waiting on it this time, and they had the range right. Pike could hear rounds plinking into its aluminum skin and knew it was in trouble. Suddenly, it abruptly nosed over and fell out of the air, crashing into the jungle in a fiery mass. He watched helplessly as black oily smoke rolled up from the green foliage and the bird's ammunition started cooking off in the blaze that engulfed its wreckage.

"Oh Shit." He thought. "The situation is about to get much worse."

"We just lost half of our fire support."

Pike was right. A second later, the second gunship also suddenly sprouted a wisp of black smoke from its engine compartment. Its pilot barely pulled it up in time and struggled to avoid the continuing ground fire and clear the treetops. It was hit badly and in trouble.

Moments later, the stricken helo somehow managed to clear the area. Seconds later, the pilot fought for control as the gunship slid all over the sky. When he finally regained it, he gained altitude as he headed back towards the firebase moments later, flying erratically and trailing even more smoke.

Pike and his people were completely alone now, waiting to be annihilated.

"Paco," Pike yelled as rounds continued to pour through the elephant grass. "get me, Redleg."

"Let's get some artillery on their asses."

"The gunships have had it."

"Dawson," he screamed. "call the CO on the company freq. and tell him we need TAC air right fucking now. "

"As much as we can get."

Dawson, across the depression, waved an acknowledgment.

"Paco," Pike asked, turning around. "where's that artillery?"

Paco didn't answer. He couldn't. The top of his head had been blown off. Blood and gray brain matter were still oozing down his shocked face. Pike saw it when he turned and stared at the mess that had been his friend a moment ago.

"Goddammit," he murmured sadly. "I told you to keep your head down, Paco."

"Now, look what you've gone and done."

"Dawson," Pike yelled, snapping out of it a moment later. "Send me a man for the radio."

"Paco's down."

A youngster named Nesbit crawled over a minute later, his face turning white when he saw Paco.

"Jesus," he said fearfully, "what happened to Paco, Sarge?"

"He's dead," Pike said grimly.

"Take his radio off him and strap it on."

"You're my new RTO, and I need you."

Nesbit gagged twice at the brain matter, and gore spread everywhere. Still, he did what he was told, finally getting the radio off Paco and strapping it to his own back.

"Good man," Pike said, smiling at Nesbit as he changed magazines.

"Now, keep your head down and do what I tell you."

Nesbit nodded and smiled back. He was terrified, and it showed.

"Pike," Dawson yelled a moment later from across the depression. "The Captain's dead, and so is the second platoon leader."

"They were both in that chopper that went down and caught fire."

"What's left of the Second platoon just called and told me."

"That means you're running the Company now, and second platoon wants to know what to do?"

"Tell them to crawl over to our position," Pike yelled, thinking.

"And make sure they bring their wounded with them."

"Their dead too, if they can get to them," He added.

"When they get here, have them fill in the perimeter around the hole."

"What about us?" Pike asked. "what's our status?"

"We got two WIA and Paco," Dawson reported. "and we'll probably have more real soon.

"Every time somebody sticks his head up and tries to return fire, they get hit."

"Then put some fire on that wood line with the M-79s," Pike ordered. "Make the gunners stay down when they do."

"I'm trying to get us some fire support, so you handle the Platoon until I do."

Dawson nodded his acknowledgment.

"Nesbit," Pike ordered. "give me that handset."

"Waco Six, this is Alpha one six," Pike transmitted on the battalion frequency.

"This is WACO six," the battalion commander answered in a quavering voice.

"What the hell's going on down there?" He screamed.

"I can't raise your Six."

"The CO and the second platoon leader are dead," Pike replied in a tight voice. "They were in the Slick that blew up on the LZ when we inserted."

"I'm running the Company now, and I need fire support ASAP."

"I've got at least two battalions of NVA dug in on the eastern wood line of the LZ with heavy weapons."

"They're shooting the shit out us, now that the gunships are gone."

"There's probably more of them on the southern and western side of the LZ."

There was silence as Pike waited for a comment or an acknowledgment from the LTC, but nothing happened. Complete silence. No answer at all. He wondered if his radio was dead, but it wasn't.

"Waco, this is Alpha six. I say again, I need air support," Pike told his Battalion CO angrily. "right now."

"And we need artillery on that tree line ASAP until the air gets on station."

"Acknowledge."

"But intelligence said there would only be light resistance," The LTC finally replied in a skeptical, childlike voice, ignoring Pike's request.

"I don't understand what's going on."

"You must be mistaken, Pike," He screamed

"Fuck what intelligence said," Pike roared angrily.

"I'm *telling* you we are in deep shit down here, Colonel."

"If you don't get us some fire support in the next few minutes, they'll shoot us to doll rags or overrun us."

"Christ, if you don't believe me, look down at us, and you can see what's happening yourself."

"I don't believe you, Sgt," the LTC shot back irrationally. "You're scared, and you're exaggerating the situation."

"Let me talk to your CO; he'll tell me the truth."

"He's the only one I can still trust."

"Everyone else is against me."

"They don't......."

Pike was astonished at the bizarre exchange as the radio suddenly went dead again. Had the man gone insane? Christ, Pike had just told him the Company commander was dead. Couldn't he see what was happening from the C&C bird circling the LZ? Suddenly, a new voice came on the radio. One that sounded rational.

"Pike, this is Captain Larson," the new voice said. "I'm the battalion S-3."

"The battalion commander's head is fucked up, and he's not acting normal, so I'm taking over."

"Tell me what you need."

Pike repeated his request for TAC air and artillery support.

"Roger," the battalion S-3 said. "I'm requesting them now."

"I'll send in the second lift as soon as possible."

"Negative," Pike told Larson quickly. "don't do that, Captain."

"There's no place for them to go."

"They'll be chopped up as soon as they try to land."

"We got beaucoup Dicks down here, Sir, and they have heavy weapons."

"That's what got the Slicks and the two gunships."

"They got the LZ covered like a blanket, so they'll shoot down anything trying to come in now."

"The only chance we've got is TAC Air support and a lot of it."

"The Dicks are dug in," Pike explained. "So, artillery isn't going to do much more than make them keep their heads down."

"It'll take TAC air to get them off our asses and move them."

"Otherwise, we're finished."

"Right now, we're barely hanging on by our fingernails," Pike reported. "Every time we try and even return fire, we take casualties."

"So, if the Dicks assault our position, they'll roll over us like we aren't even here."

"How many people do you still have left?" Larson asked anxiously. "and what's your position?"

"I've got around twenty-three effectives from my element." Pike replied. "plus, there's ten or fifteen more from second platoon that are trying to get over to my position."

"We're in a small depression in the middle of the LZ."

"That's the only thing keeping us alive."

"The Dicks have the entire LZ surrounded; if they have mortars, we're screwed."

"I understand," Larson said. "Hang in there, Pike."

"I've got TAC air on the way."

"The FAC will come up on this frequency when they get here, and Arty wi....."

Suddenly, the transmission from Larson ended abruptly. When it did, Pike realized he was listening to a dead handset. He held the handset up to Nesbit and shrugged. His new RTO checked the radio.

"It ain't us, Sarge," Nesbit yelled a moment later. "we're fine."

"It's them," He said, pointing at the chopper.

Pike glanced skyward. The C&C bird left the area wobbling dangerously, a plume of black smoke pouring out of its engine compartment. It, too, had been hit and bad enough to force it to leave the battlefield.

"Shit," Pike said unconsciously. "First the gunships and now the C&C."

"We're about to get our asses handed to us."

Nesbit's eyes widened perceptibly.

"Jesus," he thought. "If Ironman Pike is worried, I'm about to get very scared."

"Please, God," he prayed. "don't let me get killed today."

"It's my birthday."

Suddenly, a rocket-propelled grenade exploded nearby, and clumps of earth rained down on both men. Nesbit's eyes widened, and his ears rang as he tried to crawl into his helmet. Seconds later, rounds started ripping around the elephant grass like a buzz saw, tearing into it as if it were tissue paper and cutting it to pieces.

The Dicks had finally figured out Pike's position and turned their full attention towards it. As the enemy fire intensified, the pitiful remnants of the two small platoons in the depression tried to mold themselves into the earth to escape the murderous fire. They were all alone now, and death was only an eyelash away.

Suddenly, another man screamed as he got hit. An RPG exploded nearby a second later, and more screams followed. Fire coming in over the hole increased dramatically, and fear ratcheted up exponentially.

"Get ready," Pike screamed to everyone. "They're coming!"

"They're going to try and overrun us!"

"When their machine guns shift fire, let go with everything you've got."

Chapter Three

Pike had been in numerous firefights in his previous two tours, so he was not a man that frightened easily. In many, he had even been outnumbered and outgunned. Some had lasted for minutes; others had lasted for hours. One had even lasted two full days. But he had never been in one as intense and as deadly as this one.

The amount of fire being laid down on his position was devastating. Had he and his men not been protected by the depression, they would all be dead by now. This firefight had all the prerequisites for a massacre in the making, and Pike realized it. If the Dicks assaulted, Pike was sure his people couldn't stop them.

He had less than fifty men in the middle of an open field, surrounded by well over eight hundred NVA. His Company commander was dead, and his Battalion commander had gone nuts. He was at least twenty minutes by air from the nearest friendly forces, and the enemy had already shot down his only fire support; the two gunships.

Lastly, the Command-and-Control helicopter, controlling and supposedly supporting him, had also been forced to return to base because of battle damage, so he and his people were alone. He couldn't even call for artillery anymore. The firebase where it was located was too far away, and the C&C bird that was his airborne radio relay was gone. His situation could hardly get any worse.

Consequently, the NVA were now giving Pike and his pitifully small force their undivided attention. As a result, the fire pouring into his position was virtually non-stop. To raise your head above the rim of the depression was to invite death. That made trying to return fire suicide. In the last five minutes alone, four more men were killed and three more wounded because they had tried.

The air above the depression sounded like a disturbed bee hive on steroids. Hundreds of AK rounds zipped overhead continuously, sounding like angry wasps. They ripped through the stalks of the elephant grass still standing, turning it into green confetti as RPGs exploded all around the depression.

"One of them is bound to hit us," Pike thought. *"It's just a matter of time."*

"When it does, the Dicks will know the correct range and blow us to hell.

"Especially since the only fire the platoon we're able to return is from the four M-79 grenade launchers."

"And it's not even scaring them."

"So, unless we get some TacAir soon, we will cease to exist in about five more minutes."

Pike's only hope was more Tactical air support, and he knew it. But to get it, he'd have to request it through the firebase. Only their radios had the range and bandwidth to request it. That was impossible with his radios. They had neither.

Worse, despite all his efforts, he had been unable to regain contact with the C&C bird since it had departed. Without it and its radios, Pike realized he had only minutes left. The NVA were undoubtedly assembling an assault force to overrun his position at that very moment. As he waited fearfully, he wondered what they were waiting for.

"They're waiting for another lift to come in to reinforce us," he finally realized.

"When that happens, that will give them more targets to engage."

'More helicopters to shoot down and more Americans to kill."

"They can kill us anytime they want, but we're not a big enough target."

"Not yet."

"So, they're just playing with us trying to get me to call in reinforcements

"They don't want to kill us right now because if we're dead, there won't be anybody to rescue."

"That makes us nothing more than live bait for a bigger fish."

"Keep your heads down," he yelled to everyone.

Finally, after what seemed like hours but was, in fact, only minutes, Nesbit heard an unfamiliar voice come up on his radio. It was a FAC. (Forward Air Controller) When he gazed skyward, he could see him. He was in a tiny OV-1, hovering over the LZ at ten thousand feet and out of the small arms range. When Nesbit spotted the tiny aluminum speck circling overhead, he handed the handset to Pike.

"I got somebody, Sarge," he yelled excitedly. "I think it's the FAC up there," He said, pointing.

"Thank God," Pike thought as he took the handset and tried to call him.

When the FAC answered, Pike felt a wave of relief wash over him. Larson or someone had gotten through after all. Now at least they had a chance

The FAC informed Pike that he had a four-plane section of F-4s with him, loaded with five-hundred-pound fin retarded bombs, called *Snake eyes* by the grunts. Just what Pike needed to blast the NVA out of their holes. Maybe enough to give him and his men another few precious minutes.

"I've got you, FAC," he screamed into the radio. "What do you want me to do?"

"Mark his position and designate your first target," the FAC replied.

Hearing that, Pike felt a ray of hope for the first time since he had landed. At least he and his men now stood a chance of surviving now, a slim one.

"Dawson," he yelled across the depression. "throw a smoke grenade into the middle of the depression."

Dawson nodded, and a moment later, yellow smoke from the grenade billowed skyward in a bright yellow plume.

"I've got your yellow smoke," the FAC reported a moment later. "what's the target?"

"The eastern tree line of the open rice field I'm in," Pike replied anxiously.

"I've got a least a battalion of NVA dug in there with heavy weapons."

"Maybe more."

"They are my primary problem."

"If you can take them out, then we'll go to work on my other problems."

The FAC chuckled.

"You got that many, huh?" he asked jokingly.

"Yeah," Pike said, relieved at the FAC's humor. "I do."

"If you only knew."

"Hit the tree line first," Pike ordered. "Be advised the Dicks have already shot down two gunships and my C&C bird."

"That means they have heavy weapons in there up the wazoo."

"So, tell your fast movers to roll in with everything smoking."

"Roger," the FAC responded. "I understand, and I'll pass the word on."

"When they roll in, they'll be rocking and rolling with all guns blazing."

"Make sure you keep your people's heads down."

"WILCO," Pike replied.

A moment later, he yelled to Dawson and his other two squad leaders to get everybody down.

"Help is on the way." He told them. "Finally."

"I'm marking the target now," The FAC advised.

The OV-1 then rolled in, and the FAC put two white phosphorus rockets into the center of the eastern tree line. A moment later, a cloud of white smoke billowed upwards.

"That's the center of the target," Pike confirmed.

"Hit it hard."

"Get your heads down," the FAC ordered. "It's about to get very noisy down there."

Within seconds, jet exhaust screamed by, followed immediately by miniguns' rattling, then a loud explosion. The ground trembled, and suddenly, there was black oily smoke everywhere and two ugly black holes where what was left of the tree line had been. The first F-4 had screamed in and unloaded its five hundred pounders on the white smoke, and the results were devastating.

Its pass was followed moments later by the F-4's wingman, and the earth trembled again as his ordnance exploded. More death, destruction, and black smoke followed. Pike watched in satisfaction and smiled. It was payback time. Now the NVA were getting their asses handed to them for a change, which was good news. The shoe was on the other foot, and they were dying.

"Keep it coming," He yelled into the mike.

Moments later, the other two aircraft in the flight did a repeat performance. Each one dove and dropped their loads on the NVA positions. Again, with each explosion, a shockwave rolled over the depression each time a bomb exploded. It deafened everyone, and the concussion momentarily flattened the remaining elephant grass around the depression. Immediately afterward, thick acrid-smelling black smoke filled the air as bits of earth and foliage rained down everywhere and the Ia Drang had more torn up real estate.

That caused Pike's people to huddle up into fetal positions with their fingers in their ears. But they were smiling when they did. The fast movers were ripping the NVA to shreds, and they loved it.

Soon, a wave of black, foul-smelling smoke floated over the entire field and blocked out the sun. By that time, the NVA firing had slacked off appreciably. Probably because a sizable portion of the NVA were either dead or wounded. When it did, Pike called the FAC again and gave him a damage assessment.

"That got their attention, By God," Pike told him.

"Is that it, or have you got more birds?"

"I've got two more four plane sections inbound," the FAC replied.

"They'll be here in less than three mikes, and they're loaded with snake and nape."

"Just hang tight, partner."

"We'll get you out of that pocket yet."

"If the snake eyes didn't scare them off, we'll make crispy critters out of the sonsabitches with the napalm."

"Don't worry," Pike replied. "we aren't about to try and go anywhere.

"We'll just wait right here, all hunkered down nice and tight, and wait for you and your friends to start the barbeque and evict all those assholes from the premises."

The FAC laughed.

"This guy is Okay," he thought. *"he's up to his ass in alligators down there, and he's still cool as a cucumber."*

"He's too good of a man to lose."

"So, the US Air Force is going to save his ass."

"When your next group of fast movers gets here," Pike suggested a moment later. "hit the tree line again with the first section, and then hit the south end of the field with the second."

"I've got a feeling there's another bunch of assholes dug in there too, just waiting for their chance to join the party."

"After that's done, have the third section hit your current target again with napalm," Pike added.

"I'm pretty sure the first strike didn't get them all," Pike opined. "because we're still taking fire from that area."

"The stubborn little bastards just don't know when to quit."

"We can fix that," the FAC replied. "we'll hit both targets again as soon as I mark them."

"If the Gomers haven't started pulling back from that tree line by the time my next sortie gets here," the FAC predicted. "we'll either plant them there permanent like then set them on fire."

"I'd like to use your second strike as cover to try and get a Medevac bird in here," Pike explained to the FAC a moment later.

"I got three criticals down here. I need to get them out ASAP."

"If they don't get evacuated soon, they're not going to make it."

"If I can get somebody with balls enough to try it, I'll try and bring them in using your birds as cover."

"Roger," the FAC replied. "I'll have my fast movers cover their insertion and extraction, and I'll control it."

"Just give me a heads up when you're ready."

"Thanks," Pike said. "now let me see if I can raise anybody back in my rear and get a Medevac.".

"Stand by," Pike requested.

"Waco, this is Alpha Six," Pike transmitted a moment later.

"Alpha six, this is Waco," Captain Larson responded. "I'm back up on the net again in another helo."

"Sorry about having to unass the area earlier, but the C&C bird got hit pretty bad and started to go down."

"We had two aircrew wounded, and we barely made it back to the firebase," He explained.

"I've been monitoring your transmissions ever since I got back and the FAC contacted you, but we couldn't raise you."

"I had to finally take a radio and get onto a little bird and get up over the firebase itself before I could make contact."

"That's where I am now, about three thousand feet up over the firebase.

"I've been monitoring your conversation with the FAC, and I've already requested a Medevac," Larson continued.

"I explained your situation and plan to the pilot, and he's willing to try and get in."

"He's inbound to your location now, and he'll contact the FAC to coordinate his insert."

"I've also got artillery ready to begin firing as soon as you give me coordinates to support him."

"What's your current status?" Larson asked.

"I've got eleven KIA and eight WIA," Pike reported.

"Three of them are critical."

"I'm going to use the second airstrike as cover to try and get the Medevac bird in here."

"Understand," Larson answered. "I've got four gunships orbiting just north of your location, and I've got a lift package of eight slicks ready to launch to try and extract you when you're ready."

"What about using the airstrike by the third set of fast movers, plus the gunships to cover your extraction?" Larson asked.

"Let's see how much fire I'm still taking after the next airstrike first," Pike replied.

"I don't want to bring the extraction helos in too early and get them shot down."

"The Dicks are still pretty goddamned active around the LZ even after that first airstrike."

"We're still taking a helluva lot of fire from that tree line, so I got enough problems down here without having to try and rescue downed aircrew because we jumped the gun and tried to bring them in too early."

"You're the Boss," Larson said. "just tell me what you need and when you're ready."

"Maybe the second strike will calm the Dicks down long enough for us to try an extraction," Pike said, hopefully

"We'll see."

"Meanwhile, put some artillery on the following coordinates, RA 127588."

"Have them start walking it westward in twenty-five-meter increments."

"I'll have one of my squad leaders adjust it using the Company's alternate, repeat alternate, frequency."

"WILCO," Larson said. "I'll be standing by for your decision on the extraction."

"Dawson," Pike yelled. "I've got arty coming in on the tree line."

"You adjust it on the alternate frequency, and I'll keep in contact with the FAC on our primary."

Dawson waved and then got on his radio. A moment later, artillery rounds started impacting the LZ. When they hit, Dawson began adjusting them to cover the tree line. Satisfied, Pike contacted the FAC again.

"FAC," Pike transmitted, "did you copy my last with my higher?"

"I monitored," the FAC responded. "and I'm already in contact with the Medevac."

"He's already airborne."

"When he gets here, I'll bring my fast movers in North to South."

"While they hit the tree line, the medevac bird will come in from the southwest after the first pass," He told Pike.

"I'll brief him in a moment."

"That way, we can keep the arty going during the airstrike because it's coming in from the east."

"So, neither the fast movers nor the Medevac will be on the gun-target line."

"That'll work," Pike said in agreement.

"We're as ready for him as we can be right now."

"The F-4s should keep the Gomers heads down long enough to let the Dust off get in and back out again if he's quick," The FAC explained.

"Have your wounded ready because I'm going to have him land right on top of you."

"WILCO," Pike replied.

"After the second strike has been completed," The FAC suggested. "I'm going to put the gunships in over the wood line and see if they take any fire."

"If they do," the FAC explained. "I'll hit those NVA positions again with the third section of F-4's, and this time they'll use napalm."

"If they don't take fire," he continued. "we can try and bring in the Slicks while the gunships rake the area with minigun fire."

"I'll use my fast movers as cover for them."

"Have them hit the area with napalm first," Pike replied.

"I know for certain that will quiet the little bastards down."

"And the smoke it will generate will help screen the Slicks when they come in."

"WILCO," the Fac replied.

"When you bring in the Slicks," Pike added. "have them land directly on my position too, just like the Dust off."

"That way, I won't have to expose my people any more than necessary," he explained.

"I've barely got enough effectives left to carry all the wounded and dead, so I don't need anymore."

"WILCO," the FAC replied. "They're inbound to an orbit point five miles south of you now."

"When the Slicks come in, and the gunships hit both wood lines with minigun fire," Pike continued. "have your fast movers drop more napalm on the south end of the LZ. Tell them to shoot the place to doll rags."

"That should keep the NVA there occupied too."

"But keep in mind, the Dicks may be just waiting for us to try something like this," Pike said.

"So, I want to hit the entire tree line with napalm before they can open up on us from a different direction."

"WILCO," the FAC replied. "I'll wait to bring in the extraction birds until after my fast mover's second pass."

"Then I'll turn the gunships loose as soon as my guys are clear."

"After they expend, I'll hit the Gomers with more napalm."

"That should get all the bastard's attention for the next ten minutes, and that's all we need."

"I hope so," Pike prayed.

When the second section of F-4s attacked the NVA positions in the eastern and southern wood lines, minutes later, a Dust Off helo came in low and fast, over the treetops from the southwest. It sat down directly on Pike's position. Pike had his people ready for him, so the wounded were loaded aboard quickly. As a result, the Medevac bird did his pickup and lifted back off immediately.

That was undoubtedly because most of the NVA were too busy trying to keep their heads down from the airstrike to bring any effective fire on the Dust-off bird when he landed. The napalm strike had fried most of their asses, and the jungle tree line to the east and the south were burning fiercely.

Following the second napalm strike, Pike and his men were receiving only sporadic fire from that side of the LZ, which was burning fiercely. Based on that, Pike decided to employ the third set of F-4s. While they attacked the eastern side of the LZ one last time, Pike would bring in seven Slicks to extract himself and his men. Simultaneously, the four gunships would chew up any pockets of resistance that fired on the extraction birds at the southern end of the LZ.

It took a few minutes before all the birds, the gunships, the Slicks, and the FAC were briefed. Finally, everyone involved knew the plan. Afterward, Pike quickly briefed his people and got them ready to extract. Then he lined them up in loads. They would pour out of the depression the minute the extraction Slicks landed and jump on the helos as quickly as possible.

Moments later, the coordinated ballet began. The FAC brought in the airstrike and coordinated the gunship passes on the southern wood line while it was in progress. As both elements pounded their targets, he then coordinated and controlled the insertion of the Slicks.

Minutes later, while the F-4s were making their final pass on the wood line, the seven extraction Slicks came barreling in through the smoke from the west and landed astride Pike's position. Pike and his men scrambled out of the depression and leaped aboard, carrying all their WIAs and KIAs. Seconds later, all the birds lifted off again, their engines redlined and screaming for altitude. Pike ensured he took everybody, the living and the dead, when he left.

He was the last man on the last chopper when it lifted off. He watched as the four gunships raked the eastern wood line with minigun and rocket fire one last time. Unbelievably, after four airstrikes and three separate gunships run on their positions, a considerable number of NVA were still firing. Pike could see their green tracers flicking across the LZ as he lifted off.

"Jesus," he said to himself as the Slick gained altitude. "and that bozo LtCol was planning on taking this place with just two measly Companies."

"The man is a certifiable lunatic."

"You couldn't have taken this place with a regiment!"

Once the Slick gained altitude and the LZ faded into the distance, Pike let out the pent-up breath he had been holding and relaxed slightly. He could hardly believe the extraction had gone off that smoothly, and he and his men were now safe.

He had fully expected to extract under heavy fire and lose even more men. Maybe even some helos. But apparently, the airstrikes on the NVA positions had been more effective than he thought. Or perhaps the NVA had pulled back some of their forces to seek better cover in preparation for an assault. Or maybe the pall of black smoke from the napalm strikes that obscured the center of the LZ had prevented the remaining NVA from bringing any accurate, concerted fire on the extraction choppers.

Whatever the reason, Pike didn't care. With the remnants of the second platoon, his platoon was out of the deathtrap, and that was all that mattered. They would all live to fight another day, but just by the thinnest of margins. They could just have easily all wound up dead. It had been that close.

Pike's legs dangled out of the chopper, and the cool air dried the sweat covering the rest of his body as the helo flew back towards the firebase. He was so thirsty from all the action, his mouth felt like cotton, so he drank a full canteen of water in one gigantic swallow. Yet strangely, he still felt thirsty.

Afterward, Pike looked around the inside of the helo at his men. Most of them were wide-eyed and still jumpy. Some were still shaking. The adrenaline hadn't worn off yet, and they still couldn't believe they were still alive and safe. Yet, Nesbit, who was beside him, turned and smiled at him.

"Thanks, Sarge," The young RTO said softly.

"For what?" Pike asked curiously.

"Today's my birthday," Nesbit said shyly. "For a while, I thought it would be my last one."

"Now, thanks to you, I'm still alive to celebrate it."

"How old are you, son?" Pike asked at his new RTO.

"Nineteen today," Nesbit said proudly.

Pike shook his head in wonder.

"Congratulations, son," he said, smiling. "I'll buy you a beer when we get back to base."

"You deserve one."

"You did a good job today, and I'm proud of you."

"Only nineteen years old and going through a firefight like that without breaking or freezing up," Pike thought.

"How many other eighteen-year-olds could claim that."

"Jesus, I'm proud of these kids."

Afterward, he, too, relaxed and enjoyed the cool breeze.

When Pike and his men landed back at the firebase twenty minutes later, he was surprised to see the Brigade commander, a full Colonel, standing just off the LZ waiting for the Slicks to land and offload. As soon as Pike and his men exited the birds and the medics picked up the wounded, Captain Larson, standing beside the Brigade commander, waved Pike over. Pike walked over to the two men, saluted, and reported.

"Sgt Pike reporting with First and Second platoons of Alpha Company, Sir."

The Colonel returned Pike's salute, then stuck out his hand and shook Pike's vigorously.

"I'm damned glad to see you and your men back, Sgt Pike," he said. "That was one hell of a firefight and an extremely close-run thing."

"I wasn't sure you would get back for a while."

"Four separate airstrikes and the NVA were still shooting at you when you extracted," He said in awe. "That must have been some free for all out there."

"Your two beat-up platoons against an NVA regiment."

"Jesus," he shouted, expelling air.

"I've never experienced anything like that before."

"Never even heard of anything like that."

"I'm amazed you and your men are still alive."

"What happened out there, Sgt?"

"The NVA were waiting for us, Sir," Pike replied. "Two battalions, maybe more."

"They were dug in on three sides of the LZ with heavy weapons."

"It was a setup based on yesterday."

"They knew we were coming back today."

"As soon as the insertion birds touched down, they opened up on them, and their fire took out three helos and all their passengers within seconds."

"My Company commander and the only other officer on the ground were in one of those birds and died instantly."

"When I saw that, I took over the company and ordered the survivors to crawl to my position and bring their wounded."

"My platoon was lucky, Sir," Pike said. "When we offloaded, there was a small depression behind us, so when we started taking fire, we all got in it and tried to return fire."

"And the NVA......"

"It took more than luck to get out of that mess, Sgt Pike." the Colonel said, interrupting.

"It took leadership and courage, and you have plenty of both."

"Captain Larson has already briefed me on what happened in the C&C over the LZ," He said disgustingly.

"As a result, I've already relieved your battalion commander because of it."

"He's on his way back to the Division Firebase as we speak, and he's finished as far as the Army is concerned."

"I'm just sorry he put you and your men through all that because of his poor judgment," The Colonel said tightly.

I'm sorry about your company commander too,"

"I would also have relieved him for incompetence, but he's dead."

"Both were useless as leaders, and this operation should have never happened."

"It was a poorly conceived, poorly planned, half-assed abortion dreamed up by a man who had neither the experience nor the ability to conduct it.

"To make matters worse, he did it without coordinating it with my staff or me."

"We didn't even realize he was going back in with the battalion until Capt. Larson called me an hour ago when all the action started."

"Larson also told me that you tried to express your doubts about the operation before it started, but your battalion commander wouldn't listen," The Colonel continued angrily.

"That's another reason he was such a failure as a leader."

"He wouldn't listen to the advice from any of his subordinates, even though they were more experienced than he was."

"But the system isn't perfect, and now and again, it puts someone in charge, who simply isn't up to the job," He explained.

"That's what's happened here," The Colonel told Pike.

"It's just a goddamned shame we didn't find out about his incompetence earlier."

"Unfortunately, that's war," He said, shaking his head in disgust.

"Some men can handle it, and some can't."

"You just don't know who can and can't until somebody starts shooting at you and the pressure is on."

"But that mistake has now been corrected," The Colonel said tightly.

"I've got a new battalion commander on the way, and he'll be here soon."

"This is his second tour, so he's been in the field before, seen his share of combat, and performed well under it."

"I know," the Colonel said. "This time, I had his records thoroughly checked before he was selected instead of just accepting whoever the Division personnel section assigned me."

"So, he should be able to handle the job adequately."

"Until he gets here," the Colonel said. "Captain Larson will be in temporary command of the battalion."

"He did a fine job today, taking over when he did, given the situation."

"That took a lot of guts on his part to override his superior and assume command."

"So, I owe him at least that much."

"You did a fine job too, Sgt Pike," The Colonel continued.

"More than a fine job; a superb one."

"From what Larson has told me, you alone are responsible for saving not only your platoon but the second platoon of the Company as well."

"You and your people performed magnificently."

"Just managing to stay alive against that large of an enemy force was a challenge."

"The entire operation was a bad situation right from the start, but you did a superb job in making the best out of it," The Colonel told Pike.

"Unfortunately, it should have never happened to begin with."

"I'm partially responsible for that," the Colonel said bitterly.

"I put the LTC, who was your battalion commander and responsible for this fiasco, in charge to begin with."

"He failed to measure up to his responsibilities."

"Therefore, I failed in my judgment when I selected him for the job," the colonel admitted wryly. "And he failed in his job because he was incompetent."

"But you didn't fail, Pike," The colonel said, almost beaming.

"Instead, despite everything, you excelled."

"You performed superbly under the utmost stress and in the most dangerous situation imaginable."

"You did much more than what was expected of you and your position and rank," The Colonel continued.

"In fact, as a combat leader in a tough position, you performed superbly, regardless of rank."

"You took command of a Company in the middle of a vicious firefight against staggering odds and saved it from being annihilated."

"And that, Sergeant," the Colonel said. "is no mean feat."

"Very few people in this man's Army are capable of doing what you did today."

"Especially as well and as professionally as you handled yourself."

"Therefore," the Colonel told Pike. "I have recommended you for a battlefield promotion."

"We need leaders like you in this Division and experienced combat veterans planning combat operations and making intelligent decisions in the field as commanders."

"You not only meet both those requirements; you exceed them."

"Your actions today proved that."

"So, I am going to promote you and put you in a position commensurate with your new rank."

Pike just stood there dumbfounded. He was barely able to believe what he was hearing.

"Me, an officer," he thought.

"Christ, I don't know how to be an officer."

"All that will take a week or so," the Colonel explained.

"Larson will fill you in on all the details later."

"So, congratulations, Sgt Pike."

The news paralyzed Pike, so he stood there silently, unable to speak. His promotion had come right out of the blue and taken him completely by surprise. The Colonel chuckled at Pike's awkwardness.

"Now, I'm sure you want to get back to your men, Sgt Pike," the Colonel concluded. "and I have to get back to running the Brigade."

"You did a superb job Sgt and tell your men they also performed admirably."

"I'm proud of both you and them."

"Keep up the good work, and Carry on."

As the Colonel walked away, he left Pike still standing mute.

Pike stood there awkwardly, still frozen, for a few more moments as he tried to absorb the news. He was unsuccessful. The announcement of his battlefield promotion had utterly stunned him. He was still trying to recover but failing. Finally, Larson grinned and stuck out his hand.

"Congratulations, Pike," he said, taking Pike's hand and shaking it. "you'll make a fine officer."

Pike nodded numbly.

"But I don't want to be Second Lieutenant, Captain," Pike finally told Larson in a strangled croak when he recovered enough to regain his voice.

"They don't know shit!" he blurted without thinking.

Larson laughed uproariously.

"Don't worry, Pike," Larson said, still chuckling. "you won't be."

"Lieutenants don't command Companies in this Division."

"The old man told me he is getting you a direct commission to Captain."

"You are about to become the new Commanding Officer of Alpha Company."

"He's already cleared it with the Division Commander."

"He told me all about it while you were on your way back to the firebase."

Pike remained speechless, even more, shocked by Larson's revelations.

"Both he and the General are proud as hell over what you did," Larson pridefully told Pike. "And so am I."

"You did a hell of a job out there. "

"You deserve to be the commanding officer of a Company, Pike."

"So, the general is going to personally pin on your Captain's bars as soon as the paperwork goes through."

"Along with a Silver Star for saving the Company today."

"You're a hero *Captain* Pike," Larson said, smiling and shaking Pike's hand again.

"Well, I'll be Goddamned," Pike said, awed by the news but finally accepting it.

"Captain Pike," he murmured. "It makes me sound like a goddamned pirate."

Larson roared with laughter again.

"You know," he said in between laughs. "it does; it really does."

"All you need now is an eye patch and a parrot, and you'll be in character," he joked.

Then he laughed again, and after a moment, Pike joined him.

Chapter Four

Pike and his actions on the embattled LZ were all anybody talked about. Pike was promoted at Division Headquarters on the Division's firebase a week later in a small but impressive ceremony. Of course, the news of the firefight and his upcoming promotion had already spread like wildfire through the Brigade and Division.

Dawson ribbed him unmercifully the day before the ceremony. He claimed this was the last time he could talk to him like that since Pike was getting commissioned. But it was evident Dawson and every member of A Company could not have been any prouder of Pike than they already were.

He was one of them. He was a grunt just like they were. Furthermore, they all knew Pike had saved their asses from almost certain death by his actions. He deserved promotion for that and more. Much more. The fact that he had come up from their ranks made his promotion all the sweeter.

All the Brigade Commanders and staff, as well as the Division staff, attended the ceremony. Including some members of A Company, including Dawson and Lt Spence, the only officer left in A Company, and newly assigned LT Thompson, a replacement.

The Commanding General of the Division personally pinned on the silver railroad tracks of a Captain to Pike's fatigue collars following the reading of Pike's promotion orders. Then he made a speech about how badly the Division needed leaders like Pike. Afterward, he awarded Pike a Silver Star for his actions during the engagement for saving the Company, then read the medal's citation.

Suddenly, it was all over. Captain Pike and the Commanding General walked off the small stage. They joined the crowd of well-wishers attending the ceremony where Pike shook hands with everybody, even with officers he didn't know. But they knew him and what he had done to merit his promotion. And for that, they wanted to shake his hand and welcome him into their ranks. It was their way of saying Thanks, Good Job, Captain Pike. We're proud of you. So, Pike smiled a lot, shook a lot of hands, and said thank you.

After all the congratulations petered out and the ceremony finally wound down, Pike returned to the battalion firebase by helo. He was still partially stunned by what had just occurred.

Before today he had always considered himself a career NCO. He had thought he might retire as a Master Sergeant if he was lucky and didn't get killed before he got his time in. That had been his goal until recently. Now he was not only an officer and a gentleman by an act of Congress. He was a Captain, to boot. That would take some getting used to, he realized. He would have to adjust to that and change his entire way of thinking. He would have to come up with an entirely new set of goals. As he flew over the dense green jungle below him, Pike thought about his life.

Pike had been born in Linville, West Virginia, into a family that knew only great poverty. His father was an uneducated coal miner who sweated his life away, trying to provide for his family. But never quite managed to do even that. He was a man not given to shows of emotion. So, neither Pike nor his two brothers ever really got close to him. They thought of him simply as the man who kept a roof over their heads, clothes on their backs, and food in their mouths. But since just doing all that consumed most of their father's time and energy, there was little of him left to express any love. So, his mother made up for that. She also tried to ease the lack of money and the distant relationship the boys had with their father. She did all that by bestowing generous portions of her love on her three boys.

The youngest Pike was raised in western Kentucky in a mining town just south of the Pennsylvania border. His father had moved the family there two years after Pike's birth, mainly because the mine in Linville had played out. So, Pike grew up as the third son of a determined and loving mother and an increasingly alcoholic father who suffered from Black Lung, the inevitable result of his years working in the mines. It was not an ideal family to be raised in, but Pike never lacked much, especially love.

When Pike was nine years old, his father died suddenly. He left this world penniless, leaving Pike's mother to support and rear him and his two older brothers. That proved to be no easy chore. The family's existence before Pike's father's death had been bleak, with them barely getting by each month on their father's meager pay. After his death, things got even worse. There was no inheritance and no insurance. There were only bills, mouths to feed, and clothes that had to be bought.

Worse, only their mother bore the responsibility for all that now, as well as trying to keep them together with a roof over their heads. So, for the next few years, necessities were hard to come by, and luxuries were nonexistent.

Since the coal company didn't offer any widow's compensation, Pike's mother had to work as a janitor at the mine's business office and as a part-time maid for the mine's foreman just to make ends meet each month. She was lucky to have gotten both those jobs, but the foreman had known Pike's father and felt sorry for the family after he died.

Even with two jobs, she barely made enough money to get the family by each month, so the bills continued to mount. But somehow, someway, she kept the family together, and they all eked out a barebones existence, living mainly on beans and cornbread and damned little of that.

As a result, both Pike's older brothers quit school the following year to help out, having already gotten their full measure of growth. They went to work for the coal company to help Pike's mother support the family and help pay off some of the mountains of bills she had accumulated.

One became a full-time miner. The other, old enough to get a driver's license, was driving a coal truck for the company. Pike, still too young to be hired, continued school. He watched the hard life of a miner's widow gradually suck the remaining strength and life out of his mother over the next few years. That continued until there was nothing left to give.

She gradually succumbed to all the toil, pain, and hardship and grew sickly, finally becoming bedridden. But, despite that and the family's continuing trials and tribulations, she insisted Pike stay in school and finish his education. She even extracted his solemn promise to that end. That was her only dream. Consequently, Pike and his brothers were determined to make it come true, especially since it was the only thing she had ever requested.

Unfortunately, she never lived to witness her dream and died just two months shy of Pike's high school graduation. Pike and his brothers were devastated, but they eventually took comfort in the fact that their mother had at least lived long enough to realize that her dream would come true. Her youngest son would graduate from high school, even though she wouldn't be there to see it. It was enough. So, she died happily, content in the knowledge that Pike would fulfill his promise.

After her funeral, Pike expressed a desire to work for the coal company, feeling like he owed it to his brothers for supporting him while he finished school. He was determined to shoulder his share of the load and pay them back, and he told them so. After all, they worked to support him and his mother until he graduated, and Pike felt an obligation to repay the debt.

When they heard Pike's intentions, both brothers, now fully employed as miners with four years' experience, were appalled. They sat Pike down and had a long, heart-to-heart talk with him about his future. They explained the risks, poor pay, terrible working conditions, and the absence of any real future. They convinced Pike he could do much better than spending his life working in the coal mines and coming home black-faced and filthy every day, all for a measly paycheck at the end of the month that would barely pay the bills. They wasted no time telling Pike mining was a job nobody wanted or should have to endure. There were too many other ways for a man to make a living, especially if he had an education. Life was meant to be better than that.

In the end, Pike's brothers convinced him that coal mining was no fit life for him and a dead-end job. They said they were miners simply because it was the only job open to them when they had been forced to quit school and go to work.

That's all they knew. They didn't have any of the skills it would take to do anything else since they never received the education needed to acquire them. Now, years later, with no education and no other skills, they were trapped;

in the mines and the life that resulted from working in them.

They had sealed their futures when they quit school early and went to work in the mines to help support the family after their father's death. Now, they were too old and too undereducated to change careers., especially since both men now had families of their own and all the responsibilities that went with them. So even if they had the desire, they no longer had the opportunity. That made starting a new life impossible.

In short, both men told Pike it was too late for them. They were locked into working as black-faced miners and would dig coal underground until either Black Lung or a cave-in killed them. Their future was clear, intractable, and irrevocable. Their lives were on a course set the day they quit high school; now, their fate had already been decided. They would spend the rest of their lives working for coal companies and hating every minute of it.

Since they both knew what lay ahead, they damned sure didn't want their younger brother to make that same mistake and endure that same fate. They told Pike they wanted at least one family member to succeed at something else in life and become something more than a poor, black-faced miner with no hope and no future. Pike had been given an education; they had made sure of that. Now they wanted him to use it.

Pike had never seen his brothers so serious or adamant about anything before. So, on their advice, mainly due to the complete absence of any other jobs in the area, Pike enlisted in the Army after graduation. His brothers applauded his decision and saw him off when he left for Basic Training.

He initially intended to stay in the service only long enough to let the Army teach him a trade. After his initial enlistment was up, he planned to return to Kentucky and make something of himself. In the process, he intended to try and help his brothers and their families. But his brothers nixed that idea too.

They told Pike that there was nothing he could do for them. If he wanted to repay them, the best way he could do that was by becoming a success in another career, not in Kentucky. There was nothing for him there. So, Pike tearfully said goodbye and promised himself to follow his brother's advice and make something of himself. Unexpectedly, sometime during his initial enlistment, Pike found he liked the military's security and regimentation, so he elected to reenlist after his first tour.

Now, twelve years later, he had never looked back or regretted his decision. He had worked hard and made a successful career for himself. He had worked his way up through the NCO ranks, compiling an exemplary record along the way. Now, on top of all that, he was a commissioned officer and suddenly had an entirely new future to plan. He was well pleased with his accomplishments, and rightly so. He had made something of his life that would make his mother and brothers proud. Pike certainly was.

"Unfortunately," Pike thought sadly, *as he remembered his last visit back to Kentucky. "neither of my brothers have fared nearly as well over the years."*

"Their prophetic vision of their future had turned out to be true."

"One is dead, the result of a mine cave-in, and the other is rapidly going the way of my father."

"Drinking too much to try and forget his miserable life as a miner and slowly killing himself in the process."

"By contrast, thanks in great measure to both of them," Pike thought sadly. *"I'm the only one in the family that has succeeded in life."*

All that was true. By now, Pike was a hardened combat veteran, a trained Special Forces trooper, a senior NCO, and now an officer commanding a Company in an elite Division. He had come a long way from his humble beginnings back in rural Kentucky. He was proud of himself and all his accomplishments, and rightly so. He had never forgotten his mother's and brothers' sacrifices allowing him that opportunity. As a result, Pike had a burning determination to succeed and make the best of a life given to him at his mother and brothers' expense.

Pike had only one honest regret. He had never married. It was primarily because there had never been enough time during his early training or later in his subsequent assignments and deployments to Vietnam. Therefore, he could not start and develop a relationship with a suitable woman, especially one long enough to consider marriage.

But he wanted to find the right woman and have kids with her. He wanted to raise them correctly, nurture them and teach them what they needed to know to succeed in life. He wanted to give them the same chance he had been given.

He had seen too many kids drafted into the Army who had little or no parental guidance in their early lives. Nor anyone to help them plan a future. They had no long-term goals or even short-term initiatives, so they had no future. These kids lived only for the moment.

They came from small, no-name towns in Anywhere, USA, or from overcrowded cities that offered them little hope. Had it not been for the Army instilling at least some basic ideas on discipline, responsibility, and organization into their lives during their short, two-year, involuntary enlistment, they would have eventually become worthless. Just one more piece of useless flotsam or jetsam or a misdirected bit of human garbage washing aimlessly around the island of humanity for the next fifty years or so. Never contributing to society and never really mattering. Primarily just another nameless nobody that existed on a day-to-day basis with never a chance, or even a desire, to improve themselves.

But many of those young men had changed thanks to the Army and what it had taught them. Thanks to Pike's patience and teaching, they had gone on to lead productive lives after they had completed their mandatory service. Pike was proud of his contribution to that and wanted to ensure his small legacy continued. It was his way of paying his mother and his brothers back for giving him the chance to succeed at the cost of their own lives.

Pike's welcome back to Alpha Company was raucous and jubilant. The entire battalion was proud of him, and it showed. The battalion had even stood down a day to celebrate the occasion. All the troops in Alpha Company were beaming when they welcomed Pike home. They were as proud of him as he was of himself because he was one of their own. He had sweated with them in the field. He had humped endless miles with them through the dark, humid jungle. Tasted fear and endured sadness with them. He had led them through all their turmoil, disappointments, and problems.

He fought, bled, and suffered with them. But most importantly, he had gotten them through all the firefights they had endured together and kept them alive. Consequently, they were proud to say he was a grunt, just like they were. But he was no longer a simple NCO grunt.

He was now an officer and a Company commander to boot.

Furthermore, he wasn't just any officer or any Company Commander. He was *their* Company commander. Pike was their boss, leader, father figure, protector, and confessor, all rolled into one. He was their very own living legend. They trusted him so much; they would have all willingly followed him right down the barrel of a loaded gun if he had asked them.

Pike not only had the respect, trust, and admiration of the men of A Company, but the rest of the battalion as well, and that included its officers. They welcomed him into their ranks with no reservations. They had known him and respected him as an NCO. Now they had no qualms about accepting him as one of their own in the officer corps.

Pike had proven himself and his abilities and gained his rank as very few around him had ever done. In combat on the battlefield. Pike was the genuine article, and they all knew it. They were as proud of him as his men were.

One of Pike's first acts as the new A Company CO was to recommend Dawson for promotion to senior Sgt and take over his old platoon sergeant job. Thanks to his new status, that happened rather quickly. The man was also a proven leader, and Pike had recognized that. He also realized the importance of having proven leaders in sensitive positions, especially for a new unit's success. So, he and Dawson began educating the remainder of his officers and NCOs to effectively lead their men in combat.

Supposedly, they already knew how because of their training, but their training was mostly theory. Pike knew from bitter experience that there was a severe difference between theory and application, which wasn't acceptable. Especially in the middle of a war. He wanted to train his people to lead men in combat successfully.

He wanted to train them until they knew what orders to give in any given situation and when to provide them with. He wanted them to understand good leader was in charge not because of his rank but rather because of his knowledge and experience. Someone who instinctively knew what to do in any given circumstance; a leader who understood the concepts of fire and maneuver, fire discipline, and fire support. One knew how to defeat the enemy using his brains and training, not just by applying overwhelming firepower and support.

Lastly, he wanted them to be leaders who could successfully overcome their fears and stress. Then confidently lead the men under them, looking to them for guidance and direction. So, Pike set about doing just that.

He spent much of his time with each platoon leader, platoon sergeant, and squad leader over the next few weeks. He taught, explained, and patiently showed each man what was expected of him and how to effectively employ and maneuver his unit. He taught them how and when to move, when to shoot and when to wait. How to act and communicate effectively with their men while being shot at. He worked with them seven days a week, night and day. First, he explained, then demonstrated. Then he made them do exactly what he wanted them to do on their own.

Later, he watched and critiqued them as they did it. As a result, his subordinates all learned quickly. In short, they began to feel more confident and led more effectively.

At the end of a month, the results of all Pike's training and efforts were tangible and visible. The company had been transformed into a well-oiled and thoroughly trained fighting machine. They now thought, moved, and fought as a single integrated unit. Leaders at every level knew their jobs and what to do when they took fire.

Alpha Company was now an efficient, effective, and lethal killing machine, thanks to Pike. One capable of inflicting maximum damage on the enemy with minimum risk to themselves, and the men in the Company knew it. Even their attitudes had changed. They now thought of themselves as masters of the jungle rather than simply part-time intruders in it. Now they didn't fear the enemy; the enemy feared them for a good reason.

Armed with all that new knowledge and the confidence that came with it, the members of A Company all reveled in their newfound ability. Normal operations had become more than just a hot walk in the jungle. Instead, they had become a chance to take the fight to the enemy and kick his ass.

Consequently, over the next few months, almost half of the entire Brigade's monthly body count was regularly attributable to Alpha Company. And the new battalion commander, as well as the Brigade commander, knew why. That transformation was primarily due to one man, Pike.

Thanks to him, Alpha Company was head and shoulders above the rest of its sister companies in the battalion and the Brigade. It ran like a well-oiled machine tuned to perfection. Its casualties were low, its success rate high, and its morale was through the roof.

Alpha Company's transformation and success were evident at both Brigade and Division levels. Unknown to Pike, his superiors were quietly observing his abilities and success, and they liked what they saw.

Good combat leaders are extremely rare, and for that reason, they are both prized and emulated. Pike was one of those leaders, and he didn't realize it. He had come into his own as an officer. What he did naturally as a Commander, others had to learn, then practice at great length, to master. Not so with Pike. He was a born leader with all the right instincts and did all the right things intuitively.

His men loved him, his subordinates emulated him, and his superiors respected him. He had blossomed into what the Army prizes most, a capable and efficient combat leader. One who knows what to do and when to do it. Someone who knows how to command and sets the example by his actions. A man who people follow, not because of rank, but because they want to.

Chapter Five

"The area we'll be invading has been an enemy stronghold for decades," The Brigade commander told his audience.

The audience consisted of all the battalion and company commanders in the brigade and all battalion staff members. They had all been summoned to Brigade headquarters to receive the Brigade commander's operations order for an upcoming Division-sized operation that promised to be a big one.

"The North Vietnamese used this area as a base against the Japanese, then the French," The Colonel continued.

"It's been a fortified sanctuary for them for almost forty years."

"So, they have ample time to expand, fortify, and secure it."

"Now, the NVA and VC are using it against us."

"That means it will be a challenging task to take it away from them."

"That won't be an easy or quick job because they will fight tenaciously to keep it," The Colonel predicted.

"Intelligence says it has extensive tunnel systems in its mountains containing logistics storage sites and billeting areas for three regiments."

"It is also rumored to contain a complete underground field hospital," the Brigade Commander continued. "and other support facilities.

"As yet, none of that has been confirmed."

"What is confirmed says the 103rd NVA Division has its primary headquarters there, along with all three of its regiments." The Colonel explained.

"Our intelligence tells us that all those units, in addition to at least two Main Force Viet Cong Battalions, are headquartered and based there."

"Fortunately, they're not all there at the same time."

"Especially the VC Main Force units."

"Most of the time, they are out recruiting and proselytizing the population in other areas of the Corps."

"Our intelligence estimates only a Regiment of the NVA Division is usually there as a security force at any one time," The Colonel explained.

"But, again, that remains unverified."

"What has been verified is this area has numerous well-constructed logistical sites and base areas throughout the area to support all those units."

"Enough to accommodate the entire Division and both VC Battalions at the same time if necessary.

"That's our target since that's what makes this area so valuable to the NVA," The Brigade Commander told his subordinates. "its infrastructure."

"It's taken them decades to develop it."

"Destroy it, and the Division will be forced to leave the area, find a new location, and start all over again, building a replacement."

"That will, of course, take an inordinate amount of both time and effort."

"Presently, they have neither since they are engaged in and spread out through the entire Corp area ."

"However, " the Colonel continued. "the enemy will go to great lengths to retain this area."

"Because with our mobility and firepower, rebuilding a replacement would be an extremely difficult, if not impossible, task for them."

"Primarily, because most of their forces will be concerned with just staying alive after we've kicked them out of their sanctuary." He explained.

"All these areas I've mentioned," the Colonel continued. "will undoubtedly be well camouflaged and well-defended."

"So, it will be your job to locate and destroy them and the forces that occupy them."

"That will be difficult because of the terrain in the AO."

"It varies from mountains to deep, well-forested valleys," the Colonel said, turning to a larger map behind him. "Most of it is thick double canopy jungle."

"The enemy knows the area well and will undoubtedly try to control the high ground, making our job much more challenging."

"However," the Colonel stressed. "for once, he will be forced to stand and fight."

"For two reasons."

"First, he can't afford to lose this area as a sanctuary."

"And secondly, once we begin our attack, he will have nowhere to run, even if he has the desire."

"That's because the South Vietnamese 1st ARVN Division will establish blocking positions to the North and West while we attack from the South," The Colonel explained.

"And, as I'm sure you all know, the 1st ARVN Division is the best in the South Vietnamese Army."

"So, rest assured they will accomplish their part in this operation."

"It will be up to us to accomplish ours."

"All three battalions of the Brigade will participate in his operation," The Colonel continued.

"We will establish two Battalion fire bases and a third combination Battalion/Brigade firebase in the new AO."

"All these bases will be able to provide artillery fire support to the entire Brigade Area of Operations."

"Our mission is to locate, engage and destroy whatever Regiment of the NVA 103rd Division has securing the valley."

"To accomplish that, the 2nd Battalion will attack from the east while the 1st Battalion attacks from the west."

"Third Battalion will secure the Brigade firebase, form a blocking force to the south, and be in reserve."

"Gentlemen, "the Colonel said, concluding. "this will be an all-out Brigade-sized operation which will be the Brigade's main effort for this year."

"So, it will enjoy the Division's full support."

"Line companies can expect to be in the field continuously for a minimum of thirty days once they insert."

"All resupply will be by air, and right now, we are scheduling three resupply runs per company, per month."

"That may change, however, because of the weather," the Colonel warned. "so plan accordingly."

"We are on the very edge of the start of the wet season, which could adversely affect our operational and resupply efforts."

"Especially if the weather turns bad and stays that way for an extended period."

"So, we need to gain and maintain contact with the enemy from the beginning, and fortunately, for once, that may be possible on this operation."

"Intelligence expects the Regiment from the 103rd Division to stand and fight to hold this area because it is a primary sanctuary."

"Therefore," the Colonel reiterated. "as I said before, they won't give it up easily."

"For that reason," he warned. "you can expect heavy resistance once you make contact."

"However, that will work to our advantage."

"If we can engage the NVA in a stand-up fight, where they can't or won't run, we can bring our massive firepower to bear on them and destroy them."

"And that is exactly what I intend to do if given the opportunity."

"The operation will commence at 0600 hrs. two days from today with combat assaults by the line companies into the AO," The Colonel said.

"Battalion commanders have already been assigned battalion AOs, locations for their battalion firebases, radio frequencies, and call signs."

"They will assign Company AOs after they complete their planning."

"Once we get on the ground, people," The Colonel ordered. "let's get in there and engage."

"For once, we can expect the NVA to stand and fight rather than running, so let's take full advantage of that and put it to them."

"We have the advantages of surprise, mobility, and firepower, so I want to utilize them to the maximum extent possible."

"The Division expects major body counts out of this operation, and so do I, especially since this Brigade has some of the finest combat leaders in the Division."

"Therefore, I fully expect us to produce overwhelming and tangible results that will shame our two sister Brigades."

The Brigade Officer's call ended a few minutes later. Afterward, all the battalion and company commanders returned to their various firebases. On the helo ride back, Pike thought about the upcoming operation. It would be his first, real, long-term test as a Company Commander and as an officer in an extended multi-unit operation.

This operation would test his ability to employ and maneuver the Company to its maximum. Thirty days of continuous time on the ground would guarantee that. Weather, however, would be a significant factor. The wet season had already started, which meant helicopter operations could be curtailed or even suspended on certain days.

The area was also mountainous, which could mean heavy ground fog in the valleys. Especially on rainy days or days with heavy cloud cover. That could limit air or even artillery support if targets were obscured or fogged over. Pike considered all these factors as he mentally prepared to give his troops his Company operations order.

Once the helo landed back at the battalion firebase, the battalion commander told all his Company commanders he would issue his operations order at 1300 hrs. Pike, in turn, informed all his platoon and squad leaders that he would give them his op order at 1800 hrs. that same day.

Pike issued his operations order after evening chow at a meeting with all his officers and NCOs. The Op order was brief, mainly outlining the intelligence information the Brigade Commander revealed. Pike designated a MACO to handle and plan the airmobile insertion, then showed everyone where they would be inserting and concluded by giving them all the need-to-know logistics and comms information.

"That's all I can tell you at this point," Pike told his subordinate leaders unexpectedly.

"We'll decide how we'll move into our AO after we get on the ground, and I'll determine that once we've inserted and get a look at the terrain."

"Trying to devise a plan just by looking at the map is a nonstarter."

"These maps are inaccurate and don't show much anyway, so we'll have to wait until we get on the ground to develop a plan of action."

"You people remember that for future operations." He cautioned.

"But the main thing I want you to remember for this one is that the people you command will look to you for leadership and direction."

"If you project confidence, that feeling will be contagious, and that's what we want."

"Once established in the AO, I'll decide how, when, and where we're going."

"But I'll tell you now," Pike said firmly. "I have no intention of establishing a Company perimeter on our initial LZ and remaining there overnight."

"Once our recon patrols find a suitable location off that mountaintop, we'll move the

Company there and establish a new CP the same day."

"I have no idea about the terrain except that it's mountainous and has thick double canopy," Pike continued.

"I've looked at maps of the AO, but they don't show much, and I've already told you they are notoriously unreliable."

"So, once we are on the ground and get a feel for the terrain, we'll update them with information we'll collect daily."

"We'll use all that to decide how we're going to maneuver and where we're going to go as the operation progresses."

"We'll also be taking two of our 81mm mortars in with us," Pike revealed. "We'll set them up every night in the Company perimeter."

"With them, we'll have immediate, indirect fire support if we need it."

"To support them, each man, excepting RTOs and machine gunners, will carry a mortar round on his ruck, which he'll deposit at the Company CP every night."

"We'll also take extra mortar rounds, ammunition, and radio batteries in bulk when we insert."

"They'll remain in the Company CP and be dispensed as needed."

"And speaking of ammo, from now on, Company SOP will be twenty-five magazines for every individual and twenty-five hundred rounds per machine gun."

"That's excessive, but this is a bad area, and we may need it."

"If the weather turns bad on us and we can't be resupplied," Pike explained. "I don't want to run short on radio batteries either."

So have your RTOs take two extra per radio."

"I want each platoon to have a showdown inspection before insertion to ensure every man is carrying what he's supposed to carry by the new Company SOP," Pike ordered.

"We may be on the ground for up to thirty days before we get pulled out, so everybody packs what's required; no exceptions."

"I also want all medics to pack extra blood expander and morphine."

"This is going to be a long and difficult operation, and the enemy is probably going to stand and fight for once," Pike concluded.

"That means we will probably take some casualties before this is over."

"Just how many depends on how good you all are as leaders."

"Remember that."

"When a firefight starts," Pike reminded his people. "remember what you've been taught about fire and maneuver and put it into practice."

"That's going to be our edge here."

"The enemy is used to engaging us and then sneaking away while we wait for fire support."

"By the time we get it, he's long gone."

"But when the NVA engage us this time, they're going to be in for a big fucking surprise because we're not going to react that way."

"We're not going to hold in place and call for fire support when we get hit."

"That will give them too much time to fade away, and that's fighting the war on their terms."

"Instead," Pike explained. "when we get hit, we're going to immediately lay down a base of fire and pin their asses."

"While they're pinned, we're going to maneuver against them, cut them off, then destroy them."

"When they have nowhere to run, we'll call in fire support and finish them at leisure." He explained.

"That's fighting the war on our terms and maximizing our advantages."

"And that's how we're going to operate from now on."

"At night," Pike continued. "we're also going to checkerboard our AO with ambushes."

"They'll be no larger than squad size, but they'll have the advantage of immediate fire support from our mortars, so that will make up for their numbers."

"Each ambush will have a preregistered DT, which they will call in themselves while it's still light."

"Later, after dark, once they engage an enemy force, we can fire that DT for support if they need it, and they can adjust."

"While we've got the little bastards pinned down by our mortar fire, a reaction force from the Company perimeter can move to and reinforce the ambush if necessary and finish them off.

"If we use these two tactics, we can do our jobs more efficiently and take minimum casualties," Pike explained.

"All that requires is sound leadership at every level, maximum firepower, and use of fire and maneuver."

"That's going to be our three-pronged recipe for victory."

"We've all practiced this for the past month, so we know it works."

"More importantly, our troops know it works."

"Now we're going to get a chance to employ it against an enemy who has never had it used against him before, and using it; we're going to kick his ass."

"I don't want your people killing the NVA in ones and twos anymore," Pike told the assembled group. "I want you to start killing them even more in the tens and twenties."

"I want us to start putting a real hurting on those little bastards."

"I want to make them afraid to engage us because we are so lethal."

"In short, I want to make them afraid of us."

"And believe me, people," Pike stressed. "that is highly possible, considering what I am planning on doing to them."

"Alpha company is about to become the meanest mothers in the valley."

Pike little pep talk received a chorus of cheers. His people were fired up and ready. Unfortunately, fate has a nasty little way of upsetting the best-laid plans. Third Brigade was about to find that out the hard way. They were about to learn a harsh and very penal lesson and experience something no one had ever expected, least of all their intelligence section. Because of their failure, the Brigade was about to taste defeat's bile and bitter flavor.

Chapter Six

Two mornings later, the combat assault into the AO went as planned. The lift package was once again a heavy package, composed of nine Slicks, two gunships, and a C&C bird. The LZ had been prepped by artillery fire and gunship strikes ten minutes before the slicks inserted the Company.

The first lift landed without incident on the top of a small mountain whose sparse vegetation had been chopped to pieces by the artillery and gunship fire. That left a tangled mass of green confetti and knocked down trees on the chewed-up ground. However, that didn't matter since Pike wasn't planning on staying there.

As the Slicks touched down, the men in the first lift offloaded and immediately fanned out around the LZ's edges. There was no sign of the NVA and no resistance. They quickly formed a perimeter and waited for the company's remainder to come in on the second lift, with a dark, bleak sky threatening rain later in the afternoon.

Fifteen minutes later, the second lift was inserted, carrying the remainder of the Company. Meanwhile, a third lift brought in extra ammo and rations. Once the entire Company was down, Pike set up his mortars inside the perimeter, then sent out three squad-sized patrols down the sides of the mountain to recon the base and the valley below. The three patrols clover leafed the area immediately around the bottom of the mountain, looking for signs of enemy activity and searching for a new company CP.

Just as Pike had suspected, the patrols discovered signs of an enemy presence and some critical terrain features. One was a small, fast-flowing stream containing several fish traps flowing through the valley's center. That was good news because the Company now had an immediate freshwater source and wouldn't have to locate one. The patrols also found several well-used trails running along the valley floor and several tilled and planted fields.

Pike told his people to mark the location and direction of the stream, the trails, and all the fields. He then directed them to fan out and find a suitable place for a new Company CP near or on the valley floor.

1st Platoon found a small, relatively open hilltop just off the valley floor an hour later and reported its position. Pike checked its location on his map and after a conference with the patrol leader, decided it would serve as a suitable site for the Company's new CP.

While the patrol secured the site, Pike moved the rest of the Company and the mortars down to the new location. That took three long hours because of the dense foliage down the sides of the mountain and the choppers' added loads of bulk supplies.

Unfortunately, there was no let-up when the company reached the valley floor. The foliage there was also dense, usually triple canopy jungle covered with ground foliage. Worse, it had started to rain, making further movement even slower.

The remainder of the Company had to pack all the extra rations and ammo brought in by the third lift, which made the move even more grueling. It was so slow and tedious that it took the morning's remainder and the better part of the afternoon. When completed and the perimeter established, everyone was exhausted.

Only a tiny amount of sunlight filtered through the green mass of the jungle in the valley after the rain stopped. It made the entire area dim and cast everything in a yellowish tint. That promised to make any future movement that day difficult. Primarily through the jungle and off the trails. All that promised to be difficult and time-consuming, especially with the intense vegetation growth on the valley floor.

By the time Pike had reestablished his Company perimeter at the new location, it was late afternoon. Because of that, he called all his patrols back in. Once everyone was back, Pike met with all his NCOs and Officers.

"I know some of you are wondering why I moved the CP," He began as he eyed his subordinates.

"I've moved the perimeter and CP because every Dick within ten miles of here saw where we landed today."

"And since we know the NVA have mortars, I didn't want to be at that location tonight because there is a good possibility they'll hit it with indirect fire sometime after dark."

"Hopefully, the Dicks didn't have any watchers eyeballing us when we left that location and moved in here," Pike continued.

"That's why we sent the patrols out earlier, to prevent that."

"Hopefully, they flushed any NVA watchers and made them move so they couldn't follow us to our new location."

"After the three patrols had completed their initial recons and flushed any watchers," Pike explained. "I wanted them to check the area around the mountain's base to see what was down here."

"As a result, we discovered two main trail networks running through the AO that show signs of regular use."

"So tonight, 1st and 3rd Platoons will establish several squad-sized ambushes on the valley floor, along those trails, and see what's moving down here."

"Dawson," Pike ordered, "you and Pardee get your people ready to move as soon as we finish here."

"I want you both to have all your elements in position before dark."
"The NVA will undoubtedly send out patrols tonight to locate us and determine our strength.

"They will probably use the trails we found earlier to move on."

"When they do, I don't expect them to be overly cautious because I don't think they realize we've relocated the Company onto the valley floor."

"Hopefully, they'll think we're still on the mountaintop where we landed this morning."

"The three separate trails our recon patrols found this morning appear to run through the valley length, so they're probably part of the main supply and movement route the NVA use to move troops through the area."

"Tonight, we'll ambush them."

"I want ambushes on each trail about three to four hundred meters apart and some other ambushes around the jungle, all squad-sized."

"Locate them anywhere that seems a likely spot."

"However, tonight, our ambushes will operate differently," Pike revealed.

"All ambushes will report all movement to the CP and will *not,* repeat, will *not* trigger until I give them the word," Pike told the surprised group.

"There's a reason for that," Pike explained.

"I want to suck all the enemy patrols into our Company checkerboard and get them in the middle of it first," He explained.

"If we can do that after an enemy patrol triggers the first ambush, they'll bounce around inside it like a pinball and hopefully run into two or even three more before they can get out of it."

"That should chew them up pretty good," Pike said, smiling.

"We'll also position a recon team on the northern end of the three trails.

"This team will be three men, and their job will be to warn using the NVA are coming."

"Later, and most importantly, they'll determine which trail the survivors of our main ambushes use when they head back to their base areas."

"Their direction of retreat will give us an indication of where those base areas are."

"Once we determine that, we'll have an idea of where they are, and we'll move the entire Company in that same direction tomorrow and establish a new perimeter."

"By now," Pike said, summing up. "from everything I've said, it should be clear to all of you that we're going to be moving the Company CP and our Company AO daily, and there's for reasons for that."

"First, if the NVA don't know where we are, they can't hit us."

"So, we're not going to stay static long enough for them to find us."

"Second, I want to locate their main base area, and this is the best way to do that."

When everybody understood Pike's strategy, they all smiled.

"Pike's pretty damned smart, and he's thought all this out carefully," Dawson thought.

"That should be a lesson to the young leaders in the Company on how to operate in the field."

"That's why he explained everything in such detail."

"He wants them to learn."

"I want all the ambushes in place by sundown," Pike ordered a moment later.

"I've got their tentative locations already plotted on my map."

"Patrol leaders can get their coordinates when we're finished here."

"If you engage tonight, I want only Claymores and grenades used," Pike ordered.

"No weapons fire unless it's an emergency."

"That's important, so tell all your people."

"I'll explain later."

"I had extra Claymores and grenades brought in on our third lift today for just that purpose, so there won't be a shortage of them," Pike announced.

"So, when you trigger your ambush, daisy chain your claymores and blow everything."

"When we hit the Dicks tonight, I want the enemy survivors to have to return and report that they don't know who, or how many, Americans they were dealing with."

"So, if we use only Claymores and grenades and don't fire our weapons, the Dicks will have no idea about our size and strength."

"I want their patrols chewed up tonight, so take plenty of Claymores and daisy chain them for maximum effectiveness."

"We kill enough of these little shits tonight without weapons fire; that will make the NVA leadership very uneasy about who we are and what the hell is going on," Pike explained.

"That's the way I want to keep them."

"We're going to be here for a long time."

"So, we're going to try and let the NVA know as little about us as we can during that period."

"To accomplish that, we're going to move every day, and, using ambushes, we're also going to take the night away from them," Pike explained.

"That's going to force them to send out patrols in the daytime to try and find us, and that's what I want."

"I want the NVA looking for us for a change instead of us constantly looking for them."

"If we can accomplish that, then *we'll* control the situation and not them."

"Once we do that, we can determine where and when we want to engage them," Pike concluded. "And when we do, it will be on our terms and not theirs."

"That's pretty goddamn smart, Boss," Sgt Dawson said as Pike explained his reasoning.

"I especially like the idea of them having to look for us for a change."

"That will change everything."

"Yeah," the other NCOs chorused. "Then we can kill the little bastards at our leisure; while they look for us instead of the other way around."

Suddenly, in the middle of his briefing, a single shot rang out from just outside the perimeter, startling Pike and everyone in the CP. NCOs immediately grabbed their weapons, ran back to their units for SITREPS, and the entire Company readied themselves for action. Finally, Sgt Martin, a squad leader from the third platoon, returned to Pike's CP a moment later and reported.

"One of my LPs about a hundred meters outside the perimeter saw a Dick moving up the trail just below the southern edge of the perimeter."

"He was going to let him pass, but the Dick saw something, got nosy, and started moving towards the perimeter."

"When he did, my man waited until he was almost on top of him, then shot him."

"He's dead, and my guy is pretty sure he was alone," Martin continued.

"Neither he nor his buddy on the LP heard any movement in the jungle after he waxed the Dick, and they were both listening for it."

"So, I'm pretty sure this guy was by himself."

"I know you wanted to keep the CP location a secret, and this might have blown it, but my guys did what they had to."

"Tell your men on the LP they did a good job," Pike ordered. "and warn the other LPs to stay alert."

"There may be more little shits prowling around looking for us."

"They may not have waited until dark as I figured."

"No, Boss," Martin told Pike. "I think you were right in your original estimate."

"I think this Dick was just checking on his crop field or whatever and stumbled onto our perimeter by accident."

"You know the Dicks never send out lone people when they expect trouble."

"Instead, they usually send out a squad or platoon."

"I hope you're right, " Pike said.

"I'd hate to have my entire plan ruined before we even had a chance to implement it."

"Hopefully, when this Dick turns up missing, the NVA commander will think he was shot by one of our patrols reconning the valley, and our perimeter is still on the mountaintop."

"Or maybe he won't even be reported as missing until morning," He opined.

"In any case, they'll be coming to find out exactly where we are as soon as it gets dark."

"The NVA heard that shot throughout the valley, so get your people fed and then move the ambushes out while it's still light."

"I want everybody in position before it gets dark," He ordered. "And I want strict light and noise discipline in the perimeter from now on."

"I've got a feeling that it's going to be a long, exciting night, girls, so I want to be ready for it."

"We won't fire DTs for the ambushes tonight unless it's an emergency," Pike explained to everyone. "I don't want the Dicks to know that we have mortars just yet."

"I want to save that as another surprise for them," He said, smiling.

"And since, hopefully, they don't know we're on the valley floor yet," he added with a sly grin. "that'll be the third surprise."

All the platoon Sgts and squad leaders in the group smiled. Pike was preparing to stick it to the unsuspecting NVA, and they knew it. He had just told them how he was going to do it.

Engaging the enemy on your terms rather than theirs was rare. Usually, it was the other way around. Now Ironman Pike would change all that, and they would help him. Dawson just smiled and shook his head.

"Pike has certainly blossomed as an officer," *he thought.*

"He's about to become the NVA's worst nightmare.

"I plan to keep the NVA guessing about us for as long as possible," Pike continued.

"I don't want them to know who and what we are, how we operate, or what our size is," he explained.

"To answer those questions, I'm going to make them look for us instead of the other way around. "

"When they do, I intend to make it very expensive for them."

"I want to start whittling them down to size a little at a time, so we'll ambush both day and night from now on."

"Lastly, tell your ambushes they'll hear some artillery fire later tonight," Pike concluded.

"I'm going to have the Company FO fire some H, and I fire at some likely locations after dark." He explained.

"We'll probably continue that at various times throughout the night because I want to make the Dicks jumpy, and I want to keep them that way."

"So, I'm going to do everything possible to make that happen, starting tonight," Pike said, smiling nastily.

"All right," Pike said. "That's it."

"Get back to your people, brief them, get them fed, then move your ambush patrols out."

Forty-five minutes later, the ambush patrols began leaving the perimeter, with every man camouflaged and his equipment secured to prevent it from making noise. Each man wore only his web gear, a small butt pack containing his Claymore, and extra grenades. Their rucks stayed behind in the perimeter since they could move faster and more quietly without them. A little over an hour later, just as the sun set, all the ambushes were in position.

The jungle was quiet once it got dark, and that was unusual. It was almost as if its animal inhabitants knew what was coming and were getting out of the way to prepare for it. That produced a sense of expectancy inside the perimeter, with every man anticipating contact and primed for it.

Pike intended to hurt the NVA with the ambushes and also stun them. That's why he had ordered only Claymores and grenades when the ambushes triggered. He wanted to confuse the NVA regarding the size of the unit that attacked them. No weapons fire would certainly accomplish that.

Even better, once the NVA triggered the first ambush, they would bounce around inside the Company checkerboard like a billiard ball on a table, undoubtedly trigger more when they moved, and lose more men in the process. At least that was Pike's plan.

Pike intended for any survivors to report they hadn't seen their attackers yet had taken heavy casualties. A report like that would be not only unusual, but also unnerving. It would make the NVA commander wonder what type of unit he was dealing with.

Most US units didn't normally operate in that manner. They usually fired all their weapons and blew their Claymores when they triggered an ambush. Afterward, they called in artillery support and illumination rounds to sweep the area, get a body count, and police up enemy weapons. That wouldn't happen tonight. That would be atypical, causing the NVA to wonder about the type of unit and tactics used against them, and they would want answers.

The only way to get them would be to send out more patrols, precisely what Pike wanted. Make the enemy bust brush, sneak around, and look for him and his unit for a change. Force the NVA to search the green mass of jungle for a hidden enemy they knew little about and sweat bullets as they tried to find him. Scare them and make them wonder if their next step would be their last as they searched.

Pike's men would have the advantage of surprise and make the enemy look for them for a change. That would let Pike enjoy the luxury of either avoiding the NVA or engaging them. Doing that, he could fight them on his terms, not theirs.

If he could accomplish that, the entire jungle warfare paradigm would suddenly be reversed, at least in this little part of the war. The hunted would become the hunters. The unseen would suddenly have to become visible. The hidden would become targets. Surprise would no longer work just for the NVA.

Death would have Asian victims instead of just American ones.

Chapter Seven

The action started just after 2100 hrs. Sgt Blake, the man leading one of the two recon patrols watching the two trails leading into the valley, reported a large force of NVA numbering over forty, passing his location and headed south into the valley. Pike notified all the ambushes in the Company checkerboard accordingly.

Fifteen minutes later, Sgt Pardee, commanding the first ambush on the southernmost trail, reported a force moving past his position. The second ambush on the trail, led by Sgt Martin, four hundred meters further down the trail, reported the group passing their location ten minutes later. Pike notified Dawson, who led the third ambush on the trail, to trigger it once the NVA unit got into their kill zone.

Ten minutes later, the valley thundered as six Claymores detonated simultaneously, then over ten hand grenades exploded moments later. There was a flurry of random shots following the explosions, then silence.

Minutes later, Dawson reported he and his people had nailed at least fifteen NVA while the rest had fled back up the trail. Five minutes later, Martin's ambush triggered, and there was another series of Claymore and grenade detonations.

Finally, twenty minutes after that, a third ambush in the nearby jungle some fifty meters off the trail triggered another explosion of Claymores. Nobody in A Company fired a shot. During all the incidents, the only weapons fire came from the NVA, who were shooting blindly into the dark at their unknown attackers.

To add to the NVA's mounting confusion, Pike ordered illumination rounds over the Company ambush checkerboard each time an ambush was triggered. But he also ordered all his ambushes to hold in place and not leave their positions to search for bodies or weapons. The NVA still alive would expect that and rely on it as a diversion to help them escape. Not seeing the normal American response after an ambush triggered and illumination rounds exploded would further confuse them.

Any NVA survivors, now separated by the ambushes and alone in the dark, would probably be on the edge of panic because of the situation. Since they could no longer trust the safety of the trails, that would further elevate their fear. They would be forced to bust brush through the thick jungle foliage just to get away. But because of the artillery illumination rounds exploding irregularly over the valley floor, even the jungle and the surrounding landscape would be lit up. That would further expose them as targets, making their escape that much more hazardous.

That proved to be the case thirty minutes later. The ambush checkerboard survivors got spooked by something and started a large, one-sided firefight of their own with nothing but shadows. It lasted well over five minutes before their remaining leaders got control of them. However, Pike had located their position by that time and called for artillery concentration on the area, killing fifteen more. That was A Company's final going away present to the few NVA still left alive.

Finally, a few minutes after 2330 hrs. after the last artillery shell exploded, the jungle turned quiet again and remained that way until morning.

When the sun rose, all the ambushes checked their kill zones and the area where Pike had fired the artillery concentration. They reported finding forty-six NVA bodies, thirty-one weapons, and numerous blood trails. After their searches ended, Pike ordered them all back to the perimeter. When they returned, he debriefed each ambush patrol leader.

Afterward, he had the platoon previously assigned as a reaction force send out three recon patrols from the Company perimeter to locate a new company CP further north and check the area around the current perimeter for NVA watchers. When they left, Pike called battalion and reported his previous night's activities.

Capt. Larson and the new battalion commander were ecstatic at his results. They also reported the battalion firebase had been probed during the night. Unfortunately, the other companies in the battalion reported no contact. Only A Company had accumulated a body count.

Two hours later, a patrol Pike had dispatched found a suitable location for a new Company CP. They reported it was about nine hundred meters to the north of the current CP, on another small hilltop in the mountains' foothills, just off the valley floor. Pike had all three patrols link up at the new location and secure it, then moved the remainder of the company to the new location later in the afternoon. With the move completed and the new perimeter established, Pike implemented his plan for the coming night's operations.

Now positive, the main enemy base camps were still to the north; Pike concentrated A Company's nighttime activities in that direction.

The Company's morale soared that afternoon because of their previous night's successes. They had wiped out the equivalent of an NVA platoon and taken no causalities themselves. That was no mean feat. Especially considering it had been accomplished on the enemy's home ground.

The troop's success made them eager to engage the NVA again. The previous night's accomplishments were fresh in their minds, and they wanted more action. That was particularly true of the men in the squads that had not had an ambush trigger. It was also true of the platoon that had secured the Company perimeter since they wanted their share of the action.

Success in combat is infectious and breeds the desire for more action and success. The results of the previous night were a prime example. The trick, which Pike knew well, was not to let his men get overconfident and underestimate their opponents.

When Pike had reported the ambush results to his battalion commander, he had also asked for an update on the other company's activities the previous night and the location of their Company CPs. He learned that the other companies' perimeters had been probed the previous night.

In Pike's mind, that was because they had all foolishly used their insertion LZs as their Company perimeters for that first night, rather than relocating as Pike had done. Pike plotted their CP locations on his map anyway, then studied it. Afterward, he formulated his plan for the upcoming night.

Later in the day, one of Pike's recon patrols, sent out after the new perimeter had been established, reported finding a cornfield filled with ripe corn. Pike told them to pick as much as they could carry and bring it back to the perimeter. The Company enjoyed grilled corn on the cob when they returned with their noon rations. The grilled corn was delicious, especially since it was the enemies.

Later, at around 1700 hrs., Pike met with all his unit leaders to lay out the plan for the night's operations.

"Tonight," he told them. "we are going to continue our ambushes, but again we're going to do something different."

"After last night, the Dicks will expect us to have more ambushes out tonight. By now, the survivors are back with their units and have reported, so the NVA commander knows what we did to them last night. He'll likely change his tactics tonight, so we'll change ours too."

"To begin with," Pike explained. "the NVA will probably move in smaller groups tonight, and they'll also be much more conscious of light and noise discipline."

"They will undoubtedly have a recon element preceding each main body they send out, hoping it will trigger any ambush before the main element gets to it."

"If that happens, the main body will try to hit the ambush itself."

"That's what I'd do if I were them," Pike revealed. "so I figure they'll react the same way."

"So, to keep them off balance, tonight, we'll set up demolition ambushes only."

"After they're in, all our people will reassemble at a platoon NDP for the remainder of the night, and it will be well away from the demo ambushes themselves."

"That's because once a demo ambush triggers, I'm going to put artillery fire on its location."

"So, I don't want to chance hitting any of our people with that fire."

"I'm also going to call in concentrations about one hundred meters north and west of each ambush site about five minutes later."

"I figure that's where the ambush survivors and the main body will be."

"Hopefully, the arty will catch the Dicks trying to reassemble and get some more of them."

"So, tell your people to expect artillery fire in the area tonight and explain what it's for."

"And be damned sure you know where your platoon assembly areas are on the map when you call them into me," He cautioned.

"We're going to demo ambush all the trails we've found in the area and put some along the streamline, too," Pike explained.

"After they're all in, we'll pull back to our platoon locations and see what develops."

"Why are we doing all this, Boss?" one of the NCOs asked curiously.

"For two reasons," Pike replied.

"First, we've got the enemy off balance and confused as to exactly who and what we are, and I want to keep them that way."

"Secondly, I'm trying to convince the NVA that we're only a LRRP team operating in the area and not a full company."

"Everything we've done so far points to that," He explained.

"That's why we didn't fire weapons last night and used only Claymores and grenades."

"That's SOP for a LRRP Team," Pike told his men.

"The Dicks know somebody hit them last night, but because there was no weapons fire, they have no way to gauge just how big a force it was."

"Tonight, because I expect them to be organized and ready to hit an ambush once it triggers, we're going to fool them again, hopefully."

"That's the reason we're using only demo ambushes."

"When their lead element trips the ambush and their main body assaults the position, they won't find anything."

"When they don't find anything, they're going to wonder if the ambushes last night were demo ambushes too."

"Especially since they didn't take any weapons fire from them."

"So hopefully, when they add all that information up, they will conclude that they are only dealing with a LRRP team operating in the valley."

"Everything we've done so far is typical of how a LRRP team operates, and the Dicks know that."

"If we can convince the Dicks that a LRRP team is the one giving them all their headaches," Pike told his people. "they'll start sending out platoon-sized patrols in the daytime to try and find it and destroy it."

"When they do, we'll take them out."

"And for a change, we'll have the numbers advantage, as well as surprise, on our side."

"I'm pretty sure the NVA don't know they're dealing with an entire Company yet," Pike confirmed. "That works in our favor."

"So, I want to continue that deception for as long as possible, and I want to take maximum advantage of it while we still can."

"We've already taken out twenty-six of them and wounded probably another ten at least," Pike reminded his NCOs.

"Tonight, if we're lucky, we'll get another dozen or so."

"More if we're lucky."

"So far, all it's cost us is some Claymores and grenades."

"That's a pretty fair trade-off in my book."

"So, we're going to keep whittling them down for as long as we can," Pike said.

"At least until they realize they're up against a Company sized force."

"Understand?"

"I've got you, Sir," one NCO replied. "That's pretty damned smart."

"It'll fox the Dicks right out of their jocks."

"I hope so," Pike said, smiling.

"Tell your men what we're doing so they'll understand too."

"They're probably wondering what the hell I'm doing anyway."

"Remember, people," Pike cautioned. "intelligence says we're up against an NVA Regiment."

"I think there's much more than an NVA Regiment here, but that's just my opinion."

"Whatever size force is here, we're still up against at least ten battalions at a minimum, this is their home ground, so they have a home-field advantage."

"They also know the terrain, and we don't."

"So, if they find out who and where we are, we're liable to find ourselves up against at least a battalion of NVA, and I don't like those odds."

"That's why we're trying to cut them down to size by taking platoon-sized chunks out of them like we've been doing."

"That's also why I've been trying so hard to convince them that we are nothing more than a small LRRP team."

"If the Dicks think we're only a LRRP team, they won't devote much effort or manpower to try and find us," Pike revealed.

"LRRPS are more of a nuisance than a threat to them," He explained.

"Especially since they already know there's at least two battalions of Americans infantry in their AO."

"So, they'll concentrate on the bigger American units, whose locations they already know, like the firebases."

"Pike is pretty goddamn smart," Dawson whispered to Pardee quietly.

"I wondered what he was trying to accomplish with all the shit we've been doing since we inserted."

"Now I know."

"He's a sly, wily bastard, and he thinks like the Dicks.," Dawson said admiringly. "What's more, he's good at it."

"I'm damned glad he's running this outfit now."

"He knows his shit about taking care of his people and how to kill Dicks."

"The smartest thing the Army ever did was to make him a Captain."

"And the luckiest thing to ever happen to us was when the Division Commander decided to send him back to us to command Alpha Company." He added smiling

"We lucked out on that deal twice."

"Amen, brother," Pardee said in agreement. "He knows how not only to kill the NVA but how to outthink them and outsmart them as well."

"The guys in my squad all think he practically walks on water."

"And I have to admit," Pardee said. "after seeing him in action as a Company commander on this operation, I pretty much agree with them."

"He's the best goddamn commander I've ever had," Pardee admitted unequivocally. "and that's a fact."

"This plan of his tonight to use demo ambushes is slicker than shit."

"If the Dicks assault an ambush after it triggers, they won't find shit."

"And since we didn't fire a shot last night when we triggered those ambushes, they'll probably figure they were demo ambushes too."

"That's really slick."

"Pike's right," Pardee told Dawson. "when the Dicks look at all the evidence, they'll think they're dealing with nothing more than a LRRP team."

"And since LRRP teams are only ten people or less, the NVA will consider us nothing more than an annoyance and simply send out platoons to find the team in the daylight and deal with it."

"If we tangle with them in the daylight, we'll outnumber them for a change, at least three to one.

"And I like those kinds of odds, especially in this fucking valley."

"You heard what Pike told the old battalion commander about this place, didn't you?" Pardee asked.

Dawson nodded.

"Well, so did everybody else in the company."

"That's why this damn place gives me the creeps," Pardee said.

"Something bad is about to happen before this operation is over," He predicted. "I can feel it coming."

"I just hope it doesn't happen to us."

"It won't," Dawson said emphatically. "not if Pike has anything to say about it."

"He's too smart for that."

"You ever notice that he always seems to be thinking one step ahead of the Dicks."

Pardee nodded.

"He got them reacting to us," Dawson observed correctly. "instead of the other way around."

"And I like that."

"I like it a lot."

Chapter Eight

Pike watched as his NCOs left the CP and returned to their units. They were all good men and now, thanks to his time and instruction, he was sure they were good leaders too. They knew how to do their jobs more effectively, which made the entire Company a more efficient unit.

Tonight would be a break for them, a chance to throttle back slightly. They had been pushing their people hard for almost forty-eight hours. First, the combat assault into the new LZ, then the move to establish the new company perimeter, and last night's ambushes. They had been running on adrenaline during all that, and now they and their men were tired.

Tonight, after they put the demo ambushes in and reassembled their squads in a platoon perimeter, they and their men could all go to fifty percent alert and get some much-needed sleep. It was time to wind down a little and give their bodies and nerves a chance to rejuvenate. That was the hidden reason for the demo ambushes that Pike hadn't told them about.

Additionally, he needed them refreshed and alert for tomorrow because tomorrow was resupply day, and Pike had already realized that would be a problem. But he had to take the resupply because he had no choice. He needed more rations, Claymores, and grenades.

However, when the resupply came in, he would have to reveal his position, which he hated. When the helos brought in the resupply, there was a good chance the LZ would be under observation by an NVA element. If that were the case, then all of Pike's previous work in trying to convince the NVA that there was only a LRRP team operating in the area would be blown. As soon as the NVA saw how many people were on the LZ, they would know they were dealing with a Company.

Pike toyed with an idea he had come up with to prevent that from happening for the next few minutes. Maybe he could at least take the resupply without giving away the Company's location. He would think about his idea during the coming night and decide in the morning.

Meanwhile, he had to make up a resupply list and transmit it to battalion. So, he sent Nesbit around the perimeter to each platoon to find out what they needed. Ten minutes later, when he had assembled his resupply list, he transmitted his request for supplies to battalion.

When he did, he got a pleasant surprise. The battalion had gotten some new replacements, and A Company was getting ten of them. Pike decided to send eight of them to the first Platoon since they had been the hardest hit in the past two months. The other two men would go to the second platoon. He sent Nesbit to find the two platoon Sgts and tell them the news.

Dawson, now acting as the platoon leader for Pike's old platoon, took Nesbit's news with mixed emotions. On the one hand, he was glad to be getting some new people and filling some of the holes he had in his Platoon. At the same time, however, he realized introducing new people to established squads on this hairy of an operation would not be doing his squad leaders any favors. They would have to continue running their squads effectively and somehow figure out how to integrate and train the new men assigned to them simultaneously without getting them killed.

They had to also keep them alive long enough to get them appropriately indoctrinated on how the Company operated. All that would be extremely difficult, especially since he had eight newbies to deal with.

Dawson decided to talk to Pike and see if he had any suggestions. He had ambushes to brief and send out tonight, and the sun was already low in the western sky. But that would have to wait until tomorrow.

Later, after briefing his squad leaders and eating chow, Dawson picked a Platoon assembly point for the night's operation. He showed it to the ambush patrol leaders, then had them mark it on their maps. Afterward, he had a showdown inspection of the entire platoon to ensure everyone was ready and geared up properly.

An hour before dark, both 1st and 2nd Platoons left the perimeter to emplace their demo ambushes. Dawson's platoon had four ambushes to put in, and there was a considerable distance between them. Because of that, Dawson had established a platoon rendezvous point just off the main trail where two of the ambushes would be emplaced. The other two would be emplaced along the streamline about a hundred meters below the trail.

When all the ambushes were in, all the squads would reassemble at the platoon rendezvous point, and Dawson would move the platoon, as a unit, to their nighttime RON position. At least that was the plan. Unfortunately, the best-made plans tend to go wrong in combat. Dawson was about to find that out in spades.

Once Dawson reached the platoon rendezvous point, he sent all four squads out to emplace their ambushes. Afterward, he and his HQ element settled down to wait for their return as they hid in a position just off the main trail. Ten minutes after his ambush patrols had departed, Dawson suddenly heard movement coming down the trail!

At first, he thought it was one of his ambushes returning, but a quick peek out of the foliage revealed a shock. It was a squad of NVA instead! Not wanting to risk an NVA squad surprising his own two squads farther down the trail, busy establishing the demo ambushes, Dawson and his people quickly deployed online. There was no time to emplace claymores. They would have to kill them with weapons, fire, and grenades. That would mean a firefight because they couldn't kill them all at once.

When the NVA squad was abreast of them, Dawson and his men fired them up. For a moment, the jungle seemed alive, with the sounds of bullets buzzing through the foliage and grenades exploding. As Dawson expected, he and his people didn't kill them all. After the brief firefight, the NVA squad's remnants ran back up the trail the way they had come. But not all of them. Seven of them lay dead on the trail before Dawson and his men.

"Shit," Dawson thought in disgust as he inspected the kill zone. "Now, what do I do?"

"None of my squads have radios, so I have no way to contact them and tell them what's happened."

"And I'm damned sure they heard the firefight."

"I just hope they have enough sense to stay where they are and not try to make it back tonight."

"Use your heads, people," Dawson prayed. "stay put until daylight."

"Drag these bodies off the trail," he told his men, angry at himself for his mistake. "before another bunch of assholes comes trotting down here to find out what happened."

"What a fucking mess," he moaned. "and it's all my fault,"

By the time Dawson and his people had drug the five NVA bodies off the trail, it was fully

171

dark. That made Dawson's situation even worse. Any of his people trying to get back to the rendezvous now couldn't even be identified as friendlies in the dark. With Dicks in the area, that could easily result in his people getting into a firefight with each other by mistake. To top things off, Pike was on the radio wanting to know what the hell had happened. Reluctantly, Dawson told him.

"I fucked up, Boss," He reported.

"I sent my ambushes out and didn't brief them on what to do if the assembly point got compromised."

"Now, I don't know what to do," Dawson said mournfully.

"Stay put until daylight," Pike ordered. "There's nothing else you can do."

"You start wandering around the jungle trying to find them; they may fire you up by mistake."

"Those four squads will just have to fend for themselves."

"I just hope those squad leaders have sense enough to stay where they are until daylight."

"If they don't, you will have an even bigger problem than you've got now." He warned.

It was a long night. Dawson was worried about his people and what could happen to them because of his mistake. To make matters more nerve-wracking, two of Dawson's ambushes triggered around 2100hrs. Thirty minutes later, one of the second platoon's also triggered. Worse, sporadic weapons fire revealed a short-lived firefight around 2330 hrs. to Dawson's south.

"Christ," Dawson thought bitterly. "what a goddamn disaster, and it's all my fault."

"I should have briefed my squad leaders on what to do if something like this happened, and I didn't."

"So, if any of my people get killed, it's because of my stupidity." He thought bitterly.

"I just hope the squad leaders were smart enough to go to ground at their ambush sites and wait for daylight when they heard the weapons fire."

"But even if they did," he thought further. "what do I do when daylight gets here?"

"Do I remain at the RV site and wait for the squads to come to me, or do I go looking for them?" he worried.

Pike answered Dawson's question for him just before daybreak when he ordered Dawson to wait for the missing squads' at his RV site.

"They'll either come to you or back to the Company perimeter if they're able," he told Dawson.

"So, stay where you are,"

"They know where you are," Pike reminded him. "Whereas you don't have a clue where they are."

"Especially after all the activity last night."

"So, we'll wait."

"If they haven't all shown up by 0800, we'll send out patrols from the Company perimeter to try and find them."

"Keep me advised."

Twenty minutes after first light, Sgt Pardee, leading the first squad, showed up at Dawson's RV.

"Thank God," Dawson thought.

Even better, he had second squad with him. Dawson breathed a sigh of relief when he saw them too. Fifteen minutes later, the fourth squad led by Sgt Martin showed up.

Finally, thirty minutes later, just as Dawson was about to call Pike, the fourth squad arrived at the RV site looking ragged as hell with two men slightly wounded.

"*Shit,*" *Dawson cursed.* "*I knew we wouldn't get through my screw-up untouched.*"

Dawson called Pike and told him that he had all his people back and then led the platoon back to the company's perimeter. As soon as they arrived, Pike debriefed them.

"As soon as I heard weapons fire from the direction of the platoon RV," Sgt Pardee began, relating his previous night's actions. "I realized what must have happened."

"So, I went down the trail and immediately linked up with the second squad still putting in their ambush."

"But that almost turned out to be a bad mistake," He revealed. "They nearly fired my squad and me up when they heard us coming."

"Luckily, there was still enough light for them to see that we were the good guys."

"Anyways, after we linked up, we found a good RON position about midway between both ambush sites and stayed there for the rest of the night."

"Since neither of our ambushes triggered, at sunup, we took them both down and returned to Dawson's RV," he concluded.

"We had just finished setting up our ambush when we heard firing coming from up the trail," Sgt Martin, the third squad leader, continued the story.

"Since it was almost dark and I didn't have a radio, I took my squad back into the jungle about a hundred yards further south down the trail and set up a RON."

"We figured Dawson or 1st or 2nd squads must have gotten hit."

"But since it was already dark, I didn't want to take a chance and try and make it back to the RV, so we stayed where we were."

"Later, at around 2100 hrs., our ambush triggered, and about ten minutes later, we heard fourth squad's ambush, south of us, trigger."

"We figured it was probably the survivors from our ambush running down the trail and into fourth squad's.

"At first, that's what we thought too," Sgt Nolan, a brand-new Buck Sgt, and the fourth squad leader, said, picking up the story. "but that wasn't the case."

"It was another NVA unit altogether."

"I know because they came up the trail from the south, and Martin's ambush was north of us."

"So, it couldn't have been the same people."

"Anyway, after our ambush triggered, we waited for about fifteen minutes."

"When we heard movement coming back towards the ambush site, we figured it was the Dicks coming back to pick up their wounded and dead."

"When they got abreast of us, we fired them up and threw grenades."

"I know you said no firing, Captain," Nolan said, looking at Pike. "but we didn't have any choice."

"The Dicks were coming right at us, and I was afraid they would walk right into us in the dark."

"So, when they got right in front of us, we opened up on them."

"They returned some fire, but there was silence after our grenades went off."

"This morning, we found eight bodies in front of our position, and we found another nine at the ambush site, along with some blood trails."

"Two of my guys got hit during the firefight, but neither of them is serious," Nolan said in conclusion.

"One got a graze on his forearm, and the other man took a ricochet that hit his left calf and sliced it open."

"Doc's already looked at both of them, and they'll be fine."

"Doc says they won't even need to be medevacked."

Pike looked at his NCOs from his old platoon, then smiled.

"You all did extremely well," He told them proudly.

"When the shit hit the fan last night, none of you panicked, and that was the main thing."

"You all analyzed the situation correctly and made the right decision."

"That's what good leaders do, and I'm proud of all of you for that."

"Sgt Nolan," he continued. "you and your people did exceptionally well."

"You made the right decision when you fired the NVA patrol up."

"That's what I would have done too, and you and your people executed perfectly."

"Tell your people I am especially proud of them."

"Between the three ambushes and Dawson's and Nolan's firefights," Pike continued a moment later. "plus 2nd Platoon's two ambushes triggering, we racked up a total of forty-four NVA killed last night."

"That's quite a score for one night's work, and I'm sure we wounded at least that many."

"But we were lucky."

"Dawson," Pike admonished. "from now on, you make sure everybody knows what to do if your RON or your assembly point gets compromised."

"That goes for the rest of you too."

"Dawson lucked out last night, and he knows it, but he did the right thing when he set up that hasty ambush."

"He probably saved third and fourth squads from getting hit from the rear."

"So that offsets your mistake, Dawson," Pike said with a grin. "Just don't let it happen again."

"No problem, Boss," Dawson said, "I've learned my lesson."

"From now on, everybody gets briefed on a contingency plan before we go out."

"All right then," Pike concluded. "have your people get some chow and some shut-eye."

"We'll move the perimeter after our resupply, and that'll be sometime in the afternoon."

"Nesbit, get Lt Spence and bring him back to the CP."

Dawson looked at Pike before he left.

"Pike could have torn me a new asshole for my mistake, but he didn't." he thought.

"Instead, he used it as a teaching point."

"That's just another sign of how exceptional he is as a leader."

"Now, I am more determined than ever not to screw up again."

"John," Pike told his 3rd Platoon leader a few minutes later. "you and your platoon are going to take the Company resupply today."

"I don't want to move the entire Company to take it because that could give away our strength and location."

"So, you and your Platoon will handle it instead."

"No problem, Sir," Spence replied. "what do you want me to do?"

"Take your platoon to this hilltop," Pike said, pointing at a spot on his map. "and secure it."

"Take some C-4 and det cord with you because you may have to blow down some trees to make an LZ big enough for the resupply birds."

"Check the area thoroughly for watchers first, then call me."

"Once you've secured the area, wait until the last minute to blow the LZ," Pike ordered.

"That will give the Dicks less time to send people to recon you and your element because they'll have to find you first." He explained.

"As soon as the resupply is complete, have your people load everything up and haul ass back to the perimeter."

"Tell all your people to carry empty rucksacks to the LZ," Pike ordered. "They can load the supplies in them to carry them back."

"I'm also sending the ten-man mortar squad with you as extra help, plus a squad from the second platoon, but keep them out of sight once you get to the LZ, just in case it has watchers you missed."

"When you're all packed up, make your way back to the perimeter, but leave the squad from second platoon at the LZ."

"They'll ambush the LZ as a stay behind in case the NVA sends people to find out what was going on there."

"On your way back here, take it easy and stay alert." Pike cautioned.

"Your people will be packing heavy loads, and it's a long walk back down the mountain."

"I don't want them completely exhausted when they get back here to the CP because after you get back, we're going to move the Company CP to a new location."

"So, I don't want your guys so beat they can't hack it."

"To prevent that, give them some rest breaks on the way back."

"If you make contact either going or coming, stay put and set up a defensive position," Pike directed. "don't try and maneuver with all those supplies."

"I'll get a reaction force to you ASAP."

"This place is starting to crawl with NVA, so make damned sure you and your people stay alert."

"Move out in the next thirty minutes." Pike directed.

"Call me when you get to the LZ, and I'll call for the resupply birds."

"When I get an ETA on them, I'll notify you, and you can blow an LZ once you're in contact with them."

"On my way, Boss," Spence replied eagerly.

Chapter Nine

Lt Spence looked at his watch, realizing it had been almost an hour since he and his platoon had left the Company perimeter. The move back to the resupply LZ was a slow go because it was all uphill, and the jungle vegetation was extremely thick. To make matters worse, it had started to rain. That slowed things down considerably since it made the slope slick and limited his people's ability to hear. Spence didn't like that at all.

You couldn't see far in the green maze anyway, even when it was sunny. So, your people on point depended on their hearing to alert them to any danger. The rain took away that ability and that worried Spence. In his mind, all the NVA activity in the area the past two days made his move even more hazardous.

The young Lt figured he had another fifteen minutes of strenuous movement before he reached the hilltop. The platoon had already crossed one large trail running down the side of the small mountain, so he and his people were on the alert. Because of the NVA activity in AO,

Spence had already warned his people to be ready for anything when they left the perimeter.

Five minutes later, the column stopped suddenly as the point element signaled Spence to come forward. Spence ordered the Platoon down and snaked his way up to his point man.

"I thought I saw something moving to our front LT," the point man whispered.

"I'm not sure because all this rain is limiting our visibility."

"But I thought it looked like people."

"How far away?" Spence asked in a whisper.

"About twenty meters to our front," the man replied.

"All right," Spence said, thinking. "you and your slack man ease forward and see if you can spot anything."

"But wait until I move the rest of 1st squad up to cover you." He added.

"Give me a second to get them online," He ordered.

"If they did spot any Dicks this situation could get terminal in a hurry," Spence thought.

"The NVA hold the high ground above us, and if we get into a firefight, we'll be at a distinct disadvantage."

"What would Pike do if he was here?" he asked.

A minute later, 1st squad was online and covering the point's move forward. Spence had also alerted his three remaining squads, and they were ready to maneuver if something happened.

Once everyone was set, Spence hand signaled the point to move out. Moments later, the point team edged their way forward through the rain-drenched foliage for about another twenty-five meters until they stopped abruptly and went down. The point man quickly signaled Spence forward again.

"There's a big trail in front of us," the point man told Spence when he arrived. "and it's got footprints all over it."

"They're fresh because the rain hasn't washed them all away yet."

"I *did* see some people, LT!"

"Hold tight and watch the trail," Spence whispered.

He then signaled all his squads forward. When they arrived, he put them online.

"We're going to ambush this trail," he told them unexpectedly.

186

"Our point spotted people moving towards the mountaintop, so I'm going to put artillery on it."

"If the NVA are up there, when the artillery hits them, they'll head back down the mountain on this trail."

"I intend to ambush them when they get here."

"They'll be running, so be ready for them when we light them up." He warned.

"Squad leaderss, get your Claymores out now and set them up on the trail facing uphill."

"Space then about fifteen yards apart and daisy chain them with det cord."

"Sgt Franks, put two men up the trail about fifty meters as an LP," Spence ordered. "and two more out of the kill zone down the trail as rear security."

"They can kill any stragglers we don't take out in the kill zone."

"While we're putting out Claymores, I'm going to call the old man and tell him what we're about to do."

Five minutes later, Pike had been informed, and Spence's platoon had the ambush set. Pike had 1st platoon already moving to the young Lieutenant's location if Spence needed reinforcement even before he finished the conversation.

"Nobody does anything until I blow the Claymores," Spence warned his people.

"When I do, everybody let go with everything you've got; Claymores, grenades, and weapons."

"If it's a big force, I'm going to let the main body get in the kill zone before I trigger the ambush."

"So tell your people not to get anxious because some of the NVA are going to get past the ambush site."

"Hopefully, our rear security will get them."

"If they don't. they might try and double back, then hit us in the left flank or the rear after they hear the ambush trigger." He warned.

"If that happens, we may have to run," Spence warned.

"If we have to run, we'll pull back down the mountain by squad, leap frogging as we go, and under cover of the artillery fire, I'll call in."

"Everybody got all that?"

Heads in the platoon nodded, and all three of Spence's squad leaders grunted their understanding and gave him a thumbs up.

"The old man is sending 1st platoon to back us up if we need them," Spence promised. "They should be here in the next thirty minutes."

"If the NVA get here before they arrive, we'll handle them ourselves."

"So, everybody, make sure you're set."

"This is going to get nasty so let's kill as many as possible when I blow the Claymores."

"I'm calling for artillery in two minutes."

"Squad leaders, brief your squads on what's about to happen as you set the ambush."

"And tell them to break out extra magazines and grenade."

A few minutes later, artillery rounds began peppering the mountain top, their explosions echoing down the mountainside. Within minutes, the listening post LT Spence had established up the trail called and reported.

"They're coming, LT," the LP whispered. "there's lots of them, and they're running."

"We can hear them charging down the trail like a herd of cattle."

Spence signaled his platoon to get ready. A few moments later, four NVA soldiers flashed by the ambush, followed by a large body of troops, all grouped together and awkwardly running down the slippery trail

Spence let the lead element of the group get to the far edge of the kill zone, then blew his Claymores. He had six of them Daisy Chained, so they all went off simultaneously with a tremendous roar. The rest of the platoon blew theirs a second later, and the entire platoon opened fire.

The NVA in the kill zone were caught flat-footed, so most of them went down like bowling pins, knocked over by the Claymores. The platoon's weapons fire got any still standing or trying run. However, even more NVA soldiers flooded into the kill zone behind the first group because they were unable to stop quickly enough to evade the ambush. Individual claymores hit them when they tried. Soon, the trail was blocked by their bodies.

"Shit," Spence thought to himself as he changed magazines. "we've hit at least a Company."

"There must be over thirty down in the kill zone, and they're still coming."

"But we have no choice now; we're committed."

"Fire them up," he screamed. "Put it to them."

By that time, the entire platoon was laying down a heavy volume of fire. The NVA weren't returning much because they were still either jammed up on the trail or still running down the slope and into the kill zone, unable to stop. However, that didn't last very long.

After a few more minutes, the flow of NVA ceased abruptly, and the platoon started taking fire from up the mountainside. Fortunately, most of it was blind and inaccurate because the NVA couldn't get enough of a downward angle on the Platoon's position to bring accurate fire on it. Even worse for them, the rear of the NVA column couldn't even see the part of the trail containing the kill zone below them so they couldn't fire on anything. They had no targets. Worse, the jungle was too thick to allow them to lob grenades. So, their suppressive fire, little as it was, was useless.

Even the NVA that could still see the platoon's position weren't effective in returning fire. They had difficulty seeing the Americans below them because of the drumming rain and the foliage. Regardless, they continued firing.

Spence adjusted the artillery support right after he blew his Claymores, and now it was impacting up the slope of the platoon into the side of the mountain above him. He adjusted it again slightly and then started walking the impacting rounds right down the mountainside and on top of the NVA until the rounds impacted danger close, less than fifty meters from his own position.

Meanwhile, the firefight continued, with green and red tracers flying through the falling rain, causing miniature rainbows and ripping foliage to shreds. Spence could hear screaming NVA as they got hit. After the artillery barrage zeroed in on the mountainside directly above Spence and his platoon, the enemy fire abruptly abated. A minute later, as the artillery rounds smacked into the slope above them, it stopped altogether as the remaining NVA fled to Spence's flanks.

Spence covered his flanks during the respite and called for a Sitrep and casualty count. He discovered he had three wounded, but luckily nobody had been killed. A few minutes later, he called a cease-fire, then sent three men into the kill zone to get a body count. While he waited, he adjusted the security on his flanks in case the fleeing NVA tried to double back.

When his people returned from the kill zone, they reported forty-nine NVA bodies. When they checked the area further up the slope, they found twenty-one more killed by the artillery fire. Afterward, Spence told his people to hold position, then called Pike and gave him a Sitrep.

"Fantastic job, John," Pike told Spence.

"Keep the arty going, hold in place, and watch your flanks and rear."

"Put out some LPs as soon as you can in those areas because the NVA may try and get around behind you."

"From what you've told me, you may have hit more than a Company of them."

"If so, the Dicks may still be around, just waiting for the artillery fire to lift, so do that immediately."

Pike waited for Spence to issue the appropriate orders and come back up on the radio. When he did, Pike continued.

"1st Platoon should be at your location in about another ten minutes, so tell your people to be on the lookout for them."

"As soon as they arrive, let me know."

"I'm also going to move the rest of the Company once they arrive," He said unexpectedly.

"When the first platoon links up with you," Pike continued. "stop the arty and wait a few minutes to see what happens."

"If you don't hear any movement or take any fire during that time, send out a recon patrol up to the mountain top and check for bodies."

"If it's clear, go ahead and move to it, along with 1st platoon."

"When you arrive, secure the area and then blow an LZ," Pike ordered."

"I'll call for a Dust off for your wounded, then bring in the resupply birds to your location."

"I'll join you in about an hour and a half."

"We're moving now."

Pike and the entire company were on the LZ two hours later, and Pike had debriefed Spence in detail. 1st platoon had found twenty-six more NVA bodies on the mountainside killed by artillery, and Spence's people had discovered an additional three bodies more up the trail from the kill zone. That brought the total body count to ninety-seven. That many bodies told Pike Spence had hit a battalion of NVA and not a Company, as Spence had initially estimated.

That information also told him that the NVA were now actively looking for him and his company in a big way. He reported all his findings and his assumptions to the battalion commander. Unexpectedly, the LTC told Pike he and Cpt

Larson would be flying in with Pike's resupply birds for a conference.

An hour later, Larson and LTC Pizanni, the new battalion CO, flew into the LZ. Pike met them when they landed and took them back to his CP, where two ponchos had been snapped together and tied off to nearby trees to keep it dry.

"Pike," Pizanni began. "I'm very impressed with what you and your Company have done in the past few days."

"Especially with LT Spence and the way he handled that last action."

"I'm putting him in for a decoration."

"It's obvious you have trained your subordinates and men well."

"Your body counts and low casualty rates prove it."

"It also looks like you've stirred up a hornet's nest at this end of the valley."

"In addition to your contacts, the battalion firebase has also been probed once and mortared twice during the last few days," He revealed.

"But, uncharacteristically, as of yet, the other Companies in the battalion have reported minimal contact."

"That worries me," Pizzanni admitted.

"So, I wanted to talk to you personally and get your take on what's happening."

"Why are you and the firebase getting all the attention, and the rest of the Companies are reporting no contact?"

"Larson values your opinion highly and has told me you are undoubtedly the most experienced Company commander in the battalion."

"And after what I've seen the past two months, and especially the past three days, I agree with him.'

"That's the reason I wanted this conference."

"To allow you to tell me what you think is happening."

Pike nodded and took out his map, then spread it out on three ration boxes he was using as a makeshift table. Pizanni immediately noted the map had his firebase location and several other places marked on it in various colors. He wondered about that, but Pike soon explained it all to him.

"We're here, Sir," Pike began, pointing. "and here's your firebase."

"I've also marked the location of every enemy contact the Company has made since we inserted."

"They're all marked in red."

"The yellow marks indicate planted fields, fish traps, and trails we've discovered."

"I've also marked a major stream on the valley floor that we think runs down the valley's length."

Pizzanni grunted as he studied Pike's map.

"This man is thorough in addition to everything else," he thought. *"And keeping his map updated with all the intelligence he gathers is an excellent idea."*

"He's using every bit of available information to help him maneuver his company and engage the enemy, and that alone makes him a formidable opponent."

"No wonder he's such a good commander."

"You'll notice all our contacts have been just north of where we inserted two days ago," Pike continued.

"That leads me to believe the main enemy base areas are also to our north."

"That would account for A Company receiving the most attention since we are the unit furthest north in the battalion's AO."

"Your firebase is to our west," Pike said, continuing. "midway between where we have made most of our contacts and the mountains to our north." He pointed out.

"That also places it within easy striking distance of those same base areas if they're where I think they are."

"Since the NVA undoubtedly knows your firebase's location, that's another reason you've been hit."

"The other Companies in the battalion are mostly south of us," Pike pointed out. "I think that's the reason they've made little contact."

"But most importantly, we're the only unit in this valley."

"My guess is we're getting all the attention because we're the only unit currently threatening their base camps."

"And your firebase is getting probed because they know exactly where it, realize it's a static target and that your artillery is a definite threat."

"Frankly, I'm surprised they haven't mortared it every night or hit it with a ground assault since it's such an attractive target."

Pizanni considered that as Pike continued to speak. It was an astute observation worth thinking about, even worrying about.

"I think the NVA base areas are further up this valley, and the NVA are trying to stop us before we get close to them." Pike continued.

"They're not worried about the other Companies in the battalion yet, because so far, they are all operating west and south of them, so they pose no immediate threat."

"Consequently, they're concentrating their efforts on finding and destroying my people and me as a priority."

"Fortunately," Pike explained. "they don't know where we are," Pike revealed. "because I have been moving the Company CP daily, and they haven't been able to find me yet."

"But they've been looking hard," He added.

"The contact a few hours ago with my third platoon proves that."

"It's also why so many of my night ambushes have triggered recently."

"They are moving in force to locate me."

"I've moved the Company daily because I wanted to force the NVA to do that instead of my people looking for them, and that strategy is apparently working," Pike explained. "Maybe too well,"

"My third platoon tangled with what I'm sure was a battalion this morning."

"The body count proves that because it exceeded the number of troops normally assigned to an NVA company."

"That means the NVA have started looking for us in the daytime, as well as trying to find my CP at night, and they are using an inordinate number of troops to accomplish that."

"Since most of the NVA units we've engaged have come from the north, that reinforces my belief their main base areas are located there."

"Lastly," Pike continued. "the stream running through this valley runs north to south, and in my experience, the NVA normally locate their base and staging areas near a permanent water source."

"So, taking everything I've said into consideration," Pike concluded. "I believe NVA base areas are at the northern end of the valley or in the mountains overlooking it."

Pizanni studied the map intently again as he digested Pike's estimate. Pike's briefing had been astute and convincing, a real eye opener.

"What do you think, Larson?" he asked.

"I agree with Pike," Larson said. "Everything he's said points to that."

"So, do I," Pizanni agreed, a moment later. "and that means two things."

"First, the battalion firebase is in the wrong location."

"If Pike's company continues to move north, they are going to be outside the battalion's artillery fan very soon, which means we're going to have to relocate it."

"That's the first thing we need to fix, John," Pizanni decided. "so call Brigade while we're here and tell them what we're going to do."

"Schedule the move for tomorrow at first light," he ordered. "And get an engineer company in here at first light; as soon as we select a new location.

"I want that new base in before sundown tomorrow."

"After we get the new firebase in, we'll move the other line companies."

"Second," he continued. "tell Brigade to position a blocking force at the northern end of the valley as soon as they can, if that's possible."

"It looks like Pike has got the NVA moving in that direction, and we want to keep them off balance as long as we can."

"Without a blocking force to stop them, the bulk of the NVA Division will simply head north and slip away once we start putting the heat on them."

"And that brings up another potential problem."

"This valley is over twenty-five klicks long," Pizanni pointed out as he continued as he looked at the map. "and it's flanked on both sides by mountains."

"If the NVA have fortified positions on those mountains, we'll be caught in a crossfire when we try to move the companies north."

"Particularly, if we stay in the valley."

"What do you recommend, Captain Pike?" the LTC asked.

Pike thought for a moment as he considered Pizanni's question.

"If it were me, I would airlift two Companies to the two mountaintops flanking the valley here and here," he said, pointing at the map. "then let them sweep down to the valley floor while the rest of the battalion moves northwards up the valley itself."

"That sounds like a good idea too," Pizanni said. "so that's what we'll do."

"Doing that will also deny the NVA some of the high ground as we advance."

"Tomorrow, I'll relocate the firebase to this mountain top," Pizanni said, pointing at the terrain feature on Pike's map.

"Then, late in the afternoon of the next day, I'll send a lift package to you and have your Company air assault onto this mountain top," He said, pointing.

"As soon as you're in," Pizanni continued. "I'll position B Company onto the mountaintop across the valley from you."

"That way, we'll have both sides of the valley floor covered and three strong points on high ground that commands both sides of the valley and the rear."

"The next day, as you and B company move down the mountains towards the valley, I'll have D Company sweep north up the valley itself simultaneously."

"What do you think about that plan, Captain Pike?" Pizzanni asked.

"Don't be shy."

"I want my commanders to speak their mind."

"They usually have a better feel for what's happening in the field than I do because they're where the action is." He explained.
"So, I value their opinions."

"And I especially want yours, Pike, because you're the most experienced man in this battalion, including me."

"Sir," Pike replied. "before you move B company and us onto those two mountaintops," Pike suggested. "Why don't you put two LRRP teams into those areas and let them see what they can turn up?"

"I hate to take the Company in there blind."

"If the enemy is already occupying those mountaintops, the LRRPs can let us know, and you can develop a plan to counter that."

"That's a damn good idea too, Pike," Pizanni said.

"While I move the firebase tomorrow, I'll insert the LRRPs."

"Larson, tell Brigade that too."

"That will give the LRRPs two full days to recon the area before you and B Company go in."

"If anybody is on those mountain tops, they should be able to find them or at least find traces of them."

"I appreciate your input, Pike," Pizanni said, smiling. "It has been very incisive and beneficial."

"It also proves nobody has a monopoly on good ideas, me included."

"So anytime you have an idea in the future, let me know."

"I know good advice when I hear it, and what's more, I'm not ashamed to take it."

"So, don't hesitate to call me."

"Now, I want to visit with your men for a few minutes before I go back."

"They've done a fine job, and I want them to know I appreciate it," He said as he got up.

"He's a good man," Larson told Pike when the battalion CO walked off. "head and shoulders above the old CO."

"And he means what he says about valuing your opinion," Larson continued. "That's why we flew out here today."

"He specifically wanted to get your take on what was going on."

"He told me that you were out where the action was while he was stuck on the firebase.

"So, you had a much better appreciation for the situation than he did."

"Because of that, he wanted your opinion on his next step before he made any decisions."

"He also told me that this war was being fought mainly at the Company level," Larson revealed. "Your job as the Company Commander was to figure out how best to fight it."

"His job was to support you with whatever you thought you needed."

"That's the way he thinks."

"He's right about that," Pike agreed. "it is a Company commander's war."

"And he's definitely better than the CO we had before."

"By miles."

"He sounds and acts like he knows what he's doing, so that'll be a big change too."

"I like him and the way he thinks," Pike admitted.

Larson laughed.

"I wonder what happened to the old CO?" he asked.

"He probably got promoted," Pike said, smiling.

"You know the old saying, *"fuck up and move up."*

"Bullshit," Larson replied. "he's probably wondering what he'll do for a living now that his Army career is over."

"The word is, the Division Commander shipped his ass stateside the next day and advised him to resign, so his days in the Army are over."

"Christ, I hope so," Pike said. "he was a fucking train-wreck as a battalion commander."

"He didn't know his ass from his elbow about combat here in the Nam, and he and his idiot ideas got a lot of good people killed."

"And that reminds me," Pike said, thinking. "I never thanked you for taking over when he went to pieces."

"You saved my ass and the rest of the Company that day, and that took a lot of balls on your part."

Larson nodded.

"My pleasure," he said. "Where else would I ever be able to work with a live pirate like *Captain Pike*?"

Pike laughed uproariously, and Larson joined him.

"I've been looking for a parrot," he told Larson, chuckling. "but so far, I haven't found one.

Chapter Ten

By the time the resupply was completed, it was too late to try and move the company off the LZ and back into a new location in the valley because it was almost dark. That left Pike with no choice but to remain on the mountain top overnight. But to be safe, he had his men dig foxholes in case the Company got mortared during the night. He also had each platoon put out three, two-man LPs down the sides of the mountain for added security.

He then briefed the Company that there was a good chance that the perimeter would get probed after it got dark, or mortared, or both. The NVA had undoubtedly seen the resupply birds come in, and if they hadn't, the survivors of the NVA unit that had made contact with Spence's platoon would have reported Pike's position by now.

"Plot some DTs (Defensive Targets) for the battalion artillery to fire if the perimeter gets hit during the night," Pike ordered the Company FO.

"And tell them to be prepared to fire counter-battery fire."

The rain finally quit about an hour after sundown, and a slight breeze took its place. That made the temperature drop, and it was cool on the mountaintop instead of hot and stifling as it had been on the valley floor. The change perked everyone up and drove away many of the incessant insects prevalent in the valley's humid heat below. It was so pleasant being on the mountain top; for a while, you could almost forget about the war and enjoy the weather, and that's what Pike's troops did. The coolness let them back off the adrenaline surge they had experienced earlier in the day because of the firefight.

Pike met with all his unit leaders right after evening chow and told them about the upcoming Combat Assault and the battalion's overall plan. Afterward, the Company settled in for the night, with Pike ordering strict light and noise discipline after dark.

Sometime after 2230 hours, one of the third platoon's LPs reported movement down the slope. When Pike got the news, he put the Company on full alert. Ten minutes later, the 3rd platoon reported movement on the downslope below them again. Pike told them to lob some grenades and see what happened. A few minutes later, the mountainside rocked with the sound of grenades detonating; then, there was silence as the movement ceased.

At 0120 hrs., four mortar rounds landed three hundred meters below the perimeter. They were followed by another four rounds a minute later, landing in virtually the same spot, then a final four. The Company FO took a bearing on the tube's sound after the first volley and ordered counter-battery fire from the artillery battery at the battalion firebase a minute later. The battalion artillery fired twenty rounds shortly after that, and when they finished, the NVA mortar ceased firing.

Pike assumed the earlier movement had been an NVA forward observer party for their mortars. But because they had been detected earlier than expected, they had not gotten an accurate fix on the Company perimeter.

Consequently, when they transmitted their data back to the location of their tubes, it was incorrect. As a result, the NVA mortar rounds missed the perimeter. The remainder of the night remained calm, with no more activity.

As a precaution, however, Pike ordered a Company Stand To when the sun came up. Just in case, the NVA had infiltrated troops during the night for a dawn assault. But when the sun rose and nothing happened, he sent out three recon patrols to check the area out. They returned two hours later and reported finding no signs of enemy activity.

Pike moved the Company later that afternoon. He sent Dawson and three of his squads out to recon another hilltop he intended using as a Company perimeter that night and as a PZ for the upcoming Combat Assault the following morning. When Dawson and his platoon did, they reconned the hill and the area around it, then secured it while Pike moved the Company to it.

As soon as the perimeter was in, Pike had 2nd and 3rd platoons put out three ambushes each on the valley floor below the hilltop. They were all in by sundown and set, but evidently, the NVA had planned on another target that night because not one of the six ambushes triggered. Instead, it rained nearly all night, making conditions miserable.

Pike pulled all his ambushes the following morning, and the entire Company rested in the perimeter since they needed the downtime. Since the Company would depart the area later in the day, it was a perfect time for the troops to stand down until 1600 hrs., when the lift package was scheduled to arrive for the Combat Assault.

Larson called Pike two hours before the lift package arrived and reported that both LRRP teams inserted the previous day had found numerous trails on both mountainsides and signs of recent enemy activity, but no NVA. Pike wondered if he had been wrong about his assumptions about NVA base locations as he waited for the lift package to arrive.

The Company's combat assault went into the mountaintop at 1645 hrs., with 1st and 2nd platoons going in first and securing the LZ, followed by Pike, his headquarters element, the mortar section, and the third platoon. The LZ was clean, so the insertion was conducted without incident.

Dawson had sent out three recon patrols as soon as he was down on Pike's orders. One of them found a suitable location for the Company perimeter a half-hour later, right after Pike and the second lift landed. Pike moved the Company into the new location and settled in for the night.

When B Company inserted, their first lift hit a hot LZ and had to abort. The LRRPs had evidently missed the NVA in the area, or maybe the NVA had moved in after the LRRP team had departed. Pike didn't know, but the aborted Comat Assault worried him. It was a different story on the other mountain top across the valley.

"Why were the NVA massing over there?" he wondered.

"What was their intended target?"

"It couldn't be us or B company because they didn't know where our LZs were or even that we were coming."

The four gunships accompanying the lift package raked the hilltop after the failed insertion, and battalion artillery saturated it with fire for ten minutes after the abort. When they finished, B company tried it again. This time, supported by the gunships, the second Combat Assault met no resistance when they reconned the tree line by fire. After the first lift was inserted, the second lift came in a half-hour later without incident.

As Pike listened to the entire episode on the radio, he tried to figure out what the hell was going on and what the NVA were up to. He instinctively knew something was wrong but couldn't put his finger on it. He thought about the entire day's activities and the unusual behavior of the NVA at length. B Company's hot

LZ across the Valley from him especially bothered him. Finally, he called Larson at the new battalion firebase on secure when his worry peaked.

"Larson," Pike asked, "how far is the new battalion firebase from where B Company inserted?"

"About six or seven klicks," Larson replied. "maybe a little less."

"Your LZ is much further away." He added.

"That's why we put your Company in first. "

"Why?"

"I'm trying to figure out what the Dicks are up to," Pike replied. "Like why they had B Company's LZ covered and not mine."

"And why the LRRPs missed finding them when they inserted."

"There's something wrong with that picture."

"You've lost me," Laron responded. "so you'll have to explain,"

"When the lift packages arrived at the firebase, the NVA watchers undoubtedly reported that," Pike said, continuing.

"So, they knew combat assaults were about to go in somewhere up the valley."

"They're not stupid, so they figured that out as soon as they saw the helos."

"So why did they cover B Company's mountain and not mine?"

"They had to know two Companies would be inserting just by the two lift packages arriving at the firebase."

"And since both mountain tops are ideal LZs, why didn't they cover them both?"

"Why only cover one?" Pike asked. "That doesn't make sense."

"Pike, I have no clue," Larson said.

"I'm still not sure I even know what you're driving at." He admitted.

"The Dicks are up to something," Pike told Larson. "I can feel it in my gut."

"I just haven't been able to figure out what it is yet," Pike told Larson.

"What does Pizanni think is going on?" Pike asked.

"He says he doesn't know either," Larson replied. "but he agrees with you."

"Something is going on or about to happen," Pike commented. "Ask him what he thinks is happening."

"I don't have to," Larson replied. "he's sitting here in the TOC right beside me, listening to our conversation," Larson told a surprised Pike.

"He says he doesn't know either, but he wants to know what you think."

"I'd be guessing," Pike replied. "and I'm probably wrong."

"He still wants to know," Larson pressed.

"What if the Dicks are getting ready to hit your new firebase?" Pike asked suddenly.

"Jesus," Larson exclaimed. "where the hell did you come up with that?"

"Well," Pike said. "the firebase is just west of B Company's LZ, and we already know it was hot when B Company tried to insert the first time."

"What if the NVA were massing and using that mountaintop as a staging area for an attack on the new firebase?" Pike suggested.

"Then suddenly, when they got surprised, they had to move their staging area because B Company unexpectedly tried to land right in the middle of it."

"The NVA were certainly not expecting a CA to come in there." Pike explained. "at least not when it did."

"If they had been, they would have shot B Company's first lift right out of the air when they tried to insert, but they didn't."

"And I think the reason they didn't is because the CA completely surprised them."

"They simply weren't expecting it since there was no LZ prep before the actual insertion."

"So, they weren't expecting the CA," Pike continued.

"When the birds tried to land, they took some fire, but no real concentrated fire like there would have been if the Dicks had been waiting on them."

"That's the reason none of the helos got shot down."

"Instead, the NVA fled to another area instead of taking out an American company when they had the chance."

"That means their original mission had priority over that."

"To me, that means they were massing their forces and staging for an attack somewhere else."

"Somewhere on the far side of the valley just to the west of the mountain where their target was."

"Like the new firebase," Pike suggested.

"My guess is they knew a CA was going in because they saw the helos at the firebase," Pike explained. "but they thought we were going to insert further up the valley."

"They figured that's why we repositioned the firebase, to begin with."

"Because they knew the old firebase couldn't support operations in the northern end of the valley because they would be outside the artillery fan."

"So, we had to relocate the firebase so the artillery could cover our new company AOs."

"They just never figured we'd insert units so close to the new firebase," Pike continued.

"That's why B Company's CA surprised them.

Pizanni came on the radio.

"That's a pretty interesting theory, Pike," he said. "And unfortunately, it makes a lot of sense."

"It also explains several other things that happened today."

"Like why the NVA weren't expecting Combat assaults so close to the firebase."

"And why B company's LZ was covered, but your's wasn't."

"And all that worries me," he admitted.

"I only have C Company here on the firebase defending it." He explained. "and almost everything on the firebase is still uncompleted."

"Worse, we haven't even got all the defensive wire in yet,"

"Much all less the bunkers erected and operational."

"Hell, we're almost wide open." He revealed.

"If the Dicks hit us now," Pizanni admitted. "we'd be in a world of hurt."

"Sir," Pike said when he heard that, "I'd recommend you lay on a gunship and some TAC air for tonight."

"After hearing what you just told me, I think you're going to get hit."

"Everything points to it."

"You know the Dicks must have been watching the firebase ever since you established it yesterday," Pike continued. "So, they know how vulnerable you are, and we haven't spotted any sign of them in the valley since last night," He pointed out.

"They've virtually disappeared, and that's not like them at all, especially since they have been very active every day and night previously."

"To me, that means they're concentrating their troops somewhere else in preparation for hitting a new target."

"My guess is that's your firebase."

"That's why they were massed on the opposite side of the valley."

"It's a perfect staging area."

"Even worse, they know if they could take you out, the deployed Companies would be easy meat with no artillery support and no command and control."

"They also know we'd be dead commo wise because our Company radios are outside the range of any other firebase."

"I agree with your entire analysis, Pike," Pizanni said after a moment. "everything fits."

"But it's already too late to pull one of the Companies back to the firebase to help defend it."

"So, we'll have to get some TAC air support or a gunship immediately."

"I'd have D company put ambushes out on a line east of you to catch the NVA coming in for the attack or going out after it, too," Pike suggested.

"And I'd also lay on some arty concentrations from 2nd Battalion's firebase if they're in range."

"I'm way ahead of you, Pike," the LTC replied.

"Larson is already laying on air and arty support for us as we speak."

"I'll brief the artillery battery commander and C Company commander ASAP."

"If you can get a gunship in an orbit point before the attack," Pike suggested. "You could put a real hurting on the little bastards."

"I was thinking the same thing," the battalion CO said.

"I'll get Larson on that too."

"Thanks for the call, Pike," the Battalion CO said. "I'll keep you advised."

"Right now, I've got to get busy."

"Good luck, Sir," Pike said, signing off.

As Pike looked around, he realized Dawson and Spence had been listening to the entire conversation,

"Do you honestly believe the Dicks will hit the battalion firebase tonight?" Dawson asked in astonishment.

"Yeah," Pike replied grimly. "I do."

"Everything points to it."

"When they do, I think they will try to overrun it."

"They certainly have enough troops to do it," he pointed out.

"Man," Dawson said, thinking out loud. "if the battalion firebase goes under, our asses will be hanging in the wind."

"We'll be all by ourselves out here."

"Shit, we won't even have any artillery support."

"I was thinking the same thing," Pike replied.

"Nesbit," Pike ordered. "Get me B Company CO on the radio."

A few minutes later, the B Company CO came on the line.

"Pike," he began, "the old man just briefed me on what you think is going to happen tonight."

"Jesus, I sure hope you're wrong."

"We're out here all by ourselves, and if the firebase gets hit, we may not even have any artillery support if we get hit too."

"And considering what happened on our first failed insertion, I think your theory is spot on."

"I think the Dicks were using my LZ as a staging area, and we just surprised them when we tried to insert."

"We can still hear movement all around us as we speak."

"I think that's what is going to happen, too," Pike responded.

"I'm going to try and put some of my people out on an ambush line about two klicks from the firebase," Captain Art, the B Company CO, told Pike. "The rest will man the perimeter here."

"They'll at least be able to give the firebase some advance warning before it gets hit."

"But I'm really worried about supporting those ambushes if they get into trouble."

"If the firebase gets hit," Art explained, "the artillery battery may get taken out, or they may have to defend the firebase itself."

"If that happens, I won't have any fire support for my people if they get hit and need it."

"And if the Dicks do hit the firebase, considering where my people are, they will need support because they'll be up to their asses in NVA."

"Art," Pike said, "I've got two 81mm tubes with me here in my perimeter."

"If any of your guys need fire support and battalion arty gets jammed up trying to hold the firebase, have your people call my mortar section."

"We'll support them as long as we have rounds."

"I'll put my mortar section on my alternate frequency so it can be dedicated to fire your missions."

"The frequency is listed in your SOI."

"Thanks, Pike." Art said, "I am apprehensive about them, and I appreciate that."

"To be frank," he admitted. "I'm worried about the entire company."

"I've had movement reported all through my AO ever since we landed, so the Dicks are obviously still here, and there has to be a reason for that."

"So, I think it's because they're going to hit the firebase, just as you suggested."

"Where's your CP located?" Pike asked.

"I'm still on the LZ," Art moaned. "There wasn't time to relocate it before it got dark."

"I barely had time to get all my ambushes out."

"Art," Pike warned. "you better get your people dug in and your perimeter ready to repel boarders."

"The Dicks will probably hit your perimeter the same time they hit the firebase."

"That's when you'll be most vulnerable, and they know it."

"Christ," Art said, understanding immediately. "I've been so busy getting all the ambushes out; I hadn't even considered that."

"It's almost dark, so you don't have much time," Pike reminded him.

"I'll immediately put one of my radios on your Company frequency and monitor it so I can keep up with what's happening."

"Call me if you need my mortars."

"Thanks again, Pike," Art said. "I'll call you later."

"Right now, I've got to get the Company perimeter ready."

"Nesbit call Sgt Parsell in the mortar section and have him come to the CP ASAP," Pike ordered. "Tell 2nd platoon to send me an additional radio and RTO."

"I've got a bad feeling about all this." He admitted grimly.

"Also, tell all three platoon leaders to come to the CP ASAP," He added.

"We better ensure our shit is squared away, too, just in case." He told himself.

"This is bad, isn't it, Boss?" Nesbit asked, his eyes wide. "The shit is going to hit the fan tonight."

"I'm afraid so, youngster," Pike said.

"Now, get moving."

Chapter Eleven

As the evening sun slowly disappeared in the west, the atmosphere in A Company was tense. News that the firebase would get hit had spread through the unit like wildfire, and a sense of foreboding hung over the entire Company. That had created even more worry. Pike had briefed all his unit leaders on the overall situation and what he expected to happen that evening. They, in turn, had briefed their people and got them ready in case the Company's perimeter got hit.

That possibility, coupled with the news of the battalion firebase getting hit, had put the Company on edge. So, as darkness descended on the valley, it was no surprise that the entire Company was wide awake and one hundred percent alert. Everyone was expecting the worst and trying to prepare themselves for it mentally. Pike saw the tension in all their young faces as he walked around the perimeter a final time before dark, inspecting it for readiness.

When the sun finally set, although everyone was expecting the worst three hours after it got completely dark, nothing happened at all. The jungle was as quiet as a tomb, almost peaceful. That was both a shock and a relief all rolled into one for Pike's men. They clustered into small groups around the perimeter and talked in hushed whispers about the total silence and the lack of action.

"Was the old man wrong in his assessment?" they wondered.

"He's always been right before."

"Has anything happened that's affected his judgment?"

"Has he just been chasing shadows or seeing ghosts, or is he running scared?"

"Maybe, because of that, he just made the wrong assumptions about what's going to happen tonight?"

"Maybe he's gotten us all worked up over nothing?"

They were dead wrong.

Suddenly, at 2237 hrs., the sounds of a vicious firefight erupted from across the valley. They echoed through the mountains, getting everyone in A Company's immediate attention. The RTOs in A Company, who were all monitoring B Company's frequency, heard one of B Company's ambushes report that they were in deep shit and were requesting artillery fire. Pike, already monitoring B Company's internal frequency, sat and listened to the ambush's frantic call for support.

Captain Art, the B Company CO, passed the ambush's frantic fire request to the battalion, and the firebase responded immediately. Shortly after that, artillery rounds started impacting the mountainside across the valley, but evidently, the fire support came too late because there were no calls for fire adjustment calls. Nothing from the ambush period, just silence.

After five minutes of repeated attempts to contact the stricken ambush on the radio, it became apparent they were gone. The jungle quieted again when the artillery fire stopped a few minutes later.

However, seeds of anxiety and the expectancy of an upcoming disaster had now been firmly planted in all A Company's personnel. The men of A Company knew that their commander, Pike, had been right all along. A disaster was in the making, and Death was coming to the valley. It was only a matter of time. So, everybody pulled out spare magazines, checked their gear, snuggled deeper in their holes, and settled down to wait.

Less than an hour later, the battalion firebase got hit. Suddenly and savagely. The NVA attacked the base with 122 mm rockets in a direct fire mode and mortar fire, a massive uninterrupted barrage of it. Unfortunately, both the rocket and mortar barrages were devastatingly effective.

The first 122 salvo of twenty-six rockets and over a hundred mortar rounds took out the battery of 105mm howitzers and wounded nearly half the battery's personnel while destroying the fire direction center.

It also wounded and killed several C Company members who were on the perimeter defending the firebase itself. Lastly, it blew up two partially completed bunkers inside the wire. The second barrage, coming in on the heels of the first, hit the artillery ammo dump minutes later and blew it up, along with the TOC. Pike's people watched in horror as the night sky lit up in the distance, and they heard the explosion clearly, even though the firebase itself was miles away.

Moments later, the NVA hit the firebase with a coordinated ground assault from two different directions. Pike, monitoring both C Company's internal net and the battalion net, listened in horror as the massacre started unfolding. Unfortunately, there was nothing he could do to stop it or help.

When LTC Pizanni called the 2nd Battalion firebase for artillery support and counter-battery fire minutes later, he was shocked to learn that they were under attack too. The 2nd Battalion Commander told Pizanni his artillery couldn't provide any fire support to Pizanni because he was currently using all their guns to defend his own firebase. He was also under assault from indirect fire, and a ground assault by at least an NVA Regiment, and the firebase was in danger of being overrun.

He reported he had already called Brigade for reinforcements and air support. Still, he didn't think the firebase could hold unless he got help immediately. Pike got a grim look on his face at that news. He told Spence and Dawson he was positive their battalion firebase was about to get overrun since the NVA had initiated a coordinated attack on both firebases with that intent.

Two minutes later, Pike's prediction came true. The NVA hit the battalion firebase from another side with at least two more separate battalions of NVA Dog soldiers. That confirmed it was under assault from an NVA Regiment.

In response, LTC Pizanni immediately called for air support to try and stem the initial attack. It might have survived if it had been hit from only one direction. But they had no chance when the second ground assault began, with all the artillery battery's guns out of commission.

They were pitifully outnumbered and outgunned, so when the air support arrived, the two attacking NVA battalions were already through the outside wire and entering the firebase proper.

Pike listened in horror as Pizanni was forced to call for an airstrike on the firebase itself to try and save it. But even that desperate action was futile because it was too late. The NVA were already inside the wire, so the firebase fell minutes later.

In the middle of that action, just when Pike thought things couldn't get any worse, B Company's perimeter across the valley suddenly got hit. The attacking force was large because before B Company even had time to call Pike's mortars for support, the Company perimeter had been penetrated. Pike listened in anger as it too was overrun minutes later. Art's last radio call to

Pike was that he had Dicks inside his perimeter, then his radio went dead.

Moments later, despite Pike's repeated attempts to raise him on the radio, he got no answer. B Company and Art were gone too; by that time, so was the battalion firebase. Even its desperate radio calls for support ended in the next few minutes.

The news of the loss of both B Company and the battalion firebase spread like a flash fire through the Company. Within minutes, everyone knew what had happened, both to the firebase and their sister Company's perimeter. Bad news travels fast, and Pike's men had heard the short but vicious firefight across the valley. Three minutes later, when the radios from the battalion firebase went completely dead right in the middle of LTC Pizanni's transmission calling for another airstrike, they knew it was all over.

After that interrupted radio call, there was nothing but static on the battalion frequency. Pike couldn't raise anyone on the battalion net despite his and his RTO's repeated attempts. He even tried C Company's internal frequency but got no answer. In desperation, he even tried to contact D company, which Larson had told him was supposedly deployed six klicks west of the firebase. He got no answer from them either. They were out of range of his radio, or they were gone too.

"Christ," Pike said to himself in amazement and sadness. "I knew it would be bad, but not this fucking bad."

"The entire battalion may be gone."

"Maybe 2nd Battalion too."

"We may be the only unit left and are all alone now."

For the next few minutes, Pike desperately considered his options. They were few, and he didn't like any of them. But he realized he had to do something, and quickly, because come daylight, A company would be the NVA's next target, maybe even before.

That wasn't difficult to digest because it was now evident the Company was all by itself in the valley. By now, the rest of the entire battalion was either dead, running for their lives, or prisoners. Consequently, A Company could now expect no support from anyone. They were on their own.

Pike didn't even have the means to request TAC air or gunship support. He would have to go through battalion since only their radios had the range to make such requests. Pike couldn't contact Brigade either because they were also out of range. Now, they were gone too.

The entire situation now boiled down to a straightforward fact. A Company was a solitary island alone in a valley owned by an NVA Division. The same NVA Division that had just destroyed two American battalions. It was now A Company against the entire 103rd NVA Division, so it was a matter of survival now, pure and simple. That meant A Company's odds for continued existence were almost off the charts; they were so high.

Pike absorbed all the bad news and tried hard to remain calm in front of his subordinates. The last thing he needed was their loss of confidence. Afterward, he weighed all his options one last time, then decided.

"Dawson, Spence, Thompson," Pike ordered tightly, a moment later, his face grim. "Get your platoons ready to move."

"Now?" Dawson asked in amazement, his eyes wide. "In the middle of the night?"

"Yes now," Pike said sharply. "Or would you rather wait until morning and let an NVA battalion overrun us too?" Pike asked sarcastically, instantly regretting his outburst.

"Because as soon as it gets light," he told Dawson. "if we're still here, that's exactly what's going to happen."

"Those bastards are going to come after us like hungry wolves."

"Sorry, Boss," Dawson responded. "I didn't understand."

"No," Pike told his subordinate. "it was my fault."

"I should have explained myself instead of jumping your ass."

"I was mad, it was my mistake, and I'm sorry."

"I'm just pissed because of everything that's happened tonight."

Dawson nodded. Pike was under extreme pressure, and he knew it.

"We're on our own now, people," Pike continued a moment later, confirming Dawson's thoughts.

"The battalion firebase, the Companies, and 2nd battalion are gone by now."

"You all heard the radio transmissions."

"The Battalion's finished, and with it, all its radios," Pike said. "which means we can't even call for support because our radios don't have the range."

"B and C companies are also gone, and for all I know, D company too."

"That makes us the only American unit left in this entire fucking valley."

"So, come daylight, you can bet your ass the Dicks will be coming to finish us off too because that will give them a clean sweep,"

"That is an absolute given."

"They will have cleared the better part of this entire Brigade out of their base area."

"So, to survive," Pike explained. "we are about to try and disappear before they can get here."

"We need to find a secure place away from here for the Company to go to ground until I can figure out what to do next, and we can't wait until morning to start looking for one."

"We need to get out of here right now while we still have the chance."

"I don't think the Dicks will expect us to try and move at night, so that may give us an edge."

"Dawson," Pike ordered a moment later. "find me a trail off this mountain top."

"A trail," Dawson asked in amazement. "are you nuts, Boss?"

"We never walk on trails."

"You taught us that yourself."

"It's a surefire way to get killed."

"Look, Dawson," Pike explained. "and the rest of you too."

"Listen to me carefully because we're going to start doing several things you never thought of doing before."

"That means, for the time being, we start violating some of the basics I've taught you."

"We have to in order to survive, and I'm not going to have time to explain my actions in the future."

"So, you're just going to have to trust me to do the right thing."

"If you do, I'll do my damnedest to get us out of this mess."

"But you're going to have to help me. Understand?"

"Sorry, Boss," Dawson said. "That just popped out."

"Just tell us what to do, and we'll do it."

Spence and Thompson nodded in agreement.

"We're ready for your orders, Sir," they said.

Pike smiled.

"We've got to get out of here, fast, and we've got to disappear when we do."

"So, we're going to find a trail and use it to get out of this area as fast as we can."

"We don't have any choice."

"We must get as far away from here as possible before sunrise."

"We try busting brush through the jungle at night, and we'll leave a trail a blind man could follow."

"The Dicks will find us an hour after sunrise, and when they do, we'll be dog meat."

"So, I'm going to try and prevent that by using a trail."

"I'm hoping all the Dicks in our AO were either participating in the attack on the firebase or involved in the attack on the other companies," Pike explained.

"If I'm right, the area around us, including the trails, should be clear for the moment."

"If that's the case, we should be able to jump on one and get as far away from this area as we can before dawn without running into anybody."

"As I see it, that's our only chance, so that's what we're going to do."

"Dawson," Pike ordered again. "get two squads out and find me a trail off this mountain."

"The rest of you, get your people packed and ready to move."

"We'll take as many supplies as we can carry when we leave because we won't be getting anymore anytime soon."

"Ammo has the priority; rations and medical supplies come second."

"Anything we can't take; we'll leave here and booby trap."

"Get your people briefed, packed, and ready to move."

"I want to be out of this place within thirty minutes."

"It's late, and we've got a long way to go before daylight."

Twenty minutes later, Dawson called Pike. After Pike had explained how desperate their situation was, he had led one recon squad himself. Shortly after departing the Company RON, Dawson had found a trail leading down the mountain about three hundred meters downslope of the perimeter, and it was a big one. He was securing it and sending two men back to the perimeter to guide the rest of the Company to his location.

Pike moved the company out of the perimeter as soon as Dawson's men arrived back at his CP. It started to rain when they departed, and for once, Pike was glad. He and the Company linked up with Dawson thirty minutes later. Then, with Dawson and his platoon on point, A Company moved down the trail, ghostlike, for the next hour and a half.

The trail forked at that point and led off in three different directions. Pike told Dawson to take the northernmost fork, which surprised everyone, but no one questioned Pike's decision. The Company walked silently for another two hours on that trail before it started to rain heavily, drastically reducing visibility and restricting everybody's ability to hear. Despite the increased risk, Pike kept the Company moving since the rain was wiping out his tracks.

They continued walking through the driving rain until just before sunrise when the trail led to a bamboo bridge that crossed a sizeable swollen stream. Pike had Dawson leave the trail at the bridge and lead the Company northeast, up the stream itself. They walked in the streambed, the slashing rain and frothing water another three hours before Pike finally had them exit and set up a tight perimeter, about a hundred meters away, in the dense jungle.

Once settled, he put the Company on fifty percent alert and told his platoon leaders to let their men eat and sleep in shifts with strict light and noise discipline. When the perimeter was set, Pike, Lt Spence, and Dawson tried to figure out exactly where they were, under a hastily built poncho lean-to erected by Nesbit and the other RTOs. A half-hour later, they determined A Company was now probably located fifteen or so klicks northwest of their previous night's perimeter by their best estimates.

Pike told everyone they would remain there until late afternoon. Once it got dark, he intended to move again. This time, the Company would head west and try and cross the valley floor during the night.

"It's a risky move," Pike told them. "but it's the quickest way out of the valley."

"And to have any chance, we must get out of this valley as soon as possible."

The rain continued all day, ensuring everyone in the perimeter remained miserable. But again, Pike was glad since the rain had washed away all the Company's tracks. Hopefully, it also kept the NVA from mounting a significant search effort for him. Pike intended to remain undetected until he could get out of the valley.

With any luck, A Company had succeeded in its initial attempt to disappear.

Once he determined their location, Pike realized he needed to sleep himself to remain effective. He slept for over two hours until the sound of a muffled explosion from the valley's south end awoke him suddenly just after dawn. After a quick discussion with Dawson, who had taken a compass bearing on the location of the explosion, both men agreed it was probably one of the booby traps they had left in their old perimeter, going off. After their conversation, Pike called all the platoon leaders to his CP and had a conference.

"We can now assume the Dicks are actively looking for us." He told them. "That explosion we heard earlier confirms it."

"It probably came from one of the booby traps we left in our old perimeter, so they know we've moved."

"But I don't think they know which direction we went when we left the old perimeter last night because the rains washed away our tracks."

"So even if they know we used a trail to move, they don't know which direction we took

"That means they will have to work to find us."

"And now that we walked up that stream for at least two klicks, that will be no easy chore."

"Because the rain has washed out all out tracks,"

"Right now, all the Dicks know for certain is that we're still somewhere in the valley."

"But this is a big valley, and since they don't know which direction we took when we departed our old perimeter, finding us will require a major effort."

"That will mean larger numbers of troops to search, and assembling them will take some time."

"Since the obvious and quickest route out of the valley is south, the NVA realize that."

"So, I hope we fooled them by going north last night."

"At least for a while."

"If we keep moving and are careful when we do, hopefully, we can stay far enough ahead of them to get out this valley before they can locate us."

Pike platoon leaders nodded their understanding. As usual, Pike was ahead of them in his thinking and planning. If anyone could get them out of this, Pike could, and they all realized that.

"Tonight," Pike continued. "I intend to cross the valley floor and head west."

"If we can get across undetected, we will circumvent the mountain to our west and then head towards the battalion firebase, or at least what's left of it."

"Brigade will undoubtedly be searching for survivors in that area, so we'll at least have a chance of making contact with some aircraft if we can get there undetected before they call off their search efforts."

"I know that's a big if, and I know several things could go wrong with that plan, but that's all I can think of to do."

"If anybody has an alternative solution, I'll be happy to consider it."

Nobody said a word. Pike was the expert, and they knew it. If anyone could figure a way out of this mess, it was him.

"We can't stay here and just hole up," Pike explained. "If we try, sooner or later, the Dicks will find us."

"And when they do, with no support, we're as good as dead."

"Besides, we're running out of rations, so we have no choice but to move and keep moving."

"And when we move, we have to have a final destination."

"We can't just wander aimlessly in the jungle hoping some help will miraculously find us."

"So, we'll head for the firebase."

"I'm sure Brigade will already be scouring the area for survivors, and I'm hoping they'll have aircraft up over the rest of the Brigade AO, looking for the deployed companies."

"But we can't count on that," Pike warned. "so we're going to concentrate on getting ourselves out of this mess by heading for the firebase because I know they'll have aircraft in that vicinity."

"I figure it will take us at least two or three days to cover the distance between here and there, but that's presuming we don't run into trouble."

"Regardless, that time will eat up just about all our available supplies."

"Especially our radio batteries, and we can't afford to lose them since they're critical."

"So, from now on, unless we make contact, I want all radios turned off except mine and whoever is running point."

"We have to have a way to contact help if we can make it to the firebase, and to do that, we have to have operational radios."

"Therefore, I don't want to take the chance to run our few remaining batteries down or use up what few spares we have left."

"So, we'll use the radios as little as possible for the next few days."

"I'll keep mine on if anyone tries to contact us and keep up with the point element."

"Everybody else turns theirs off unless we make contact or get separated."

"Meanwhile, we'll use runners."

"Clear?"

Everyone nodded.

"I don't have to tell any of you that we are in deep shit," Pike said a minute later. "You all already realize that."

"But I promise you I'll do everything in my power to get us all out of this mess, and I want you to tell your people that."

"They have to have confidence we're going to get back safely, and it's your job as leaders to project and maintain that confidence while keeping their morale up."

"If we're careful and watch how we move, we can make it."

"Trust me, I've been in worse spots than this on previous tours, and I've survived."

"So, I know from experience it can be done."

"But it's going to take time, and it's going to take a concerted effort by everybody."

"It isn't going to happen tomorrow or the next day, or maybe even the day after that."

"But it will happen eventually."

"But to do that, we've got a long way to move, and we have to do it stealthily and carefully."

"In the process, we can't afford to leave a trail, get detected, or get into a firefight with the Dicks anywhere along the way," Pike said grimly.

"If we do, we lose."

"So, tell your people just to hang in there, follow orders and trust me."

"Also, tell them we're probably going to do some unorthodox things in the next few days too."

"Like turning off platoon radios or walking on trails, for example."

"But we *will* make it back," Pike promised.

"They have my word on that."

"We'll rest here the remainder of the day," Pike concluded. "After evening chow, as soon as it gets dark, we'll start moving across the valley floor.

"Before we leave, make sure your people drink their fill of water and fill all their canteens from the stream."

"I don't know when or even if we'll find more water."

"I also want you to check every one of your people for loose gear personally," He cautioned.

"We can't afford to make any noise when we move."

"From this point on, this Company moves like a ghost."

"I want no noise, no lights, and I don't want to leave a trail."

"As far as the Dicks are concerned, A Company has disappeared and no longer exists."

Chapter Twelve

Later that evening, as the Company moved out, every platoon had its orders and assigned mission. Every man in every platoon also knew the gravity of the current situation and what was expected of him. He also knew what to do if the company made contact and was very aware of the importance of strict noise and light discipline and the requirement to move as stealthily as possible.

Walking on trails was like trying to boil raw gasoline on an open flame. One wrong move, one unlucky break, and one unforeseen accident, and it was all over. If A Company was discovered, the NVA would be all over them within hours, and they would never get out of the valley alive. Pike realized the danger and gave each platoon a specific mission in the upcoming move.

Dawson and 1st platoon would act as the Company's point element and provide frontal security and early warning. 3rd Platoon, under Lt Spence, would provide rear protection and erase the company's trail. 2nd Platoon would be the maneuver element if either 1st or 3rd platoon made contact.

Dawson's people had reconned a portion of the area Pike intended to move through earlier and found several trails across the valley. Dawson had chosen one that seemed to be headed generally in the right direction and had sent a three-man element ahead of the point squad as a roving LP. Their job was to locate any NVA checkpoints on the trail and alert Dawson to them. Their secondary mission was to act as a tripwire for any NVA element coming down the trail from the opposite direction and provide the rest of the company early warning.

Both Pike and Dawson fervently hoped that neither of those scenarios wouldn't occur. A firefight in the valley would be akin to a death sentence. There was little cover and nowhere to run, so both men realized the risk.

Unfortunately, there was no choice. The Company had to get closer to the destroyed firebase to have any chance of survival. Furthermore, it had to be done quickly; before the NVA sealed off the entire valley.

According to Pike's map, the valley floor was four klicks wide where the Company intended to cross. By his estimate, even using the trail and hurrying, it would take at least two hours, probably longer, to cover that distance.

That was a long time to be on a trail the NVA probably used daily, even worse if it was under observation.

The valley was flat, offered little to no cover, and parts were devoid of concealment, making the company extremely vulnerable. If the NVA saw them, they could hit them with mortars, putting forces in blocking positions to their rear and front, then finish them off at leisure.

That was a real possibility if the NVA had watchers on the mountainside observing the valley. If they were spotted, the NVA would undoubtedly be on them immediately. Failing that, they would send tracker teams to follow the company to its next RON position and then hit them there the following day. Pike prayed none of that would happen.

Instead, Pike hoped most of the NVA searching for him and the Company were still concentrating their search efforts in the valley's south end. He was also hoping a significant portion of the other NVA forces in the area were probably still concentrated near the destroyed firebase, preparing to repel any reinforcement or ambush any rescue attempts.

If Pike's assumptions were correct, that would mean the north end of the valley where he and A Company were now located should be relatively clear of any large NVA force concentrations. But the area wouldn't be completely devoid of them either. The NVA wouldn't be that careless.

As a result, they would certainly leave at least token forces, at a minimum, to observe the area, secure their base areas, and report any movements or attempted intrusions. They had more than enough troops to accomplish all that since they had three regiments.

Worse, they may have moved up some of those troops as reinforcements to help their forces already in the area repel any future attempted incursion into the valley. Despite that, as far as the company was concerned, none of that mattered. They had to cross the valley to have any hope at all.

Pike moved the Company out a little after 2030 hrs, all those thoughts weighing heavily on his mind. There was a sliver of a moon peeking through a cloudy and heavily overcast sky and the hint of oncoming rain heavy in the air. So he felt sure there would be rain sometime during the night. That was good on one hand because the rain would wash away any tracks. But it was bad, on the other hand, because the precipitation would significantly restrict the Company's hearing and vision. That heightened the chances of an accidental meeting on the trail, but that possibility couldn't be helped. Pike had to use the trail to cross the valley floor since the Company would leave a track through the elephant grass and other vegetation on the valley floor the NVA would see and follow as soon as it got light.

Accordingly, Pike had Dawson keep his platoon radio on during the move, along with his forward. element That was all Pike could think of to do. Everything else, he would just have to trust to luck.

Dawson felt like he was walking on eggshells as he led his men out onto the trail as the move began. The move was dangerous but necessary. It wasn't usually done because it was too dangerous. Still, it unnerved him because it went against everything he had been taught.

"Jesus," he thought to himself. "I hope to Hell Pike's right about the Dicks being south of us."

"We meet anybody coming down this trail in this terrain; we're fucked for sure."

"Once we get on the valley floor, there won't be any place to hide."

"But we must cross this valley without leaving a trail and put as much distance as possible before the Dicks realize we've crossed."

"Even though we have no choice, just thinking about it gives me the shakes," he admitted. *"Now that we're actually doing it, I'm scared shitless because we're wide open out here."*

The Company had been moving for over an hour when Pike got the call. Dawson's point element had heard movement on the trail ahead of them. When they did, they had immediately stepped off the trail, then watched an NVA squad pass. Moments later, they had called Dawson and alerted him. Dawson had, in turn, warned Pike.

Pike had the entire Company melt into the nearby elephant grass and get down in the thick foliage once informed. Minutes later, as they held their breath and listened, an NVA squad calmly walked down the trail and past them, completely unaware of their presence. Afterward, Pike waited a full five minutes before getting the Company back up, on the trail, and moving again. They reached the far edge of the valley thirty minutes later without further incident.

The trail out of the valley ran north, and Pike wanted to go south or west. Since he didn't want to leave the trail and bust brush in the jungle for the remainder of the night, he sent Dawson's element further down the trail to try and find another trail leading in those directions. Meanwhile, he and the rest of the Company quietly circled up into a tight perimeter about fifty meters off the trail and waited.

While they were waiting, the rain started coming down hard, almost like a monsoon. It was unabated, with huge droplets falling in sheets, driven by the wind. They soaked everybody to the skin in seconds, and the wind chilled them. The entire company huddled up in the jungle went from sacred, to scared, wet, and miserable, in seconds.

But that couldn't be helped. They were too close to the trail to erect temporary shelters to shield them from the weather. And since Pike needed a trail going in the right direction before he could move, everyone had no choice but to wait until Dawson found one. So, he and everyone else in the Company just sat in the small perimeter and endured the pouring rain and wind while they waited for Dawson to report.

After almost two hours of being pounded by the weather, Pike finally got a call from Dawson. He reported finding a trail leading west. It was a small one, but it branched off the trail the Company had been following and was headed west.

That was the good news. The bad news was that they had met another squad of NVA on the trail. Because of the rain, they had walked right into them. At first, the startled NVA thought Dawson and his people were another NVA Squad, but that changed immediately when Dawson shot the first three Dicks at point-blank range. The situation then turned into a wild free for all. Sgt Nolan, whose squad was with Dawson, shot two more as they turned to run, and his people sprayed the trail, downing two more and finishing the last of them. They were saved from a firefight because the Dicks had been moving with slung weapons, thinking the area was secure. As a result, they had all been killed before they could get them off their shoulders and bring them to bear.

Dawson called Pike when the action was over and told him what had happened.

"Did you get them all?" Pike asked anxiously.

"I think so, Boss," Dawson replied. "I counted seven bodies, and that's a normal squad of NVA."

"But I'm not sure; there could have been more." He admitted. "Sorry, we had no choice."

"Don't be sorry," Pike replied. "It was bound to happen sooner or later."

"I've been pushing our luck from the beginning as it is," He admitted. "But we didn't hear any firing where we are, so maybe the rain drowned it out up your way too."

"Stay in place and observe the trail."

"If nobody else shows up in an hour, we may have gotten away with it."

}If they do, ambush them."

"WILCO, Boss," Dawson replied.

That had been an hour ago. Dawson called Pike and reported everything still clear minutes later.

"What do you want me to do now?" He asked.

Pike looked at the map where he had plotted Dawson's position and then at his watch. Dawson and his people were almost five klicks from where Pike and the rest of the company were, and it was now 0243 hrs.

"Will that be enough time for some of Dawson's people to come back here and then lead the Company back to his location?" Pike wondered.

"Then move from that location to a suitable RON before dawn."

"It will be damned close," He decided.

"We will have to run to make it," He calculated.

"But one thing is certain," he told himself. "we can't stay here."

"That NVA squad will be missed by sunrise, and the Dicks will undoubtedly send search parties to find it."

"We can't be in the area when that happens."

"So, there's no choice; we have to move," He decided.

Pike ordered Dawson to send a squad back to Company immediately to act as guides. Meanwhile, since there were no other trails between the two, he would move the Company in his direction. While they were moving, Pike told him to sanitize the scene and hide the NVA bodies in the jungle.

Dawson's squad arrived, met Pike, and less than five minutes later, Pike had the Company running up the rail towards Dawson to save time. He knew he had to be off the trail and into an RON before dawn because the NVA would probably be using that same trail sometime later during the day since it was a popular one. Proof positive was the NVA squads encountered earlier.

Consequently, the Company slogged up the slippery trail as fast as they could move, no longer worried about leaving tracks because of the driving rain. The pace Pike set was a killer, but somehow, everyone managed to keep up. The Company reached Dawson's location half an hour later, but the rapid movement was not without cost. Everyone was exhausted.

Dawson immediately led Pike and the remainder of the Company another two klicks down a new trail into an RON position he and his platoon had already found and secured. Once arrived, the Company formed a small perimeter then literally dropped in place. Half slept, even in the rain, while the other half watched. Everyone was so tired some of the watchers even slept.

Dawn produced a weak sun and no letup in the rain. Pike's senior medic reported several men with oncoming colds and chills because of the weather. That was not good news since sneezing and coughing people would make stealth in the jungle impossible.

Time was running out, and Pike realized it. He had been fortunate so far, but he was pushing that luck, and he was smart enough to realize that it wouldn't last forever.

He calculated he had one or two more days before running his course because all the signs were there. Dawson's encounter with the NVA squad had been the topper. Very soon, some NVA commander would realize the company was in the northern end of the valley, and the NVA would shift the focus of their search operations there. When that happened, it was only a matter of time.

On top of everything else, rations had been exhausted, even though they had been rationed. Consequently, Pike had to maximize what little time he had left. So, after morning chow, Pike asked Dawson what he thought about moving during the day.

"That'll be risky because we already know the NVA use these trails regularly." He replied.

"But right now, the weather is so bad; I doubt very many NVA are out in it unless they have to be, especially in this part of the valley."

"I'm hoping they're still looking for us further south because that's the logical direction we would have headed when we moved."

"But I'm sure most of them are still located around the firebase waiting for a rescue attempt and not searching for us, because they know we aren't going anywhere."

"So after they mop up around the firebase, they can run us down at their leisure."

"Because they know our radios won't transmit outside the valley to call for help, and we certainly can't walk out of it."

"As to the weather, I know I wouldn't be out in this shit if I didn't have to be," He said miserably. "And I'm betting they feel the same way."

"So my guess is they'll wait until it clears before coming after us bigtime."

"If all that's true," he said. "maybe this lousy weather will work to our advantage for a change by lessening our chances of contact."

"But then again, after what happened last night, we know at least some NVA are moving in the area." He admitted. "So basically, it's a crapshoot."

"Anyway, I say we try it," Dawson concluded.

"Since we can't have any fires here in the RON, and the men are starting to get chilled; in my mind, there's no sense in remaining static."

"They'd be better off moving because that will keep them warm."

"My thoughts exactly," Pike said, agreeing. "and the sooner, the better."

"This rain won't last much longer, and I want to take advantage of it while we still can."

"Nesbit," Pike ordered. "tell the other two platoons to wake their people up."

"We'll be moving again in ten minutes, so have them get their people geared up and ready."

"Dawson," Pike asked. "you still want point, or do you want to take a break after what happened last night?"

"We'll stay on point," Dawson replied. "My guys are starting to get a feel for it now."

"I'll get my forward element moving right away." He said, getting up.

Ten minutes later, the Company was moving again. The move continued slowly but steadily around the mountain's base on a small trail for the next three hours. Luckily, the weather continued to be lousy. Finally, Dawson led them off that trail onto a much smaller one that went west-northwest. It wasn't much more than a footpath, and it didn't appear to have been used lately because it had vegetation that had crept out of the jungle on its sides.

The Company walked on that trail for another three hours. Still, everyone was utterly exhausted by that time because of fatigue and lack of sleep. Pike had Dawson lead them off the trail and into the jungle for another three hundred meters, where he established an RON position.

It was still raining, so those that could, slept, even though they were miserable. Those that couldn't kept watch and stayed miserable until it was their turn to sleep. Rations were now gone, and water was rapidly getting that way. Pike had ponchos erected to catch rainwater to refill canteens.

Food, however, couldn't be replaced that easily, which meant he had to find a way to get extracted soon, and he knew it.

"As close as I can figure," Pike told his platoon leaders, now gathered under a makeshift shelter made of ponchos. "we're still about five to six klicks from the firebase."

"That means if this damn weather ever lifts, we should be able to spot, or at least hear, friendly choppers looking for survivors."

"But, unless something has changed, the area around the firebase is probably still crawling with NVA."

"They're just waiting for a rescue force to be inserted so they can jump on it."

"So, there's probably NVA units as far west as we are right now."

"The trick," he explained. "is to contact a friendly chopper without attracting the NVA's attention."

"If we can do that, we'll try to figure out how and where to get extracted without getting our asses shot off."

"However, I don't want even to try and attempt anything like that until the Company has rested for at least four or five more hours," He told his platoon leaders.

"Between the weather, the constant stress, and the lack of proper rations, the men are dead beat."

"They made it here but were on their last legs when we arrived."

"So, they've got to rest before we can even attempt an extraction because they have to be fresh and alert since we may have to extract under fire."

"Because of that, we'll wait here until the weather lifts and we hear aircraft before we try anything."

"And," he said, looking up at the dark cloudy sky. "that may be some time."

"Unfortunately, this damn weather front doesn't appear to be going anywhere."

Pike was right. It was still raining when the sun went down that evening. Nesbit shared the last ration he had been saving, a can of ham and lima beans, with him. It was lousy when it was heated. Cold, it was almost inedible. Pike would have killed for a cup of hot coffee, but that was out of the question. The Company was too close to the old firebase to risk getting discovered by lighting a fire.

The rain continued throughout the night without let up. That ensured everyone spent another miserable night soaked to the skin, cold, and unable to sleep. Finally, an hour before sunrise, the weather front started moving out of the valley, and the rain began to slack off, stopping entirely just after dawn. An hour later, with a weak, cold sun shining intermittently through the low-hanging clouds, Pike heard the first chopper.

Pike ordered all the RTO's turn on their radios and search for a frequency that had American voices on it. He had Nesbit begin sending out a constant MAYDAY call on all the battalion frequencies. Fifteen minutes later, Nesbit excitedly handed Pike the radio's handset and told him that he had contacted a chopper and had the pilot on the horn. Pike took the handset from him and transmitted.

"Unknown aircraft, this is Alpha Six." Pike transmitted. "For security purposes, use your SOI and authenticate Alpha Romeo."

"Alpha Six, this is Wolfpack Three Zero." The pilot responded. "Wait one for authentication."

"Alpha Six, this is Wolfpack Three Zero." The pilot transmitted a moment later. "I authenticate Alpha Romeo as Sierra Bravo. Now you authenticate Tango Sierra."

Nesbit thumbed to the correct page in the SOI authentication table and put his finger on the proper authentication.

"I authenticate Tango Sierra as Bravo Yankee," Pike transmitted.

"That's correct," the pilot transmitted a moment later.

"Now, answer some questions, so I know who I am talking to," The helo pilot said.

"Since the firebase went down with all its SOIs, we aren't taking any chances."

"Spell the CO of Alpha Company's last name phonetically and give me his home of record."

"Papa India Kilo Echo," Pike transmitted. "Home of record is Linville, West Virginia. Over"

"This is Wolfpack Three Zero. Copy. Wait." The pilot responded.

Five long minutes passed before the chopper pilot came back on the radio again.

"Welcome back, Alpha Six," the pilot said. "your next higher just verified your answers, and they want to know your status and location."

"I and my entire element are tired and hungry but otherwise intact," Pike replied. "We have been evading for the past four days."

"We have moved from our previous AO to the vicinity of where Capt. Larson used to work, but the entire area is alive with little people."

"I also have to assume they are monitoring this transmission on captured radios."

"So, for right now, I'm going to keep my location secret until we can figure out where and how to set up and execute an extraction."

"Roger Alpha Six," The pilot replied, "I'll relay your traffic to your next higher. Anything else?"

"Yes," Pike said. "have my higher contact me on my alternate frequency plus Jack Benny's age."

"I'll be monitoring that channel as well as this one."

"WILCO," Wolfpack Three Zero said, "Out."

When Pike handed the handset back to Nesbit, everyone else in the CP was smiling.

"All Right," Pike said happily. "pass the word to the Platoons; we've made contact with a chopper and will be in contact with Brigade shortly."

"Now, we have to figure a way to extract, so have all the Platoon leaders come to the CP."

"Right away, Boss," Nesbit said, still smiling as he got up.

Five minutes later, Pike talked to a member of the Brigade staff via a radio relay through the chopper. Despite being thoroughly soaked and chilled because of the weather, everyone in the perimeter was all smiles.

Chapter Thirteen

"Alpha Six, this is Ranger Six." the Brigade commander transmitted on secure. "You don't know how good it is to hear from you."

"Unfortunately, you're the only element in your battalion we have heard from so far."

"What's your location and situation?" he asked anxiously.

"Currently, we are approximately five or six klicks east of the place Pizanni worked," Pike replied. "My entire element is intact, and everyone is accounted for."

"We evaded Dicks for the past four days and nights, so we're tired and hungry, but otherwise okay."

"The area around the here is still crawling with NVA, just waiting for a rescue force to land or for any survivors to try and extract."

"If and when that happens, they'll jump on them."

"Fortunately, they don't know where my element is, and they don't know I plan on extracting."

"However, I have a plan I think will work if we time it right."

"Let's hear it," Ranger Six transmitted.

"There's a cleared rice paddy at coordinates RA 1364 6764." Pike told him. "that would make a good LZ."

"When I am in position, I want you to start prepping that area with artillery fire, just like you would if you were getting ready for a normal insertion or extraction."

"After the artillery prep, have a pair of gunships circle it and hit the wood line with minigun fire too."

"Hopefully, by the time all that's finished, the NVA will think that's the LZ we intend to use to either insert or extract a force."

"When they do, they'll move their forces in the area towards it."

"However, that will be a diversion."

"While the gunships hit the wood line," Pike continued. "Move the lift package towards the LZ and orbit them at ten thousand feet where they can be seen from the ground."

"While they're orbiting, have the gunships make several more gun runs on the LZ."

"After the guns have finished, have the lift package begin descending toward the LZ."

"However, just before they reach it, have them change course and overfly it instead, then proceed to coordinates RA 1355 6761."

"That's another cleared area about six klicks further west."

"My Company will be there waiting for pick up."

"That's a pretty slick deception," Ranger Six transmitted. "If we execute it correctly, it might just work."

"When do you want to try this?"

"Have the artillery start prepping the fake LZ in one hour," Pike transmitted. "Continue the prep for fifteen minutes, then orbit the lift package."

"I should be in position at the real LZ by that time, and I'll keep you advised of my progress."

"I'll lay everything on," Ranger Six advised.

"I'm also going to lay on some TAC air for this op too."

"We may need them if this plan starts to go south and the NVA catches on to what we're doing."

"Advise me when you get your people to your extraction LZ," He ordered.

"WILCO," Pike replied. "Alpha Six out."

"Dawson," Pike ordered, handing the radio handset back to Nesbit. "everything's set, so get your people moving."

"The trail we used to get here looks like it goes right by the extraction LZ, so move your point people out and have them follow it to the LZ."

"The Company will follow n five minutes."

"When your people get to the LZ," Pike continued. "have them put in demo ambushes on both ends of the trail to block any reinforcement by the NVA, and make sure they're big ones," Pike ordered.

"Use all your Claymores and get extras from the other two platoons before you leave."

"This will be a one-time shot, so I don't want to take any chances."

"As soon as the ambushes set, have your platoon join us on the LZ."

"We'll be in the wood line on the western edge of it."

"Gotcha, Boss," Dawson said, turning and moving towards his platoon.

"Nesbit," Pike continued. "tell the rest of the Company to be ready to move in ten minutes and tell the platoon leaders what we're going to do."

"Also, have them send all their Claymores to Dawson's people right now."

"I want everybody on their toes when we move out, and that will be in ten minutes."

"We got this one last thing to do," He said. "We do it right, and we're home free."

"We fuck it up, and we're dead."

"So, I don't want any screw-ups."

"I want all weapons checked and loaded before we move, and I want everybody primed and alert for anything."

Ten minutes later, the Company was moving with everyone alert and ready. Dawson's lead element neared the edge of the LZ five minutes after that and reported everything clear. As the Company moved down the small trail, Pike could hear the rumbling of multiple explosions in the distance as the artillery prep of the fake LZ began, and artillery rounds started to impact it seconds later. The NVA would have heard them too, and knowing the area, hopefully, they would take the bait and start moving towards the explosions' sound.

A drizzle in the air made the morning light dreary and dim, matching the Company's mood as they slogged down the small trail as quietly as they could for the next fifteen minutes. Finally,

Pike's lead element linked up with Dawson's point element just off the LZ.

Dawson's people were on the edge of the tree line surrounding the LZ, so Pike moved the Company past them into the sparse jungle towards the cleared area.

The rice field serving as the LZ was almost a klick long and about three hundred yards wide. Pike surveyed it carefully when they arrived but detected nothing to indicate any NVA were around.

"Spence," Pike ordered. "have two men with a radio and some smoke grenades move to the center of the LZ and tell them to keep low when they do it."

"When they get there, have them get down and wait for my radio call."

"I'll call them when I want them to throw smoke."

"Meanwhile, you and Thompson break your platoons into ten-man groups and assign each group a helo to board."

"Your two platoons will take the last eight choppers, four per platoon."

"Dawson, your people, and the mortar section will take the first four."

"I and my HQ element will be on the last chopper out."

"Getting the entire company out in one lift is going to be tight," Pike said. "so, tell everybody to squeeze in when they on load."

"We'll only get one shot at this, so everybody goes out on this one lift."

"Dawson," Pike asked, "your demo ambushes ready?"

"They're both in and set," Dawson confirmed.

"Each one has fifteen Claymores, and they're daisy-chained and hooked up to a tripwire across the trail."

"Anybody that trips them will be hamburger meat."

"I've also moved both the squads that set them back to just off the trail beside the LZ for additional security to cover our rear."

"I'll call them both in when the birds are inbound."

"Okay," Pike said, taking a last look around. "then I guess we're about as ready as we're going to be."

"I'll call the old man and tell him we're set."

"Ranger Six, Alpha Six," Pike transmitted a few moments later.

"Ranger Six here," The Brigade Commander replied immediately. "send your Traffic."

"This is Alpha Six," Pike transmitted. "We are at the LZ, and set."

"I have an element in the center of the LZ that will pop smoke when the birds are inbound."

"Advise the lift package C&C; we will have to put ten people in each chopper because there will be no chance for a second lift."

"The wind is nominal from north to south, and the LZ is clear of obstacles."

"The C& C can contact me on this frequency."

"WILCO," Ranger Six answered. "we're passing your traffic to him now, and he'll be switching over to your frequency."

"Be advised I have a FAC with two A-1 Sky raiders on call and orbiting five miles west of the LZ."

"His callsign is Osprey 12, and he is also monitoring this frequency for your call."

"Use him if you need him."

"Are you ready for the lift package?" the Colonel asked.

"Roger," Pike replied. "We've already broken down into loads."

"Have the guns working the fake LZ divert and cover the Slicks for my extraction."

"WILCO," Ranger Six replied. "Good Luck."

"Osprey 12, this is Alpha Six," Pike transmitted moments later.

"This is Osprey 12," the Lead Sky raider pilot replied.

"Alpha Six," Pike continued. "If we need an airstrike, the target will be on the southwestern tree line just inside the jungle's leading edge."

"There's a trail there leading to the LZ, so if the Dicks attempt to stop the extraction, that's where they will be coming from."

"I have a large demolition ambush rigged on that trail, so if the Dicks trigger it, you should be able to see the smoke from it."

"If you do, have your birds hit that area immediately.

"Don't wait for my consent or corrections; just have your birds hit it as soon as they see the black smoke."

"I'll be too busy controlling the ground situation and getting my element out to adjust your fire."

"Roger, Alpha Six," The FAC replied. "I'll brief my people.

"And don't worry," he added. "we'll cover your extraction, and I'll take care of any fire adjustment."

"Any Dicks try to get to that LZ, I guarantee you, we'll chew them up good."

"Alpha Six, this is Pony 22," Pike's radio chirped. "I'm the C& C bird for your extraction."

"My lift package is ready to commence the extraction."

"ETA, your location is four mikes."

"Have your element pop smoke in two mikes."

"WILCO," Pike said.

Artillery and gunships' strike continued to rumble in the distance as the fake LZ continued to get hammered.

"Just give us another five minutes, Lord," Pike prayed silently. *"then we'll be out of here."*

Two minutes later, Pike ordered the element in the center of the LZ to pop smoke, and a moment later, a plume of yellow smoke streamed skyward. However, just as the yellow smoke plumed out over the LZ center, the demolition ambush on the trail's western end suddenly triggered. A huge explosion thundered through the area as fourteen Claymores detonated simultaneously, and a massive cloud of black smoke erupted from the nearby jungle a second later.

"Shit," Dawson said disgustedly as he stared at the black smoke rising from the ambush site. "one more goddamn minute, and we'd have been gone."

"Cover the trail," he yelled to his people.

"Osprey 12," Pike screamed into the handset. "hit the black smoke west of the LZ and the area behind it right now."

"The Dicks just triggered my ambush, so they're coming up the trail from west of the LZ."

"Pony 22," Pike transmitted urgently. "Get the Slicks in here fast."

"I've got Dicks headed for the LZ, and they'll be here any minute."

"Have your birds land south to north."

"My people are already on the LZ."

"Also, be advised I have a FAC working the western end of the LZ with two fixed wings to try and delay the Dicks."

"Roger Alpha Six," Pony 22 acknowledged. "I monitored your last to Osprey 12, and my birds are inbound as we speak.

Pike signaled his men to move onto the LZ, and the twelve helo loads immediately ran out to the LZ and got down on one knee, waiting for the helos to sit next to them.

"Dawson," Pike yelled. "get your security in now."

"The FAC will take care of the Dicks."

Dawson nodded and then yelled to his two squads on rear security. They all ran for the LZ seconds later.

A moment later, the earth shook as a Sky Raider unloaded two five-hundred-pound bombs just off the western side of the LZ, into the jungle, just behind the cloud of black smoke generated by the ambush triggering. A vast, much denser plume of black smoke appeared immediately, rapidly eclipsing the first cloud, and suddenly the damp air reeked of cordite.

As the Sky Raider roared overhead, Pike saw the Slicks coming in low over the south's tree line. He caught a glimpse of the Sky Raider's wingman out of the corner of his eye and realized the second A-1 was already on final, getting ready to drop his ordnance.

When the Slicks touched down moments later, Pike's people loaded them quickly. Pike saw two gunships roar overhead, firing miniguns into the tree line as he and Nesbit ran for the last chopper. As he loaded the helicopter a moment later, he heard the Sky Raiders unload again, and the ground shook. Moments later, the dark green jungle was streaming by beneath him as the chopper lifted off quickly and gained altitude. Pike saw a huge dirty cloud of smoke on the western corner of the LZ as the bird banked northward.

"Nesbit," he yelled above the screaming wind pouring into the Huey through the open door. "call Pony 22."

"Find out it all the Slicks made it off the LZ."

Nesbit nodded and started talking into his radio handset, his free hand covering his other ear. He nudged Pike a few moments later as he smiled and nodded yes, giving Pike a thumbs up. Pike smiled back and relaxed as the gunships and Sky Raiders continued to pound the tree line, rapidly fading in the distance. He then gazed out of the helo and watched all twelve helos of the lift package in a single line execute a slow turn westward. Afterward, there was only the sound of the damp wind rushing by as the package flew west towards the Brigade firebase. That's when Pike noticed that he was sweating furiously.

The lift package landed at the firebase twenty-five minutes later, and the Brigade commander himself was waiting for them when the birds touched down. As Pike's Company unloaded, the Colonel waved and walked out to meet Pike when he saw him.

"Spence," Pike yelled when he saw the Colonel. "take the company to the mess hall," He ordered. "The Colonel wants to see me."

Lt Spence nodded as the Brigade commander walked up to Pike, shook his hand, and patted him on the back.

"Welcome back, Captain Pike," he said with a smile. "You don't know how good it is to see you and your men."

"Let me buy you a cup of coffee."

"I figure you could use one."

Pike nodded and followed the Colonel.

A few minutes later, in the mess hall, Pike watched his men file in and eat. He was sitting at a table with the Brigade commander and some staff members in the officer's section where he had been relating some of the events of the past four days.

"LTC Pizanni called me and told me about your conversation before the firebase got hit," the Colonel revealed.

"That was pretty perceptive on your part, Pike."

"I want to hear how you figured that out, but that can wait until later."

"Unfortunately," the Colonel continued. "your assessment was too late for me to get a gunship to him in time, and the TacAir we sent wasn't enough."

"Did he make it?" Pike asked.

The Colonel shook his head sadly.

"No," he said simply.

"How about Larson and the rest of the battalion staff?" Pike asked. "and how about C Company?"

"We haven't heard a word from any of them since the firebase got overrun," The Colonel said grimly.

"The TOC took a direct hit by a 122 mm rocket and was destroyed."

"We confirmed that when we overflew the area at first light the next morning."

"We've had choppers overflying the area every day since, but like you said when you called me, the entire area is still crawling with NVA just waiting for us to try and insert a search and rescue force."

"Division has decided to hit the area around the firebase with a B-52 strike at first light tomorrow morning."

"We'll try and put a battalion on the ground as soon as it's over to search for survivors."

"How about second battalion?" Pike asked.

"Their firebase went down too," the Colonel said sadly.

"We haven't heard from any of their companies, so we assume they're gone too."

"But we're putting another battalion in to search for them tomorrow after the Arclight."

"We got our ass handed to us, son," The Colonel revealed angrily. "Intelligence had no idea how many NVA were in that base area when we started the operation."

"They figured a regiment at most, but they were dead wrong."

"We now know the entire 103rd NVA Division was in there, just waiting for us."

"You're the first survivors we've even gotten a call from since night before last; much less extracted," He revealed bitterly.

"Jesus," Pike said, sucking in his breath. "I figured the news would be bad, but not this bad."

"Two entire battalions gone?"

The Colonel nodded.

"What are we going to do about that, Colonel?" He asked.

"After the B-52 Arclight in the morning," the Colonel revealed. "we're sending First and Third Brigades in."

"We're going to Arclight the entire valley in addition to hitting the area around both old firebases."

"After the B-52s are through," he explained. "First Brigade is inserting in the north end of the valley and establishing two firebases there."

"Third Brigade will go in from the south."

"We've also got a Brigade from the 1st Cav in reserve."

"COMUSMACV has ordered us to clean out the entire valley and the mountains around it," He explained. "so, the Division has priority on all TACAIR in the Corps area for this operation until it's finished."

"We went in too light the last time," The Colonel admitted. "and the NVA took advantage of that."

"We won't make that mistake again."

"The Division Commander wants some payback, and he also wants to see you, Pike," the Colonel revealed.

"So, get something to eat," The Colonel ordered. "then get cleaned up."

"Afterwards, we'll fly up to Division."

"The Old Man wants to talk to you."
Chapter Fourteen

"Captain Pike reports to the Division Commander," Pike said as he saluted the two-star General sitting behind the desk in front of him.

The General got up from behind his desk, returned Pike's salute, walked around the piece of furniture, and shook Pike's hand.

"I am happy to see you again, Captain Pike," he said sincerely.

"Apparently," The General continued with a smile. "you're a hard man to kill."

"The NVA of the 103rd Division obviously couldn't manage to do that."

"In fact," the General said, motioning Pike towards a chair. "they couldn't even kill any of your men."

"Yet they managed to wipe out the rest of your battalion and second battalion with no trouble."

"How do you account for that?" he asked curiously

"I was just lucky, Sir," Pike replied.

"No," the general said. "it was more than that, Pike."

"That's twice you managed to save the men under your command in the last six months, so it's more than luck."

"It's something else: skill, experience, leadership ability, maybe a combination of all those things."

"But whatever it is, it seems to be working."

"That's why I wanted to see you, Pike," the general explained. "to find out how you managed to survive when every other unit in your battalion couldn't."

"So, tell me, Pike," the General said curiously. "how come the NVA couldn't manage to take out you and your company?"

"I'm not sure, Sir," Pike answered. "maybe I was just at the right place at the right time."

"Or maybe they had other more important targets at the time."

"Or, as you said earlier, maybe we just got lucky."

"No," The General said. "it was more than that; much more."

"That has to be because you're not the type of man to trust luck."

"I knew that about you when I promoted you."

"Even LTC Pizanni confirmed it after the operation started.

"He was highly impressed by you, Pike, and he told your Brigade commander and me that before he was killed.

"You're a thinker, Pike," The General said. "and a good one."

"Your analysis of the NVA strength in the valley with your old battalion commander, and then your conversation with him before the firebase got overrun, proves that."

"Your Brigade commander told me all about both of those conversations."

"He knew because Captain Larson, and later LTC Pizanni, told him."

"So, I know when you're given a mission, you think it through; all aspects of it."

"You're older and have more experience than most Captains in the Division," the General said. "so I suppose that accounts for some of your command ability."

"But certainly not all of it."

"You're obviously running your Company differently than most other Captains in this Division."

"You monthly body counts prove that."

"And since whatever you're doing seems to be working, I want to know what it is so I can pass that along to the rest of my commanders and get them to start doing the same thing."

"So, I'm serious, Captain Pike," the General continued.

"I want you to tell me what you did to keep yourself and your men alive during that time."

"Your Company not only had the highest body count during that period, but it was also the only unit that not only didn't have any KIAs but also survived intact."

"I want to know the reasons for that."

"I'm getting ready to send two more Brigades into that same valley, and I want them to be able to benefit from your knowledge and experience."

"Sir," Pike answered. "I'm not doing anything special in how I command and employ my company."

"And I didn't do anything special during the last operation either."

"I just used my common sense and my training to plan and execute an operation whenever I'm given one."

"How, for example?" the general asked.

"You can start by telling me what you did from the time you and your Company were inserted."

"When I was inserted, I immediately moved my Company off the LZ to a new location and set up a perimeter." Pike began.

"I didn't establish my initial night's perimeter on the LZ as the other companies in the battalion did."

"I make that something that I never do if it can be avoided."

"I established my Company NDP away from the LZ because I was sure the NVA saw where my LZ was located once I inserted on it."

"And since they knew my location, I didn't want to take a chance that my perimeter would get probed or mortared that night."

"Go on, Pike," the general ordered eagerly. "this is exactly what I'm looking for."

"As soon as I established my new perimeter," Pike continued. "I sent out squad-sized recon patrols to recon the valley around it."

"They discovered two major trails and a large stream, all running north to south in the valley in my Company AO, so, I marked them on my map, and that night I put out six squad-sized ambushes on and around those trails and the stream."

"They also discovered other signs of enemy activity which I also noted on my map."

"So, what you're saying," the general said. "is that you normally use your Company assets to recon the area and collect intelligence for you as soon as you get your new NDP set up."

"Then you mark anything they find on your map."

Pike nodded.

"Why do you do that," the general asked. "other than the obvious reasons?"

"The maps we're using are just reprints of the old maps the French had when they were here," Pike replied. "and they are notoriously inaccurate."

"I learned that in Special Forces on my first tour."

"So, I continually update mine while I'm on the ground in my AO by marking everything my Company finds, all contacts in the entire battalion AO, and all Company CPs as well as the battalion firebase."

"And I update everything daily, with reports from battalion."

"That way, I have an appreciation for what's going on in the entire battalion AO, and that helps me plan my Company operations accordingly."

"That sounds like something every Company Commander should be doing automatically," The general said.

"But how did you know the maps are inaccurate?" The General asked curiously. "I've never heard that before."

"I found out my first tour with SF, Sir," Pike replied.

"The Agency told us about the maps when we asked them," he explained.

"We had a lot of trouble with them initially, especially when we used them to navigate, and we wanted to know why."

"Well, I'll be damned." The General said. "That's the first time anyone has ever mentioned that to me."

"Did you know that, John?" He asked Pike's Brigade Commander.

"No, Sir," the Brigade commander replied. "That's the first I've heard of it too."

"But it sure makes sense and explains why our pilots sometimes have navigation errors, and our artillery is sometimes off."

"Yes," the General agreed. "it does."

"And I'll make a note to pass that on to everyone else in the Division."

"But continue Pike," he ordered. "you were saying you put squad-size ambushes out every night."

"Weren't you afraid one of your ambushes would get hit and overrun since a squad-sized ambush is so small?"

"No, Sir," Pike replied. "I wasn't, and neither were my squad leaders, for two reasons."

"First," Pike revealed. "everyman in the Company carries a Claymore, so when a squad sets up an ambush, they may put out as many as nine Claymores."

"That's a lot of firepower, especially when all the Claymores are daisy-chained and can be detonated simultaneously, and I make that Company SOP."

"A squad-sized ambush with nine daisy-chained Claymores can effectively cover almost a hundred yards of trail," He revealed.

"That means they can take out at least two full NVA platoons when they are detonated."

"Since my squad leaders know that, and so do their men, they aren't afraid to take on a unit two or three times their size because they know they can take almost all of it out with Claymores alone."

"They've not only seen it done before, but most of them have also done it themselves."

"Secondly," Pike continued. "my squad ambushes know if they get into trouble, I can immediately support them."

"How?" the General asked.

"Unlike most other companies," Pike explained. "I carry my mortars to the field when I deploy, Sir," Pike replied.

"So, each squad-sized ambush has its own DT it can call in if it needs it."

"And that DT is registered with my mortars and battalion artillery."

"So, my squads know when they call for it, they're going to get fire support immediately."

"Not minutes later when it may be too late, but immediately, because they've got their Company mortars shooting for them."

"Plus, I maintain a reaction force in my perimeter ready to reinforce any squad ambush that needs it."

"Where do you get the mortar ammo for your tubes?" the general asked curiously.

"Each man in my Company, excepting RTOs, machine gunners, and the mortar section itself, carries a mortar round on his ruck, " Pike replied. "including me."

"That normally totals up to around eighty rounds."

"That's enough for me to provide initial fire support to my people until the battalion artillery can take over."

"I get additional rounds every time I get resupplied." He added.

"My men also carry two empty sandbags," Pike continued a moment later. "That allows us to construct two separate sandbagged mortar pits in my Company perimeter to protect the tubes, as well as sandbag our machine gun positions."

"Don't you trust your battalion artillery to support you?" the Brigade commander asked.

"Yessir." Pike replied. "of course, I do, and they do a fine job."

"But it takes as much as five minutes to get battalion artillery fire on a target once we call for it," Pike explained.

"Remember, Sir, the fire request has to come from the squad to me and then be relayed to battalion, and then finally to the artillery battery."

"Afterwards, for any adjustments to their fire, the entire process has to be reversed."

"It has to come back down the same chain and then go back up it again."

"That's a long time if you're a squad in contact and you need help immediately."

"More importantly, during that time, my squad leader needs devote his time to running the squad during the contact and not talking on the radio," Pike explained.

"Controlling the situation is his priority, and he knows that."

"By contrast," Pike continued. "my mortars can have rounds on a squad target in less than ten seconds, and it's accurate fire."

"My squad leaders also know that, and they trust their Company mortars implicitly."

"That's another reason they have no fear of running squad-sized ambushes or jumping on enemy units two and three times their size."

"And yes," Pike added. "we do use Battalion artillery and gunships too for normal support, especially during daylight operations when we're moving."

"During those operations, if we make contact, my squads and platoons also immediately employ fire and maneuver if they make contact because I've trained them to do that."

"We don't stop in place when we take fire, call for support and then wait for it to come in," Pike explained.

"By that time, the Dicks are usually already gone."

"If the Dicks hit any element of my Company," Pike continued. "the unit taking fire immediately lays down a base of fire to prevent them from getting up and moving."

"The units behind it then begin maneuvering against the enemy force's flanks to pin it down and prevent the Dicks from escaping."

"After they're pinned, we call for support and use it to finish them off."

"So," Pike said in conclusion. "I guess if I have a secret to my Company's success, that's it."

"I just do what the Army taught me to do when I became an NCO."

"And I ensure that my squad and platoon leaders do the same."

"I also employ all the equipment allocated to my unit, like my mortars."

"I figure the Army spent a lot of time figuring out tactics that work in combat and what equipment a Company should have to support itself."

"So, I just do what they taught me to do and try and employ the equipment they gave me effectively."

"And that seems to work nicely," Pike ended simply.

"Well, I'll be goddamned," The Division Commander said, shaking his head in wonder. "could the answer be any simpler?"

"My God," he said, shaking his head in awe. "I thought we were already doing all that."

"What about that, John?" He asked the Brigade Commander.

"I don't know what to say, Sir," the Brigade commander said in astonishment.

"I just assumed my Company Commanders have been using fire and maneuver, but evidently, I've been wrong."

"But after thinking about it for a moment, I think Captain Pike is right."

"With all the firepower we have at our disposal, I guess it's natural for most Company Commanders to call for fire support as soon as they get hit as their first reaction."

"Then they wait for it to come in before they start to maneuver."

"That's where they make their mistake," He concluded.

"That accounts for us getting so few body counts whenever we have small unit contacts."

"In most cases, from the after-action reports, it appears the enemy has already fled before the supporting fire comes in."

"And by that time, it's also too late to maneuver because there's nothing left to maneuver against."

"The NVA have already gone."

"Well, we can certainly change that operating procedure," The General said firmly. "and we will."

"I'll see to that."

"We'll have an Officer's Call before the next operation, and I want every officer in this Division to attend."

"And in it, I'll make sure everybody from Battalion Commanders on down understands the correct principles of fire and maneuver."

"And I'll also make sure they know to employ that tactic *before* calling for support."

"Captain Pike is one hundred percent correct," He said firmly.

"The Army spent a lot of time coming up with that tactic, and when employed correctly, it works."

"We just haven't been using it correctly."

"Thank you, Captain Pike," the CG said, standing up and offering his hand. "your thoughts have been extremely illuminating, and they will undoubtedly save some lives in the future."

"You deserve much of the credit for that."

"I like to think I've done a lot of smart things in my career, but I can truthfully say that one of the smartest things I've ever done was promoting you to Captain."

"Keep up the good work."

"Now, I need a word with your Brigade commander, Pike."

"You can wait for him in the outer office."

"He'll join you in a moment."

"Yes, sir," Pike said.

Pike saluted and left the General's office.

"John," the Division Commander said after Pike had left the room. "I want you to take a special interest in that young man from now on."

"He's smart, he thinks, and he is a hell of a leader."

"I've never seen one better."

"When he explains how he does things, he makes it all sound so simple and easy."

"Anyone listening to him, including me, I'm ashamed to say, almost feels like he's an idiot for not already doing the kinds of things Pike just does naturally."

"Hell, he's just doing the basic things the Army has trained him to do, and he does them so easily and well."

"He even adjusts them naturally to fit the terrain and situation here in Vietnam."

"He'll make a hell of a battalion commander one of these days."

"I agree with you, Sir," The Brigade commander replied. "I talked with him earlier."

"When I had to relieve his old battalion commander."

"Pike impressed me then, and he's continued to impress my staff and me ever since."

"Pizzani told me he was head and shoulders above any other Captain in his Battalion."

"He said Pike was the best Company Commander he had ever met in his entire career."

"So, I plan to leave him in the field for a few more months, then bring him up to Brigade as my operations officer."

"I think that's an excellent idea, John," the Division Commander said. "working at the Brigade level will broaden his horizons and prepare him for a battalion."

"Meanwhile, I'm going to contact the Corps commander and the Pentagon and see what I can do to get him promoted."

"He needs to be on the next Major's List."

"We're wasting his talents as a Captain."

"He's just what we need at the senior level in this Division."

They had good news when Pike and the Brigade Commander returned to the Brigade firebase. Captain Larson, three other battalion staff members, and twenty-one C Company troops defending the firebase had been found and rescued. Two platoons of D company had also been in contact with searching helicopters and were also in the process of being extracted.

Hearing the news about Larson, Pike immediately went to the Brigade aid station where Larson was being treated. When he walked in and saw Larson, he was chagrined. He had bandages on his head, chest, and legs and was lying on a stretcher with an IV drip.

"Is it okay if I say hello to him?" Pike asked the doctor.

"Sure," the doc replied. "but make it quick."

"We're evacuating him in a few minutes."

Pike nodded and walked over to the stretcher.

"It's good to see you again, Tom," Pike said warmly as he walked up. "I'm glad you made it out."

"Did you get the tag number of the truck that hit you?" he joked.

Larson smiled.

"Good to see you too, Pike," Larson said, looking up. "I knew you'd make it out."

"I even told Pizzani that."

"You're too smart and crafty to let the NVA nail your ass."

"I'm just lucky," Pike said. "How do you feel?"

"I'm in la-la land," Larson said, smiling dopily. "I got no pain."

"The doc gave me something that took it all away a few minutes ago."

"But I can tell you I was hurting like a sonofabitch until we got picked up."

"Pizanni?" Pike asked hopefully.

Larson shook his head.

"He's gone," Larson said tearfully, "along with almost everybody else on the firebase."

"He bought it when a 122-rocket hit the TOC."

"I would have bought it too, except for some guys from C Company who dug me out of the wreckage, patched me up, and then carried me into the jungle with the rest of the survivors."

"We hid for the last four days and nights, dodging the NVA and waiting to get picked up."

"Man, I thought I would die for sure then."

"Luckily, one of the guys finally signaled a chopper this afternoon with a panel, and we got picked up a few minutes later."

"It's too bad about Pizanni," Pike said sadly. "he was a good man."

"I liked him."

"It's funny," Larson replied. "Pizanni said the same thing about you."

"He said you were the best Company Commander he had ever seen."

"He valued your opinion about the situation on the ground, and he told me that."

"It's too bad he didn't make it because he was one of the good guys."

"So, what happens now?" Pike asked.

"Division will build a new battalion around you and A Company," Larson said. "

"They're probably already getting the officers and men for it, fresh from the replacement depots in Saigon and Bien Hoa."

"So, they should start arriving here in the next few days."

"But you've got to get out of this nasty habit of losing battalion commanders, Pike," Larson joked. "It's not dignified."

Pike smiled.

"I'll try," he said.

"How about you?" Pike asked. "What happens to you now?"

"My war's over," Larson said. "I'll be shipped stateside for a nice long hospital stay, where they'll wire me back together again, according to the doc."

"After I heal up, they'll probably medically retire me."

"So, my career in the Green Machine, short as it has been, is over."

"And that's ironic because I've spent my entire life preparing for an Army career."

"Hell, I even went to West Point."

"But you, Captain Pike," Larson said mysteriously. "are destined for bigger and better things."

"The Army has big plans for you."

"A very reliable little birdie told me that earlier today."

"Is there anything you need or want?" Pike asked, ignoring the comment.

"Nothing," Larson said, "except to shake your hand."

"It's been a real pleasure knowing you, Pike," Larson revealed.

"You're a hell of an officer and the best combat commander I've ever seen."

"I'll be amazed if I don't see your name on the General's promotion list one of these days."

"Thanks," Pike said. "coming from you means something."

"But I'll just be happy to retire as a Captain."

"I've found I like commanding a Company."

"I get a real sense of accomplishment out of it."

"You ought to," Larson said. "you're the best I've ever seen at it."

"And it all just seems to come naturally to you," Larson said, almost in awe. "that's the amazing part."

"I loved watching you work, you old pirate." He snorted

"Good Luck, Pike."

Moments later, two corpsmen came in, picked up the stretcher, and took Larson to a waiting chopper. Pike watched them load the stretcher, and then the chopper took off. Seeing Larson leave, Pike felt like another chapter in his life had just closed. As one of the few surviving officers left in the battalion, he felt strangely alone. As an officer, Tom Larson and he had shared a common bond, and Tom was about the only officer outside the Company that he had been friends with. He thought about his miserable first battalion commander, and then he thought about Larson and Pizzani.

"Why does it always seem to happen to the good guys?" he wondered. *"How come the assholes are always the ones that seem to skate by?"*

"Pizzani is dead, and Larson is screwed up for the rest of his life, while that asshole first battalion commander got sent back to the states and was probably allowed to retire."

"That's not only unfair; that's a goddamn travesty."

Chapter Fifteen

Pike walked slowly back to his Company area, thinking about Larson. He remembered him risking his career and taking over from his first battalion commander when he had to and getting Pike the support he needed. And he remembered Larson and Pizzani working to build a better battalion after that incident. Now both were gone. One was dead, and one was so severely wounded he would have to be medically retired. Yet, here he was, still alive and kicking.

He wondered if he led some sort of a charmed life for a moment, then quickly disregarded that thought.

"No," he told himself. *"I just did what I've been trained to do to the best of my ability and try and take care of my men in the process."*

"And so far, that seems to be enough."

"But how long will that last?" he wondered.

He had escaped almost certain death twice now while the rest of his sister units had bought it. Just how good or how lucky was he?

The Company was now manning a portion of the Brigade firebase's perimeter as its new mission, so it was a cushy job compared to what they had been doing. But they had earned it. Almost everyone was sleeping when he arrived except Dawson. He was sitting in the CP smoking a cigarette, and he looked up at Pike when he entered the bunker.

"How'd it go?" He asked.

"Fine," Pike replied.

"Then why the long face?" Dawson asked.

"I just came from the aid station," Pike said.

"I spoke with Larson before they medevacked him, and he was pretty fucked up."

"He told me that after they put him back together, the Army will retire him medically, and that's a goddamn shame."

"He was a good man and a good officer."

"The Army was his life, and now he's done."

"Yeah," Dawson said. "That is a goddamn shame."

"We heard he and about twenty other guys got rescued earlier."

"That was good news because they were also good men."

"Hell, a lot of them still laying out there dead were good men too."

"But Larson was sort of special," Dawson remembered.

"He sure saved our ass when the old battalion CO went batshit."

"Yes, he did," Pike said, remembering.

"We also heard by way of the grapevine that two platoons from D Company have also been found and are waiting to be picked up too."

"Is that true or just a shithouse rumor?" Dawson asked.

"I heard the same thing," Pike said. "except I heard it from the Brigade Commander, so it's a pretty safe bet it's true."

"And there's probably more of our guys out there waiting to be rescued too," Pike said.

"It's just a question of finding them before they run out of time and the Dicks find them."

"So, it's a race as to who gets to them first; us or the Dicks."

"What happens now," Dawson asked. "to the Company, I mean?"

"Did the old man tell you?"

"Not exactly," Pike said. "but I'm pretty sure we aren't going anywhere for a while."

"We don't have a battalion anymore, remember?

"Apparently, we're the only unit left."

"But I do know the Division is going back into the valley in a few more days," Pike replied.

"No shit," Dawson yelped in surprise. "Again?"

"Yeah," Pike said. "again. "The CG told me himself."

"But this time, he's putting two full Brigades on the ground."

"What about us?" Dawson asked. "Are we going back in too?"

"I don't think so," Pike said.

"Larson told me they'd probably start building another battalion around A Company, and that'll take some time."

"At least a month or more, probably longer."

"They don't even have the people here to do it with yet."

"And after they get here, the units will have to be organized, then trained," Pike explained.

"At least I hope that's what's going to happen."

"Sending a brand-new battalion into the field filled with green replacements would be crazy."

"Especially here."

"So, I think we'll probably spend the next few weeks right here guarding the Brigade firebase while they do all that."

"We could use a break," Dawson said. "Besides, I can use the time to train my new replacements."

"They need it because none of them know shit."

"You think we might be part of that training process for the new battalion?" Dawson ventured. "After all, we're the only ones left with any combat time in the field."

"Jesus," he gasped as the thought struck him. "you don't think they'd start pulling some of our people out and assigning them to the new units as a cadre, do you?"

But Pike didn't hear him. Dawson noticed Pike had fallen asleep sitting at the field table he used as a desk. So, he shut up and reached over, draping a poncho liner over Pike's shoulders. Afterward, he lit another cigarette and then tiptoed out of the bunker. When he did, he met Lt Spence on his way in.

"The old man back yet?" Spence asked.

"Yes, sir," Dawson replied quietly. "but he just fell asleep as I was talking to him."

"He's in there now with his head on a field table, passed out."

"He's tired, LT, and he needs the rest, so let him be."

"He's had a lot on his mind lately, and he hasn't slept since the night before last."

"So, whatever the problem is, it can wait."

"Or, if it's too important to wait, we'll handle it ourselves."

"It can wait," Spence said.

"You're right; letting the old man sleep is more important."

"I got some coffee brewing over at my CP," Spence told Dawson a moment later. "Want a cup?"

"You know LT," Dawson said with a smile. "you're a good man."

"I could use a cup of coffee right about now."

"So, lead on, and when we get to your CP, I'll tell you what Pike told me before he fell asleep."

"Believe it or not," Dawson quipped. "It's good news for a change."

"No shit?" Spence said. "We could use some of that."

"I just heard a rumor that the Division is going back into the valley," Spence said. "That's what I was about to ask the old man about."

"Bad news travels fast," Dawson said.

"Jesus," Spence said, sucking in his breath. "You mean it's true?"

"We're going back in there again."

Dawson nodded.

"It's true," he said. "The CG told Pike, and he told me."

"Christ, we just got out of there," Spence said, in astonishment. "my poor platoon."

"Easy, LT," Dawson said smiling. "*we* aren't going back in."

"2nd and 3rd Brigades are going in this time."

"The Company is staying here at the firebase for the next few weeks until they can form a new battalion around us."

"Man," Spence said. "you scared the shit out of me there for a moment, Dawson."

"I felt the same way thirty minutes ago when Pike told me," Dawson admitted. "Liked to shit a brick when I heard about it."

"Still want to buy me a cup of coffee?" Dawson asked.

"Shit," Spence replied, grinning. "with good news like that, Dawson, you can have the whole pot."

Minutes later, both men were enjoying a cup.

"You've known Pike for a long time, haven't you?" Spence asked Dawson.

"Not really," Dawson replied. "only about seven months now," Dawson said, counting.

"He was already here when I joined the Company. Why?"

"I was just curious," Spence said.

"He never talks about himself, and I've never seen him get a letter at mail call."

"Doesn't he have any family?"

"A brother, I think," Dawson said. "that's all."

"He never talked about himself to me either."

"Even when we were NCOs."

"I only know about the brother because he asked me to sign his GI insurance form as a witness."

"I guess he's pretty lonely then," Spence said.

"I don't think so, LT," Dawson replied. "I don't think that at all."

"I think he considers the Company his family, and the men his children."

"Especially the younger troops."

"Haven't you ever noticed how he goes out of his way to ensure they're always looked out for?"

"That's why he's on us NCOs and you officers all the time to take care of them."

"He told me once that *If you take care of your troops, they'll take care of you*," and he's right."

"He's the best damned commanding officer I've ever seen since I've been in the Army, and I got sixteen years in."

"We're damned lucky to have him."

"Well," Spence said. "he's the only Company Commander I've ever had, but when I compare him to other officers I've met since I've been in the Army, he's heads and shoulders above them."

"And in a combat situation, he's like the iceman."

"He always knows what to do."

"He sure saved or asses on that last operation."

"So, I'm like you; I think we're damned lucky to have him too."

When Pike woke up, it was quiet in the bunker, and long shadows told him it was almost sundown. He heard choppers landing in the distance, then cheering. So, he got up, walked to the bunker's door, and peered out curiously. About forty men, all of them tired, dirty, and looking like they were on their last legs, were getting off the choppers.

"It's the two platoons from D Company," Pike thought instinctively. *"they made it back."*

"Jesus, they look like they've been through the wringer."

"I wonder if there's anybody else still out there waiting and praying to be rescued?"

Dawson walked up a second later.

"How was the nap?" He asked.

"Not long enough," Pike replied with a smile. "I'm still groggy."

"Do I look like shit?"

"Yeah," Dawson said, "you do."

"But I got a cure for that."

"It's called hot food."

"Come on," Dawson said. "it's time for evening chow, and you need something hot in you."

"I heard about those cold Ham and Lima's you had to share with Nesbit."

"Man, you're a braver soul than me." He snorted. "I wouldn't eat that shit even if I was starving."

Pike nodded and put on his boonie hat. Later, both men walked towards the Brigade mess.

"The food's good here," Dawson said. "not like that shit they fed us at battalion."

"You'll like it." He predicted.

"Unlike the Mess Sgt we had back at battalion, the one here knows what he's doing."

"Probably because he has to cook for the Colonel."

"Any word from Brigade or anybody else?" Pike asked.

"A runner from Brigade HQ came by while you were asleep," Dawson said

"He wanted to see you, but I told him he could give the message to me."

"He told me our mission, until further notice, was to secure our portion of the Brigade firebase's perimeter."

"Why didn't you wake me? Pike asked.

"Because you've only had six hours of sleep in the last four days," Dawson said. "and the message wasn't that important.'

"You needed the sleep more."

"Besides, if you had an XO like every other CO in the Brigade, he could handle things like that for you."

"Are you applying for the job?" Pike asked.

"No," Dawson said. "but I know who I'd recommend if you asked me."

"Who?" Pike asked.

"Lt Spence," Dawson said. "he'd be perfect."

"He cares about the men and the Company almost as much as you do."

"How do you know?" Pike asked.

"Because I've talked to him," Dawson replied. "several times."

"He treats his platoon the same way you treat the Company."

"He learned that from you, and he's a damn good platoon leader because of it."

"Thanks, Dawson," Pike said, thinking about Dawson's suggestion. "that's not a bad idea."

"But if we moved Spence up to XO, who would we give his platoon to?"

"Pardee," Dawson said without hesitation. "he's ready."

"I've been using him as my Platoon Sgt for the past two months."

"Letting him run it most of the time."

"He's done a damn good job, so he could handle a platoon easily."

"You know, Pike," Dawson said. "you won't be here forever, so you better start training your replacement."

"Otherwise, we're liable to get stuck with some asshole Brigade sends us, and that could turn out to be fucking disaster."

"And with all those replacements coming in to form the new battalion, you're moving up to battalion or brigade staff is a real possibility."

"You know, Dawson," Pike said, thinking. "for a dumb-assed NCO, now and then, you come up with a good idea."

"Fuck you, Captain Pike," Dawson said, grinning. "Sir."

Pike laughed.

As usual, Dawson was right when both men arrived at the mess hall. The food was good, so Pike ate like a horse. He hadn't realized how hungry he was. Afterward, as he sat drinking a final cup of coffee, Pike thought about Dawson's suggestion.

The following day, Pike called his three platoon leaders and the senior NCOs to the Company CP.

"We're going to be securing this part of the Brigade firebase perimeter for the foreseeable future," Pike told them. "while they build a new battalion around us."

"So, we'll use this downtime to train our people and refit."

"And we'll do the training round-robin style."

"Each Platoon will be responsible for presenting and conducting a block of it."

"The men in the Company will rotate through all three blocks every day, and we'll have three new blocks each week."

"We'll keep training for the entire time we're here, and I estimate that may be about a month, maybe more."

"The man who responsible for coordinating and delivering all this refresher training is our new Company XO, Lt Spence."

Spence stared open-mouthed at Pike; he was so surprised. Everyone else grinned since it was a welcome appointment.

"Sgt Pardee," Pike continued. "I have recommended you for promotion, and it should come through in the next few weeks."

"You'll take over as the new platoon leader of 2nd Platoon, effective today."

"And you'll remain as the new platoon leader."

"I've already spoken to the Colonel about that, so there won't be any second lieutenant coming in to replace you."

"You've earned the job, so you get to keep it for a while."

Pardee and Spence looked at each other in surprise.

"Well, don't kiss each other," Dawson quipped. "smile."

Everybody laughed.

"John," Pike told Spence a moment later. "unlike other Company XOs in the Division, you'll be going to the field with the Company."

"Among other things," Pike told him. "you're going to be the Company MACO when we have airmobile operations, the resupply officer, responsible for keeping us in beans and bullets, and you'll be responsible for setting up the company perimeter every night."

"You'll also oversee the mortar section."

"Lastly," Pike said smiling, you'll also handle all the Company paperwork."

"You are about to discover the Army is like a ship, Spence," Pike quipped. "it floats on a sea of paperwork."

"And your job will be to ensure all A Companies is correct and filed on time."

"Think you can handle all that?" Pike asked.

"Yes, Sir," Spence replied, beaming. "I think so."

"Good," Pike said. "you can get started on the training schedule I mentioned earlier right away."

"I want to see a rough draft by noon today."

"Concentrate on the basics, like first aid, fire and maneuver, fire discipline, and ambush procedures."

"The things all the old hands already know."

"When we finish that, if we have time, we'll get into calls for fire support, indirect fire adjustment, and recon procedures."

"I'll send Pardee over to your platoon a little later today, and you can introduce him to your people."

"Afterwards, you and he turn can over, and you can move your gear into the Company CP."

"Sgt Pardee," Pike said after Spence had left. "get with Lt Spence after you turn over your squad."

"You and he can coordinate the turnover of 2nd platoon."

"We'll be here in the firebase for at least the next four weeks, so you can use that time to get to know your new platoon, get it completely reequipped and resupplied, and get it running as you want it."

"Thanks, Captain," Pardee said. "I appreciate your confidence in me, and I think I can handle the job."

"I think you can too," Pike said. "and so does Sgt Dawson."

"He's the one that recommended you."

Later as Pike and Dawson sat smoking, Pike asked. "Who you going to replace Pardee with?"

"I think Sgt Nolan," Dawson said. "he's pretty damned sharp for a Buck Sgt."

"He's been doing a good job running the third squad, so it's time he grew a little."

"He would have been my choice, too," Pike said in agreement. "I'll put him in for another stripe to go along with his new job."

"Thanks, Boss," Dawson said. "I think all these new changes will work out well for the Company."

"A little new blood is good now and then."

"It brings in new ideas."

"Meanwhile," Dawson said, getting up and crushing out his cigarette. "I need to get back to my monkeys and get them doing something useful."

"If they aren't busy, they got too much time to get into trouble and to bitch, and I hate bitching."

"I heard enough of that from my ex-wife to last me a lifetime."

"She was the bitchiest, most unhappy one woman I've ever met."

"She didn't like the Army; she didn't like the posts I was assigned to; she didn't like the lifestyle, and finally, after a while, she got so she didn't like me either."

"Before I divorced her ass, she bitched about all that and everything else too."

"Every single fucking day."

"That woman needed an on-off switch for her mouth."

"She was the unhappiest person I think I've ever seen after we got married."

"I think she realized she'd made a mistake as we walked out of the church, but she didn't want to have to admit it."

"Sometimes, I wonder if some other poor bastard married her."

"If he did, I feel sorry for him."

Pike laughed. Dawson was a good man too, and an excellent NCO. He always sensed when Pike needed a little humor to cheer him up and was quick to provide it. Pike considered himself lucky to have Dawson as a friend and a subordinate.

Chapter Sixteen

The next few weeks flew by for Pike and the Company. They spent their nights guarding their section of the perimeter and their day's training. Three new companies were formed during that time, and new officers and NCOs arrived to cadre them.

On the Brigade CO's orders, all the new NCOs and officers underwent a five-day training program conducted by Pike himself on the correct employment of fire and maneuver. While Pike was busy training the new personnel, Spence ran the Company.

When that program had been completed, the Colonel ordered Pike to develop and implement a training program for all the new companies that would be part of the new battalion. Because of that action, after the first two weeks of the training program, Pike became the de facto battalion commander for the new unit.

He drew up and initiated a training schedule for all the new companies that included classes and hands-on training encompassing all his hard-earned combat knowledge, along with every technique he used to command and employ his own Company effectively. But when the actual training began, he had to draft Dawson, Pardee, and Thomson to help him.

During the training of the officers and NCOs, the Companies began filling up with troops. When the units were up to strength, the final phase of instruction began.

That consisted of all the newly formed Companies running day and night combat and recon patrols and conducting night ambushes in the jungle around the firebase. Of course, all those operations were conducted under Pike's watchful tutelage, his three platoon leaders, and Lt Spence, all acting as on-site instructors and evaluators. Pike even included A Company in some of the exercises to refresh their knowledge and had all the Companies maneuver as units, as part of a battalion-sized operation. Unknown to Pike, The Brigade commander watched all of Pike's training and exercises with silent approval and quietly passed on his observations to the Division CG.

Finally, after four weeks of nonstop and often grueling day and night training, Pike pronounced the three new Companies ready for combat operations.

By that time, the battalion staff had also been fleshed out, and Pike had succeeded in training them too. Again, with the help of his platoon leaders and Lt Spence.

"How's the Company doing under Spence?" Pike asked Dawson one evening after chow.

"Running like a Swiss watch," Dawson told him.

"Spence commands the same way you do; takes care of the troops as you do too."

"And if he has a problem or doesn't know the answer to something, he's smart enough to ask his senior NCOs what to do about it before he makes a decision."

"You may not know it, Pike," Dawson said. "but that boy learned a lot working under you, and in the last four weeks, he's come into his own and blossomed."

"He could run the Company by himself if he had to."

"He watched you like a hawk when you trained those new Company commanders," Dawson told Pike. "and he absorbed every damned thing you taught them."

"He's a quick study, plus he already had the advantage of working under you as a platoon leader in combat."

"He'll make a hell of a Company commander when he gets his own company."

"Well, that's a relief," Pike said.

"Why?" Dawson asked curiously.

"Because the Brigade Commander wants to see me in the morning," Pike replied. "And I think he may be about to move me out of the Company to a new job."

"Shit," Dawson said. "I was afraid something like that was about to happen."

"That explains why he's had you training all those new Company Commanders instead of just running A Company."

"He wanted to see what you could do when you were dealing with more than just a Company, and he liked what he saw."

"Where do you think you'll be going?"
Pike shrugged.

"Beats me," he said. "probably somewhere on battalion or Brigade staff maybe, but that's just a guess."

"And since I don't know shit about Intelligence, supply or Admin and Personnel, it'll have to be a job in Operations."

"That's all I'm qualified for."

"And I'm not even qualified for that." He added.

"Remember Dawson; I haven't been to Basic Officer's school yet."

"I'm just an ex-NCO wearing Captain's bars, trying to get by on my experience and what I picked up over the years."

"Well, so far, that seems to be enough," Dawson said. "You got the best Company in the Division, and everybody from the CG on down knows it."

"I just hope I can keep it," Pike said.

"But keep all this to yourself, Dawson, because I'm just guessing about what's going on, and I may be wrong."

"I sure hope so."

"I'll find out tomorrow and let you know."

"You aren't wrong," Dawson predicted. "the Old man has plans for you, sure as shit."

"Hell, I knew that when the CG promoted you."

The following day Pike reported to the Brigade commander. Over a cup of coffee, the Colonel asked Pike about the training program progress for the Company Commanders.

"We're finished, Sir," Pike reported. "I've got all the Companies out running daylight patrols and conducting night ambushes around the firebase now, under the watchful eyes of my three platoon leaders and my XO."

"By now, I'm confident they all know what they're doing."

"My people are just tweaking them up a little before turning them loose on their own."

"As the last item on the training schedule," he added. "I've got my guys giving them a few hard-earned tips on movement, ambush techniques, airmobile operations, and the tactics the NVA use."

"When they digest all that, the company's new COs and their officers and NCOs will all be fully capable of running their operations," Pike explained.

"The stuff we're teaching them now is just good sound combat tips my people got from hard-earned experience."

"How about the new battalion staff?" the Brigade commander asked. "What's their status?"

"I've been working with them too," Pike replied.

"After I took them through the basics by having them plan and schedule all the training, I had them shadow one of second Brigade's deployed battalion staffs for a week."

"That let them get a real feel for how a battalion functions in combat and what a staff has to do to support the line companies when they're in the field."

"The battalion they went to was working the same valley we were in earlier, so the staff got a chance to see how an operational battalion staff has to function in a combat environment when its deployed companies are in daily contact with the enemy."

"They learned a lot from that experience," Pike observed.

"Lastly, I've had them functioning as a complete staff for the last week and controlling the Companies I've had operating around the firebase."

"They've just about got the hang of all of that now."

"The big thing is knowing where to go and what procedures to use, to get fire support and air support, and how to process those requests from the Companies in the field."

"So, next week, I'm going to have them spend two days with the artillery battalion fire direction center here at the firebase to give them some experience in handling requests for fire support," Pike revealed.

"They'll also spend a day at your Brigade TOC seeing how things work operationally at the next higher level and how Division Support Command handles supplying battalions in the field."

"After that, they should be fully capable and operational."

"I heard about them spending a week with the battalion in 2nd Brigade," the Colonel told Pike unexpectedly. "The Brigade commander told me."

"He thought it was a hell of a good idea."

"Said he wished he would have been smart enough to think of it himself."

"And I think the idea of sending the staff over to the artillery for two days is a good move too, as well as letting them spend some time with my staff."

"In truth, I am extremely pleased with everything you've done to get the new battalion up and running."

"Your training program has been innovative, practical, and extremely well thought out."

"You have a flair for command, Pike," The Colonel said approvingly. "and it seems to come naturally."

"Your instincts for what you need to do to train people in their jobs, and the methods you use to accomplish that, are nothing short of amazing."

"You use a hands-on approach, do what I do, and only stress what's important."

"Both I and the CG have watched you take this battalion from scratch and transform it into an effective operational element."

"Now, its leaders not only know their jobs, but they also know how to employ their men in combat situations they're going to be faced with when they have to take their units to the field."

"And I especially like your instruction to them on how the NVA operates and what tactics they use," The Colonel said.

"That should serve them well and let them know what to expect when they get into contact for the first time."

"But the most amazing thing about your entire program," the Colonel continued. "is that you managed to accomplish it in just over four short weeks and virtually all by yourself."

"With help only from your Company NCOs and officers."

"You should be extremely proud of yourself for that."

"I don't think I've ever witnessed anything like it before in my career."

"Now that the training program is complete and the battalion operational, all it needs is a new commander."

"Yes, Sir," Pike said in agreement. "I think everything else is pretty much ready."

"All the new commanders will have to do is get acquainted with the Brigade SOPs and with the new battalion commander."

"Will he be getting here soon, Sir?" Pike asked.

"I think so," the Colonel said. "I'll know in the next few days."

"The CG is personally requesting the man he wants, so his assignment just has to be approved by higher."

"How's your Company doing?" The Colonel asked a moment later.

"I know your XO, Lt Spence, has been running it while you've been training the new battalion, and I also know he's been assisting you in the training program as well."

"He appears to be a very capable young officer."

"The Company is in fine shape, Sir," Pike replied.

"Lt Spence has done an excellent job getting it refitted, re-equipped, and retrained."

"And you're right, Lt Spence is a competent young man."

"I met him the other day, you know," the Colonel revealed.

"I briefly talked with him while inspecting the firebase perimeter."

"I was very impressed with his knowledge and his manner."

"You trained him well, Pike, so he thinks as you do."

"I could tell by the way he briefed me."

"He'll be ready for a Company of his own soon."

"In fact," the Colonel said. "that's what I called you up here for, Pike."

"To talk to you about moving to a new job."

"I know you don't want to give up your Company, but you can't keep it forever."

"And after talking to Spence, I think he's capable of taking over for you."

"How do you feel about that?" the Colonel asked

"Well, Sir," Pike said. "you're right."

"I don't want to leave the Company."

"I trained it, tweaked it, and it's working just the way I want now, so I'd like to keep it a little longer."

"But, if I have to give it up, I feel sure Lt Spence can run it effectively after I'm gone."

"He enjoys the full confidence of all my senior NCOs, and I trust their judgment."

"And I know they would rather have him as their new CO than someone from outside the battalion."

"I realize he's only a Lieutenant, but he's a much better commander than many Captains I've seen."

"So, if I have to leave, and I have any say in the matter, I would like to see him take my place."

"Excellent," the Colonel said. "your recommendation for your replacement is good enough for me."

"Lt Spence will get the job, and he'll keep it, despite his rank."

"So, I want you to plan on turning A Company over to him no later than Friday."

"That should be enough time, shouldn't it?"

"Yes, Sir," Pike said. "that'll be enough."

"Where will I be going when I leave the Company?" Pike asked.

"That hasn't been determined," the Colonel said unexpectedly.

"Both I and the CG want to use you where it will best benefit the Division."

"I've already given him my recommendation, but I haven't gotten any decision from him yet."

"But I should know by Friday, and I'll let you know then."

After his talk with the Colonel, Pike walked back to the Company area with mixed feelings. He would hate leaving the company; he already knew that. He had trained it, nurtured it, and led it in combat. He was proud of it, and it would be tough to let go of his first actual command. But, on the good side, Spence would get his chance at command when Pike left, and he deserved it. Pike had no doubt the young Lt would do a fine job. He already had the respect and confidence of the rest of the Company, and he knew how it operated, so the transition would be smooth and easy.

Dawson met Pike when he arrived back at the Company CP. As usual, he was standing outside the CP bunker with a cigarette dangling from his lips, squinting into the morning sun.

"Don't bother to say it," he said disgustedly as Pike walked up. "it's written all over your face."

"You're leaving, right?"

Pike nodded.

"Shit," Dawson retorted. "I knew it."

"Even though I expected it, the news still sucks."

"Just when we get everything running like a greyhound, the Green machine comes along and fucks it up."

"It never fails."

"Sorry, Pike. I know you don't like it any more than I do, but I told you this would happen."

"That's why I asked Lt Spence to have all the platoon leaders and NCOs assembled at the CP when you got back."

"So, you could tell them."

"They're all inside waiting on you."

"I figured you'd want to break the news to them personally and as soon as possible before the rumor mill cranks up."

"Thanks, Dawson," Pike said. "You're right; I might as well tell them now."

A second later, he and Dawson walked into the bunker.

"Smoke 'em if you've got 'em," Pike said as he sat down.

"I have some news that affects everybody here," He said, gazing at his NCOs and Officers.

"Effective this coming Friday morning, I will leave the Company."

"I guess I don't have to tell any of you how I feel about that."

There was a chorus of curses and groans. "Goddamn Army," somebody said in the middle of the grumbling.

"But the good news is that you'll be getting a good CO to replace me," Pike continued. "and not some know-nothing, unknown asshole from Division."

"What's his name?" somebody asked.

"Your new commander will be LT Spence," Pike revealed with a smile.

"Congratulations, John," Pike said, grinning and looking at the young Lieutenant.

Spence was thunderstruck. He couldn't even find his voice for a reply.

The smiles on his NCOs' faces told Pike they were pleased with Spence's selection as the new Company CO.

"Where will you be going, Boss?" newly promoted SSG Nolan asked.

"I don't know," Pike said, shrugging. "I'll find out Friday after I turn over the Company."

"Probably to some REMF job at Brigade or Division where I'll screw up royally because I don't know shit about staff work."

"Bullshit, Sir," Nolan said. "the Brigade commander isn't that stupid."

"He wouldn't have moved you if he didn't need you somewhere else more important."

"He is not a stupid man, and we all know that."

"I hope you're right, Nolan," Pike said. "but that doesn't make leaving any easier."

"Well," Dawson piped up to change the mood. "I am appointing myself and 1st platoon as the official organizers of your going away party and of Lt Spence's assumption of command party."

"We'll combine them, and we'll buy the beer."

Everybody cheered., then congratulated Spence and shook Pike's hand. It was an emotional moment. Later Pike talked to Spence alone. Spence was happy to be assuming command of the Company, but he was also a little anxious about it, and Pike saw that.

"You'll do just fine, John," Pike told him.

"You already know how the Company operates, and everybody in it, and every NCO in the Company is happy that you're taking over."

"That should tell you something right there."

"They have confidence in you."

"They've seen you command your platoon under fire in a tough situation and know you take care of your men."

"So, they know you'll do a good job as the new CO and take care of them too."

"Thanks, Sir," Spence said. "but I'm still a little nervous."

"It's my first Company, and I don't want to screw up."

"It was my first Company too," Pike told him. "remember?"

"And I felt the same way."

"Just trust your instincts and your training."

"If you want advice, ask Dawson or Pardee."

"They're both pretty damned savvy and have a lot of experience between them."

"So, you can depend on them offering sound suggestions if you ask them."

"The rest of the noncoms in the Company are top-notch, too, so you won't have any problems if you give mission-type orders and then let your NCOs handle the details."

"The noncoms thrive on that, and they'll give you their best effort when you handle taskings that way."

"You're already way ahead of all the other Company COs in the new battalion."

"You're a combat veteran and have already successfully commanded in combat, whereas they haven't."

"None of them have ever even been shot at before, which is a huge advantage you already have."

"That means you have a wealth of hard-earned experience going for you that they don't have and can't replicate."

"Combat experience is something they're going to have to get the hard way, and, as you already know, that's not easy."

"Lastly and more importantly, John," Pike said. "you're smart."

"You think before you act."

"That's an excellent trait to have as a commander."

"It will serve you well when you get an order for an operation from battalion."

"You'll think it through before acting, and using your experience, you'll make sound decisions."

"So, I want you to quit worrying."

"You'll do fine."

"If I didn't think you could handle the job, I would have never recommended you as my replacement to the Brigade Commander."

"He thinks you'll do well too; he even told me so."

"That's why he approved your selection even though you are still a Lieutenant when he has Captains already here in the Brigade that are still waiting for their chance at command."

"So have some confidence in yourself and quit worrying."

Spence smiled shyly and nodded.

"Now," Pike concluded. "between today and Thursday evening, I want you to inventory every piece of equipment in the Company."

"If it's worn or broken, turn it in and get a replacement."

"If it's missing, replace it."

"Now's a perfect time because Brigade Supply is issuing all new equipment to the new battalion."

"Make sure we get our share."

"Doing the inventory will let you know exactly what the Company's status is equipment-wise and what you'll be signing for when you take over."

"When you're satisfied everything's accounted for, I'll sign the Company over to you."

Chapter Seventeen

Pike turned over A Company at 1000 hrs the following Friday, an event he was not looking forward to. It was a small change of command ceremony at the firebase attended by the Officers and NCOs of the new battalion and the Brigade Commander who officiated since the new battalion commander hadn't arrived yet. Lt Spence was beaming when he accepted the Company's command, so at least someone there was happy.

After the ceremony had been completed, everybody migrated back to the A Company area, where there was iced beer in coolers and a cake Dawson had scrounged from somewhere. Once everybody had arrived and gotten themselves a beer, Dawson called for quiet. When the noise subsided, he walked up to Pike, standing next to the CP bunker. As for Pike, he felt like he had just been demoted back to Sgt.

"Pike," Dawson said. "everybody in the Company is sorry to see you go."

"Everybody here owes you their life, and we all know it."

"You've been the best Company Commander all of us NCOs have ever served under, and you have taken care of your troops and still accomplished every single mission A Company has been assigned."

"We all feel proud to have served under you."

"Because of all that," Dawson continued. "we wanted to give you something to remember us by when you left."

"So, everybody chipped into the hat when it was passed."

"We wanted your going away present to be something special that would always remind you of your first Company and how your men felt about you."

"We wanted it to be something useful you would always have with you in the field."

"We didn't want to give you some plaque or trophy that would just wind-up gathering dust somewhere," Dawson said,

"So, we decided on this."

He then handed Pike a brand-new Gerber Mark I Combat Knife in a black leather sheath. It was beautiful, efficient, and deadly, the knife a professional carried.

"It's got an inscription on the blade," Dawson said as Pike looked at the gift.

Pike looked at the blade. Then he read the inscription aloud.

"To Cpt Pike from the men of A Company. You always made us proud to be the best and saved us from the worst. You made us as hard and efficient as this blade, and we thank you for it."

Pike held up the blade as he looked over the men.

"Thank you," he said huskily. "thank you all very much."

"I appreciate the gift and the sentiment."

"You have all made me proud, too; every single one of you."

"You have all excelled as soldiers and always accomplished every task and mission you have been assigned, no matter how difficult."

"It's been a privilege to command you and a pleasure to work with you."

"My only regret is that I couldn't have served with you longer."

"This was my first command, and there may be others in my career, but there will never be another as special as this one."

"And all of you are responsible for that, so I thank you."

"I wish every one of you good luck in the future, and rest assured I'll miss you."

"But this knife will always remind me of you and the bond we share, and from this day forward, I'll carry it on my web gear."

Almost overcome by emotion, Pike then turned and walked away. Later, a runner from Brigade found him at the Company CP and told him the Brigade CO wanted to see him in his office.

Pike reported minutes later. When he did, he was surprised to see the Division Commander standing in the office.

"Good to see you again, Captain Pike." the general said with a smile. "How did your Change of Command ceremony go?"

"Good to see you too, Sir," Pike replied. "and the ceremony went well."

"I can't say I enjoyed it because A Company was my first command, and I hated giving it up."

"What brings you down to the firebase, Sir?"

"Pike," the General said. "to be perfectly frank, I'm here because of you and what you have done ever since I promoted you."

"I don't understand, Sir," Pike said with a confused look.

"Now and then in the Army," the General explained. "a soldier comes along, who by his abilities alone, proves he is exceptional."

"He doesn't merely separate himself from the soldiers around him by his actions; he stands heads and shoulders above them because of what he does."

"He exhibits such a talent for organization and a flair for leadership that it is unequaled by either his peers or his superiors, and it's apparent to everyone."

"I have been in the Army for almost forty years now, and this is my third war," the General continued. "and I have seen only two such men in all that time." The General revealed.

"One was a young lieutenant in WWII that was in the same unit I was in."

"He was truly exceptional, and all his peers and superiors knew it."

"Back then, he distinguished himself commanding a company during a most violent engagement, just like you did about six months ago."

"Today, that ex lieutenant is a Lieutenant General commanding a Corps here in Vietnam," The CG said.

"The other man I have known that had those same attributes is you, Cpt. Pike."

"From the time I promoted you, I have been watching you because I suspected you possessed those same unique talents that the young lieutenant I was talking about earlier did. And I've been proven right."

"You have that same level of ability and talent," The CG revealed.

"Your Brigade commander and I have watched you save your company from being annihilated on a hot LZ; then later, safely lead it into an NVA stronghold and begin destroying the enemy there when your sister Companies were accomplishing nothing."

"Finally, we watched you lead your Company out of a two-battalion-sized massacre without so much as a scratch."

"A massacre that you predicted to your superiors."

"And if all that wasn't enough," the CG concluded. "recently, we've watched you form, organize and train a collection of brand-new replacements and turn them into a cohesive military unit."

"You took an unorganized collection of men and turned them into three functional and trained line Companies from scratch."

"Then you transformed those Companies into a cohesive Battalion that is now fully trained and combat-ready."

"And you accomplished all that almost by yourself."

"But the most astonishing thing," The CG said in admiration. "is that you did all that in a little over four short weeks in the middle of a combat zone."

"Believe me, son, that feat is nothing short of amazing."

"I have never met a commander who possesses a more natural talent for command than you, nor one who has exhibited more ingenuity, inventiveness, and intelligence than you did in training the line Companies and the Battalion staff of this new Battalion, as well."

"I have been so impressed with your training and techniques; we are going to incorporate them into a new course we're instituting for all our new replacements before assigning them to battalions in the Division," The CG told Pike.

"After completing that course, those new men should be much more ready to be assimilated into the field units and have a much better chance of survival when they get into a combat situation."

"So, you should be justifiably proud of your accomplishments, Pike."

"Because you and your training program for the new Battalion were the inspiration and basis for that course."

"But even as important as all that is," the General told Pike. "that's not the real reason I'm here."

"You're here because neither your Brigade Commander, nor I, nor even the Corps Commander, when I told him about you, were satisfied that your talents were being put to good enough use here in the Division."

"So, we decided to do something to remedy that situation," The CG said.

"Something very unusual."

"That's why we had you turn over your Company." The General explained.

"You've outgrown it, Pike," The CG said unexpectedly.

"You're ready to take on a bigger challenge."

"So, based on the Corps Commander's and my recommendations," the CG revealed further. "the Army has allowed us to take an extraordinary step."

"One that we think will allow the Army at large, and this Division, in particular, to fully capitalize on all your talents."

"So, Congratulations, *Lt Colonel* Pike," the General said smiling. "as of this moment, you are the new battalion Commander of 1st Battalion, 1st Brigade of this Division."

Pike was so stunned his breath caught in his throat, and he struggled to breathe for the next few moments. He wasn't even sure he had heard the General right as he blinked in amazement. He had expected several new possible jobs when he came into the office but coming out of it as the new Battalion Commander wasn't one of them. He had never imagined that in his wildest dreams.

Yet here he stood, struck dumb by the news, as the General and the Colonel removed the Captain's bars and pinned the silver oak leaves of a Lt Colonel to his collar points.

Afterward, he stared mutely as both men shook his hand.

"Well, say something LTC Pike" the Brigade Commander finally said, chuckling.

"I can't, Sir," Pike stammered. "I'm in total shock."

"I'm not even sure this is happening."

"I'm numbed by it all, almost frozen."

"Well," the CG said smiling. "you better unfreeze yourself pretty quick, Colonel, because, in about two minutes, I'm going to take you outside and introduce you to your new battalion."

"We assembled them after we called you into the office," he revealed.

"General," Pike protested. "I don't know how to run a battalion."

"Hell, I was barely getting by trying to run a Company."

"And I know I don't know enough to be a Lieutenant Colonel."

"Bullshit, Pike," the General said, completely dismissing Pike's protests. "You've been running a battalion for the past four weeks and doing an excellent job."

"My other Brigade commanders and I have all watched you do it."

"In the process, we all marveled at how easily and naturally you instinctively did the right thing and made the right decision."

"It was never that easy for any of us when we were doing it, and we realized that." He admitted.

"Unlike you, it took time for us to become good at it," The CG said smiling, "and we had to work hard to achieve any success at it."

"You don't, Pike."

"Command comes as easily to you as breathing."

"So, when I went to the Corps Commander and talked to him about what you'd done, and your remarkable capacity for command, even of a battalion, he decided to give you command of one of your own," the CG said.

"And since a LTC commands a battalion, he decided to promote you too."

"You have a rare gift, Pike," The General said. "You do all the right things instinctively when you're in charge."

"That's what makes you so very rare, like the Lieutenant General I told you about earlier."

"He's the same way."

"He's our Corps commander now, by the way." The CG revealed.

"He's also the man who convinced the Pentagon to take the unusual step of promoting you and giving you this battalion."

"His word carries a lot of weight in Washington," The CG revealed. "because people there know he is extraordinary too."

"You and he are alike in many ways," The CG told Pike. "Command comes easily to him too."

"So, when I told him about you, your remarkable ability, and all you had done, he agreed that you needed a job more commensurate with your capabilities."

"That's how you're becoming a battalion commander came about."

"Simply put," the general said. "you're the best man for the job."

"I think so, and so does he."

"He wants to meet you later to congratulate you personally."

"But right now, Colonel," the General said. "your new Battalion wants to meet you, and we've kept them waiting out in the sun for too long."

"So, follow me," The General ordered.

A few minutes later, the General addressed the assembled battalion.

"Men," he said, "I won't keep you long."

"I just wanted to introduce your new Battalion Commander to you."

"I think you're all going to be very pleased with the man we've selected for the job."

"All of you already know him well because he's already trained every single one of you."

"He's one of those rare men whose ability knows very few boundaries."

"He's an expert on training and a proven commander in a combat situation."

"He's already proven that several times since I've known him."

"So, under him, this battalion will excel."

"There is absolutely no doubt of that in my mind about that."

"And one of the reasons for that is because he follows one basic rule when he commands."

Take care of your men, and they will take care of you.

"And he's proven that old Army adage works."

"Gentlemen," The General said proudly, stepping aside.

"Your new Battalion commander; newly promoted LTC John Pike."

There was stunned silence for a moment as all the assembled men looked at Pile, now wearing the rank insignia of a LTC. There was a collective intake of breath in amazement and a sense of almost complete disbelief. There was Pike. Yesterday a Captain, and today a Lt Colonel. Yesterday their Company Commander and trainer, and today their new battalion commander. It was almost beyond comprehesion.

When that happened, A Company, led by Dawson, naturally, started cheering; wildly. They were immediately joined by the other Companies and even the Battalion staff. A moment later, reality finally kicked in, and everyone realized t was true. Everyman in the Battalion not only knew Pike by sight but had worked with him and seen him instructing them and training them in the past two months. They knew he was good.

They had seen him at work as a Captain and heard about his exploits in the old battalion. Now, they realized their good fortune in getting him as their new Battalion commander. The cheers swelled and soon grew until everyone on the firebase heard them. Pike stared at his new unit with a smile as a tear ran down his cheek.

The General and the Colonel pounded him on the back and smiled too. The cheers of the troops told both men that they had made the correct decision. Seconds later, the troops broke ranks and engulfed the small group. Everyone wanted to congratulate Pike and shake his hand, and everyone seemed to be smiling.

The General just shook his head in admiration at the scene. He had never seen a new commander welcomed by his unit like that before in his entire career, and he was envious of Pike. His new command adored him, so he was now positive he and the Corps Commander had chosen the right man for the job and made the right decision. Pike would make a superb Battalion commander. He had the talent, and the experience, and his men loved him. That was an extremely rare combination that he had rarely seen before in his forty years of service.

Dawson just stared in wonder at the troops milling around Pike and congratulating him.

"Would you look at that," he told Lt Spence in amazement. "ain't that something, LT?"

"I can't believe the Goddamn Army finally did something exactly right."

"I didn't think I'd ever live to see the day that happened, but it has."

"I was pissed when I heard Pike was turning over the Company," he admitted.

"I thought the Army had just made another bad decision, but, by God, I was dead wrong."

"Now, I see why they had him do that."

"I'll be goddamned," he said in awe. "Lieutenant Colonel Pike."

"I can hardly believe it." He said, grinning.

Spence looked at Pike with unabashed admiration while he listened to Dawson.

"Enjoy this moment, Dawson," he said thoughtfully. "you've just seen history being made."

"Pike is not only our new battalion commander," the young Lt pointed out. "The Army promoted him directly to LTC."

"I've never heard of that being done before, much less seen it."

"But they damned sure picked the right man," Spence said smiling.

"They damned sure did," Dawson agreed.

"Come on," Spence said to Dawson, "I want to shake the old man's hand too."

"So, do I," Dawson said, getting up. "so, do I."

"He was our very own Company Commander," he said proudly, "and now, by God, he's our very own Battalion Commander."

"It just doesn't get better than that, especially in the Nam."

"Lt Colonel John Pike," he said in awe. "and he and I were Sgts together a few months ago."

"Goddamn, I'm proud of him."

Chapter Eighteen

Pike had his first battalion officers call that evening after chow. All the officers in the battalion and all the NCOs that were acting platoon leaders attended it. There was an air of anticipation among everyone as they waited for Pike's comments. Many, especially those who hadn't served under Pike before, were expecting a stern no-nonsense *"this is the way we're going to do things"* type lecture, but that's not what they got. They got a sensible, logical, low-keyed talk about what Pike expected of them as commanders and his ideas on the best way to operate in the field.

"All of you know me," Pike began as he looked over the assembled group, settling on Spence. "some of you better than others."

"Most of you know that my last command was A Company."

"Now, all of a sudden, I'm a Lt Colonel in command of this battalion."

"So, I 'm sure there must be a lot of questions on how and why that happened."

"So, let's get that out of the way to start with before the rumor mill cranks up."

"When I came to this Brigade, I was an NCO," Pike told them. "During an operation that went terribly wrong, I was forced to take command of the Company because all the officers got killed."

"Evidently, my handling of that situation was viewed very favorably by both the Brigade commander and the Division Commander as well."

"Because after it was over, I was given a battlefield promotion to Captain and command of A Company as a result."

"Months later," Pike continued. "when this Brigade went into the Ia Drang valley, the NVA massacred two entire battalions of it."

"This battalion was one of them."

"My company was the only unit to survive that operation."

"As a result, and for reasons I still don't fully understand myself, I was promoted again; directly to Lt Colonel and given command of this battalion."

"To be perfectly honest, I have never commanded at this level before." Pike revealed. "so, commanding a battalion will be new to me, just like commanding a company or a platoon will be new to most of you."

"But the Army has seen fit to give us both the rank and responsibility to run our respective units."

"Unfortunately, the Army hasn't sent me to school to learn the basics of command like it has many of you," Pike said.

"Everything I know about the subject is based on my experience and hard lessons learned over the past four years I have been in the country."

"Those lessons were the basis of the training program I just put all of you through earlier."

"And," Pike explained. "they are going to be the basis of how I intend to run this battalion."

"If some of my decisions seem unorthodox or different than what you have been taught in school, that's the reason."

"So far, the tactics and procedures I've instituted and utilized seem to have worked out well for me and the units I've commanded," Pike said. "mainly because they were all based on what works in this war and what doesn't."

"And the Commanding General of this Division told me that it was because of those tactics and procedures, and the way that I implemented them, that I was being given command of this battalion."

"So, we will continue to implement them."

"Now command of any size unit is an awesome responsibility," Pike told the assembled group a moment later. ", especially in wartime."

"When you're a commander in combat, the decisions you have to make can either save people or get them killed."

"And you must make those decisions in the most urgent and immediate circumstances."

"Usually while you are being shot at."

"Consequently, you have very little time to think about them."

"That makes decision-making for you even harder."

"Many of you may not realize it," Pike continued. "but this war is a Company Commander's war."

"I know," Pike told the group. "I've been fighting it for over four years."

"Our enemy rarely stands and fights," Pike explained.

"He uses the age-old guerrilla tactics of hit and run instead."

"When he attacks, he does so at a time and place of his choosing, and he rarely employs units larger than a Company."

"Because of all that, engagements in the field usually occur at company level or below."

"That means most of the combat decisions in this war will, by necessity, be made by you, the company commander or the platoon leader," Pike told his leaders. "and those decisions will be critical ones."

"They will determine whether you win or lose the battle, how many casualties your unit takes, and how many you inflict on the enemy."

"So those decisions have to be right."

"I realize most of you have never been in combat before," Pike continued. "As leaders, you are understandably anxious or nervous about that prospect."

"You wouldn't be normal if you weren't."

"So, the first piece of advice I'm going to give you is to not worry about how you'll react."

"You'll do fine once the shock wears off; believe me, that won't take long."

"You'll also realize that once you get into contact, your men are going to look to you to make the right decision, and that's going to be difficult to do."

"But because of the way we will operate in the field and because of the tactics we will employ, some of that pressure and anxiety you're going to be feeling will be alleviated," Pike told them. "and that will happen automatically."

Several of the officers looked at each other, wondering what Pike was talking about.

"That's because," Pike explained. "in this battalion, we will use fire and maneuver at every level of command."

"Not just because I believe in it," Pike explained. "and not even because I trained all of you on how to employ it."

"But because it works, and it works extremely well."

"Ask the Officers and NCOs of A Company," Pike said.

"They have been using it against the NVA for almost six months now."

"They'll tell you how effective it is."

"They kicked the NVA's ass all over the southern half of the Ia Drang Valley using it, and they didn't take a single KIA in the process."

"Since most of you have never been in a firefight before," Pike continued. "you're probably wondering what that will be like too."

"And you're also wondering how you'll react when you start getting shot at."

"Well," Pike said. "I'll tell you how you're going to react."

"You're going to employ fire and maneuver, and you're going to do it automatically."

"Without even thinking about it.

"Just like A Company does."

"And so are your squad leaders."

"Because you are going to drill them on it repeatedly, every chance you get," Pike ordered.

"And you're going to keep drilling them on it until they react instinctively when they take fire."

"Therefore, when your unit gets into contact and starts taking fire, your troops will know what to do automatically, and they'll do it without even having to think about it."

"They will either lay down a base of fire or begin to maneuver against the enemy."

"That action," Pike explained. "employed immediately by your squad leaders, will give you a chance to assess the situation and make an intelligent decision on what to do next."

"That's why you're going to practice and stress fire and maneuver to those squad leaders repeatedly until they can do it in their sleep."

'Until it becomes automatic."

"Until it becomes an instinctive reaction for both them and the members of their squads."

"And that, gentlemen," Pike said with a smile. "is going to be the big secret to our success."

"When we make contact, the unit taking fire will immediately return it and lay down a base of suppressive fire."

"That will pin the enemy, and he won't be able to move without taking significant casualties."

"Simultaneously, the unit behind them will then automatically begin to maneuver against the source of the fire on their flanks."

"And when they start taking fire themselves, the first unit that initially took fire will begin maneuvering itself."

"And your squads will continue that tactic until you have the Dicks pinned completely."

"Once you have them pinned in one place, you will keep up the fire to force them to stay there."

"*Then* you will call for fire support," Pike emphasized.

"When it arrives, you will use it to finish the NVA off."

"I know that sounds simple," Pike said as he looked at the young faces watching him. "and it is."

"But believe me when I tell you, it works."

"And it works for one simple reason," Pike explained.

"Because, up to now in this war, the Dicks have been used to starting the firefight, then watching our units just stop in place and call for fire support."

"And that support, either from gunships or artillery, usually takes a minimum of at least five to fifteen minutes before it arrives."

"Unfortunately," Pike explained. "99% of the time, by the time that supporting fire starts coming in, the Dicks have already done their damage and are already gone."

"They've melted back into the jungle."

"So, we wind up taking casualties and shooting at nothing but shadows."

"But that's not going to happen when the Dicks fire at one of our units," Pike continued.

"When they fire at us, they will get a great big surprise instead."

"When we take fire, we will return fire immediately and begin maneuvering against them."

"We've got guns too, and by God, we're going to use them."

"So, the Dicks aren't going to have a chance to get up and run while we call for supporting fire because we aren't going to call for supporting fire immediately."

"Instead, we will use our organic weapons to lay down a base of fire on them the second we get hit."

"And if they get up to run, they will get killed by that fire."

"So, they will be forced to find cover and stay in place."

"And once they stay in place, our maneuver elements will come in on their flanks and rear and pin them down before they can fall back and escape."

"When they can no longer get away," Pike concluded. "*then* we will call for supporting fire and finish them off at our leisure."

"That's the way we are going to do business in this battalion."

"And as of today," Pike continued. "there will be some other changes in the way we operate too."

"From now on," Pike ordered. "it will be battalion SOP that each Company takes two mortar tubes to the field when it deploys."

"You will use those tubes to support your subordinate units with indirect fire until battalion artillery can take over."

"And if they don't already know how, Company commanders will ensure that every squad leader in this battalion knows how to call in and adjust indirect fire."

"It will be your responsibility to train them, and you will have ample opportunity to do that when you get to the field."

"That's because every time a Company deploys an ambush, that ambush will have a DT registered by Company mortars to provide it fire support if it's needed."

"So, if they don't already know, you need to train your squad leaders and fire team leaders on just how to do that," Pike ordered.

"Next," Pike continued. "each company will checkerboard their Company AO every night with squad-sized ambushes."

"And, as I've already said, each of these ambushes will have a preregistered, on-call mortar DT to support it if necessary."

"To also support those nightly ambushes, everyman in every Company will carry a Claymore."

"Each ambush will use daisy-chained Claymores when it sets up the kill zone."

"How many will depend on the terrain and the situation."

"So, if your people don't know how to do that, in the jungle and at night, then you will train them until they do."

"Those squads will also learn to set up unmanned demolition ambushes inside their Company checkerboards nightly, too," Pike added.

"How many will be determined by you as the platoon leader and Company Commander."

"A Company's people are experts on all this, so they will help train your people when you ask them."

"Up to now, the Dicks have owned the night," Pike told his people.

"They use it to move, to resupply, to stage, and to attack."

"But starting today, we will take the night away from them."

"We are going to ambush their trails, their avenues of approach, and their water sources, among other things."

"When we do, the NVA will be forced to start moving in the daytime, when he can spot a potential ambush and avoid it."

"When he moves in the daytime," Pike explained. "he will be more susceptible to detection by our units and therefore more vulnerable to our direct and indirect fire."

"So, in summary," Pike said. "you as platoon leaders and Company Commanders will use every spare moment to train your people on everything I have just stressed.

"Teach them until they can do it day or night, in any kind of weather and under any type of conditions."

"That means I expect to see your people in training anytime we are not in the field."

"Remember," Pike warned. "the more you sweat in training, the less you bleed in combat."

"So, when your people start to bitch about not having any downtime, tell them that."

"Units that are good in combat don't just happen."

"Their leaders train them hard before they ever get into combat."

"That's what makes them good."

"And good units don't take a lot of casualties either."

"Instead, they inflict a lot of casualties on the enemy."

"That is what you and your units will do when you get to the field."

"Lastly," Pike said in conclusion. "starting today, it will be battalion SOP that you never use an LZ you've just landed on as a Company perimeter for that same night."

"After the CA has been completed, you will immediately send out recon patrols from the LZ and have them locate a new site for a Company CP, then secure it while your Company moves into it."

"You will also move your Company CPs daily, throughout the operation; never spending two nights in the same location."

"In summary, we are going to start operating like the enemy does," Pike stressed. "and we are going to force him to start looking for us, instead of us constantly looking for him."

"Because when he does that, he becomes vulnerable."

"That's the way we want him, and that's the way we want to keep him."

"Gentlemen, these are all combat-proven techniques that work," Pike explained.

"A Company can confirm that."

"If you implement them in the field," he continued. "you'll find that you suffer fewer casualties and have greater body counts."

"We are better trained, better equipped, better supplied, and have the advantages of mass, mobility, technology, and firepower on our side."

"So, we will take full advantage of all those assets."

"We are also going to use our heads and try and stay one step ahead of the NVA when we are in the field."

"That's how we're going operate."

"One last thing," Pike said in conclusion, "I'm still a Company commander at heart."

"So, I know all the problems you're going to face and most of the challenges you will have to overcome in the field."

"Consequently, if you need advice, don't be afraid or ashamed to call me."

"Nobody knows everything, including me, and nobody has a monopoly on good ideas."

"Lastly, smart commanders use good advice and don't care where it comes from."

"So, I want you to use your senior NCOs as a source of that advice too."

"They have a lot more experience than you do," Pike reminded his officers. "so give them mission-type orders and don't try to micromanage."

"Let them do their job."

"I see part of my job, as your Battalion Commander, as being your instructor, and your mentor, as well as your commander," Pike said a moment later. "and the other part of my job will be to ensure that you get all the support you need when you're in the field."

"But remember," Pike cautioned. "I can't kill the enemy for you."

"You and your people will have to do that."

"You are the tip of the spear; therefore, your people will be the ones that meet the enemy."

"Therefore, it will be up to you to ensure you are innovative, careful, and exacting when you carry out your day-to-day operations to defeat them."

"When the sun comes up in the morning," Pike said. "you should already have a firm plan as to what you want your Company to do that day."

"If you don't, you haven't done your job."

"I will give you guidance and answer all your questions, but the actual ground plan for how you implement that guidance will be up to you."

"Primarily because you are on that particular piece of ground, and I'm not."

"So, you must devise a practical plan to complete your mission."

"If the sun rises, and you haven't got one," Pike told the group. "you are already behind the power curve and not doing your job."

"Your primary job, people, is to locate, close with, and kill the enemy."

"That's what you were recently trained for, and that's why we are all here."

"So, let's do that job efficiently and effectively, and let's take maximum advantage of all our training and our assets to help us."

"In another week or so, we will be deploying to the field," Pike told them. "Unless I miss my guess, we'll probably be going back into the Ia Drang Valley again."

"It's a bad area, and the Dicks still own most of it."

"This Division is in the process of trying to take it away from them, but the NVA won't give it up easily."

"They've already proved that," Pike said grimly. "so, we'll have to fight for it, and that fight will be yours to make."

"You have seven days to ensure you and your units are ready to make that fight."

"Seven more days to complete any training you need to give your people before we get into that fight."

"And let me assure you, training time in a combat environment is very rare," Pike warned. "so, don't waste any of it."

"Use the next seven days and nights to get your people ready."

"Especially in the areas I have emphasized."

"I will entertain any necessary support requests to allow you to do that."

"Remember, I'm always as close to you as your radio," Pike said. "so call me if you need advice or have a problem.

"And also remember," Pike told everyone. "The only dumb question is the one that doesn't get asked.

Chapter Nineteen

The next day, Pike met his new XO, the young major arriving at the Brigade firebase from Division HQ on an early chopper. After he got to the battalion and reported, Pike sat him down in his office and got acquainted.

"My name is Pike," Pike told the youthful-looking major as he shook his hand. "welcome to the battalion."

"I'm Major Jim Potter," the Major said. "and thank you, sir."

"You don't know what a pleasure it is to be here."

"Why's that?" Pike asked curiously.

"Mainly," Potter said bluntly. "because you're the commander here, Sir."

"Everybody in this entire Division knows who you are and what you've done."

"You've become somewhat of a living legend."

"You may not know it, Sir," Potter continued. "but you have people practically fighting to get assigned to this battalion because of that."

"So, I considered myself extremely lucky when I got offered the job as your XO."

"Well," Pike said. "I don't know about my being a legend and all."

"Most of that kind of talk is probably just exaggerated rumor, but it's kind of you to mention it anyway."

"All I told the Brigade commander was that I needed a strong major as an XO who had commanded a company in combat before and who knew admin and logistics."

"Since you fitted that bill, you got the job, which speaks well of you."

"Thank you, Sir," Potter said, smiling.

"You may not thank me when I tell you what all I want you to do as my XO," Pike said with a wry grin.

"Where did you command your company?" Pike asked.

"I was in the 1st Division a year and a half ago," Potter replied. "I had my Company when we were in III Corps."

"Afterwards, I went to Command and General Staff College at Ft Leavenworth."

"When I graduated, the Army sent me here to the Division."

"I worked in Division operations when I was selected to be your XO."

"Well, after all that, you probably know more about commanding a battalion than I do," Pike said.

"I know how to do it in theory," Potter admitted. "I learned that in school."

"But you know how to do it for real," Potter told Pike.

"You've been doing it for over two months all by yourself."

"The CG told me that himself."

"He thinks you're a hell of a soldier and a world-class commander," Potter revealed. "He told me so."

"Well, Jim," Pike explained. "what I really am is just an ex-NCO who has somehow managed to get this far in the Army because of my performance in some difficult situations."

"And even then, I didn't do anything extraordinary."

"I just did my job."

"That's not how I heard the story, Sir," Potter said.

"Well," Pike said. "that's about the way things really happened."

"Anyway," Pike continued. "I know a little about command and operations because I learned about them through experience."

"But Admin and Logistics are foreign to me." Pike admitted. "especially at this level."

"And I learned long ago that the Army is a ship that floats on a sea of paperwork and that without supplies, operations just don't happen."

"Unfortunately, I know very little about either of those areas."

"Certainly not enough to successfully run a battalion."

"That's why I requested a man like you," Pike revealed. "To handle those areas for me."

"At the same time, you can teach me about them as well."

"And in turn, I'm going to teach you what I know about command."

"That way, we both help each other, and the battalion as a whole benefits."

"How does that sound?" Pike asked.

"I think that's a formula that will work well, Sir," Potter smiled.

"Good," Pike said. "then I think we are going to get on well together."

"The only other thing I require of you," Pike told Potter. "is that you always speak your mind to me."

"If you don't agree with me on something or think you have a better idea about how to do something," Pike ordered. "I expect you to tell me."

"I don't pretend to know everything," Pike said earnestly. "and no one has a monopoly on good ideas."

"So, I expect you to speak up if you need to and to keep me out of trouble if you see me headed that way."

"If you can do that, we can work together as a team to make this battalion operate efficiently and effectively," Pike told his new XO., "and I think we can make that happen if we both use our experience and talent."

"So welcome to the battalion."

Potter smiled.

"Now," Pike continued. "since I know you just got here, have the S-1 show you where everything is on the firebase and where you'll be bunking."

"Afterwards, once you get settled," Pike told Potter. "come back here, and I'll introduce you to the staff and the Company commanders."

"Then we'll talk about the upcoming operation and what we're going to do in it."

Later that afternoon, Pike, Potter, and the staff sat in the TOC, and Pike told everyone about the upcoming operation.

"We'll be going back into the valley sometime next week," Pike told everyone.

"3rd Brigade will be replacing 1st Brigade."

"1st Brigade has gotten a little chewed up over the past two months, and they need a stand down, so we're going in to relieve them."

"This will be our new battalion Area of Operations," Pike said, pointing to an area of the map outlined in red grease pencil.

"As you can see, our battalion will be further north than anyone else."

"The other two battalions of the Brigade will be operating south of us."

"The Brigade commander wants us to be in a position to cut off any NVA units trying to escape from the valley as our two sister battalions push northward," Pike said.

"I want all of you to scrutinize our new AO and come up with at least two potential locations where we can establish a battalion firebase."

"When you do, ensure it's in an easily defensible area."

"All of you know what happened to our last firebase in that area," Pike reminded everyone.

"Consequently, I have no intention of letting that happen again."

"So, ensure you select an area that can be easily defended and where we support the deployed companies in the battalion AO with indirect fire."

"Once you've picked the location," Pike told them. "I have some specific ideas on how I want the firebase established and laid out."

"I'll brief you on those later on."

"After you've done that," Pike continued. "I want you to locate the Company AOs within our battalion AO and then select some potential landing zones where they can Combat Assault into the area once we have the firebase up and running."

"Once our firebase is established," Pike explained. "I intend to have the Companies push northward to the northern limits of our AO before establishing a blocking force for the rest of the Brigade."

"And there's a reason for that."

"I've been looking at after-action reports and talking with the Division staff about 1st Brigade's contacts the past two months and where most of them have been," Pike told his staff.

"I've also looked at all those contacts' size and frequency."

"After plotting them and reviewing the intel reports and operational summaries," Pike explained. "I still believe the significant portion of the enemy forces in the valley are north of where our two Brigades are currently operating."

"Especially since neither 1st nor 2nd Brigades have found any major staging areas or logistics sites in their current AOs."

"Because of that, I think the earlier attacks on this battalion and second battalion's firebases were coordinated and planned by the NVA to make us think we were getting too close to their major base areas."

"I think the NVA moved two regiments down the valley to destroy those firebases and after achieving that, moved them back north into their base areas," Pike opined.

"All the contacts 1st and 2nd Brigades have made over the past two months have been platoon and squad-sized NVA units."

"They haven't made contact with Company or Battalion sized NVA units since they inserted."

"I think the reason is the major NVA units are based in this mountainous area at the northern end of the valley.",

"Their commanders are holding them there in preparation for another major attack on our units when they get into range."

"We haven't found them yet," Pike said. "because our operations have all been in the southern portion of the valley."

"I have talked to the Brigade and Division Intelligence officers about this, and although there is no hard proof to back up my assumptions," Pike continued. "they both agree that so far, none of the Division's elements have found any of the NVA base areas where they expected them to be, or in the mountains adjacent to the valley itself."

"So, to confirm my assumptions," Pike explained. "I have requested IR overflights of the area north of our battalion AO, and they have been approved."

"If I'm right and those flights turn up any major hot spots in that area, then we, as a battalion, may be relocating soon after we insert."

That statement got the entire staff's attention. Shortly after it had been established, relocating a firebase would be no mean feat, and they knew it.

"I realize that if we have to relocate our firebase, it will be a giant pain in the ass," Pike told his staff. "but it can't be helped."

"If the main NVA base areas *are* north of us, that means they will hold the high ground, and if that's true, our Companies will have to fight their way uphill almost the entire operation."

"I don't want them to have to do that."

"That puts us at a disadvantage, and the area is bad enough as it is."

"I know," Pike said. "I've been there."

"So, I'd rather stick our new firebase on the top of the mountain in the middle of Indian territory and fight our way downhill instead."

"Plus, it'll be easier to defend if we put it there."

"Why don't we just locate it there, to begin with?" Captain Larry Bell, the battalion S-3, asked. "then we wouldn't have to move it."

"I asked the Brigade commander that same question," Pike said with a smile. "but he said we would be outside the other two battalion's artillery fans, and he wanted all the battalions to be mutually supporting, at least initially."

"And remember," Pike said. "there's always the chance I'm completely wrong about all of this."

"If I am," Pike admitted. "and we inserted to the north, we'd be all by ourselves up there, and we could suddenly find ourselves in a world of shit."

"So," Pike concluded. "we're going to err on the side of caution and insert to the south first."

"If my assumptions prove correct and that area doesn't turn up any major base or staging areas, then we will relocate north."

"And when we do, so will the rest of the Brigade."

"I've discussed this entire idea with the Brigade commander, and he's tentatively approved it as an option," Pike explained. "But he won't exercise it unless we can turn up some proof that the NVA base areas are further north."

"If that happens," Pike explained. "I want you to plan for our relocation as a contingency we will probably execute in a concise period."

"If we have to relocate, I'm going to CA A Company onto a mountain top we'll use as a firebase to secure it."

"They have the most experience, and that will be a hairy operation."

"As soon as A Company has it secured," Pike continued. "we'll send the engineers in to clear the area and start building a firebase."

"And I expect the firebase to be ready to occupy in a maximum of two days, even earlier if the engineers can manage it."

"When it is, we'll bring the remainder of the battalion, so include that contingency as a part of your planning."

"We have a little over a week before we go in," Pike told his staff. "so, I want to see a draft plan, with the contingency for relocation, no later than sundown tomorrow."

"That will give us time to try and shoot holes in it and then fix them before we give the Companies an operations order."

"I've got overflights of potential AOs scheduled for first light tomorrow morning," Pike told his staff.

"I want the XO and the S-3 to take the first one."

"After they get back." Pike continued. "Then I and the S-4 will go up."

"S-2, while we're gone, I want you to get with both the Division and Brigade S-2s and garner every scrap of information you can find about both those two AOs."

"Ask our Vietnamese liaison officer to use his sources too and see what he can get from his people."

"I want you also to request the Division LRRPs be inserted into the northern AO the same day the battalion goes into our southern AO."

"I want them to start reconning the mountains there while we are still operating down south."

"And I want to talk to the LRRP team leader before he takes his team in," Pike added. "So, arrange that."

"Tony," Pike said to his S-1. "You just ensure all the required paperwork goes in on time and keep me out of trouble in that department."

"Run it all through the XO before you submit it so he can get familiar with it."

"That should be enough to keep all of you busy for the next two days," He said, concluding.

"And while you are all slaving over the new op order," Pike told his staff with a grin. "I'm going down to visit the Companies and see how their training is going."

"Jim," Pike ordered. "mind the store while I'm gone."

"I'll see you all at the mess hall for evening chow." He said as he departed.

Later, Pike visited each of his companies and inspected their training, deliberately saving A Company for last. When he arrived at Spence's CP, Spence had all his platoon leaders there. Someone on the staff had alerted them and told them Pike was coming.

"Welcome back to the Company, Colonel," Spence said smiling.

"Thanks, John," Pike said, genuinely pleased. "It feels like I'm coming home."

"I know I have to be equally fair in the way I treat all my companies now," Pike said. "but it's tough sometimes because I miss you guys."

"We miss you too, Sir," Spence said. "You can always call A Company your home."

"What brings you down to see us?" Spence asked.

"I wanted to talk to you about the upcoming operation," Pike replied. "and I didn't want to do it in front of the other companies."

"I wanted this talk to be private," Pike said. "just between you guys and me, and I want it to stay that way."

"No problem, Boss," Spence said. "we know how to keep our mouths shut, so what you tell us will stay right here."

Pike nodded. Then he began to explain.

"A Company has more experience, field time, and combat time than any other company in the battalion, and you have more experienced officers and NCOs."

"All of you have successfully led men in combat, while none of the other Commanders in this battalion have. They're all still green."

"They are all good men," Pike said. "but they haven't been blooded yet, and until they get into and through their first firefight, they will be an unknown quantity."

"To be honest," Pike said. "A Company and you people here are my only known quantities in this battalion."

"You're all combat veterans, you all know how to function under fire, and I know without a doubt I can depend on you."

"Basically," Pike said. "when the shit hits the fan, I know how you will react, so I don't worry about you."

"But I don't know how the other companies will react," Pike explained. "Because they haven't been in a firefight yet."

"Because of that," Pike explained. "I'm going to have to give A Company what I consider the most dangerous of the new AOs when we go back into the valley next week."

"I just can't take the chance of one of the other companies getting hit and screwing up because it's their first combat action."

"Our northern flank is critical, and I have to have somebody on it that I can depend on, and that means A Company."

"I wanted to tell you guys that personally so you'd know why you got the most difficult assignment," Pike said. "I didn't want you to think I was screwing you."

"No problem, Boss," Dawson piped up, "we can handle it."

"I'm sure you can," Pike replied.

"But there's another reason why you're getting the job, too," Pike said.

Then he briefed A Company on his plan to relocate the battalion firebase to the mountain top.

"I want you to be ready to cut an LZ when I give you the word, John," Pike told Spence. "then get picked up and CA onto the mountaintop when I give the order."

"Once you get the area secured and certainly before sundown, I'll send the engineers in, and they can clear the area and begin putting in the new firebase."

"When you get there and secure the area, I'll send in at least another Company to reinforce you, followed by the engineers."

"When the engineers are through," Pike concluded. "I'll CA the rest of the battalion into the new firebase and relocate my CP."

"But all that means you will be all by yourself for at least the first day or two."

"That's what makes the job so difficult."

"Because there's a good chance you'll get hit before I can reinforce you."

"That's why I want A Company to handle the mission."

"John," Pike ordered, "I want you to think about my plan and tell me what you want me to send in with the engineers once you have the mountaintop secured, like extra mortar rounds, Claymores, concertina wire, things like that."

"Compile a complete list, let me know what you think you're going to need, and I'll make sure it gets to you on time."

"I'm also going to lay on some TAC air for you to use if you need it," Pike told Spence. "and a gunship for you to use when we break down the old firebase and start moving the battalion."

"And as soon as the move begins," Pike explained. "I'm going to send my XO to your location with a skeleton staff to control the relocation itself."

"That will let you concentrate on defending the place while the move is in progress and allow the engineers, directed by the XO, to complete the interior of the firebase."

"I'm almost certain when the Dicks realize we intend to put a firebase on that mountain top, they will try and kick you off it before we can get the new base firmly established."

"So, think about what you'll need, the sequence of the operation, and how you want it to proceed."

"You're going to be the commander on the ground initially, and I won't," Pike said. "So, I'm going to depend on you to make the decisions in those areas until I can join you."

"That's a big responsibility," Pike told Spence. "but I know you can handle it."

"And you have my word that if and when I send you in," Pike said. "I'll reinforce and support you."

"You just take that mountaintop and hold it until I can bring in the cavalry and relieve you."

"We get that firebase up and running," Pike promised. "we'll tear the Dicks in that area a new asshole."

"I want some serious payback for our firebase they overran."

Chapter Twenty

"We go in at first light day after tomorrow," Pike said, walking into the Battalion TOC. "I just got the word from the Brigade commander."

"Larry," Pike said to his S-3, "alert B company."

"They'll CA into the location for the battalion firebase and then secure it."

"Twenty minutes after they land, if the area is secure," Pike continued, "Chinooks will fly in the engineer company."

"Once they land, they should have the area cleared, the perimeter bunkers and trench system in, and the wire up for the firebase before sundown."

"The next day, they should have the interior bunkers and the TOC built and all the outer defenses in."

"If everything goes as scheduled," Pike told Bell and Potter. "we should have the battalion firebase fully operational by evening chow."

"I want you on the ground with B Company when the engineer Company goes in," Pike ordered.

"Take a radio and an RTO with you so we can maintain contact and keep me advised of the construction progress."

"As soon as the firebase is complete, I'll bring in the remainder of the battalion staff and headquarters element, and we'll also bring the artillery battery in with us."

"Unless we run into trouble, by no later than sundown of the second day, we should have the firebase fully staffed and ready for business," Pike said.

"That means we'll CA the Companies into their AOs the morning of the third day and begin combat operations."

"So, call the staff together, brief them on the schedule I just laid out, and get them busy."

"They all have a lot of work to do in the next twenty-four hours."

"I want a timeline and a priority list for the operation firmed up by noon today," Pike ordered. "I'll want to give the Companies a warning order at 1800 hrs."

"Call the CO's of the artillery battery and the engineer company and set up a meeting right after noon chow."

"Jim," Pike ordered. "you chair it."

"Larry, count on issuing the order of the actual operations at 0900 hrs. tomorrow."

"Can you get everything coordinated and completed by then?" Pike asked.

"Yes, sir," Bell replied. "most of the op order has already been drafted."

"All we have to do is fill in the times and locations and ensure all coordination for the lifts has been laid on."

"Good," Pike said. "I wanted to be here with you for all that, but now that's impossible."

"Instead, I'll be at Brigade CP for the rest of the day if you need me."

"The Old Man has a commander's conference scheduled there in an hour, and I expect it to last all afternoon."

"He's got some of the Division staff and the Corps S-2 coming in to brief us," Pike explained.

"That means that you and Maj Potter will have to finish the op order, issue the appropriate warning orders and make sure all the required coordination has been done."

"Make sure the Engineer CO knows how we want the firebase laid out before he leaves," Pike added as an afterthought as he turned to leave.

"And just in case," Pike said, thinking about the operation and what had happened to the battalion's previous firebase in the area. "Give D Company a warning order to go in and reinforce B Company at 1500 hrs. the first day."

"I don't want to take any chances of anything happening to the firebase that first night that we can't handle."

"We are not going to let this firebase get overrun like the last one," he said firmly.

After briefing his staff, Pike boarded a helo and departed for the Brigade firebase and the officer's call.

"The NVA appear to have pulled their major units back into their base areas after they overran our two firebases earlier last month," The Division G-2 said, briefing everyone attending the Commander's conference.

"But unfortunately, we still don't know exactly where those base areas are."

"We suspect they are in the mountain at the valley's northern end, because none of our operations in the valley's southern end have turned up anything yet."

"3rd Brigade," he continued. "operating to our west, on the other side of the mountain chain, hasn't found any major base areas either."

"So, by elimination, that leaves the mountains to the north."

"But there are several mountains in that area." He cautioned.

"The mountain chain they are part of runs across the border into Cambodia."

"So, pinpointing the exact location of any NVA base area will be extremely difficult because it may be located inside one of those mountains."

"Especially because there are several reports from the South Vietnamese indicating that."

"For all we know," the intelligence officer said in summary. "the base areas may even be across the border in Cambodia."

"The NVA may be using the Ia Drang as nothing more than a staging area for their in-country operations here in II Corps."

"We know for certain there is a major trail network in the area that seems to run back across the border into Cambodia," The G-2 revealed. "but as yet, we don't know what the NVA are using it for."

"They could be using it as an infiltration route or as a series of logistics routes from log depots in Cambodia to their base areas in the Ia Drang."

"We don't know the answers to any of those questions."

"That's one of the things we hope to uncover before this operation ends."

"I have given everything in my briefing to your battalion and Brigade S-2s, along with maps marked with the Division's contacts for the past thirty days," The briefer said. "I have also given them our operations summaries for the past month."

"Those should give you an idea of where our hotspots have been."

"That completes my briefing," he said. "I'll now entertain any questions you have."

"What assets are you using to gather intelligence on the area to the north?" Pike asked.

"We've been using low-level photo recon missions and some IR flights by the Air Force," The briefer replied.

"To be honest," the briefer admitted, "they haven't turned up very much to date."

"We have also inserted the Division LRRPs into the area on two occasions, but they haven't found much more than the major trail network."

"Thanks," Pike said, nodding.

The briefer answered a few more questions, then the conference ended.

"Okay, Pike," the Brigade commander asked after the conference was over. "let's have it."

"What do you mean, Sir?" Pike asked.

"I saw your face when the G-2 answered your question," the colonel said. "You weren't happy."

"You expected something more, and he didn't give it to you."

"That means you must be aware of more information on that area than the he gave us."

"And if that's the case," the Brigade commander concluded. "then I'd be interested in finding out about it too."

"So, tell me, Pike, what do you know about intel on that area that I don't?"

Pike hesitated. He wondered just how much to tell the Colonel. He considered whether he should tell him anything at all. After all, the information was classified Top Secret, and the Colonel did not need to know. But he thought about all the lives that had been lost on this operation already, some of them unnecessarily, in his opinion. After that, he decided to tell the Brigade commander about SOG.

"Sir," he asked, moments later. "do you know what MACVSOG is?"

"No," the Brigade commander replied. "I've never heard that term before."

"Should I have?"

"Not really, Sir," Pike replied. "It's hardly known outside the Special Forces community."

"But it's something that could have a significant impact on our upcoming operation."

"Unfortunately, it's highly classified, so I have to have your word that what I'm about to tell you won't go any farther than between us," Pike said.

The Colonel looked at Pike evenly. Then he nodded.

"You have it," he replied.

"The US has established a Joint Unconventional Warfare Task Force here in South Vietnam," Pike began.

"The Pentagon runs it, and its headquarters is in Saigon, but it has been tasked to support MACV."

"Its mission is to conduct unconventional warfare operations against the North

Vietnamese, and all of its missions are therefore covert and classified Top Secret."

"That's because they are conducted in Cambodia, Laos, and North Vietnam."

The Colonel raised his eyebrows when he heard that, but he remained silent.

"Among the other things it does," Pike continued. "SOG conducts ground reconnaissance operations into the border areas of those three countries."

"They execute these missions using small joint Special Forces and Montagnard or Nung Chinese recon teams, and they are conducted almost daily."

"They are controlled by SOG's three Forward Operational Bases here in South Vietnam."

"Therefore," Pike explained. "SOG has up-to-date intelligence on NVA logistics sites, base areas, and staging areas in the border areas of those countries, because they insert recon teams into them regularly."

"How do you happen to know all this, Pike?" the colonel asked curiously.

"Because I pulled a tour in SOG before coming to the Division, Sir," Pike replied. "I ran recon into northeastern Laos when I was assigned to CCN."

"I thought that might be the case," the Colonel said.

"And how do you suppose we could get access to that information?"

"I don't know the answer to that, Sir," Pike replied. "I was never privy to the dissemination of what we collected."

"But I do know that it's pretty close hold stuff because the missions are covert."

"I assume that if the CG or the Corps Commander requested it, they would be granted access."

"Get your hat, Pike," the Colonel said, deciding. "We're going to see the CG."

"Sir, I'm a little uncomfortable with that," Pike said.

"I don't know if I should have even told *you* about SOG."

"Don't worry, Pike," the Colonel replied. "The CG can keep his mouth shut too, and this is too important to let just slip by without at least trying to get access to that intel."

Pike and the Colonel were in the Division Commander's office an hour later, where Pike briefed the CG on MACVSOG.

"I knew we had an intelligence source that gave us information on what was going on in the border areas of Cambodia, and Laos, " the CG said after Pike's briefing. "I've been briefed on intel out of that area before."

"But until now, I didn't know where the information came from."

"So, I can understand your reluctance in pursuing this, Pike."

"Because to ask for the information, you would be admitting that you knew it existed and where it came from."

"And you understandably don't want to put yourself in that position."

"But," the CG said, thinking. "if the Corps Commander requested access to that intel, that would be a different matter altogether, and your name would never have to come up."

"So that would solve that problem."

"And there's no question we could use it," The CG said.

"I'll see him today and ask him to make the request."

"And thanks for trusting us enough to make us aware of all this, " The CG said, smiling.

"I assure you that knowledge will go no further."

"Is your battalion ready to go back into the Valley?" the CG asked, indicating the subject was now closed.

"Yes, Sir," Pike said, feeling better. "My people have already issued the warning order to my Companies."

"They get my op order at 1800 hrs. this evening."

"I'm putting Pike's battalion out on the Brigade's northern flank," The Brigade commander told the CG.

"And, after listening to his reasoning, I may let him move his firebase into the mountains at the northern end of the valley later this week."

"I'd be interested in hearing the reasoning behind all that," the CG said.

So, for the next few minutes, the Brigade commander briefed the CG on Pike's reasons for thinking the main NVA base areas were in the mountains at the north end of the valley. He also told him how Pike had arrived at those conclusions and a tentative contingency plan he had developed.

"That's a very incisive analysis, Pike," the CG said.

"Now I understand why you'd like to get the information from SOG on what they have found across the border from the valley."

"That information could be extremely valuable to us if your reasoning is correct."

"That was why I decided to tell the colonel and you about MACVSOG, Sir," Pike replied. "even though technically, I probably committed a security violation when I did."

"You did right, son," the CG said. "That information could save many lives, and I'm sure the Corps Commander will feel the same way."

"So, don't worry about your revelations going any further."

"Both your Brigade commander and I know how sensitive that information is, so we will keep our mouths shut about it."

"I just hope what you've told us generates some positive intelligence," He said, concluding.

"Now, both of you get back to your units."

"I'll let you know if and when I hear anything."

An hour later, Pike was back at his battalion headquarters. After he arrived, Potter briefed him on his meeting with the engineer company commander. He also brought him up to speed on where the staff was on the Battalion Op order.

"After some reflection, I've decided to put both B and D companies into the firebase the first day," Pike told Potter unexpectedly. "I want you in there too with radios and a skeleton ops staff."

"Have Larry lay on some on-call TAC air support for you to use, too."

"Also, have both B and D companies send recon patrols around the firebase during the day and put out LPs around it at dusk."

"Lastly, ensure the entire firebase perimeter is ringed with daisy-chained Claymores before the sun sets," Pike ordered.

"Take a pallet load in with you when you go in, along with a few rolls of det cord and some boxes of electric and nonelectric caps."

"I want both B and D Companies, as well as the Engineer Company, to be as ready as soon as possible, to repel an attack in case there is one."

"Also, have both Companies take in extra mortar rounds when they insert and consolidate their mortars into a central location." He added.

"They'll be your only source of indirect fire support until we can get the artillery battery in the next day."

"You're worried about us getting hit that first night, aren't you, Sir? Potter asked.

"Yeah," Pike said, "I am, and you should be too."

"Don't ever underestimate the NVA, Jim, especially when you're dealing with them at this level."

"Proof of that is the two firebases they overran with a coordinated attack when this operation started."

"They may not be as technically sophisticated as we are, but they have an excellent intelligence system, and their troops are well trained."

"It wouldn't surprise me a bit if they didn't already know about us going in to relieve 3rd Brigade day after tomorrow."

"You think that's possible?" Potter asked in almost disbelief.

"Not only possible," Pike replied. "but also probable."

"I just hope like hell they don't know where we're going to be putting in our firebase."

"How could they possibly know that?" Potter asked in astonishment.

"How many people know where we're going to put that firebase, Jim?" Pike asked patiently.

"Just us and the engineer battalion commander," Potter replied. "that's all I've told."

"What about the Brigade and Division staffs?" Pike asked. "We told them where it's going to be, didn't we?"

"And the Engineer Company knows because they're going to do all the construction."

"The helicopter company inserting them and their equipment in certainly knows, in addition to the helicopter company that's going to insert B and D Companies."

"Not to mention any artillery batteries supporting the initial insertions."

"That's a lot of people, Jim," Pike said. "and people talk to other people, especially about things like this."

"That's human nature."

"When they do, other people hear them, and they repeat what they've heard."

"So, it's almost impossible to keep a secret on something like this because too many people have to know about it to make it happen."

"So, with that much knowledge floating around, among that many people," Pike continued. "keeping it a secret is impossible, especially from an enemy whose specializes in HUMINT collection like the NVA."

"Don't ever underestimate the NVA's intelligence system," Pike warned. "That would be a serious mistake."

"They are very, very good."

"Hell," Pike said, "I'm sure they have agents right here on the firebase working as hooch maids or laborers."

"So, you'd be better off assuming the NVA already knew about the upcoming operation and planning what countermeasures they want to conduct to prevent us from taking advantage of that knowledge."

"Jesus," Potter said, sucking in his breath and realizing he had just learned a valuable lesson from his new commander. "I had no idea."

"When you go in tomorrow, Jim," Pike ordered, "go in loaded for bear and expecting the worst."

"That way, if something happens, you'll be prepared for it."

"From now on, I want you to start thinking proactively and not reactively."

"Yes, Sir," Potter said.

Chapter Twenty.One

Just after dawn, Pike watched B Company load the heavy-lift package of fourteen helicopters taking them to the new firebase site. Potter had already joined the Engineer Company at the PZ. CH-47 Chinooks would pick them and their equipment up as soon as B Company landed and secured the LZ.

"Please don't let them hit a hot LZ," Pike prayed. *"not on their first time out; at least give them that."*

Five minutes later, Pike watched as the helos disappeared into the morning sky, headed for the Valley. He turned and walked back to the Battalion TOC, where he would wait for B Company to report it was down on the LZ and their status.

Twenty minutes later, when the B Company commander reported a cold LZ, a wash of relief flooded over Pike. Ten minutes later, B Company commander reported the area secured and that he was sending out three squad-sized recon patrols into the jungle around the LZ.

Pike breathed a sigh and uttered a silent "Thank You." Immediately afterward, he had Bell call the Engineer Company and give them and Potter the news that the LZ had been secured. Forty minutes later, the Engineer Company and its equipment's first load was also down on the LZ.

By noon, Potter reported the entire site, as well as a three-hundred-yard area outside its intended perimeter, had been bulldozed and cleared. The engineers would start putting in the perimeter berm, its bunkers, and wire shortly. B Company also reported t their recon patrols had found several trails in the area but no sign of any recent NVA activity. Pike ordered them to keep looking. By sixteen hundred hours, the firebase perimeter was completed, all perimeter bunkers were in, with three lines of concertina wire erected around the site. D Company had also been airlifted into the new location to reinforce B Company.

Just before sunset, Potter reported the entire firebase perimeter had Claymores surrounding it. Both company's mortars had been consolidated, and both companies had all their people dug in, with LPs already out in the nearby jungle. Potter reported that they were as ready as they could be for any trouble.

Pike was still extremely nervous about the entire situation, so, he stayed in the TOC glued to the radios in the event of any trouble. He remained there through evening chow. Later, he ate a sandwich Bell brought him from the mess hall and sipped coffee while he continued to wait.

He had a gut feeling the NVA would not let the new firebase get established without any sign of resistance; at the very least, a token show of force to let the Americans know they were aware of their new intrusion. He was right.

At 2144 hrs. mortar fire hit the firebase. In response, Potter called in counter-battery fire from a 155 mm battery. But not before 28 mortar rounds impacted inside the new firebase's perimeter. Fortunately, there were no casualties since everyone had either been in a bunker or a foxhole, ready for just such an event. The only damage sustained was to one of the Engineer Company's bulldozers hit during the barrage. The remainder of the night passed without incident.

Pike remained in the TOC all night and finally fell asleep at a field desk. He didn't awaken until 0700 hrs. When he did, Bell told him nothing significant had happened during his nap and to go eat at the mess hall since everything was under control. Pike smiled sheepishly, went back to his hooch, shaved, showered, changed clothes, and then ate breakfast. When he got back to the TOC, Bell updated him telling him Potter had called and reported no enemy activity that morning and that the engineers were building the TOC and the interior of the firebase.

Potter had also recommended headquarters company personnel be airlifted into the new base at noon along with the Artillery battery. Pike okayed the move and then packed his ruck in preparation. Thirty minutes later, he had a final meeting with A and C Company commanders about their upcoming combat assaults and afterward prepared to depart for the firebase along with the rest of the battalion staff.

They landed at the new firebase at 1500 hrs. Minutes after touchdown, Bell began setting up the TOC and started getting the radios and antennas in, while Potter gave Pike a tour of the firebase. Pike was satisfied with the layout and engineer's progress. It was apparent they would have the firebase completed by sunset that day. They had done an excellent job, so Pike met with the Engineer Company commander and told him so.

By 1730 hours, the artillery battery was in and registered, and the mess hall, which had also been established earlier, served a hot meal for evening chow. Afterward, Pike had Bell report to Brigade the firebase was operational.

That evening Pike had both B and D Companies put out ambushes on the trails they had found around the firebase. After sunset, everyone settled in for the night.

One of B Company's ambushes triggered after midnight, and a brief firefight followed. The remainder of the night was quiet. The following day, the ambush reported finding ten NVA bodies with weapons, and the news spread through the firebase like wildfire. The Company had been blooded and was victorious. The Company commander was so excited about his Company's first kill; that he reported the ambush results to Pike personally. Pike had to force himself to keep from smiling at the young Captain's eagerness.

At 0700 hrs. A Company inserted into their AO, and forty minutes later, C Company inserted into theirs. Both LZs were clean. After the lift package refueled, it returned, picked up D company, and combat assaulted them into their new AO. By 1130 hrs, all three companies moved off their LZs, located a new Company CP site, and occupied it. No one reported any contact the remainder of the day despite the recon patrols that all had sent out. The patrols found several trails in the area but little else. All the Companies put out squad-sized ambushes on trails they had discovered earlier, but none triggered that night.

The following day Pike ordered all three Companies to move northward another six klicks and set up new perimeters. A Company reported finding several planted fields near a significant north-south stream and several well-used trails. D Company found an abandoned bunker complex, but C Company found nothing during their move. That night was a repeat of the previous one, except there were no contacts by any deployed companies.

Consequently, the following day, Pike again moved all three companies northward and told them he wanted their AO's cloverleafed by the end of the day. The recons took the better part of the day but again produced no tangible results. That was the clincher for Pike. He was now firmly convinced the NVA base areas were in the mountains to the north.

That afternoon, Pike called the Brigade Commander on secure and told him about his lack of results and contacts and his firm belief about the major base areas' location. He also told the Colonel that his Companies were now at the firebase's artillery fan's extreme edge. Moving them further north would require movement of the firebase to support them regardless. The Colonel told Pike neither of his sister battalions had found anything significant either.

Pike asked if there had been any developments on their intel request to SOG. The Colonel told him no. Pike asked permission to relocate his battalion to the mountaintop he and the Colonel had discussed earlier. The Colonel told him to give it one more day in the AO. If none of Pike's Companies found anything significant by that time, he would green-light the move.

As soon as he got off the radio, Pike told Bell to start planning the firebase's relocation and start laying on another Engineer Company and lift assets to construct the new base. That evening A Company had two of its ambushes trigger. They resulted in a total of twenty NVA KIA. C and D companies reported no contacts. Pike gave Spence a warning order to be ready to cut an LZ the following morning and be prepared to combat assault A Company onto the mountain top he had shown him earlier and execute the plan he had discussed. He also told C and D Companies to cut LZs and be prepared to be extracted NLT than 1700 hrs.

Pike told Potter and Bell that while the firebase was being relocated, he, Bell, and a skeleton staff would immediately enter the new location after A Company secured it. Afterward, he would lift C Company into the new firebase and the artillery battery. D company would be airlifted back into the current firebase to help B company secure it overnight. The following day, if everything went well, everyone at their current firebase would be flown into the new firebase by 1600 hrs.

Pike also revealed that he expected a firefight on the new firebase as soon as the NVA could move their forces into position to attack it, maybe even as early as their first night on the ground, but certainly, no later than their second night. He ordered his S-4 to ensure extra ammunition was airlifted into the new base on the first and the second day. He also told Potter to coordinate indirect fire support from the 155-

howitzer battery and have TAC air and a gunship, coordinated and on call.

"Why are you so sure the new base is going to get hit, Sir? Potter asked.

"Because I think it's going to be located right in the middle of the NVA's major base area," Pike replied. "And they can't afford to have us sitting on a mountaintop overlooking their main sanctuary with an artillery battery."

"So, they will hit it and try to get rid of us as soon as possible, and they'll commit as many troops as necessary to accomplish that."

"That's why I am locating all the Companies at the firebase initially," Pike explained. "and that's why we laid it out so carefully when we planned its construction."

"I wondered about that," Potter said. "I couldn't understand why you wanted it to be bigger than this one."

"Now I understand."

"You wanted it to be large enough to put more line companies on its perimeter to defend it."

"That's right," Pike said. "that was the primary reason."

"The second reason was to ensure it would be large enough to accept reinforcements directly into its interior in case they were needed."

"And we may very well need them before this operation is completed," He cautioned.

"Because I am positive that the NVA will commit whatever size force they think necessary to overrun it," Pike said bluntly.

"How large a force do you think the NVA will attack us with?" Bell asked.

"At least a Regiment," Pike replied calmly. "maybe two."

"They'll want to eliminate us quickly because they won't want this to turn into a prolonged fight."

"That's why I want TAC air and a gunship laid on for every single night we're there."

"And that reminds me, Larry," Pike added. "we'll centrally locate all the Company mortars on the new base too."

"They'll be more effective that way."

"So, ensure we bring in plenty of ammo for them that first day, as well as extra water, ammo, and Claymores."

"If I'm right about the NVA," Pike concluded. "this is going to be a hell of a firefight, and it's probably going to last more than one day whether they want it to or not."

"I've talked to the Brigade commander about all this at length, and he agrees."

"So, he's going to be prepared to airlift both our sister battalions into the area around the base of the mountain if we can get the NVA committed to trying to kick us off its top," Pike revealed.

"Christ," Potter suddenly realized as the light bulb clicked on. "That's been the plan all along."

"Pike has thought out this entire scenario beforehand."

"Hell, he had all this planned before we ever left the Brigade firebase."

"We're going to deliberately draw out the NVA, get them to deploy major forces against us, and engage them in a huge stand-up firefight."

"Once they're committed," he realized. "the rest of the Brigade will combat assault in behind them and cut them off to prevent them from escaping."

"Christ, that's a classic textbook maneuver."

"We studied that same tactic at Command and General Staff College at Ft Leavenworth, but this is the first time I've ever seen it planned for and employed for real."

"I should have picked up on this much earlier," he told himself angrily

"This will be a Brigade-sized operation for sure; maybe even bigger," Potter thought, remembering Pike's exact words. "

"No wonder they wanted to make him a battalion commander."

"He's at least one step, maybe even more, ahead of the NVA and even own his contemporaries."

"Potter, you better start paying close attention to everything Pike says and does from now on," he told himself. "even his nuances."

"Because you can learn a lot from this man."

"The rumors about him were all true."

"He does know what to do instinctively in any given situation, and he's never even been to school for it."

That evening, Pike had another talk with the Brigade commander on secure. The intelligence from SOG had come in and confirmed what Pike had already assumed. The NVA had several large logistics complexes across the border in Cambodia in the same general area as the Brigade's AO.

But to date, SOG recon teams had found no major base areas on the Cambodian side of the border. But they had found several major trail complexes from the staging areas that led back across the border into the Ia Drang Valley. That seemed to confirm Pike's suspicions the NVA Division's main base areas were in the mountains at the north end of the valley, just as he thought, the exact area Pike was preparing to establish a firebase.

Pike requested Division LRRPs be sent to his firebase at first light. He planned to brief them on the areas he wanted reconned, and afterward, they would launch directly from the firebase. The Colonel okayed the request and confirmed the LRRPs would be there at first light.

After his conversation with the Colonel, Pike decided it was time to brief his staff on the actual plan and the reason for the new firebase. He also told Pike that everything they had planned had been coordinated and was ready to be executed. All he needed was the word from Pike.

"Okay, people," Pike told his assembled staff. "this is what this entire operation is all about and what our part in it is."

"We will establish a firebase right in the middle of what we assume to be the 103rd NVA Division's main base area."

"This operation has been planned for some time, but for security reasons, none of you were told about it earlier."

"The CG, the Brigade Commander, and I all think our earlier entry into the valley was compromised," Pike revealed.

"The NVA knew we were coming, and that's why they were so ready for us."

"That's the only logical explanation for them being able to mass enough of their forces in the right positions in that short of time, and execute a coordinated attack on two separate firebases simultaneously."

"They had to have definite foreknowledge to allow that to happen."

"As a result, this operation, as well as its primary mission, was kept very close hold, and our replacing 1st Brigade was a deliberate cover plan to get us into the AO without the NVA suspecting we were about to assault their main base areas."

"The plan itself is simple," Pike explained.

"This battalion will establish a strong point on the mountaintop I showed you earlier."

"The NVA will immediately attempt to overrun it because they can't afford to have a US battalion with an artillery battery sitting right in the middle of their primary sanctuary."

"When they commit themselves, they will discover this strongpoint is not a normal firebase usually defended by only one infantry company."

"They will find it is a much harder nut to crack than they originally expected because we are eventually putting all the battalion's line companies into the base to defend it."

"In addition, we will retain the engineer company as our battalion reserve."

"Consequently, the NVA will be forced to commit major forces to remove us."

"When they do, the remainder of our Brigade, along with elements of 1st Brigade, will combat assault five or more battalions into the AO around the base of the mountain and surround it."

"These forces will not only cut off any NVA forces on the mountainside that attempt to escape," Pike explained. "they will also prevent all the NVA forces already there from being resupplied or reinforced."

"The Brigade will then tighten that noose and finish off the trapped forces with indirect fire and TAC air."

"If the thought hasn't already occurred to you," Pike told them with a smile, "we are the cheese in a big trap."

"This operation commences tomorrow morning when we combat assault A Company onto the mountain top."

"From the time A Company hits that LZ until this operation is over, we will all be in a position of maximum risk."

"I considered all that when I proposed this plan to the CG and the Brigade commander over a month ago, but I consider that risk acceptable."

"We will establish this strongpoint on the mountaintop, and we will hold it," Pike said firmly. "In the process, with the help of the rest of the Division, we will destroy the major portion of the 103rd NVA Division."

"This battalion owes it to all those who died the last time we were in this valley to extract a full amount of retribution from the NVA that killed them."

"And I will assure you, I fully intend to exact that retribution."

"In blunt terms," Pike barked, "I am going to do everything in my power to make sure that the NVA realize they made a big mistake when they overran this battalion two months ago."

"I intend to take a huge chunk out of their ass for that, one so big that they will never again even consider screwing with this Division."

Potter looked at Bell in awe. He had never seen Pike like this before. His intensity and determination were almost tangible.

"Christ," he said as Pike walked away. "The old man is really serious about all this."

"Yeah," Bell replied. "He is."

"And you couldn't pay me a million dollars to be a member of the 103rd NVA Division right now."

"They may not know it yet, but they are in for a world-class ass whipping, and the LTC that is going to give it to them just walked out of this TOC."

"He has been planning this payback for more than two months," Bell said. "ever since he brought A Company back out of the valley as the only survivor of the battalion, and they promoted him to LTC."

"I just realized that," Bell said quietly.

"He's worked this whole thing out in great detail, and we even helped him do it, although we didn't know it at the time."

"Yeah," Potter said. "I know."

"He as much as told me so earlier."

"He told me never to underestimate the NVA, especially their intelligence system."

"I should have picked up on that hint then, but I didn't."

"I guess we both better start paying closer attention to what the old man says and does.

"We'll learn a lot more."

"Right now, we better start planning this relocation," Bell said.

"Now that I know what is at stake, I want to make damned sure everything about this operation goes off without the slightest hitch."

"I'm with the old man," Bell snarled. "I want some serious payback from these NVA sonsabitches."

Chapter Twenty Two

The following day in the predawn hours, Pike called Spence and told him to cut an LZ at first light and have A Company prepared as soon as the LZ was usable. Spence would have the 155-howitzer battery on call for indirect fire support if he needed it, and the lift package would have four gunships flying escort for it for Spence to employ in case of a hot LZ. Their mission was to combat assault onto the mountaintop at the valley's north end.

There would be no LZ prep before the insertion because Pike didn't want to lose the element of surprise and let the NVA know they were coming or exactly where the LZ was. He also told Spence to secure the mountaintop as soon as possible because the lift package would pick up C Company as soon as they dropped off A Company. Afterward, they would insert them onto the mountaintop LZ to support A Company.

"Understand, Boss," Spence transmitted. "we'll secure the area as soon as possible."

"I know the insertion sequence is tight, and you want to get the engineers in as soon as possible."

"If we don't make any contact, you should be able to have the Chinooks bring them and their equipment in as soon as I can get C Company positioned on the new perimeter."

"That should be about twenty minutes after they land, max."

"Okay, son," Pike said. "keep me advised of everything that's happening from the time you hit the LZ, and watch your ass."

"WILCO," Spence replied.

At 0555 hrs, just as the sun cleared the jungle treetops, A Company cut an LZ out of the jungle floor using C-4 and det cord. The explosion echoed up the valley, and a cleared area magically appeared in the mass of green. Simultaneously, two helos departed the firebase with two LRRP teams aboard, bound for the valley floor. Both team leaders had specific instructions from Pike on what they were to do once they inserted. Shortly after, a heavy lift package appeared over the newly blown jungle LZ and picked up A Company. The pickup took ten long minutes since only three birds at a time could land on the small jungle LZ.

When the Company had been picked up, the lift birds formed up into a line formation, with two gunships on either side, and headed northward through the morning mist. Fifteen minutes later, A Company was inserted on the mountaintop in a light fog. Vegetation on the mountaintop was sparse, so all the birds landed simultaneously.

Spence's heart was in his mouth when his bird touched down since Pike had warned him to be prepared for anything, including a hot LZ. What he got was nothing, complete silence. The LZ was clean. His platoon leaders already had their people moving to secure the area before the birds were even out of sight.

"Chicken man, this is Chick One," Spence transmitted a few moments later. "we're down, and the LZ is clean, repeat clean."

"LZ surface is a three hundred meter by four-hundred-meter rectangle with only sparse vegetation, no trees or other obstructions."

"It can accept any size bird without a problem." He relayed.

"My people are moving to secure the area now."

Pike, sitting in the TOC, blew out a pent-up breath.

"Alert C Company the birds are on their way," he ordered Bell. "tell them to blow their LZ now."

"Jim," Pike ordered. "give the engineers and the Chinook pilots a ten-minute warning order."

"As soon as C Company is down, I want the engineers and their equipment already on their way."

"The next hour or so are critical if this plan is going to work."

"If the NVA decide to hit A Company," Pike explained. "it will take them at least an hour or more to mass enough forces, and another hour or more to get them up the mountain and into position to launch an attack."

"That gives us a little over two hours to get ready for them."

"If we can get the engineers onto the LZ, and they can get a perimeter dozed around the top of that mountain before the NVA forces get in position," Pike predicted. "then we are good to go."

"So, from now on, it's a race against time, and the morning fog will help us."

"If it covered the mountaintop when A Company inserted," Pike explained. "and that's good."

"The NVA know we inserted somewhere, but because they couldn't see where the helicopters sat down, they can't be sure exactly where."

"So, they'll have to send out recon patrols to find out before they can send larger units to the site."

"That will give us even more time to get the mountaintop cleared and secured."

Bell went to work immediately. So did A company on the mountain top/

"Thomas," Dawson ordered. "send three of your people down that trail three hundred meters or so and set up a demo ambush, a big one."

"And make sure you camouflage it."

"Jerry," Dawson continued. "you take two men and do the same thing on the other trail."

"And both of you make it quick." He added.

"Every Dick in this valley knows we're up here by now, so they'll be coming Moshe skosh."

"Everybody else, cover them."

"Charley," Dawson ordered his RTO. "call Nesbit."

"Have him tell the old man we found two large trails leading down the east side of the mountain, and we're putting demo ambushes on them."

"Give him their coordinates."

"The rest of you spread out, find some cover and get set; ten meters between positions."

"I want a machine gun covering each trail and Claymores out in front of everybody's position."

"I want all that done right now, so let's move it, ladies."

"We got company coming."

"C Company is airborne," Bell reported back in the TOC. "So alert Spence and tell him they're inbound," he told his Operations Sgt.

"And tell the Chinook pilots to start cranking."

"I want those engineers into that LZ right on C Company's ass."

"Forward element," he continued. "start breaking it down and get ready to move."

"We go into the new firebase about thirty minutes after the engineers, and that's about a half-hour from now."

"Part of Headquarters Company will be going in with us to provide CP security for us, so let the Headquarters Company Commander know to get his security element down to the PZ and ready to be picked up."

"Also," Bell added. "make sure we have contact with the FAC before we depart."

"I want a radio set up, operational, and in contact with both him and the TOC back here within three minutes of our touchdown."

"What's the status on the LRRPs insertion?" he asked

"Both teams are down and moving," a TOC RTO reported. "No contact thus far."

"Tell the old man when he comes back in," Bell ordered. "He'll want to know."

"C Company is down on the mountaintop," another RTO reported a moment later. "and the Chinooks are airborne."

"ETA to the mountain is one five mikes."

"Make sure Spence knows that," Bell ordered.

"The lift package that took C Company in will have to return to base and refuel," Bell said, calculating and looking at his watch.

"So, get an ETA from the C& C on when they will be back here to pick us up."

"Everybody stay on top of the situation."

"We've got a lot going on right now, it's on a tight schedule, so I don't want any mistakes."

"Make sure when you get the word on something, you pass it on, so everybody is up to speed on the situation as it unfolds."

"You're doing a fine job, Larry," Pike said, startling the young Captain. "and so are your people."

"I've been listening from just inside the TOC entrance."

Pike had been standing off to the side and watching his Operations Officer handle all the details concerning the new firebase's establishment. Bell had done everything just as Pike would have himself and Pike was impressed. His battalion operations section was solid, and it showed.

"LRRPs are down and moving, Boss," Bell reported. "C Company is in, and the engineers are airborne and en route."

"Spence reports no contact thus far."

"If the Dicks will give us one more hour before they try anything," Pike told Bell. "We'll be set."

"After that, we can handle anything they throw at us."

"I'm about to start giving them something else to think about besides the LZ," Pike said mysteriously. "that will hopefully confuse the hell out of them."

"What's that, Sir?" Bell asked curiously.

"Lt Spence reports hearing two large explosions in the valley," an RTO reported before Pike could answer.

"That," Pike said with a smile. "is what I'm referring to."

Bell looked confused.

"I told the LRRPS to plant two-pound blocks of C-4 on the jungle floor as soon as they landed and then put them on a long-time fuse," Pike explained.

"The first two just went off," Pike said smiling. "and there'll be more detonations in the next hour."

"The NVA will wonder what the hell is going on when they hear those explosions."

"I'm hoping they think we're cutting LZ's into the valley floor for some incoming combat assaults."

"That will force them to halt the deployment of any forces moving towards our new firebase until they can find out what's happening on the valley floor."

"That will delay any action against A Company until they can figure out what's happening."

"They may even figure that A Company's landing was just a ruse to draw off their forces while we combat assaulted our major forces onto the valley floor itself," Pike opined.

"Regardless, until they can determine what the situation is, they will hesitate to commit anyone anywhere, in force."

"And while they are trying to sort through everything, we will get the extra time we need to clear the mountaintop and get set to repel any attack."

"That's why I wanted to insert the LRRPS this morning," Pike revealed.

Bell just smiled.

"Pike knows his shit," he thought. *"He not only dreamed up this entire operation, but he also planned a diversion to give us time to get the firebase in and set."*

"Potter was right."

"Pike may have never been to Leavenworth, but he already knows instinctively what they teach there."

"Chinooks are setting down on the mountaintop," an RTO reported a moment later. "first chalk is going in as we speak."

"I'll bet Lt Spence is busier than a one-legged man in an ass-kicking contest about now," Bell joked.

"Get your people and equipment ready to move," Pike ordered. "The lift package will be here in a few minutes."

"Jim," Pike said, turning to Potter. "you take over the TOC now."

"We'll call you as soon as we're down on the new base."

"Keep me advised on what's going on back here, and keep the resupply schedule going."

"We'll see you and the rest of the battalion tomorrow morning if everything goes well."

Ten minutes later, the lift package arrived, and Pike, Bell, the forward headquarters, and the HQ security element loaded the helos. They were airborne minutes later. The flight to the mountaintop took fifteen minutes. When they arrived, Pike told the pilot to let the rest of the helos land first and to circle the mountaintop so he could get a good look at the new firebase from the air.

"Christ," Bell said in amazement as he and Pike looked down at the mountaintop below them. "those engineers have been busy."

"They've already cleared the entire mountaintop of vegetation and put a berm around the entire firebase."

"It looks like they are already putting in the perimeter berm and trenches along with the TOC too."

"Yeah," Pike acknowledged happily. "they've obviously been going at it hard."

"Give us another hour, and we'll be set for sure."

"Okay," Pike told the pilot. "I've seen enough; take us down."

The bird landed a minute later, and Spence met them when they stepped off the helo.

"Good to see you again, John," Pike said, slapping Spence on the back. "I can see that you've been busy. What's the situation?"

"We're all set to repel boarders, Colonel," Spence replied with a smile.

"A Company and C Company are all tied in on the perimeter, and we have demo ambushes on all the trails leading down the mountain."

"They're about three hundred meters downslope from the edge of the perimeter."

"We also have two-man LPs out about five hundred meters further out."

"So far, everything's quiet except for the explosions we heard in the valley earlier," Spence reported. "We don't know what the hell they were."

"That was the LRRPs," Pike told him. "I inserted them at first light and told them to blow some C-4 in the valley after they inserted as a diversion."

"I'm trying to convince the NVA the LRRPS are cutting LZs on the valley floor for upcoming combat assaults into the valley."

Spence smiled.

"That's pretty slick, Boss," he said. "No wonder the Dicks haven't sent any recon teams up here yet."

"They're worried we're about to insert into their rear."

"We won't fool them for long," Pike said. "When they find out those explosions were only diversions, they'll be up here pretty damned quick."

"We're ready for them, Sir," Spence said smiling.

"Most everybody on the perimeter is not only dug in, but we also have sandbagged positions for the crew-served weapons, three lines of concertina up, and Claymores out."

"I've also consolidated the mortars in the center of the firebase, and they have an earth berm around them for protection, so they are ready to provide fire support on command."

"In another half hour," Spence said proudly. "we'll have an earth berm around the entire perimeter, and the TOC will be finished."

"Then we can dig in and wait."

"Everything looks great, John," Pike said, "You've done a fine job."

"Now show us where the new TOC will be so Larry can get the radios operational."

"Then you can give me a tour of the perimeter."

"Follow me, Sir," Spence said.

Twenty minutes later, Bell had an operational TOC set up, and the lift package had returned, bringing in extra ammo, water, and rations. Pike was just finishing up his tour of the perimeter when Nesbit came running up to Spence.

"Our LP on the eastern trail just reported heavy movement coming up below them," Nesbit reported. "they're on the way back in now."

"I also ordered our other LPs back in."

Spence nodded.

"Tell C Company to pull in their LPs too and to get set," Spence ordered. "and alert all our platoons and the engineer company commander we got visitors coming."

"What have you got the engineers doing if there's a firefight, John?" Pike asked Spence.

"They're my reserve," Spence replied. "I told the Engineer Company Commander to have all three of his platoons ready to act as reaction forces and to be prepared to reinforce any hotspots on the perimeter."

"Good," Pike said. "that's exactly what I wanted."

"Now get back to your Company."

"I'll take over now, and I'll be at the TOC."

Spence ran off with Nesbit to his Company CP while Pike ran back to the nearly finished TOC.

Running into the sandbagged enclosure, Pike yelled.

"Larry, call the FAC and get me some TAC air ASAP."

"The Dicks are on their way."

Just as he started to say more, there was a massive explosion on the eastern side of the mountain.

Spence called Bell a moment later.

"That was our demo ambush detonating," Spence reported. "The Dicks are now three hundred yards from the east side of the perimeter."

"Larry," Pike ordered. "have the mortars open up on that side of the mountain and call for the 155's."

"Let's get them working that area too."

"Spence's people can adjust their fire."

"Then get me Brigade," he ordered.

Moments later, the mortars in the perimeter began firing, and rounds started peppering the area below A Company's portion of the perimeter. Pike could hear Dawson adjusting their fire on a nearby radio as he waited for the Brigade Commander to come onto the line.

"It's started, Sir," Pike told the Colonel a minute later. "the Dicks are on their way up the mountain."

"Their lead element just detonated a large demo ambush on the eastern side of our perimeter, and we're hitting them with our mortars."

"Any idea on the size of the NVA force yet?" The Colonel asked.

"Negative," Pike reported. "I should have a better idea in the next few minutes."

"What's your status?" the Colonel asked.

"The mountaintop has been cleared," Pike reported. "and we have two Companies dug in on the perimeter."

"We also have an eight-foot-high earth berm around the entire site."

"We've got wire up, Claymores out, and the TOC, although not finished, is operational."

"We're not as ready as I would like," Pike admitted. "but we can hold this hill from anything up to a regiment."

"That's what I wanted to hear," the Colonel said. "Tell me what else you need in the way of support, and I'll see that you get it."

"I'm hoping this is only a probe," Pike told the Colonel.

"I think when the NVA find out how strong we are up here, they will back off and wait for reinforcements before they try an all-out assault on us."

"And I don't think they'll try that until dark."

"I'd like to bring in another of my companies before dark to beef up the perimeter, but I don't want to leave our old firebase with only one company to defend it," Pike said.

"I'll send you a Company from second battalion before sunset," The Colonel told Pike. "You can replace them with one of yours in the morning."

"Thank you, Colonel," Pike said. "That will give me four complete companies up here to defend this place, including the engineer company I already have."

"I'm hoping that will be enough."

"Me too," the Colonel echoed. "As soon as the NVA commits in force, let me know."

"I've got everybody back here on standby ready to move."

"WILCO," Pike replied.

As he finished, a series of Claymores in A Company's section of the perimeter detonated. They were immediately flowed by a heavy volume of weapons fire. Pike listened to Spence on his Company frequency as he directed his forces.

"Larry," Pike ordered, "alert the Engineers to get a platoon ready to reinforce A Company and get those 155's working."

"John, this is Pike." Pike transmitted.

"Spence here, Sir," Spence replied immediately.

"We're getting hit hard in my second platoon sector."

"Roger," Pike said, "I've been monitoring."

"Send the engineers a guide; I'm sending you one of their platoons for reinforcement.:

"And tell your 2nd platoon leader to stand by to adjust some 155-fire coming into his front."

"WILCO," Spence replied.

"I've got the FAC online," Bell reported. "He's got four F-4s loaded with snake and nape ready to unload as soon as we mark our perimeter."

"Tell Spence to have his platoons mark their leading edges with smoke," Pike ordered. "And tell them to get their heads down."

"I'm going to order the FAC to hit the entire eastern side of the mountain just outside the perimeter."

A minute later, the earth shook as the first F-4 rolled in and unloaded five hundred pounders on the eastern side of the mountain. The first airstrike was immediately followed by other three aircraft unloading on the same area.

First, they hit the mountainside with five-hundred-pound bombs, then napalm. After the last aircraft dropped its napalm, there was complete silence on the perimeter as fire engulfed the nearby jungle.

"I think that stopped them," Pike told Bell. "They won't try that again, at least not in the daylight."

"Contact Spence," Pike ordered, "And get a SITREP and a casualty count."

"And as soon as it's clear, send somebody outside to guide in a lift package."

"The Brigade commander is sending us another Company from second battalion."

"Have Spence meet them and put them on the perimeter, then adjust everybody's sectors accordingly."

"By God," Bell exclaimed excitedly. "that will beef up our defensive capability considerably."

"The Dicks hit us again; they're in for a big fucking surprise."

"Line us up a gunship for tonight too," Pike ordered. "we get Spectre working for us; we'll have something big going."

"Already done, Boss," Bell said happily. "I coordinated that last night while you were asleep."

"Spectre will be on station at 2200 hours unless we need them sooner."

Pike nodded.

"We're nearly set then," Pike said. "So, I'm going down to A Company."

"Call Spence if you need me and get a SITREP from all the other units too; then send a battalion SITREP to Brigade."

"And while we've still got some daylight, have the engineers finish the TOC, and sandbag it."

"We'll need all that completed before dark."

Chapter Twenty Three

As the sun set that evening, Pike felt much more confident about his ability to defend the firebase against an all-out NVA assault. The engineers had finished the TOC and the earth berm around the perimeter had been reinforced. On Pike's instructions, they had also reinforced all the firebase's main structures with extra layers of sandbags on their roofs and sides.

The engineers had also constructed another large interior bunker Pike was planning to use as an aid station and several other interior bunkers that Pike had ordered built but had never explained their intended use. All four line companies were firmly dug in on the perimeter behind the earth berm, in sandbagged positions and embedded bunkers. Three more strands of concertina wire were erected outside the berm itself and expended Claymores had been replaced..

Lastly, Pike had positioned the three engineer platoons at strategic points in the firebase behind the four line companies so they could quickly reinforce them if necessary.

None of the Companies on the perimeter had reported any movement since the failed NVA attack earlier. The only evidence of the event was the mountainside's burned side stretching from the perimeter for six hundred meters down the mountainside. So, A Company and part of C Company now had a clear field of fire from the berm to the edge of the downslope and two hundred yards beyond that.

Consequently, Pike ordered them to put out a series of trip flares in the cleared area as an early warning precaution. He had also had extra ammo delivered to all platoon CPs on the perimeter. Pike realized there would be no time for a resupply once the NVA attacked again because the firebase's next attack would be a major one. The NVA would be intent on overrunning it, so they would be fully prepared to commit whatever size force necessary. Pike realized that, and he had already planned for it. That's why he wanted all his subordinate units to be as ready and prepared as possible.

By sunset, the entire battalion went on full alert; everyone waited. That was the hard part because everyone on the firebase knew what was coming; they just didn't know when. So, the anticipation was nerve-wracking. Anxiety was extraordinarily high and, left unchecked, could quickly become overwhelming and consuming fear. Pike knew that too, so at 2030 hrs. Pike sent out an all-call to every unit on the firebase to alleviate some of it.

"We are going to get hit tonight, people," Pike told everybody. "That's a certainty, and I realize that every man on this firebase is already aware of that."

"That knowledge may cause almost overwhelming concern and fear for some of you because you know it will be an all-out assault by the NVA, using all their available forces."

"And all of you know what happened the last time this happened in this same valley."

"This Brigade had two firebases overrun."

"But I can assure you, that's not going to happen tonight; for several reasons."

"First, we have four complete companies defending this firebase."

"The two other firebases that got overrun earlier this year only had one."

"Secondly, we already know what the NVA intends to do, and we have prepared for it."

"Thirdly, we have fire support from ground and aerial assets that have already been coordinated and laid on."

"They are just waiting for our signal to support us."

"Lastly, the firebase has been specially constructed to withstand an all-out NVA assault."

"That's why the earth berm and all the reinforced bunkers on our perimeter were constructed."

"So, when the NVA hit us, they are the ones that will be surprised, not us."

"However, I think the NVA will precede their attack with indirect fire from their mortars," Pike warned. "And they'll keep the barrage going up to and including the beginning of their ground assault."

"They will also hit two points on the perimeter simultaneously, maybe more," Pike told his battalion.

"Probably the eastern slope because the airstrikes and their units have already cleared it, and they can move faster through the open area and also from the western side of the perimeter."

That's so our supporting mortar fires will be forced to split into two opposing directions."

"I've already directed the combined mortar section to focus on those two areas."

"Consequently, we'll have half our tubes firing HE and the other half illumination rounds."

"So, ensure your people stay in their holes once the action starts."

"You have good cover from indirect fire and direct weapons fire there, and you can bring accurate fire on the enemy from those positions."

"Consequently, I don't want to see anybody exposed in the open when the attack begins."

"The concept behind our defensive plan is to make them come to us; when they do, we're going to make them pay for it."

"I also have artillery and a Spectre gunship on call to support us once the attack starts," Pike revealed.

"I plan to let the NVA fully commit to an all-out ground assault, then turn Spectre loose on them."

"But you people will have to keep them outside the wire with your organic weapons until Spectre can arrive and commence firing."

"That's a must."

"We can't let them get inside the wire because Spectre or artillery fire is no good to us if they breach the perimeter."

"Finally, I don't think the NVA know just how strong we are here," Pike continued.

"Hopefully, they think we only have one company defending the perimeter since that's our normal operating procedure."

"Each company on the perimeter will also have an engineer platoon behind them as a reserve force, ready to provide immediate reinforcement if necessary."

"All you Company Commanders have to do is call for it."

"The engineers have their radios on the battalion frequency."

Lastly, we'll have 155 howitzer support when we need it."

"It's already been called for, and their pieces are already registered."

"This won't be an easy fight when it starts," Pike warned everyone in conclusion. "but it will be a crucial one."

"It will be the start of an all-out, Division-sized operation to wipe out the entire NVA 103rd Division."

"If we can get the NVA to commit major forces against us tonight, the Division will combat assault five battalions into the valley around the mountain at first light to surround and trap them."

"So, you people must hold your positions and keep up the suppressive fire in your assigned sectors."

"If you do, we should be able to turn back any NVA attack, especially with Spectre helping us."

"Company Commanders and platoon leaders," Pike ordered. "make sure your people exercise fire discipline and deliver accurate, aimed fire once the action starts."

"And I want SITREPS from all of you on your situation at regular intervals.

"I can't assess the overall situation and react unless I get accurate, up-to-date information, as to what's going on, so have your RTOs feed the TOC regular reports."

"I know we are as ready as we can be and that once the action starts, we will give a good account of ourselves."

"So just do what you've been trained to do, and we'll all survive. Good luck."

All the Company commanders acknowledged Pike's orders, and afterward, everyone settled down to wait for the NVA attack."

"*Now, thanks to Pike's pep talk, the waiting is a little easier.*" Dawson thought.

Finally, at 0247 hours, A Company reported movement outside the perimeter to their front. That started it. Moments later, C Company, diagonally across the firebase on its western side, also reported movement. Three minutes later, two trip flares in front of C Company went off, lighting up the cleared area. They illuminated an NVA sapper team trying to sneak in and blow the concertina wire. The enemy sappers were all quickly killed by grenades thrown from the perimeter.

Five minutes later, an NVA mortar barrage began, a big one. Bell had the battalion FO call for counter-battery fire from the 155 battery. Still, the counter-battery fire was only marginally effective because the firebase was being hit from several different positions by several other NVA mortar crews. Consequently, more than a hundred mortar rounds fell on the firebase in the next few minutes.

With mortar rounds still impacting the perimeter, the NVA initiated their ground attack. Dawson's platoon was the first to engage them after a trip fire in front of them ignited and revealed an NVA company advancing on their section of the perimeter. The platoon lit the lead NVA elements up immediately, and within seconds, all A Company was engaged. Less than thirty seconds later, C Company was also in heavy contact when an NVA company was spotted moving towards them.

"Chicken man, Chick One," Spence reported minutes later. "We got at least two companies advancing on us now, with more coming up the slope."

"This is no diversionary attack," Spence reported. "this is the real thing."

"The NVA are wall to wall in front of us, with more coming."

"Give me mortar fire two hundred meters outside the wire right now," Spence ordered. "illumination first, then HE."

"Keep it coming, and I'll adjust."

C Company called a moment later and requested mortar fire, reporting heavy contact to their front.

"Okay, Larry," Pike ordered. "call Spectre and get him on station."

"This looks like the main attack."

"We got at least two NVA battalions committed, one coming at A Company and one at C Company."

"As soon as Spectre gets here, shift the 155 fire down the mountain, so the NVA can't retreat."

"Then tell Spectre to start chewing up their lead elements."

"When they start to fall back, shift our mortars out from the perimeter down the mountainside too and have them begin using airbursts.

"Boss," Spence reported a minute later, "we got them stacked up like cordwood in front of us, and they're still coming."

"I'm starting to run low on ammo and grenades."

"Understand, John," Pike replied. "I'll have the engineers bring you more ammo."

"Keep putting it to them."

"Spectre is on the way; ETA is ten mikes."

"Stand by to mark your front with strobes."

"Larry," Pike ordered. "tell the Engineer platoon behind A Company to take some more ammo and grenades to A Company's positions and to stand by to reinforce them."

"Also, pass the word to the other two Companies to stand by to mark their forward positions with strobes and check on their ammunition status."

"Get me, Brigade," Pike ordered an RTO.

A moment later, the RTO handed Pike a handset.

"The Colonel's on the line, Sir," he said.

"Pike here, Sir," Pike began. "we are being hit by at least two battalions from both the eastern and western sides of the perimeter."

"They started the attack a few minutes ago with a large-scale mortar barrage."

"I suspect we are up against at least an NVA regiment, with more probably on the way."

"I don't think the NVA knew we had four dug-in companies defending the perimeter when they attacked."

"Now that they have committed, they're going to realize that very soon."

"When they do, they 'll know they'll need a larger force to take this place."

"I estimate we have killed at least two to three hundred of them in the initial assault alone, but my Company Commanders report they're still coming." Pike continued. "so, I have called in Spectre."

"His ETA is ten mikes."

"So far, we are holding the perimeter with organic weapons, but if the NVA hits us from a third direction, I'll have a problem."

"My mortars can only support two sections of the perimeter simultaneously."

"So, any attack from a third direction will be unsupported by indirect fire."

"What's your casualty count so far?" The Colonel asked

"Unknown at this time," Pike replied. "my Company Commanders have been too busy to give me one so far."

"But all of my people are well dug in, in sandbagged positions, so I have no reason to suspect that it's high."

"I think we'll probably have a lull in the action in the next few minutes." Pike opined.

"When the NVA discover just how strong we are on the perimeter, I suspect they will pull back and wait for reinforcements before committing a final all-out assault."

"When their reinforcements arrive, I think they'll commit everything they've got, and that's what I'm waiting for."

"When they attack in full force, I'm going to turn Spectre loose on them."

"They don't know he is on station yet, because I have him orbiting at twelve thousand feet about twenty-five miles away, gathering target data."

"Hang in there, son," The Colonel said. "I have four heavy-lift packages ready to launch at first light."

"That's an hour and a half from now."

"The LRRPs are already positioned to cut four LZs at the mountain's base on the northern, eastern, southern, and western sides."

"Second battalion will combat assault into the northern and eastern LZs while Third battalion combat assaults into the southern and western ones."

"As soon as they're down," the Colonel confirmed. "Third Brigade will start bringing their people in."

"We'll have that entire area around the base of the mountain surrounded by 0700 hrs. with two full Brigades."

"Roger, Sir. Out." Pike replied.

"Colonel," Bell said, interrupting a moment later, "Both A and C Companies report that the NVA are pulling back."

"They're still taking fire, but the ground assault has stopped for the time being."

"Have the engineer platoons take fresh ammo, grenades, and water to the line companies and evacuate any wounded back to the battalion aid station," Pike ordered. "and get me a casualty count from all the Companies."

"Tell A and C companies that this is just a lull in the action while the NVA brings up more troops."

"So, use the next few minutes to reorganize and resupply."

"They can expect an even heavier attack on their perimeters within the next half hour."

"When that happens, and the NVA are fully engaged, I'll call in Spectre."

"Casualty count coming in, Colonel," an RTO said.

"Let's hear it," Pike said.

"A Company reports five KIA and eleven WIA, three serious," the RTO replied.

"C Company reports two KIA and eight WIA, three serious."

"B Company, 2nd Bn reports two WIA."

"Have the engineer Platoon behind A Company reinforce them," Pike ordered. "And tell the Company commander from 2nd battalion to expect his section of the perimeter to get hit hard in the next attack."

"So, resupply his people with extra ammo and water now."

"There won't be time once the attack starts."

"This time, the NVA will throw everything they have at us."

"Spectre is on station, Colonel," Bell said. "The pilot wants instructions."

"Spectre, this is Chickenman," Pike transmitted a moment later.

"Spectre here," the pilot replied. "We are on station and ready to provide fire support."

"Have your forward elements mark their leading edges."

"WILCO Spectre," Pike replied. "They'll turn on their strobes as soon as the next attack starts."

"I don't want the NVA to know you're on station yet, so continue to orbit and gather target data."

"Meanwhile, let me tell you how we're laid out down here."

"We occupy the top of the mountain," Pike told the pilot. "Our center of mass is RA 13316246, and my perimeter is a two-hundred-meter radius around that point."

"We have a large earthen berm around the firebase itself that takes up almost the entire mountain top."

"The Dicks own the rest of it."

"So, consider anything outside my perimeter as hostile."

"I expect to be hit from three separate directions in the next attack, the east, west, and north, and I expect all those attacks to occur simultaneously, by a minimum of a Regiment of NVA."

"We'll let you know when that happens, but I expect that attack to begin sometime in the next half hour."

"When the attack begins, I want you to hold your fire until the Dicks are fully committed."

"When that happens, we'll mark our perimeter with strobes, and I'll give you consent to fire."

"Then you can start chewing them up."

"Meanwhile, you can maintain your orbit and start marking potential targets on your target acquisition computer."

"I estimate I will be hit by the better part of two full NVA Regiments when the NVA fully commit," Pike explained.

"So, when you roll in, I'll initially need maximum firepower just forward of my perimeter's leading edges to break their assault."

"Once that's done, you can finish off any targets of opportunity you detect, at will."

"But primarily, I want you to prevent as many NVA as possible from escaping back down the mountain."

"I have assets coming into the valley at the base of the mountain at first light to cut them off," Pike explained.

"So, I want you to contain them on the mountainside until after my other elements arrive and are in position."

"WILCO, Chickenman," the pilot replied. "We're all locked in and standing by."

"Let us know when you want us to commence firing."

"WILCO. Out," Pike replied.

"Larry, tell all the companies Spectre is now on station and the plan."

"And tell them to ensure all their forward elements have their strobes in position and ready to turn on when I give the word."

"Son," Pike said to a nearby RTO, "call Brigade and give them a SITREP and a casualty count."

"Yessir," the youngster said with a stammer.

"And relax," Pike told the youngster seeing the anxiety on his face. "now that Spectre is on the station, we're practically home free."

"Why's that, Colonel?" the young RTO asked.

"Because there has never been a firebase overrun in this country since the war began while Spectre was supporting them," Pike said.

"That means we are about to put a world-class ass whipping on the 103rd NVA Division."

"They don't know yet, but they are about to be had and in spades!"

The young RTO smiled. Pike exuded confidence, which was contagious; every other RTO in the TOC had been listening, and they were smiling too.

"Everything is set, and everybody has gotten the word, Colonel," Bell told Pike a moment later. "I think we're ready."

"I've even put an extra radio and RTO in the Aid bunker in case we get hit with another mortar barrage and lose our antennas."

"That's good thinking, Larry," Pike said. "I hadn't thought of that."

"Neither did I," Bell admitted. "my Ops Sgt suggested it."

"While we've got time," Pike ordered. "call Potter and give him a SITREP."

"Tell him to have D Company ready to be picked up at first and flown here."

"We'll use them to replace the Company from 2nd Battalion."

"I'll call him right….."

Bell's sentence was drowned out by somebody screaming *"INCOMING."* Suddenly, NVA mortar rounds started falling like rain on the firebase. The explosions echoed through the TOC, and the structure shook as at least three rounds impacted the sandbagged roof. The NVA didn't need to adjust their fire this time. They were dead on target with their first barrage.

"Okay, Larry," Pike ordered. "This is it."

"Call Brigade and tell them the main attack has now started."

"Then wait five minutes and call Spectre."

"Roger, Sir," Larry replied.

Chapter Twenty Four

"Oh shit," Bell yelled a moment later. "I can't raise anybody."

"I was right in the middle of talking to C Company when I lost contact."

"So, either our radios are down, or theirs are."

"It's us," the Operations Sgt confirmed. "I can't raise anybody either, and I was just on the horn to Brigade."

"That last barrage that hit the roof must have taken our antennas out."

"I'll send some people outside and get them back up, but that'll take a few minutes."

"From the sound of things on the perimeter," Bell shouted above the rising staccato outside the TOC. "we don't have a few minutes."

"We've got to have commo right now."

"Spectre is still waiting for our command to commence firing."

"And before we can give that command, we must tell the companies to turn on their strobes and mark the perimeter."

"You'll have to use the spare radio in the aid bunker," the Ops Sgt yelled. "meanwhile, we'll try and get the antennas back up here."

Bell nodded and ran out of the TOC. Pike, who had been listening to every word of the exchange, was right behind him.

Outside the TOC bunker, the entire firebase was one big explosion. The sound of continuous gunfire was everywhere, with green NVA tracer rounds flying through the night sky nonstop and mortar rounds impacting inside the firebase every few seconds. The situation appeared ominous between all that and the sound of the ongoing firefight raging on the perimeter. The NVA had committed everything they had to breach the wire and overrun the firebase, and now they were remarkably close. Fire was pouring in from every direction with no slowdown.

Pike had to call in Spectre immediately to save the firebase, and he knew it. There was no more time. Unless they got fire support, the Dicks would break through and be inside the wire in a few minutes. The Companies on the perimeter were already outnumbered at least ten to one, and they couldn't stem the rising onslaught by themselves. They had to have some support; they had to have Spectre. The battalion was finished if Pike couldn't contact him in the next few precious minutes. He and Bell had to get to the spare radio in the Aid bunker.

Pike ran behind Bell in a bent-over crouch, ducking and cringing every time a mortar round impacted close to them. There was no time to try and duck for cover or run between the incoming rounds. There were too many of them, and they were coming in too fast. So, he and Bell ran directly through the barrage, hoping they didn't get hit. They had to get to the one remaining operational radio in the Aid Station and contact the gunship before the NVA breached the wire. If that happened, Spectre would be ineffective because it would be unable to differentiate between friendlies and hostiles.

Both men's legs churned as they ran headlong through the explosions for the bunker. Rounds were zipping everywhere, and the firefighting and mortar explosions lit up the night sky. Their run was dangerous and made more difficult by the darkness.

Halfway to the aid bunker, there was a colossal explosion directly in front of both men. Pike felt his body suddenly being thrown violently through the air. When he landed, he crumpled, the wind knocked out of him, and he lay dazed for a moment. When he finally recovered and sat up a moment later, he was woozy, his ears were ringing, and he felt blood running down his left arm. When he tried to move it, it seemed to still function. Then he saw Bell, face down in front of him, crimson bloodspots all over his fatigue jacket, and not moving.

Grunting with pain, Pike got up, scooped the young captain up in his arms, and ran the last few yards towards the door of the aid bunker. Still, the barrage was so heavy that he was almost knocked down twice more by near-misses before he finally made it. Running inside, he put Bell down and searched through the dimly lit interior for the radio and RTO. He finally spotted them in the front corner.

"Is your radio still working, son?" he asked the frightened young RTO.

"Yes, Sir," the youngster said.

"Give me the handset," Pike ordered.

"All companies, this is Chicken Man," Pike transmitted. "Activate your strobes; I say again, activate your strobes. Acknowledge and report."

A moment later, all three Companies reported their strobes activated.

"Spectre, this is Chicken Man," Pike transmitted as soon as he got the word.

"This is Spectre," the pilot replied anxiously. "What the hell happened down there?"

"We've been trying to raise you for the last five minutes, and all we got was static."

"We lost our antennas," Pike answered. "so all our TOC radios are down."

"We're operating on a spare until we can get them back up."

"We have now activated our strobes that mark the perimeter," Pike transmitted.

"We've got them." the pilot acknowledged.

"Commence firing immediately," Pike ordered. "Danger Close."

"The Dicks are almost through our outer wire."

"Roger, Chicken man," Spectre replied. "Get your people's heads down."

"We are rolling in hot."

Pike called all the Companies and told them to get down.

A moment later, the elephant farted. Not really, of course, but that's what it sounded like when Spectre cut loose with its five-barreled electric 20 mm Gatling gun. The loud BRRRRRRUUUUPPPP was followed by a stream of red fire erupting from the night sky and tracing its way down to the ground just outside the perimeter.

The noise was unmistakable, but the effect on the NVA was horrific. The twenty-millimeter Gatling gun was firing at a rate of almost a hundred rounds per second. So when the first burst hit the attacking NVA lines, it cut them to shreds in nanoseconds, slashing its way effortlessly through their leading elements like a giant buzz saw. The lead NVA Companies were chopped to pieces with bodies and body parts flying everywhere in a mist of red gore, flesh, and bone, all around the perimeter's outer wire

Spectre's first pass killed at least four hundred NVA, mainly because they were jammed up almost on top of each other as they attempted to breach the outer wire. Their bodies were blown to pieces as the twenty-millimeter shells tore into them and ripped them to shreds. Even their screams were cut short by the instant death descending on them in relentless waves.

Spectre's second pass, a moment later, tore into the massed second wave of NVA forces directly behind the assault elements, waiting to pour through the wire once it had been breached.

They never got the chance. They were eviscerated two seconds later. When the NVA formation's rear elements saw their assault elements being blown to pieces in front of them, they immediately stopped their forward movement, reversed their direction, and attempted to run the other way. But they were too late, so they didn't get far. They were too bunched up for any rapid movement, especially in the opposite direction. So, when Specter started its second pass, they too were cut down by the twenty-millimeter fire, like a scythe going through ripe wheat.

They died by the hundreds, many never even realizing what had killed them. Their mangled bodies were heaved skyward, and the remains fell back to earth in bloody heaps as the rounds tore into their ranks.

The aircraft was the only thing still firing by Specter's third pass. The NVA's back had been broken, and they were no longer interested in attacking the firebase.

What few remained alive were only interested in trying to escape Those still able were in headlong flight back through the black jungle and down the mountain's side. But even they couldn't escape. Spectre's target acquisition equipment picked them up and the aircraft set about methodically relieving them of their existence as they attempted to run or hide. Overall, it was a slaughter of the first magnitude.

An hour later, the better part of the 103rd NVA Division's two Regiments no longer existed. Between Pike's battalion and Spectre, the two elements had killed or wounded almost three thousand NVA, and it wasn't over yet!

The remaining Regiment of the 103rd NVA Division was now surrounded by two entire Brigades of Americans, supported by TAC air and a battalion of gunships. Payback is a sonofabitch, and the remaining regiment of the 103rd was about to find that out the hard way. Their lesson would be extremely penal, so most wouldn't survive. Pike's plan to suck them in and get them committed to destroying the Firebase while the rest of the Division combat assaulted in behind them and cut off their line of retreat had worked perfectly.

Having watched the entire spectacle from the bunker's door, Pike was awestruck. He had seen killing before, but never on a scale like this; This had been a massacre, a killing of the first order, a slaughter. He was startled when the radio suddenly squawked.

"We're back up, Colonel," the Operations Sgt's voice blared over the radio.

"Get a SITREP from everybody," Pike ordered, somehow finding his voice. "I'm on my way back to the TOC."

"WILCO," the Opns. Sgt replied.

"How's Captain Bell?" Pike asked the medic.

"He's dead, Sir," the medic replied.

"Goddammit," Pike said in a choked voice.

A moment later, he started to walk out of the aid bunker and back to the TOC.

"You better let me look at that arm, Sir," the medic said.

"It's Okay," Pike said. "just put a field dressing on it for now; I'll let you treat it later."

"I've got to get back to the TOC."

"This isn't over yet."

So, Pike waited a few additional minutes while the medic slapped a field dressing on his arm.

"What's the situation with the Companies?" Pike asked the Opns. Sgt when he walked into the TOC minutes later.

"They all report the NVA assault has been broken by Spectre, Sir," the Opns, Sgt reported.

"The few NVA left aren't even returning fire now; they're just running."

"And since none of the Dicks breached the wire, the Companies are reorganizing and evacuating their wounded to the battalion aid station."

"It was close," the Sgt reported. "especially in C Company."

"It got down to hand to hand at one point, but they held."

"Have you got a casualty count yet?" Pike asked.

"Yes, Sir," the Ops. Sgt said, picking up a clipboard and looking at it.

"A company reports 4 KIA and 13 WIA, and C Company has 12 KIA and 19 WIA. They got hit the hardest."

"B Company, 2nd Bn has 5 KIA and 10 WIA, and the engineer Company has 1 KIA and seven WIA.'

'Headquarters Company has 3 WIA."

"We got hit pretty hard, Sir, but we held," He said proudly. "and against at least two NVA regiments, but we kicked their ass."

"By God," he said tightly. "That's something."

"Call for the medevacs," Pike ordered.

"Already done, Sir," the Ops, Sgt said, noticing the bloody field bandage on Pike's arm for the first time. "They're on the way."

"Where's Captain Bell, Sir?" He asked, fearing the worst.

"He's dead," Pike said tightly. "The mortars got him as we were running to the aid bunker."

"Shit," the Ops Sgt moaned angrily. "Shit, Shit, Shit."

"He was a damn good man," he said in a tight, choked voice. "I'm going to miss him."

"They were all good men," Pike said.

"Yessir," the Ops, Sgt said in a choked voice. "but I didn't know the others, and I knew Captain Bell."

"Consider yourself the acting S-3, Sgt," Pike told him. "and take charge of the TOC."

"Yes, sir," the Sgt replied.

"Get Brigade on the horn and give them a SITREP and a casualty count," Pike ordered. "And find out how their half of this operation is going."

"Then call Major Potter."

"Fill him in on what's happened and tell him to get the artillery battery in here and set up ASAP."

"The battalions coming into the valley will need fire support, and we're the only ones that can reach them."

"So, we need to get that battery in here and operational ASAP, along with all the artillery rounds they're going to need."

"So have him send in extras."

"After the arty is in, tell Potter to get the rest of the battalion up here as soon as he can, especially the rest of Headquarters Company."

"I want a hot meal for the people here NLT 1100 hrs."

"So, tell him to get the mess hall set up and operational first thing."

"I'm going down to the perimeter to check the companies then walk around the firebase to see what's left," Pike said.

"While I'm gone, call the Companies and have them bring all their casualties to the aid bunker."

"Then get somebody outside to guide the medevac birds in when they get here."

"Did you get all that?" Pike asked, his ears still ringing. "I was probably rambling because my ears are still ringing."

"I got it all, Colonel," the Opns. Sgt said with a smile.

"Watkins," he said, turning to two men just inside the door. "you and Smith grab M-16s and go with the Colonel."

"I don't need anybody, Sgt," Pike protested.

"Do what I told you," the Opns Sgt told the two men, ignoring Pike. "We're not going to take the chance of losing you now that this thing is almost over, Colonel."

"And when the Colonel's finished with the Companies," the Opns. Sgt added. "escort him to the aid bunker and have his arm tended to properly."

"No excuses. Got all that?"

Both men nodded.

"We'll look after the Boss, Sarge," one said." We ain't going to let anything happen to him."

Outside the bunker, it was just starting to get light. Smoke from the firefight and the smell of cordite hung in the humid morning air, and the entire area had a pall of death over it. The interior of the firebase was one big shell hole. Sandbags surrounding the TOC were leaking sand, slashed by shrapnel from the mortar attack. Black scorched earth and shell holes were everywhere, and the sickly smell of death and fresh viscera hung in the morning mist like a cloud.

The sound of Spectre still working the mountainside thundered across the valley now and then as they found and annihilated another pocket of NVA. The faint sounds of helicopters landing in the valley below could also be heard from time to time.

As Pike walked up to A Company's CP, Nesbit was outside the bunker crying.

"Lt Spence took one in the head," he told Pike raggedly. "there wasn't nothing I could do, Sir."

"I put a bandage on him and tried to get him to wake up, but I couldn't. He's dead." He sobbed.

Pike put his hand on Nesbit's shoulder to comfort him. He wanted desperately to say something. To tell him it was all right. But he couldn't find the words. Tears ran down his cheeks as he patted the youngster on the shoulder.

Dawson walked up a moment later. He had a bloody field dressing on one leg and his habitual cigarette hanging out of the corner of his mouth. He was hollow-eyed and looked utterly drained.

"That's one youngster you can be proud of, Pike," he said, pointing to Nesbit. "He ran the entire company after Lt Spence got it."

"Never missed a beat."

"Kept all the platoons supplied with ammo, repositioned the engineer platoon continually to fill in the gaps, and called all the shots all by himself."

"He obviously learned a lot as your RTO."

"And Lt Spence in another one you can be proud of," Dawson said wearily.

"He was plugging a hole in the wire all by himself after delivering a box of ammo to 1st platoon when he bought it."

"He must have killed twenty of the bastards all by himself before he died."

"Lt. Thompson in second platoon got hit too."

"It was pretty bad, but he'll make it."

"Even Pardee got nicked, along with me."

"It was a hell of a firefight, so I guess we're lucky to be alive."

"But by God, you can be proud of you old Company.

"Everyone in it did their job and a hell of a lot more."

"They all deserve a medal."

"I guess we killed the better part of at least two battalions before Spectre got here."

"That's mainly because you trained us so well.

"Hell, we all learned how to lead thanks to you."

"With Spence and Thompson gone,'" Pike said, looking at Dawson. "That makes you the new CO of A Company, Dawson."

"Think you can handle it after you get your leg patched up?" Pike asked.

"I think I can," Dawson replied. "I had a good teacher."

"I think you can too," Pike said. "and the job will be permanent, *Lieutenant* Dawson.".

"Lieutenant?" Dawson said in astonishment.

"That's what I said," Pike echoed. "I just gave you a battlefield commission."

"Shit," Dawson said. "I don't know how to be no officer."

"I didn't ask you how you felt about the job," Pike said in mock seriousness. "I just told you to assume command, Lieutenant."

"And get your leg seen too," He ordered. "I've got to check on the other companies."

"Yes, sir," Dawson said. "right away."

"And Dawson," Pike added as he turned to walk away. "Come see me at the CP after you get everything sorted out."

"I got a rucksack jug with about four snorts left in it."

"That should be enough to wet down your new Lieutenant's bars."

"We'll just be two old ex-NCOs who somehow got to be officers."

"Yes, sir," Dawson said with a grin. "I'll be there just as soon as I get my Company squared away."

Epilogue

When Major Potter arrived with the remainder of the battalion, he was shocked at the damage he saw as he flew in an hour and a half later. He wondered how anyone had survived, considering what the shot-up firebase looked like. Later, after Pike had given him a quick recap of the previous night's action, he understood. Then as he realized what the entire operation had been about, he had to almost kick himself for not seeing it earlier.

Pike's plan had been to sucker the entire 103'rd NVA Division into an attempt to overrun the new firebase, just as it had done two months ago with the previous firebases. They had expected the Americans to use the same tactics and the same battle plan when they established the new firebase, so they fully expected to overrun it with ease.

But Pike had counted on that, and he had fooled them by putting four Companies instead of one into the new firebase to defend it. He had also anticipated their actions and had Spectre and all the battalion mortars in readiness to support his Companies when the NVA attack began. The NVA hadn't expected any of that, so when they attacked the firebase, they failed to overrun it with their first assault.

Afterward, they compounded their mistake by calling for more reinforcements rather than pulling back as they should have. But those reinforcements did them no good because Pike had also anticipated that and had Spectre already on station and ready to support him. The result was the 103rd Division got massacred; the few remnants that escaped down the mountain, running right into two brigades of infantry now surrounding them. That took care of the last few NVA survivors.

Two days later, the Brigade found and destroyed the actual Headquarters of the NVA Division itself. It was in a massive cave complex carved into the mountain's side at the valley's northern end. Just where Pike had suspected.

As for A Company, the Division Commander approved Dawson's battlefield promotion, and he formally assumed command of A Company three days later as a 1st Lieutenant. Nesbit, Lt Spence's RTO, was also awarded a Silver Star for his actions during the battle and promoted to Staff Sgt. He became a platoon Sgt in A company when he had to give up his radio. And as for Pike, he survived the action and later trained the replacements for his now battle-hardened battalion. Afterward, he commanded it for another seven months before he had to turn it over to his replacement.

He later rotated back to the States and spent another two years training lieutenants at Ft Benning, Georgia, to lead troops in the hell called Vietnam. During that time, he met a charming southern belle from Alabama, whom he courted and later married.

When he completed his twenty years of service, he retired. Dawson, Nesbit, Potter, Pardee, and many of the old hands of A Company attended his retirement ceremony and threw a big party afterward.

Pike and his wife now have three children, and Pike is the principal at an elementary school in Alabama. He is still teaching and instructing, something he does best. But he attends the Division reunion every year as an honored guest and a Division hero. Even though he's retired, his exploits and his name live on, and his training methods and procedures are still taught to every new Division member. It's a legacy that is well remembered and will live on. The same is true for Pike.

The End

GLOSSARY

A

A-4 SKYRAIDER WWII vintage, prop-driven fighter bomber, capable of carrying huge weapons loads and with a long loiter time, these aircraft were a favorite of teams calling for air support.

A-6 INTRUDER A US naval strike aircraft capable of all-weather operations. Usually operated off an aircraft carrier.

AO Military acronym for Area of operations

A TEAM The fundamental operational detachment in a Special Forces Group. It has 12 SF troops: 2 officers and 10 NCOs.

A CAMP A permanent camp or operating location established in enemy territory by an SF

A-Team. It housed the A-Team and a battalion of ethnic strikers recruited by them. Its mission was usually border control or area denial.

ACROSS THE FENCE / LINE Across the border. Inside Cambodia, Laos, or North Vietnam. In denied territory.

AGENCY The Central Intelligence Agency (CIA)

AIR AMERICA A wholly-owned CIA proprietary; it served as the Agency's private air force during the Southeast Asian conflict.

AIRMOBILE OPERATION An operation in which helicopters are used to either insert or extract troops into or out of an AO.

AIRSTRIKE An attack on a target by aircraft. It usually involves the employment of bombs, rockets, napalm, strafing runs, or all four.

AK-47 The standard assault rifle of the Soviet Army. A rugged, reliable 7.62mm weapon that operates in semi-automatic and automatic mode. The AK has become the primary weapon of communist-backed insurgents worldwide. Copies of the Russian version are also produced in China, Poland, and Czechoslovakia.

ALTIMETER The instrument on an aircraft that indicates how far above the ground the aircraft is flying.

AMMO Short or slang for ammunition.

AO Area of Operations is where a unit conducts combat operations.

ARC LITE A B-52 bombing mission/strike.

AREA OF OPERATIONS The area where the operation or mission takes place.

AVGAS Aviation gas; fuel for aircraft

B

B-47/ B-50 A Russian-made anti-tank and anti-personnel rocket launcher that used rocket-propelled grenades to engage targets. An extremely effective and feared weapon used by the enemy in Vietnam.

B-52 The primary heavy bomber of the US Air Force.

BAHNAR A tribe of Montagnards living in the Central Highlands of South Vietnam; member of the Degar nation.

BAR Browning Automatic Rifle; a 30-caliber box-fed light machine gun.

BASE CAMP Rear area in a combat zone where the unit has its fixed installations; a place where the unit's headquarters, personnel, logistics, maintenance, housing, messing, training, and other combat support sites are normally located.

BASE STATION   The radio station that normally controls all the other radio stations on the net; usually, the base station is a fixed site with a large, fixed antenna array capable of sending and receiving long-distance radio transmissions.

BATTLE DRESSING: Each soldier carries individual first aid dressing to dress wounds.

BDA   Bomb Damage Assessment; an on-the-ground assessment of the effectiveness of a bombing raid.

BEAR   "Meet the Bear," face death, or get killed.

BEAT FEET   Leave quickly, get away.

BEAUCOUP   A French adjective meaning many; a favorite of the Yards to describe how many VC or NVA they had seen; it could mean one or one hundred, you never knew.

BINARY A two-part system used to store or employ chemical weapons.

BLACK BOX   A lie detector; when an individual is black-boxed, he is given a lie detector test.

BLACK PSYOPS   Psychological operations that are non-attributable.

BLOW AWAY   Kill

BODY BAG   A green rubber bag with a zipper used by the military to temporarily store bodies or human remains.

BOOK CODE   A simple code in which both the sender and the receiver use the same book to encode and decode their messages.

BRASS The metal casing of the round containing the powder; it has a primer on its base and a projectile on its other end.

BRITE LITE TEAM   A reaction force that SOG employed to conduct operations to recover downed airmen or to locate and recover POWs.

BROWNING A-6   A WWII vintage, 30 caliber, belt-fed, air-cooled machine gun.

BUF   Big Ugly Fucker; a nickname for a B-52.

BURMA   The former name of Myanmar. Also, the name of the largest ethnic tribal majority in Myanmar.

C

C-4   Plastic explosive used by the military.

C-7A   A two-engine, STOL, medium-lift cargo aircraft; nicknamed the Caribou.

C-46   A WWII, two-engine, prop-driven cargo plane; used in Southeast Asia by many countries in a commercial capacity and by Air America in other ways.

C-47   A WWII vintage, two-engine, prop-driven cargo plane, sometimes used in Southeast Asia as a special operations aircraft.

C-123   A two-engine prop-driven cargo aircraft used in Southeast Asia for conventional and special operations. It also mounted two small jet engines because it was so underpowered.

C-130   A modern four-engine turboprop aircraft used by the USAF in several variants. i.e., Cargo, Gunship, ELINT, Weather, Command and Control, and Spec Ops.

C-141   A modern, four-engine jet, heavy-lift cargo aircraft currently used by the USAF.

C&C   Command and control

CAMO, Short for Camouflage

CAS   Controlled American Source; an indigenous agent controlled by a US intelligence agent; a euphemism for the CIA.

CASE OFFICER   A nonmilitary intelligence officer employed in various roles by the Central Intelligence Agency.

CCC   Command and Control Central, a subordinate headquarters of SOG; an FOB located at Kon Tum.

CCN Command and Control North, a subordinate headquarters of SOG, an FOB located in Da Nang.

CCS Command and Control South; a subordinate headquarters of SOG; an FOB located in Ban Me Thouit

CEP Circular Error of Probability

CHOLON The Chinese section of Saigon.

CIA Central Intelligence Agency

CIDG Civilian Irregular Defense Group; a paramilitary organization composed of ethnic or religious minorities; these groups were organized, equipped, trained, employed, and commanded by US Special Forces throughout the Vietnam War.

CLANDESTINE Secret; usually refers to a mission or an operation.

CLANDESTINE COMMUNICATIONS A form of communication using other than normal means to send and receive secret or coded messages between operatives or agents and their handlers.

COMBAT ASSAULT A heliborne or airmobile assault into a landing zone.

COMMO Short for communications; usually radio communications.

COMPANY A military unit normally composed of a command element and three platoons. It usually numbers anywhere from 120 to 160 personnel, based on the unit type, and a captain commands it.

COMPARTMENT/COMPARTMENTATION A security procedure that breaks a mission or tasking into levels or tiers. Personnel working in a tier know only the information available to them in that tier. They are deliberately kept unaware of information available in the tiers above them and below them. Only the overall commander or manager of the project/mission knows all its details. Everyone else is aware of only enough information to do their jobs within their tiers.

COMUSMACV Commander US Military Assistance Command Vietnam; the supreme US military commander in South Vietnam.

CONCEPT OF OPERATIONS A basic idea of how a commander intends to conduct an operation; is normally fleshed out to form a complete operations plan.

COSMOLINE A thick, greasy, preservative used to coat metal items during their shipment or storage to prevent rust or corrosion.

COUNTERINSURGENCY Operations and actions designed to combat/defeat the insurgent/guerrilla and rally the indigenous populace to support the government.

COURT-MARTIAL   The military equivalent of indicting a person for a crime. In this proceeding, a soldier is brought before a military court under the Uniform Code of Military Justice.

COVER   A false identity or background used by an intelligence or undercover operative to hide or protect his real identity or mission.

COVERT   A secret operation in which the sponsor's identity is concealed and protected; he is given plausible denial about the operation.

COVEY   Call sign of the airborne forward air controllers who supported US covert missions into Cambodia, Laos, and North Vietnam.

CROSS TRAINED   Trained in a second military specialty; all SF troops are cross-trained in at least two military specialties.

CUT OUT   A deliberate break in communication or operational chain so that no single person will know all the personnel in the chain or all the aspects of the entire mission.

D

DA   Department of the Army

DANIEL BOONE   The code name for the SOG covert ground reconnaissance program in Cambodia

DCI   Director, Central Intelligence; another hat of the Director of the CIA; in this role, he controls all US intelligence efforts.

DEA   Drug Enforcement Administration

DEAD DROP   A technique used in or a method of clandestine communications.

DEBREDE   To clean and disinfect a deep wound.

DEEP SHIT   Big trouble

DEGAR TRIBE: The name of the five hill tribes living in the Central Highlands of South Vietnam; later redubbed the Montagnards by the French, which translated means "Hill People."

DENIED AREA   An area into which the entry of US troops is legally prohibited.

DEROS   Date Expected to Return from Overseas; the actual date your tour was completed and you left Vietnam.

DET CORD   Detonation cord; a stringlike explosive with an extremely high detonating velocity. Det cord is often used as an initiator when connecting bundles of explosives for simultaneous detonation.

DIA Defense Intelligence Agency; the US intelligence agency that supports the Department of Defense.

DICK An enemy soldier; an NVA soldier.

DINK Another name for a VC insurgent.

DOG SOLDIER A nickname for a North Vietnamese soldier since they lived in the jungles like dogs.

DO MAMY Vietnamese slang for Goddamn.

DOWNTOWN Slang for where the enemy is.

DROP Slang for a parachute drop.

DROP OFF POINT A preselected point on a map or on the ground where men or material are deliberately dropped off their insertion platform and left.

DROP ZONE A preselected area on the ground where personnel or equipment are dropped by parachute from an aircraft.

DZ Acronym for the drop zone.

E

END USER CERTIFICATE A legal document entitling the holder to buy and transport arms, ammunition, or explosives across international borders.

EXFILTRATION/ EXFIL Being extracted from or getting out of the area.

F

FAC Forward air controller

FAST MOVER A jet aircraft; a fighter or fighter-bomber in Vietnam.

FIELD EXPEDIENT Using available equipment to jury rig something in the field and make it temporarily operational.

FIRED UP Shot at; attacked.

FIREFIGHT An engagement with the enemy; when both sides exchange weapons fire.

FLASH The highest precedence of classification available within the military communications system.

FLYING COLUMN A formation used in the early 1900s by the IRA when they battled British troops in Northern Ireland.

FOB Forward Operations Base; a forward headquarters or operating base for UW units

FOXTROT UNIFORM Slang military communications jargon meaning Fucked Up.

FUBAR A slang military acronym meaning Fucked Up Beyond All Recognition.

FUSION CENTER A collection and analysis center for all-source intelligence.

G

GENERAL GIAP The Military leader of all North Vietnamese forces during the Vietnam War.

GET HAT To move out quickly.

GET OUT OF JAIL CARD A laminated identification card issued to all personnel assigned to MACVSOG.

GET SOME To shoot something; to kill the enemy.

GOLDEN TRIANGLE The confluence of the borders of Thailand, Laos, and Burma; this area is home to the largest opium-growing area in the world.

GREEN MACHINE The US Army

GRID SQUARE A series of north-south and east-west lines overlayed on a military map; they are numbered and make it possible to locate objects and pass on their location by transmitting their "coordinates."

GROUP A Special Forces Group.

GUNS Helicopter gunships

GUNSHIP A fixed or rotary-wing aircraft mounting various weapons to provide aerial fire support to troops on the ground.

H

HARD   Tough

HATCHET FORCE   A platoon-sized reaction force used to reinforce or assist SOG Recon Teams in extractions under fire.

H E   High explosive; a type of artillery or mortar round.

HELIOCOURIER   A small, fixed-wing monoplane with STOL capability; used in Vietnam by special operations elements.

HILLSBORO   Call sign of the Air Force airborne command post operating over Laos in the daytime.

HIT   Wounded.

H & K   Heckler and Koch. German firearms manufacturers who produce the finest submachine guns in the world.

HO CHI MINH TRAIL   A network of trails beginning in North Vietnam and stretching to South Vietnam through Laos and Cambodia; they composed the primary logistics artery used by the North Vietnamese during the Vietnam War.

HOUMG   The largest tribe in Laos. They were recruited by the CIA and used as mercenaries against the communist Pathet Lao and the NVA.

HUSH PUPPY A silenced 9mm Belgian Browning pistol.

I

ID Acronym for Identification.

ID CARD A laminated military identification card issued to everyone in the US military; it had his service number as well as his picture on it.

IMAGERY Satellite photography.

IMMEDIATE The second highest precedence in the US military communications system.

INFILTRATION / INFIL Clandestine insertion of personnel or equipment.

INDIG Short for personnel indigenous or native to the country or region

INSERTION Introduction of men or material into an operation area by ground, aerial, or maritime platform.

INSERTION PLATFORM How an insertion is accomplished, usually by a vehicle, an aircraft, or a watercraft.

I P Initial Point

The IRA Irish Republican Army is a paramilitary Irish nationalistic organization dedicated to ending British rule in Northern Ireland.

J

JARAI   A tribe of Montagnards living in the Central Highlands in South Vietnam.

JIMMY DICK   To jury rig; to make a field-expedient use of an available asset.

JOINT OPERATION   An operation involving forces from more than one military branch.

JOLLY GREEN   A CH-53 heavy-lift helicopter

JUNGLE BOOTS   The distinctive footwear worn by ground personnel during the Vietnam War; They were designed for wear in a tropical climate and made of nylon and rubber with a cleated sole.

JUNGLE FATIGUES   The nylon uniform worn by military personnel during the Vietnam War. They were breathable, durable, fast-drying, and came in olive drab or a mottled green camouflage pattern.

JUWTF   Joint Unconventional Warfare Task Force; a multiservice task force charged with conducting unconventional warfare operations in a selected region.

K

KACHIN An ethnic minority hill tribe living in Burma.

KAREN An ethnic minority hill tribe living in Burma.

KIA Killed in Action.

KILL ZONE A preselected area in which you intend to kill the enemy.

KLICK One thousand meters on a military grid map

KMT An abbreviation for Kuomintang.

KUOMINTANG The Nationalist Chinese Army or Party; formed by Dr. Sun yet Sen and later controlled by Chang Kai Chek.

L

LANDING ZONE A relatively flat, unobstructed area on which fixed or rotary-wing aircraft are landed or take off from.

LANGLEY Langley, Virginia; Headquarters for the Central Intelligence Agency

LAOS A country in Southeast Asia that borders Vietnam, Thailand, and Burma. The NVA used its border regions to establish a permanent large-scale logistics artery and basing area from North Vietnam to South Vietnam called the Ho Chi Minh Trail. Laos was supposedly neutral during the

Vietnam War. Yet, it turned a blind eye to the NVA efforts and activities in its border areas during that period.

LAUNCH SITE   A forward operations site is normally established to launch or recover UW operations.

LITTLE PEOPLE   What many Americans called the South Vietnamese or Montagnards

LOG SITE   Short for a logistics site.

LORAN   Long Range Navigation system used by aircraft.

LZ   Landing zone.

M

M-5 KIT   A portable medical surgical kit used by SF medics.

MACV Military Assistance Command Vietnam; the overall headquarters for the American war effort in South Vietnam

MACVSOG   Military Assistance Command Vietnam Studies and Observation Group; cover name for the Special Operations Group operating in Southeast Asia during the Vietnam War.

MAGUIRE RIG   A personnel extraction system consisting of a rope with four to six harnesses attached was dropped from a helo. Personnel on the ground hooked themselves up to the harnesses and were lifted directly up and exfiltrated. The system was used when there was no landing zone available.

MAN The Man; the nickname for the President.

MEO A hill tribe located in northern Laos; they were recruited by SF and used as paramilitary forces against the NVA and the Pathet Lao.

MIA Missing in action.

MIKE FORCE Mobile Strike Force: a company or battalion-sized force composed of Nung Chinese or Montagnards and cadred and commanded by SF; used as either a strike force or a reaction force.

MILPERCEN Military Personnel Center.

MONTAGNARD An ethnic hill tribe in Vietnam; they were recruited and employed as paramilitary forces against the NVA and VC by SF throughout the Vietnam War.

MOONBEAM Code name for the US Air Force Command and Control aircraft operating over Laos during the hours of darkness.

MOSHE SKOSHE Korean/American slang for very quick.

MSGT Abbreviation for Master Sergeant.

N

NCO Non-Commissioned Officer
NOE Nape of the Earth; the flight profile of an aircraft when it flies at approximately 250 ft above the earth's surface and mimics its terrain.
NSA National Security Agency
NUMBER TEN Slang Viet/American term meaning bad.
NUNGS Ethnic Chinese minority living in Vietnam. A sect of Tay Chinese that was originally a part of the Chinese Nationalist Army that fled from China when Mao Tse Tung defeated Chang Kai Chek and resettled in South Vietnam.
NVA North Vietnamese Army
NVN North Vietnam
NVGs Night vision goggles; light amplifying goggles that allow the wearer to see images at night with almost the same clarity as daylight.

O

OPERATIONAL Functional; ready to be implemented or employed.
OPSEC Operational security

PAPER GOODS   False documentation; fake ID or passports.

PATHET LAO The communist insurgents in the country of Laos allied with the NVA during the Vietnam war

PAVE LOW   A heavy modified CH-53 heavy-lift helicopter used as a Spec Ops insertion platform.

PISSER   The toilet

PLASTIQUE   Plastic explosive.

PLATOON   A military unit containing three squads and commanded by a lieutenant.

PLAUSIBLE DENIAL   The ability of the sponsor to deny any knowledge of a covert operation because there is no link or proof available to tie them to it.

POP SMOKE   Detonate a colored smoke grenade on an LZ to mark it for incoming helos.

PORTER   A Heliocourier; a high mono wing, STOL aircraft used by SF and the CIA for various missions in SE Asia.

PRAIRIE FIRE   The code name for the SOG covert ground reconnaissance program into Laos. Also, the code word for an emergency on the ground requiring the immediate extraction of a Recon Team in contact.

PRC 25   A short-range portable voice radio used during the early part of the Vietnam war.

PRC 77   The upgraded version of the PRC 25.

PRC 74   A man-portable, long-range voice and CW radio used by SF units; it had its own secure burst transmission device and could transmit and receive voice or Morse code.

PREP   Preparation of an area or LZ by artillery fire, airstrikes, or both before the insertion of troops.

PRIORITY   The third highest precedence in the military communications system.

PONCHO   A plastic military raincoat or ground cloth.

R

RAT LINE   A clandestine communications or transportation system established by intelligence agents when conducting unconventional warfare operations.

RECON   Short for reconnaissance

RECON TEAM   A small joint US/indigenous reconnaissance team consisting of two or three

Americans and four to six indigenous personnel. The RT was the element inserted into Laos or Cambodia to accomplish reconnaissance, locate targets or installations and call in airstrikes to destroy them.

RECOVER In militarise, to return to a certain point.

REMF Rear Echelon Mother Fucker; what grunts called support troops who were based in rear areas and never got shot at.

RESISTANCE POTENTIAL The likelihood of a group of citizens rebelling against their government and willing to try and overthrow it by force of arms.

RHADE A tribe of Montagnards living in the Central Highlands of South Vietnam; members of the Degar nation.

RICKY TICK Slang for quick or very fast.

ROGER Codeword in military communications meaning Yes or I understand.

ROUND Military term for a cartridge or bullet

ROUTE PACKAGES The designated air corridors used by USAF aircraft when departing Thailand to conduct combat missions in North Vietnam.

ROUTINE The lowest precedence of classification in the military communications system.

RP Rendezvous point

RPD A Russian light machine gun in 7.62 mm Parabellum caliber.

RPG Rocket-propelled grenade.

RT Recon Team

RTO Radiotelephone operator

S

SAFE HOUSE A secret location that intelligence organizations maintain to house personnel and secure them.

SAFETY The feature on a weapon that prevents the operator from pulling the trigger and firing the weapon.

SAM Surface to Air Missile

SARIN A type of nerve gas.

SECURE Safe from detection. No enemy around the area.

SENSOR: An electronic device that detects personnel or selected equipment types.

SF Special Forces.

SFG Special Forces Group.

SGT Abbreviation for Sergeant; an NCO

SGM Abbreviation for Sergeant Major; the highest rank an NCO can attain.

SHAN A large ethnic minority in the country of Burma

SHEEP DIPPING Moving funds/people through a series of numbered accounts/identities in a series of foreign banks/situations to eventually make them untraceable. Or giving personnel false identification and papers identifying them as any nationality desired.

SILENCED When a sound suppressor has been affixed to the end of a weapon's barrel to make the sound of the round being fired almost unnoticeable, it is a silenced weapon.

SILENCER: The implement allows the report/firing of the weapon to be silenced.

SLICK An unarmed helicopter; used to transport troops and equipment; a UH-Ih Iroquois; nicknamed a HUEY.

SMOKED Killed; eliminated.

SNAFU Military slang acronym meaning Situation Normal, All Fucked Up

SNAKE A helicopter gunship: an AH1G helicopter specifically designed to provide aerial fire support.

SOG Special Operations Group.

SOG CARD A laminated card issued to all personnel assigned to SOG which allowed them to carry weapons anywhere and have priority access to transportation assets.

SORRY Lazy, no good, worthless.

SPECIAL FORCES A specialized element of the US Army that conducts unconventional warfare; also called Green Berets.

SPECIAL OPERATIONS Unconventional warfare operations.

SPECTRE A C-130 gunship with target acquisition and electronic sensors carries awesome firepower and can attack ground targets with surgical precision.

SPONSOR The initiating, authorizing, and supporting power behind an operation.

SPOOK An intelligence operative.

STABO RIG A newer, more efficient version of the Maguire Rig

STAGE Prepare, provision, and rehearse for a mission.

STAGING AREA The area in which a unit stages for the mission. Usually different from its launch site.

STARLIGHT SCOPE A light-enhancing night scope that allows the user to see in the dark

STERILE Nonattributable equipment used on a covert mission that could never be traced back to the sponsoring power.

STOL Short Take-Off and Landing

STRIKER A member of an ethnic paramilitary force.

STRIP ALERT Aircraft are sitting on a runway with their pilots already in them, ready to launch at a moment's notice.

STROBE LIGHT A small high-intensity light used as a marking device by downed aircrew or recon teams to mark their location at night. Later versions had an infrared filter.

SUPPRESSED A modification to a weapon that reduces the noise level when it is fired.

SWEDISH K A Karl Gustav Swedish 9 mm submachine gun with a folding wire stock.

SYRETTE A syringe, sometimes with an auto-injector. Atropine is carried in syrettes by the military.

T

TAKE OUT Another name for kill.

TAI A hill tribe living in the north Laotian and Vietnamese border areas.

TATMADAW The Burmese army or government.

TERMINATE A euphemism for kill.

TET Vietnamese NewYears; a holiday period.

TOC Tactical Operations Center.

TOUR OF DUTY A year-long assignment in Vietnam.

TIGER STRIPES A uniquely camouflaged fatigue uniform worn primarily by SF and their strikers during the Vietnam War.

TRADECRAFT The secret techniques and operating procedures particular to intelligence work.

TRAIL SIGN Inconspicuous and secret signs or markings left on trails by the VC or NVA indicating mined areas, water, rest areas, the direction of movement, etc.

U

UAV Unmanned aerial vehicle; an aerial drone capable of being controlled from the ground.

UNCLE Short for Uncle Sam; the US government.

UNLOADED ON Came down hard on verbally.

UNTENABLE SITUATION A military situation where it is no longer possible to maintain control, to win, or in some cases, even to survive.

UW Unconventional Warfare: the type of warfare prosecuted by special operations forces.

UZI A 9mm Israeli submachine gun

V

VC   Victor Charlie; the name of the South Vietnamese insurgents.

VETTED   Insured the reliability and loyalty of an employee of an intelligence organization by various background investigations and other means.

VIENTIANE The capital city of Laos

VIET CONG   The ununiformed guerrillas in South Vietnam who aided the NVA in the Vietnam War. They were dedicated to overthrowing the Saigon government.

VR   Visual Reconnaissance; is usually conducted by overflying the area.

VT FUSE   Variable time fuse: artillery or mortar fuse that allows the round to detonate in an airburst at various heights above the ground.

VX   Military name for non-persistent nerve gas.

W

WA   An ethnic Chinese minority located primarily in the Burma and Laos border regions.

WASTE   Another word for kill or terminate.

WETSU A slang military acronym meaning We Eat This Shit Up

WHACKED Killed

WIA Wounded in action

WILCO Military acronym used in communications. It means I understand and Will Comply.

WING A large Air Force military organization; usually consists of a headquarters and staff, three or more flying squadrons, and maintenance and support squadrons.

WP White Phosphorus: A type of artillery, mortar, or aerial rocket round normally used to mark targets. It also comes in grenade form. It ignites on contact with the air and produces voluminous white smoke.

X

XO Executive officer. The second in command of a unit.

X OUT/ XERO OUT Get rid of; kill.

Y

YARD   Montagnard tribesman. Member of the Degar tribe.

Z

ZERO   An individual's sight settings on his weapon allow him to bring accurate fire on his target.

Advance preview

Hitler's Revenge

Now available on Amazon.com or at LegionBooks.net

Chapter 1
The Sahara Desert
Unnamed Oasis
December 1940

The Egyptian let out a sigh of relief after topping the edge of the wadi. Although he had alternated between camelback and walking to save his strength, he was still tired, dehydrated, and wanted to get paid and go home. After more than ten long days of hard trekking through the desert and enduring its withering heat and blazing sun, it was time to end his arduous journey.

"*Alhamdulillah*," he said in relief as he gazed at the oasis. But after scanning its bleak and unforgiving surroundings and realizing he was in the middle of nowhere, he realized expressing gratitude to Almighty Allah was probably a regrettable choice of prayer.

The small oasis was as remote as it was insignificant, a mere flyspeck of relief in a vast sea of sand. However, since it was the only water for over a hundred miles in any direction, that alone made it important.

Even with that, the place hadn't been used for decades, since it was well away from the customarily traveled caravan routes. Also, because of its remoteness, it was just as far from everything else, civilization included. As a result, over the years, it had been almost forgotten about.

Inexplicably, however, the German hired him knew about it. He was also confident of its location and had been the first to tell him of it. He even showed him its supposed location on a German map, and German maps were renowned as the best available at the time. Even so, maps of the Sahara were notoriously inaccurate, even German ones. The Egyptian had known that, so he had consulted with the old ones in his village before agreeing to the proposed bargain and undertaking the arduous and dangerous trek.

When asked, the older men of his village had confirmed the oasis' existence and, with a bit of prodding, even told him how to get there. They remembered the place only because their fathers had told them about it, as their grandfathers had done before them. Only by word of mouth, passed on religiously from generation to generation, was the oasis's existence still even remembered. And then only because it contained the most precious resource in the desert. Water.

So, the Egyptian had agreed to the German's proposal and taken a down payment in gold coins to seal the bargain. Afterward, he had provisioned himself, loaded his camels with the German's mysterious cargo, and made the arduous trek. Now, fourteen days later, he had finally arrived, exhausted, dehydrated, and relieved that his navigation had been so accurate.

As he gazed at the oasis below him, he heard the faint sounds of its water lapping at the pool's edges, like some temptress, enticing victims with their wares. The oasis, however, was no bargain, at least by itself. However, it contained water, and water meant life in the desert.

Staring at the pool hungrily, the squat Egyptian suddenly realized it was full. Apparently, a leftover of a recent but rare rainfall in the arid region. Its moisture was even evident in the dry arid wind near it. So, he, along with the camels, could even smell it. Water was limited at best during most seasons, but today it was here. The elixir of life was surrounded by a sea of sand and encircled by clumps of thirsty, browning scrub grass, with a few tall date palms that signaled its presence.

He toyed with the idea of climbing one to check for fruit, but a second look at their height, coupled with his fatigue, changed his mind. His sense of adventure had been more than satisfied by the long exhausting trip. After such an arduous journey with eight camels in tow, each loaded with heavy cargo, he was thankful to Allah for even getting there. So, he didn't want to press his luck. Besides, his wife's insistence on packing extra food and supplies to sustain him until he arrived had more than satisfied his needs.

A moment later, gently tugging on the lead camel's reigns, the Egyptian encouraged her forward with a patient "*Yalla*" and then successive clicks of his tongue off the roof of his mouth. Walking down off the surrounding wadi, the small caravan made its way off the edge of the dune to the oasis proper.

The trailing seven animals, hitched to one another in convoy formation, took their queues to move from the tension and tugging of their reins. Surprisingly, after ten days of travel, they were quite eager to move, probably because they smelled water. Even so, minutes later, after drinking their fill, they displayed their fatigue and displeasure.

They were tired, hungry, and cranky; the trek having taken its toll on them. They needed to rehydrate then rest before their long journey home. Following their descent into the wadi and the quenching of their thirst, they would be unloaded and begin satisfying all their needs after a few days' rest.

The Egyptian's respite, however, was not going to be quite that forthcoming or occur that quickly. He had much to do before resting. But that didn't bother him. He was motivated by the remainder of the gold he had been promised if he followed the rules of his agreement and successfully delivered the mysterious packages, currently making his camels so irritable. He had even been given a taste of it with a few coins as a down payment. Now he hungered for the remainder.

The amount of gold he had been promised would be life-changing for him and his family, and it was this dream that kept him on his sore feet and working. There was much to do before the German's arrival. As he diligently accomplished all the tasks, he thought of a thousand ways to spend his new fortune.

Ten kilometers northwest of the Wadi, on a small mountain of sand, a man stood atop a German-made half-track, a *Hanomag*. He was peering into heavy, long-range, tripod-mounted binoculars that looked more like erect rabbit ears mounted in its cargo compartment. He was facing southeast towards the Wadi, spying on the Egyptian, verifying his arrival, and ensuring he kept his word about not tampering with the cargo. Not that it mattered now. He had other plans for him when they finally met.

"Gute Arbeit, mein Arabischer Freund," he thought when he sighted the Egyptian."

"You're late, you squat little toad, but at least you're finally here."

"I wasn't sure about you initially, but despite my reservations, you made the trip after all."

"Let's just hope you haven't tampered with any of my cargo."

Afterward, he turned to his two companions, below him, who were resting in the shade of the Hanomag.

"I believe the time has finally come for us to begin packing and get ready to depart," He told them.

"We're leaving, Herr Professor Scheer?" asked a surprised voice on the ground below. "Now, in the heat of the day?"

Travel in the Saharan Desert, especially in the daytime, was a dangerous and exhausting undertaking. Between the blazing sun and the British airpower, travel at night was much safer and easier. The man was obviously aware of that.

"Not right away," Scheer said, trying to appease his subordinate.

"We'll wait an hour or two more to ensure our Arab friend has come alone."

"When I'm satisfied, then we'll depart."

"That should be around sunset." He predicted.

The two Wehrmacht soldiers sitting on empty metal water cans while using their armored vehicle to shield themselves from the blinding sun simply nodded. They didn't care about some filthy Arab one way or the other. They merely wanted to travel at night since it was cooler and safer. Besides, they were enjoying their beer.

They didn't even wonder why the professor cared about some filthy Arab. Since he was an odd, abrasive man, they didn't care about him either. They were there only because they had been ordered to accompany the asshole and follow his orders. Accordingly, they considered this another bothersome detail they would have to complete before returning to their unit.

After all, they were soldiers, not nursemaids or errand boys for some eccentric, superior acting civilian, out wandering around in the Sahara on what they considered a fool's errand.

They were warriors, not servants. Their tan-colored Afrika Korps uniforms were disheveled, dirty, and sweat-stained. Sure, signs of men who were battle-wearied and combat-hardened. Their faces reflected the past horrors of war they had already witnessed. Consequently, they had already had their fill of combat, as well as the desert, and their eyes reflected it with thousand-yard stares that revealed its horror.

Because of that, they were not nearly as zealously dedicated to the 1000-Year Reich as they had been two years before when the Afrika Corps had owned everything north of the Sahara and had reveled in its victories. The situation was vastly different now since victories were few and far between, and their side was losing. Consequently, there was little to celebrate and much to regret.

Still, they were loyal soldiers, so they obeyed orders. The orders assigning them to this detail, however, in their opinion, were unproductive and a waste of time. They had little to do with serving the Fatherland. Yet they had abruptly been issued by their commander, and the two men were reassigned and ordered to comply with any instructions given them by their new interim Kommandant. Naturally, he had turned out to be some verdamnt civilian asshole of a professor. The man above them in the Hanomag.

Neither soldier was happy about that. And the fact that the professor, their temporary boss, had turned out to be an elitist egotistical ass didn't escape either man. Not to mention, they were supposed to be in Tunis to start a well-deserved leave. Not running around the desert and playing errand boy for some arrogant goddamned scientist

Scheer, however, had anticipated both men being less than enthusiastic about being assigned to him. That was why he had brought an abundance of contraband American Lucky Strikes and two cases of beer as a bribe to urge them on and keep them compliant. The two soldiers had been enjoying both until he had ordered them to break camp and get ready to move.

Scheer had been amused earlier, listening to their childish bickering about how and where to hide the leftover *Zigaretten und Bier* to avoid sharing with their Kameraden in Tunis when they returned. Their squabbling reminded the professor of the level of intelligence he was being forced to deal with on this mission.

He disliked ignorance in any form, yet, in this case, he had been forced to accept it. That was the price he was being forced to pay for destroying his lab, months earlier when the British had overrun the area where it had been located. Fortunately, they had not discovered it before Scheer had destroyed it, then escaped with his staff back to German-held territory.

"Meine Herren," Scheer said after another hour had passed.

"Finish your cigarettes and beer and prepare to depart."

"Our Arab friend appears he is alone," Scheer announced.

"Now it's time to see if he had done as he has been told and brought my material without tampering with it."

Neither soldier seemed too eager to comply, simply staring up at him in disgust.

"Schnell! Schnell," The professor ordered sharply. "I am in a hurry."

"We must ready ourselves and depart without delay."

"I want to complete our business here and be on our way back to Tunis before it gets dark."

"Or would you rather spend another night in this miserable place because of your laziness?"

With that, the two soldiers gave him a dirty look, then started packing the few remaining supplies into the belly of the *Hanomag*. They had already been here waiting for two days, so that task didn't take long. Afterward, they strapped the empty water cans to one side of the vehicle, planning on refilling them at the oasis. Finally, they nodded their readiness to move as Scheer covered the binoculars, climbed down from his perch, and seated himself in Hanomag's front passenger's seat.

After checking the action on their MP 40 Schmeisser machine pistols and climbing into the half-track, the two soldier's final pre-departure task was to make sure the top-mounted 7.92mm MG 42 machine gun was loaded. According to

Herr Professor Scheer, it might be needed in the upcoming task. However, since they were only facing one lone Arab, they doubted it.

When they finished, they both climbed into the half-track and awaited Herr Professor's next stupid order. Moments later, Scheer simply waved his hand forward, signaling them to start the engine and head for the oasis.

In the meantime, back at the oasis, with all eight camels securely tied to a nearby date palm tree and reasonably placated, the Egyptian had begun unloading the cumbersome packages from each animal. They were one by one-foot cubes made of metal. Probably lead, which accounted for their weight. They were very heavy, weighing at least eighty pounds apiece. The Egyptian carefully removed each metal cube from his camels, then placed the burlap-wrapped package on a tarp he had laid out on the sand, all the while wondering what they contained.

He had entertained similar thoughts for the past ten days and had thought about opening one many times during his journey but remembered the tall German's explicit instructions.

"Bring the packages to the oasis untouched," Scheer had demanded.

"If they are opened or show signs of tampering, you will forfeit the remainder of your fee."

"Instead, I'll use it to pay others to find you and punish you for your disobedience."

"And I promise, you won't like that."

"Because if you fail me or don't obey me, you will not be receiving any more gold."

"Instead, you will pay with your life."

Since the German was a brittle, cruel acting man, who looked capable of almost anything, the Egyptian had believed him and had let his greed win out over his curiosity. Still, he couldn't help but wonder what the mysterious packages contained.

What the tanned unsmiling German had not told him was that if he discovered the wily Arab had tried to open any of the packages while they were in his care, he would cut out the squat Arab's entrails and leave him to the wandering jackals.

He was the type, A man who was perfectly capable of an act like that and would probably enjoy it. He had the look, the demeanor, and the capability. One glance at his arrogant posture and cold hard eyes told you that. He was someone who considered everyone else beneath him and therefore wholly expendable. Consequently, if you betrayed him or his trust, he would not hesitate to kill you and not think twice about it.

"Why are these packages so important?" *The Egyptian wondered as he unloaded them.*

"Why did the mysterious foreigner seek me out and hire me in secret, then pay me in gold to pick them up from the railway station at Wadi Al Rub?"

"When I had accomplished that, why did he then offer me even more gold to transport them to this desolate place secretly?"

"What possible value could they have way out here in the middle of nowhere?"

"More probably, he intends to take them back to German lines once I deliver them," He decided.

The squat Egyptian had asked himself these questions hundreds of times during his journey, yet as he unloaded his cargo and placed the last of the sixteen packages that composed it onto the small sheet of canvas, he had still no answers. Still, he picked at it.

"What makes them so valuable?"

"Why did he have an Arab like me collect them, then bring them here, to the very ends of the earth?"

"He knew the location of this oasis, and he's no stranger to the desert." he remembered.

"He also speaks our language and has the mark of the sun on his skin."

"That alone proves he has spent much time in the desert, so he could have done all this himself."

"Maybe it's because of the war," he thought. "Yet he is not a soldier."

"He's a civilian, but in the middle of a war zone."

"But he is not English."

"I have seen them before and heard them talk."

"This one is German, even though he tries very hard to hide it."

"I'm certain of that."

"I could tell by his accent."

"Is he a spy, I wonder?"

"Is that why he couldn't be seen picking up the packages at the railway station at Wadi Al Rub because it is in the British sector of control?"

"Do the British already know of him and hunt him?"

"Will I be hunted too when I return because I picked them up for the German?"

"OOOH Allah," he whined. "These are things I should have considered before I made my bargain with him."

"These are questions I should have asked before he tempted me with his gold."

However, it was too late for remorse or recriminations, and the Egyptian realized that. What was done was done, and there was no going back. He would have to accept his fate, regardless of what it might cost him, and that frightened him.

Breaking his train of thought, suddenly, the Egyptian head the faint sounds of a vehicle engine in the distance. When he ran to the top of the nearest dune, he saw a German half-track, slowly approaching the oasis, and realized it was the German who had hired him.

He was at first filled with joy at the prospect of being paid the remainder of his gold. Then, remembering the complex, cruel face of his employer and recalling his cold, unforgiving eyes, he suddenly had another thought. One that sent a chill of suspicion down his spine.

"What if my employer decides it will be easier to simply kill me rather than pay me the rest of the gold he promised?"

"That would be much cheaper, and what would prevent him?"

"We are miles from civilization, and there would be no witnesses, so no one would ever know."

"The bald German looks like he is perfectly capable of cutting my throat and watching me bleed to death, as easily as he would order a cold beer at Shepard's Hotel in Cairo."

"I have no trust in him." he suddenly realized.

He considered that gruesome possibility for a moment as the vehicle continued to approach, then made what he hoped, at the very least, was a decision that would give him some bargaining power if he were threatened. Accordingly, he quickly ran back down to the oasis to the pile of wrapped packages and selected two at random.

Afterward, he awkwardly carried them towards the western edge of the oasis, one at a time. When he had moved both items, he put his back to a nearby palm tree, then paced off thirty steps westward, towards the setting sun. Afterward, he knelt and dug furiously into the hot sand with his bare hands.

When he had dug a hole large enough and deep enough, he put the two packages into it, then refilled it. Afterward, he brushed the sand lightly with a dead palm frond to erase any signs of either the hole or his digging. He then wiped away his tracks that led from his campsite to his cache. Satisfied, he returned to his small fire and had another cup of tea, pleased that he had taken adequate precautions to ensure he got the remainder of the gold he had been promised.

The vehicle he had been hearing finally pulled into the small oasis five minutes later. It was, indeed, a German half-track, painted in tan desert camouflage, complete with the faded German Army insignia of the *Afrika Korps* palm tree on its doors. It had spare gas and water cans strapped all over it, and they alone told him it had traveled far.

Three men were in the vehicle. Two were dressed in German Wehrmacht desert khaki uniforms and were German soldiers. The third was a civilian and wore a khaki-colored twill jacket and tan pants. That was, of course, Her Scheer, his mysterious employer. When the vehicle stopped, Scheer, dressed in the khakis, got out first, followed by the two uniformed Germans.

"Greetings, main Freunde," Scheer said in Arabic with a thin smile. "I see you have made the journey safely."

"Have you brought my cargo?"

"I have," The Egyptian confirmed.

"But it was an arduous and dangerous journey," he complained.

"Worth much more than you agreed to pay me when you hired me," he whined.

"Even so, I have kept my promise and fulfilled my end of the bargain."

"Did you bring my gold?" he asked excitedly.

"First, I want to see my packages," the German replied.

"They are there," the squat Egyptian said, pointing. "and they are all unopened as you instructed."

"I have done all that you have asked of me," he said impatiently. "Now, I want to be paid."

After seeing the packages laid out on the tarp, Scheer turned and looked at the Egyptian contemptuously, with a thin evil-looking sneer.

"Yes," he said coldly. "I guess it is time to pay you."

Then he turned to the two soldiers and nodded.

One of the Germans behind him raised his MP40 machine pistol and put a short burst into the Egyptian. The copper-jacketed 9-millimeter rounds tore into the wiry Arab and killed him instantly. His body arched as it was flung backward, so his corpse landed in an awkward, ungainly heap almost a yard away, his red blood staining the sand where he fell. His mouth had sprung open in surprise, and his lifeless eyes stared upward in the rictus of death. They revealed how completely unexpected his death had been and how unprepared he had been to face it. His last thoughts were a complete shock. He never had the chance to even bargain with the German for his life.

However, Scheer was not shocked by the event. He had planned for it, and as such, looked down at the Egyptian's corpse with complete indifference as he spat in contempt.

"There's your payment, you filthy little savage," He said nastily.

"The only payment you'll ever get."

"And even that's more than you deserve."

"Your entire race is scum and needs to be eradicated."

"You are all subhuman and a stain on the rest of humanity."

"You deserve the same fate as the Jews."

Of course, the Egyptian didn't hear him. He was on his way to paradise and the twenty-nine virgins that awaited him. Suddenly, the German remembered where he was and what he was there for.

"Collect the packages and load them into the vehicle," He ordered the two accompanying soldiers tersely. "Be careful with them."

"They can't be damaged by rough handling."

"If they are, and the containers spring a leak, their contents will kill us all."

That statement got the two soldiers' immediate attention, so they obeyed instantly. Returning their weapons to the half-track, they walked over to the stack of packages and began carefully carrying them back to the Hanomag, two at a time. The task required several trips, and when they had finished and had all of them safely stowed in the half-track's cargo compartment, one of them frowned slightly, then turned and asked.

"I thought you said there would be sixteen packages, Herr Professor?"

"There are," Scheer confirmed, still staring at the Egyptian's corpse and wishing he had killed him himself.

"But we only loaded fourteen," The German Sgt reported, puzzled.

Scheer whirled around anger etched into his hard, tanned face.

"Are you sure your count was right?" he asked furiously.

"Jawohl, Herr Professor," the Army Sgt confirmed. "I counted them twice."

"There are only fourteen."

The Professor threw down his hat in anger and swore violently in German.

"The little bastard stole two of them," he screamed afterward.

"I'm sure of it."

"Check the oasis," He ordered.

"Maybe he hid them somewhere."

But after twenty minutes of fruitless searching, the professor grudgingly called the two soldiers back to the half-track.

"We're wasting our time," he admitted, his fury barely contained. "The filthy little shit could have hidden them anywhere."

"He could have even left them back at Wadi Al Rub and never brought them here, to begin with."

"Probably hoping to extort more gold from me."

"Goddamn thieving Arabs."

"They are all alike."

"Worthless *unter menschen* who are, a stain of humanity that should be erased as soon as possible."

"I was a fool to trust the little bastard, but I had no choice," Scheer told himself angrily.

"Someone native had to pick the packages up at the railway station, then transport them here."

"Any Caucasian attempting that would have been suspected immediately and picked up by the verdamnt British, so I was forced to recruit a native."

"But, in hindsight," Scheer muttered angrily. "I should have taken one of his ugly children hostage and held them as a guarantee against his treachery."

"Instead, I thought his greed over the promise of more gold would guarantee our bargain."

"I was wrong," He ranted as he kicked the corpse.

"My only regret now is that I can't kill this thieving little swine again."

"This time with my bare hands."

The two soldiers just stared at Scheer in astonishment. He was extremely close to being psychotic, and they realized it.

"We're wasting our time continuing to look for the two missing parcels." Scheer finally told the two soldiers angrily a moment later.

"The little shit had plenty of time to hide them if he even brought them."

"I'll just have to make do with the fourteen units I still have left."

"They should be enough to complete the project's field trials if I'm careful." He told himself, rationalizing.

"Let's go," he ordered a moment later.

"We have a long journey back to base, and it's almost sundown."

"That means we'll have to travel all night."

"Jawohl, Herr Professor," the two NCOs said, hurrying back to the vehicle.

"What about the camels?" one of them asked.

"Cut them loose and leave them," Scheer ordered.

"They'll find their way home or eventually be picked up by some wandering nomads."

"It doesn't matter either way."

A few minutes later, the Hanomag was headed west once again, back towards German-controlled territory, from where it had originally

come. It disappeared over the *
horizon twenty minutes later, jus*
setting. Exactly where it went was *
remained unsolved and utterly unhear*
next forty-odd years. It took long before*
whiff of what had all started at a remote d*
oasis to ever emerge again.

By then, even the poor Egyptian's bones *
eroded into nothing by the blowing desert sand.
However, the two packages he had buried lay
undisturbed in the desert silica where he had put
them over four decades ago. Ultimately, their very
existence would eventually set off a chain of
events with the potential to trigger a war., Even
worse, if their contents were released, they would
kill half the entire population of the northern coast
of Africa!

_ ᴊʋ୵ was a Type VII, long-range, ocean-going submarine and was fully equipped with all the latest German U Boat technology. She was the latest in her class, had a full complement of the newly developed acoustic torpedoes, and was equipped with enough supplies and fuel to remain at sea for over sixty days with ease. Her prime hunting ground was the Allied convoy routes in the North Atlantic, where she would be a real threat with her veteran skipper and experienced crew. But that was not to be. At least not yet. She had another duty to perform first.

Her original sailing orders, issued just two days prior, had informed her Captain that was his destination, and he eagerly awaited cast off time. But unfortunately, that was not where the U 507 was now headed. Instead of preparing to launch for the target-rich North Atlantic and begin stalking her prey, she was bound for the

Mediterranean. There she would be used as nothing more than an overpriced, undersea taxicab.

Kapitan Willie Klepper, her skipper, was furious about his sudden change in orders, and he did not attempt to hide it. He was looking forward to taking his ship and crew on another hundred-thousand-ton war patrol, during which he planned to sink an equal amount of Allied commercial shipping. He had done so on his previous war patrol and was looking forward to doing it again. He and his crew had been trained for that, and over the preceding year, they had become highly proficient. They had even been awarded medals for their success. That was why Klepper was the leading U Boat ace in his entire flotilla, and he and his crew were the acknowledged experts at sinking Allied shipping in the North Atlantic.

Consequently, they were eagerly looking forward to another chance to once again cruise to their prime hunting grounds and replicate their previous mission. However, that was not to be. Not just yet anyway. First, another little chore had to be performed, and it had nothing to do with sinking Allied shipping.

Just hours before departing his home port in Brest, Willie had been unexpectedly summoned to the Flotilla commander's office. There he was informed, his orders had been unexpectedly revised. He would still conduct his scheduled war patrol in the North Atlantic, but only after he had picked up a German agent off the coast of Libya and ferried him across the Mediterranean to Salerno's Italian port. Since that was a dangerous and time-consuming chore that had nothing to do with his real mission, Klepper was understandably perturbed.

Worse, that chore would require sneaking past Gibraltar twice. Once in and once out. Worse, afterward, the boat would have to return to Brest to be refueled and re-provisioned before heading into the North Atlantic to accomplish its fundamental mission. So, when the flotilla commander informed Willie of his change of orders, Klepper became so furious, he bordered on becoming insubordinate.

"What idiot ordered this?" he demanded furiously.

"This is the grossest waste of resources I have ever heard of."

"I can't believe a fully-equipped German submarine, already repaired, fueled, provisioned, resupplied with torpedoes, will be diverted over fifteen hundred miles to transport one lousy individual less than two hundred nautical miles."

"Have they gone completely insane in Berlin?"

"Or has that fat idiot Goering and his glorious Luftwaffe run out of fucking airplanes?" he asked disgustedly.

The flotilla commander just looked at Klepper stone-faced and decided to let him vent. He also thought the tasking was idiotic. Besides, Klepper had earned the right to voice his displeasure over being ordered to perform it.

"Why is this agent so goddamned important?"

"Why do we have to risk an entire U-Boat and its crew to extract him?"

"Why can't he fly to Italy on a regular aerial resupply run?

"It's less than a two-hour trip for Christ's Sake," he ranted.

"Or if he is afraid of flying, why can't one of our E boats in Sicily pick him up and take him there?"

"Hell, they have three squadrons of them, and the trip would take less than four hours."

"Certainly, they could spare one for this simple a mission."

"Willie," his commander told him calmly after Klepper had vented his wrath. "there's no good answer to any of your questions."

"Furthermore, there's nothing I can do to change your orders."

"I know, "He admitted. "I've already tried."

"There's nothing you can do either," He added.

"The orders straight came from Admiral Doenitz himself."

"He even called me about them earlier this morning."

Klepper just glared at his Boss in frustration, unsure whether that was the truth or just something to appease him. Even if it was, that still did not explain the absurdity of his new mission. He was the Captain of a German U Boat. Not a goddamn taxi driver.

"If it makes you feel any better," The Captain continued. "the Admiral didn't have any choice in the matter either."

"So, he's not any happier about having been ordered to do this than you are."

"Just like you, he thought this entire mission was a gigantic waste of resources, dreamed up by some maniac in the Furher's inner circle."

"He even told Berlin that in short and very terse language and initially refused to do it."

"His objections did not affect the decision at all. and he was overruled."

"It appears that Hitler himself wants this agent picked up and brought back to Germany."

Furthermore, he insists that his evacuation from Libya be accomplished by submarine."

"He's afraid this agent could be shot down if he went to Italy by aircraft, and he's probably right about that."

"Especially since the Allies now control most of the airspace over the Mediterranean."

"When the Admiral asked about using E-boats, that option was also turned down as being also too risky."

"Probably for the same reasons."

"So, the order stands," the admiral said. "and since it came directly from the Fuhrer, neither Doenitz nor you, nor I, have any choice."

From the look on Willi's face, he was still obviously unimpressed by Der Fuehrer's decision. As Willie's flotilla commander stared at him, it was obvious he agreed with his ace U Boat commander. He, too, wondered if the Third Reich had gone utterly insane in ordering Admiral Doenitz to perform this seemingly idiotic task. So, he decided to explain his decision further to calm his subordinate down.

"According to Doenitz, some scientist has convinced the Fuehrer that he has the key to some wonder weapon that could win the war all by itself."

"He's developed a prototype in Egypt and is ready to transport it to Germany for field trials and production."

"And you already know how the Fuhrer feels about wonder weapons."

"He's enthralled by them."

"Especially lately."

"Der Fuhrer forgets that the Wehrmacht, the Luftwaffe, and the Kriegsmarine have already won every single battle in this war for him."

"All by themselves, and without the aid of a single wonder weapon." The Admiral pointed out.

"Despite that, our Fuhrer seems to be addicted to new technology and weapons systems."

"So, the old time-tested methods, used by the services to win thus far, although one hundred percent effective in the past, are no longer glamorous enough to suit him."

"So, humor me and run this little errand, Willi," He pleaded.

"And don't try going out of channels and raising hell about it either."

"It won't do you any good."

"That kind of thing nowadays is extremely unwise." He explained.

"The Reich Chancellery and the Gestapo might take something like that as a sign of defeatism."

"If that happens, we may both find ourselves in some Gestapo dungeon, hanging by piano wire for disobeying orders."

"I don't know about you, but I would much prefer to die like a sailor rather than a traitor."

Hearing that, Willie's blood pressure soared, but he kept his mouth closed. He knew what his boss had just told him was true. It was not wise to offer your opinion on the stupidity of Germany's leadership nowadays in any forum. Since even the walls seemed to have ears lately, any private, much less public comment that bordered on defeatism or hinted at Germany's problems could get you killed by the thugs in the Gestapo.

Klepper was already aware of that, having seen two of his comrades reduced in rank and sent to a penal battalion because they voiced their opinions to the wrong people with those types of comments. They were duly reported to Gestapo and the men accused of defeatism, then stripped of rank and sent to the coal mines of Silesia. They would probably die there. Klepper didn't want to join them. Even knowing that, Klepper still couldn't keep his displeasure from registering on his youthful face.

"Just go and get this Professor and take him across the water to Salerno, Willi," The flotilla commander told his most successful U Boat Kapitan.

"Then you can return to the Atlantic and win the swords for your Iron Cross, you little glory hunter."

Willie snorted and then smiled. His commander knew he didn't give a damn about medals. He knew him well enough to know that he was more concerned with getting his boat and his men back home safely after he had completed his mission. Lately, however, that was becoming increasingly more difficult. Still, it was a job he did exceedingly well.

Besides, Willie couldn't be mad at one of the few friends he still had left that hadn't already been killed in the U boat Service.

"Okay, Poppa," he said, smiling once again. "I 'll be a good boy."

"I won't bitch or offer any more of my defeatist opinions."

"I'll just go get my passenger without any more squawking."

"Just tell me where he is and where to send the taxicab bill for this idiocy when I'm through."

"Get out here, you troublemaker," the flotilla commander said, laughing.

"And take these new instructions with you," he said, handing Willi a sealed envelope. "Follow them, and don't get yourself sunk in the process."

"I'm getting tired of going to funerals," He told his subordinate.

As a result, Willie and his crew had sailed out of Brest later that afternoon to the somewhat off-key sounds of *Deutschland Uber Alles*, the

German National Anthem, played by a less than professional German Navy band. Picking up their escorts at the harbor entrance, they made their way to the open ocean protected by them, then turned south for the Mediterranean, running on the surface because of the darkness.

All that had been ten long days ago. Since then, Willie had successfully steamed from Brest south to Gibraltar, evading British aircraft and sub hunters the entire way. After daylong surveillance, he had penetrated the treacherous Straits of Gibraltar and entered the Med under cover of darkness.

Still, his entry had not been without incident. The damned British Navy had almost succeeded in stopping him cold at the entrance to the straits by setting up a moving blockade of warships that had nearly proven to be Klepper's undoing. Willie had barely succeeded in evading them and saving his boat, doing so by only by a hair's breadth and his considerable skill.

The Straits of Gibraltar were like the cork in the wine bottle. Everything in the Atlantic Ocean to their west and the Mediterranean Sea to their east narrowed down to them. Moreover, other than the Suez Canal, there was no other way of entering or exiting the Mediterranean. As such, the Straits were getting harder and harder to penetrate as the war continued.

The Brits were determined to defeat Rommel in North Africa, and one of their strategies was denying him supplies. So, they were determined to seal the Mediterranean Ocean from any German shipping as a means of accomplishing that. Closing the Straits of Gibraltar was critical to that strategy.

After successfully reaching the Mediterranean proper, Willie had carefully and silently navigated his way eastward, following the North African shore to the designated pickup point on the Libyan coast outlined in his secret orders. Once arrived, he had succeeded in picking up his important passenger, along with his almost five hundred goddamned pounds of cargo that he had insisted on bringing aboard with him. Something that both Hitler and Doenitz had failed to mention in his original set of orders. It was now taking up valuable space in the boat's after torpedo room.

That alone had been enough to raise Willie's ire about the mission further. Now he knew why Hitler had insisted the agent be transported by a submarine. All the cargo he brought with him would not have fit into any German aircraft or on an E-boat.

Worse, once underway again, the *agent,* Klepper, had been sent to fetch, turned out to be a scientist instead of a spy. When Willie discovered that, his anger turned to all-out fury.

"All this trouble for some *verdamnt* scientist," He practically screamed at his Executive Officer in frustration.

"I've risked my men and my boat, just getting here, for some screwball professor."

"That's the final straw," he fumed. "the frosting on the fucking cake."

"There's no doubt about it now; the goddamned Fuhrer is completely insane," He told his XO.

However, all that proved to be just the tip of the iceberg for both Klepper and his crew. After safely picking up his passenger and all his baggage, things got worse.

His passenger turned out to be overbearing and obnoxious, letting everyone he met on board know just how smart he was as soon as he met them. Worse, he also claimed he was a high-ranking member of the Nazi Party with influential friends. Consequently, if he weren't accorded every courtesy and offered every convenience, he would let his influential friends know about it once he reached Berlin, and heads would roll as a result. That was the last straw, and Willie had to forcibly gain control of his emotions lest he tell the silly ass what he thought of him before throwing the sonofabitch overboard.

Herr Professor, however, blissfully dismissed Klepper's anger and immediately installed himself in the XO's cabin, claiming it was barely fit for habitation. But it would have to do, given the circumstances. Afterward, true to form, the miserable prick turned out to be what everyone on the boat already suspected; a typical self-centered Nazi asshole who thought the world revolved around him. He was both a dedicated Nazi and a self-proclaimed scientific genius. Worse, as an egomaniac, he would gladly inform you of his exalted scientific stature anytime the occasion arose.

Willie despised him precisely thirty seconds after meeting him. Since then, the man had made a complete nuisance of himself, bitching and carping about the conditions, the food, the smell, and everything else on the U Boat. In short, he had made a complete ass of himself with the officers and crew of the entire boat, infuriating everyone he met. As a result, the crew thoroughly detested him and could not wait to be rid of the egotistical bastard.

Unfortunately, all the asshole professor's pompousness and failings had become a moot point the third day following his pickup. It started only hours before he was due to be put ashore in Salerno. That was when the British destroyer had found Klepper and his U boat, using its newly installed sonar.

Even worse, the discovery of the submarine could not have come at a more inappropriate time. The boat was out of the deeper waters of the Mediterranean proper and near the northwestern Italian shore, where the water was much shallower. That meant it could be detected much easier. As a result, the British warship was in the process of depth charging the hell out of Willie and the U 507 and doing a thorough job of it.

Although Willie had already tried every trick he knew to get away from the destroyer, nothing had worked. The sub killer was like a terrier that had caught a rat. He just would not let go and was determined to kill his catch. So, even though Willie and his crew were doing everything they could to save the boat, it was rapidly becoming a futile exercise.

While Willie and his crew worked desperately to save the boat, Herr Professor sat huddled in the corner of the XO's cabin, terrified and crying like a sick infant. However, his continuous sobbing stopped several minutes later, when the U 507 took two depth charges on her port side, close in. They ripped a gaping hole in her pressure hull, immediately flooding her and drowning most of her crew in the process. The trapped remainder died in their sealed compartments, hours later, from the lack of oxygen. Therefore, it took only minutes, for Willie and his entire crew, along with their arrogant passenger, to all eventually perish as the doomed sub sank to the bottom.

Consequently, the small, heavy packages Herr Professor had brought aboard and had been stored in the sub's aft torpedo room were also lost forever, as the dead sub settled into her watery grave in the soft sand of the bottom. Hitler would never see their capabilities, and their original purpose would never be realized. Unknown to the world, they would be far better off for that.

When ten days passed with no radio contact with U 507, Willie's Flotilla commander was sadly forced to report to Doenitz that Willie and the U 507 were overdue and presumed lost. Doenitz, in turn, duly reported that fact to Adolph Hitler that same day. When informed, Hitler, along with his staff, was not happy with the news, especially his Chief Scientific advisor. He was appalled because he was the only man who knew the real purpose behind Herr Professor's ultra-secret project and what all it had entailed. Later in the day, when Hitler discussed the loss, Der Fuhrer became enraged at being denied his wonder weapon.

"The Professor is dead, and all the items he created are at the bottom of the Mediterranean, so the project is finished," He screamed in frustration.

"And I had high hopes for it in the future."

"Now that those hopes dead and Germany will fight on, losing more of her sons in the process."

"That means your failure is unacceptable, Karl!" he snarled hotly.

"If what you said about the weapon's capability is even half true, Germany has lost a chance to end this war early, and much of the blame for that is yours."

"You should have arranged for the professor to be brought back to Germany much earlier."

"So, you share the blame for this inexcusable mistake."

"All may not be lost, Mein Fuehrer." The advisor replied unexpectedly, trying desperately to save his skin.

With that statement, Hitler's rage disappeared instantly, and his face brightened unexpectedly. He hated terrible news, and the bearer usually suffered accordingly. Good news was what he needed now, so, he grabbed for it hungrily.

"You have a plan to make more of these weapons?" he asked hopefully.

"Possibly, Mein Further," the Advisor confirmed.

"Tell me," Hitler ordered, the eagerness evident in his tone.

"After the sinking of the U-Boat and the death of Professor Scheer, I talked to the other scientists that worked on the project with the Professor, by radio," the Advisor revealed.

"They are still in Libya, you know."

"According to them, aided by copies of Scheer's research notes, they know enough about the process the Professor used to create the sixteen items, to recreate some of the same material themselves."

"Especially since they have copies of Scheer's original formulas, notes, and procedures."

"All they need is a new laboratory and some raw materials."

"That's better, Klaus," Hitler said smiling. "even encouraging."

"How long will it take them to reproduce the weapon?"

"I'm not sure, Sir," Klaus replied. "Right now, they don't even have the raw materials to begin the process."

"And as for the scientists themselves, as I said, they are still in Libya."

"How long will it take to get them back, acquire the necessary materials and restart the program?" Hitler asked irritably.

"If we have to find and then mine a new source of ore ourselves," the advisor replied. "then transport it back to Germany and refine it, the entire process may take as long as another full year."

"That's too long," Hitler interrupted angrily. "I'll need this weapon long before then."

"You'll have to find some way of cutting that timetable."

"However, if we can locate enough previously mined ore," the Advisor added hastily, in response to Hitler's new timeline. "then it will take much less time."

"We might be able to produce some new material in as little as three months, maybe less."

"Right now, however, all that's a moot point."

"Why?" Hitler demanded.

"The Project is at a complete standstill because of the recent British advances in Africa, Mein Further.

"Their forces have already overrun the area where our primary laboratory was located."

"Fortunately, they didn't discover it initially, so Scheer had time to destroy it before he and his scientific team were forced to flee."

"Consequently. we'll have to create an entirely new laboratory in a more secure area even to begin production again."

"Why didn't we do that to start with?" Hitler asked angrily.

"Because of the danger of a lab accident, Mein Fuhrer." The advisor explained.

"That's the primary reason we established the original lab in the middle of the desert, so far from civilization."

"The material we are dealing with is extremely hazardous."

"So toxic it almost defies description."

"If an accident were to occur near a populated area, the results would be catastrophic."

"The number of people dead could be in the hundreds of thousands."

"We could wind up killing ourselves off even faster than the Allies are doing."

Hitler didn't like that remark, but he ignored it because he was more concerned with reproducing the weapon.

"If you can resurrect this project and produce a weapon, just how effective will it be?" Hitler demanded.

"You asked me that same question when I first proposed the project, Sir," The advisor replied.

"I gave you a conservative answer then."

"However, that answer was based on what we originally projected as results when the material was still in the initial process of being created."

"Now that we have produced the prototype items, even though we still need to make the weapon operational and run some preliminary tests on its potency, we have a much better feel for its effectiveness."

"Quit waffling," Hitler ordered. "just tell me how many people we can kill if we use it."

"Hundreds of thousands," the Advisor exclaimed proudly. "Probably more."

It depends on the climatic conditions where the weapon is released."

"I can now tell you now that our first estimates on the causalities that the weapon would produce were extremely conservative."

"We grossly underestimated just how toxic this weapon is."

"If we deployed it in England, for example, in its current form, we would only need to emplace two liters of it in a maximum of three separate locations on the entire island."

"Once the weapon is released into the air, in less than a month, virtually the entire population of that island will either be dead or dying."

"It's that deadly."

"Even better, it has no antidote."

"Once you ingest it, you die."

Hitler's eyes gleamed in anticipation at that thought.

"Mein Gott," he said softly to himself, already contemplating how and where he would use it.

"We could kill the entire population of England in one single blow."

"Almost overnight."

"Later, over half the population of Russia."

"And we could do all that without firing a shot."

"I could win the war with this in the space of months!"

"Once the Americans saw its effects, they would also be forced to sue for peace or face annihilation, lest we unleash it on them."

"With them gone, I could rule the world."

"That's entirely possible, Mein Further," The Scientific Advisor said in agreement.

"Then I must have this weapon as soon as possible," Hitler ordered.

"We can field test it against the Russians along their western border."

"They breed like flies anyway, so they'll be an ideal target."

"We're going to have to fight them anyway, sooner or later, you know." He revealed.

"When we do, I don't want to have to fight them conventionally, like we did the British in France because there are too many of them."

"So, I want a weapon that will kill them by the hundreds of thousands, without our troops ever having to get near them."

"Mien Gott, if this weapon is only half as effective as you say it is," he said excitedly. "we could take the majority of Russia with a minimum of casualties."

"Most of it without firing a shot."

"And do it in a matter of weeks," he said happily.

"If what you told me about this weapon is true, this may even be our chance to win the war in the next few months!" he said excitedly.

The Scientific Advisor simply nodded.

"But how long does it take for it to become harmless?" Hitler asked as the thought occurred to him.

"We won't know that exactly until we test it," The Scientific advisor reported.

"But Scheer estimates it will no longer be toxic after a week."

"Maybe two at the most."

"It depends on the weather," he explained.

"Sunlight affects its molecular structure and eventually breaks it down and renders it harmless."

"That's the reason England would be such an ideal target.

"The weather during the fall and winter there is so bad; the sun doesn't shine that much."

"That means it could still be lethal weeks after it was employed."

Hitler's eyes gleamed with the thought of such an easy victory.

"Do whatever is necessary to get the project going again," Hitler ordered eagerly. "and do it immediately."

"I want this weapon, and I want it now."

"You have my full authority to requisition whatever resources you need."

"And this time, don't fail me, Klaus," He warned coldly.

"If you do, you will forfeit not only your position but your life."

"Do you understand?"

The Advisor nodded, his face turning ashen. He had just pledged his life, and he knew it.

"See Bormann before you leave," Hitler ordered.

"Let him read the file."

"Afterwards, he will arrange all the details of getting you what you need."

"And keep him advised of your progress," He added.

"He'll keep me up to date on the project's status."

"You just get me that weapon and do it as quickly as possible."

"You are a good man, Klaus," Hitler said smiling icily, "but not irreplaceable. "

"Remember that," Hitler emphasized.

"Yes, Mein Fuehrer," Klaus replied, swallowing hard and realizing his life now hung on him reproducing the weapon Scheer had created.

"No excuse will satisfy Hitler if I fail." He thought.

"If I don't give him what he asked for, I'm a dead man."

"Thank you for your time and your support, Mein Furher," he said, getting up and noting he was sweating.

"Sieg Heil."

An hour later, the Advisor sat in Martin Bormann's office, anxious and uncomfortable. His face and manner reflected it. Hitler may have been the Fuehrer, the head of all Germany as far as the public was concerned. But Martin Bormann was the man that ran the Third Reich and with an iron fist. As such, he was the single most powerful man in Germany. Party insiders and shakers and movers in Germany knew that and feared him because he controlled everything. His power was virtually absolute and his authority unlimited.

Worse, Bormann was a man not known for his warmth or pleasant personality. Instead, he was a ruthless result getter who absorbed facts like a sponge. He had a phenomenal recall and possessed an enormous intellect. As such, he considered his time valuable and hated having to waste it.

Consequently, he hated whiners and could not stand excuses or excuse-makers. But most of all, oddly enough, he hated things that he considered dishonorable or unconscionable. His skewed sense of morality would not abide anything that fell into that category. Consequently, he considered most products of that line of reasoning the result of faulty assumptions, unrealistic ideas, faulty planning, poor execution, or low intellect.

Oddly, his moral code did not include the Reich's program to exterminate the Jews. He was aware of it and knew more than he wanted to know about it. It was repugnanat, despicable and a waste of resources in his opinion. Yet it had been ordered by Hitler himself and he was adamant on the subject. That left Bormann no choice but to support it, even though he abhorred it. It was a dichotomy that he despised but could could do nothing about. So he simply ignored it and concentrated on things that he had influence or power over.

Furthermore, in his opinion, projects like that, including this one, were all based on flawed logic or inbred hatred and racism to begin with. And flawed reasoning such as that was something he thoroughly detested.

In contrast, as a realist, he based his decisions on logically thought out and proven actions and procedures. Accordingly, when someone violated those procedures, especially by going around him and directly to the Further with anything concerning the Third Reich, that infuriated him. He was the Reich gatekeeper, and he tolerated no interlopers. Violate that rule, and you found yourself at considerable risk and in great peril, usually with your life at forfeit.

Lastly, unlike his boss, Hitler, he did not place much faith in unproven technology or things he considered iniquitous. Worse, having just read the Advisor's file on the project for the first time, Bormann was furious: for two reasons.

First, it was evident the Scientific Advisor had gone over his head and directly to Hitler with the project to get it started, bypassing Bormann completely. That fact alone infuriated the ReichLieter, although he took pains to avoid showing it to the little weasel who was now seated in front of him.

Secondly, to Bormann, the entire project was insane, and the work of a mad man. If the Allies were to get one whiff of the existence of the weapon the project was designed to produce, much less have it employed against them, Germany would simply be erased from the face of the earth. The Allied fury would be that intense, and their anger would demand it. Consequently, Germany would be bombed into extinction, maybe using something other than conventional explosives.

German intelligence had already told Bormann that the Americans were working on a super bomb. It would undoubtedly be used to obliterate Germany should she employ the weapon described in the project's file. Of course, Bormann was not about to reveal that secret to this lowly little weasel of a Scientific Advisor, so he took a different tack.

"Don't come to me with generalities or with promises without proof, Mein Herr," he barked, as he held up the file he had just read. "I need specifics if I am to act."

"Don't try and lecture me on resources or priorities either," Bormann added icily.

"The Reich has several important projects already in being that have to be supported."

"They all have a priority higher than yours, and they must also have resources."

"Resources that Germany has only in limited supply nowadays.

"So, those resources have to be carefully allocated."

"In truth," Bormann continued testily, "although this project of yours may very well have great potential, in reality, you don't even know if it will work."

"It has yet to be tested," he pointed out. "much less proven to be effective on the battlefield."

"You only have its inventor's word that it will perform as efficiently as he says it will, and now you can't confirm even that because he's dead."

"So, since the weapon has yet to be even field-tested, it remains simply an unproven theory, and not even a real weapon."

"Instead, it is merely its creator's untested brainchild."

"As such, it is just one more drain on the Reich's resources until it has been proven to be effective."

"So, based on all that, in my opinion, its priority is a rather low one."

"Besides," Bormann added. "right now, the German military does not need a doomsday weapon like you propose here."

"We are already winning the war with our conventional weapons and our armed forces."

"But the Fuehrer told me that this project was of the highest importance and priority." Klaus protested.

"He said that he wanted it immediately."

"He even promised me that I was to get whatever I needed to produce it."

"So that it could be employed as soon as it could be produced in sufficient numbers."

"And so, you shall," Bormann said, smiling thinly. "but that may take some time, Mein Herr."

"As I said, resources are stretched extremely thin at the moment."

"The Fuehrer may not have been as aware of that as I am when he gave you those orders."

"Remember, Mein Herr; we're currently fighting a war on the continent, as well as in North Africa."

"So, supporting both those efforts is a tremendous drain on the Reich's limited resources."

"Besides, your need for resources doesn't matter at present anyway, does it?"

The Scientific Advisor looked at him, obviously confused.

"Right now, you haven't even got a laboratory to continue the project with," Borman reminded him.

"You haven't even found a suitable site to establish a new one as yet."

"And you state, in this very file," Bormann said, holding it up again. "that its location is essential. "

"*The project cannot continue until we reestablish our laboratories at a suitable location*," your own words, Mein Herr, Bormann said, quoting.

"Worse, even after you establish a new laboratory, you still need to locate some scarce resources and relocate all of the scientific personnel still in Africa, before you can even continue the development of the material."

"So, until you can accomplish those three tasks," Borman said with finality. "this discussion is entirely moot."

"Since nothing can be done until you accomplish all those tasks, the entire project remains at a standstill."

"As such, no resources need be allocated to it until those first three conditions have been satisfied."

The Scientific Advisor suddenly realized that what Bormann had just said was true. He did not have any of the things Bormann had just mentioned. And if Bormann's obvious dislike of the project was any indicator, he never would. Unless he did something to resurrect the project on his own, it was apparent Bormann would let it die a natural death.

However, he was also enough of a political realist to realize that Bormann, having just been made aware of the project, would not be an avid supporter of it. Under any circumstances. His original plan to back door the Reich Leiter and go directly to Hitler had suddenly backfired. Angering Bormann any further by trying to force the issue guaranteed its demise.

"Why don't you devote your initial efforts to finding a suitable location to build your new laboratory as an initial step," Bormann suggested silkily.

"Then, after you have found that site, you can come back to see me and tell me exactly what else you need to develop it and get your Project going once again."

"Afterwards, we can set about acquiring the resources you're going to need, getting them to your new site, while simultaneously reassembling your necessary personnel."

"Doesn't that sound like the most efficient way to get your project back up and running again?" Bormann asked with a thin smile.

The Scientific Advisor realized by Bormann's unyielding smile he would abide no argument. So, he had no choice but to accept Bormann's decision. Like it or not, it was final.

Therefore, it was either do things Bormann's way or the project was finished.

"Maybe Bormann considers it finished anyway." He thought.

"But I certainly don't."

But the Scientific Advisor wasn't crazy. He had no intention of overruling or getting into an argument with the second most powerful man in Germany. That would be the equivalent of committing suicide, both politically and literally and he wasn't that stupid.

"Yes, Sir, Party Leiter," The Advisor replied. "as always, you know best."

"I will concentrate on finding a new and suitable home for the Project's laboratory as my primary task."

"Once I have found it, I will come back and see you," he promised.

"Or even better, I will find a way to begin the Project again without your knowledge, you egotistical ass."

"Because I am certainly not going to let it die because you dislike it."

"Because you are such a moron, you have no idea of its real potential."

"Excellent," Bormann said, raising his hand and dismissing the Advisor. "Heil Hitler."

When the Advisor had left his office, Bormann buzzed his private secretary, going her explicit instructions.

"When that idiot Scientific Advisor calls or comes back for an appointment to see me, make up some excuse and put him off."

"I don't want to be bothered by him again."

"The man may be one of Der Fuhrer's favorites, but he's a lunatic, and I don't have any more time to waste on either him or his idiotic projects."

"Yessir," she responded. "I'll see to it."

"Madness," Borman thought as he reflected on Scheer's Doomsday Weapon. "complete insanity."

"I won't be a party to trying to win a war with this kind weapon and possibly destroying mankind in the process."

"And apparently, this project can do just that."

"What was that maniac Scheer even thinking when he came up with this idea." He said, shaking his head in amazement.

"He's insane."

"Thank God that submarine sank and took all the Items the Scientific Advisor talked about in this summary, to the bottom of the ocean."

"That's where they belong."

"Along with the maniac that created them."

"They should have never been created to start with."

"My God, we may be at war, but despite everything we've done in this war to date, some of us are still rational enough to want to survive when it's over."

"Consequently. only a madman would even consider supporting something like this."

"Much less employing it as a weapon."

"And that includes our beloved Further!"

"If the Allies get one inkling of this Project's existence, there will no place on earth that any survivors of this Glorious Third Reich can hide."

"They will bomb Germany into rubble."

"Destroy us a nation and as a people."

"Eradicate us."

"And that must never be allowed to happen," Bormann vowed.

"And it won't."

"Not if I have anything to do with it."

"Because I, for one, intend to survive this madness."

"So, this abomination dies, right now."

Afterward, he threw the entire file into the Burn basket, intending to forget about it, along with the Scientific Advisor. But try as he might, the project was so grotesque; he couldn't rid his mind of it. A few moments later, he had an inspiration and buzzed his secretary again as he retrieved the file

"Get me, Himmler," he ordered. "I've got a special job for some of his SS thugs."

"Yes, sir," She replied.

"Better yet, cancel that," Bormann said, suddenly changing his mind.

"Instead, have my car brought around, then call Himmler's deputy, Brigade Fuehrer Krantz, on his private line."

"Tell him to meet me at my private room at the Adlon in half an hour."

"Advise him that I have some urgent business to discuss, and I don't want to do it over the telephone."

"This is much too sensitive to reveal to Himmler," Bormann told himself as he reviewed the file from the wastepaper basket.

"That egotistical little chicken farmer doesn't need to know anything about it."

"His deputy Krantz can easily handle what I want done." Bormann decided.

"And since Krantz's primary loyalty is to me and not to Heinrich, I can ensure Krantz will do exactly what I tell him with no questions."

"Afterwards, I can put this whole insane matter to rest once and for all and be rid of it."

"This abomination should never have been proposed, much less created as a weapon, to begin with." He murmured softly.

"I remember what happened to us when we used gas against the Tommies in the First War."

"In the end, they made us pay dearly for that mistake."

"Both during the war and after it ended."

"So, I won't let something like that happen again."

"Especially with a weapon a hundred times more lethal."

"If we used this weapon and wound up losing this war, as is genuinely possible," he told himself. *"Germany would never survive its aftermath."*

"And neither would I."

To be continued

Made in United States
North Haven, CT
19 April 2023

35639907R00323